In the Summertime

Maeve Haran is an Oxford law graduate, former television producer and mother of three grown-up children. Her first novel, *Having It All*, which explored the dilemmas of balancing a career and motherhood, caused a sensation and took her all around the world. Maeve has written seventeen further contemporary novels and two historical novels, plus a work of non-fiction celebrating life's small pleasures. Her books have been translated into twenty-six languages, and two have been short-listed for the Romantic Novel of the Year.

She lives between North London and a much-loved cottage near the sea in Sussex.

Maeve Haran

In The Summertime

PAN BOOKS

First published 2023 by Pan Books
an imprint of Pan Macmillan
The Smithson, 6 Briset Street, London EC1M 5NR
EU representative: Macmillan Publishers Ireland Ltd, 1st Floor,
The Liffey Trust Centre, 117–126 Sheriff Street Upper,
Dublin 1, D01 YC43
Associated companies throughout the world
www.panmacmillan.com

ISBN 978-1-5290-3521-6

1 3 5 7 9 8 6 4 2

A CIP catalogue record for this book is available from the British Library.

Typeset by Palimpsest Book Production Ltd, Falkirk, Stirlingshire
Printed and bound by CPI Group (UK) Ltd, Croydon, CR0 4YY

Visit **www.panmacmillan.com** to read more about all our books
and to buy them. You will also find features, author interviews and
news of any author events, and you can sign up for e-newsletters
so that you're always first to hear about our new releases.

For Cresta Norris, for years of fun and friendship and for coming with me to a lot of car washes. Also to her wonderful family who almost feel like my own.

One

'Bad luck always comes in threes.'

Gina tried to ignore the sound of her grandmother's voice in her head. She'd loved her gran but the old lady had been ludicrously superstitious, always telling you that seeing a lone magpie was bad luck, or that you shouldn't cross on the stairs, or pick red and white flowers. She'd also had a firm belief in horoscopes, predictions and even the fortune teller on the end of the pier in the seaside town where Gina had grown up.

Besides, should you call the fact that your husband was a compulsive gambler, who had been lying to you and taking money from the antiques business you ran together, one piece of bad luck or two?

Gina held on to a French armoire to steady herself. She mustn't break down for her daughters' sake.

Ever since she'd discovered his addiction to betting on horses, she'd tried to persuade him to seek help but he'd laughed in that irritatingly charming way of his, telling her she was such a killjoy. It wasn't as if he was some sad addict stuck in his bedroom gambling away the household budget. Maybe he overdid it a bit occasionally, but he had it all under

1

control. All the same, he kept disappearing without saying where he was going. Like today.

She told herself she wouldn't think about Mark and what to do about him until she felt a bit stronger. Instead, she tried to focus on the holiday in Sicily she was supposed to be going on with her friend Evie. But should she even go? Gina closed her eyes, imagining the small and charming Hotel Siciliana, right on the beach, with its own vineyard in the hills behind, run by the delightful Bambieri family.

Instead of a grey English spring there would be sea, sunshine and Prosecco! It was exactly the balm for the soul she needed. For months now she'd been feeling anxious and harassed, wondering what to do about her husband's problem.

Gina straightened her back. It was painfully stiff from moving stock around. She really ought to do some yoga again and she'd promised herself this holiday would give her the chance. She smiled, imagining herself doing sun salutations on the Sicilian beach. Then reality bit. Of course, she couldn't go. She'd have to persuade Evie to make it another time.

A message pinged on her phone. It was from the Villa Siciliana:

> Cara signora Lewis,
>
> I regret to have to tell you that we are closing the hotel for the month due to a sudden death in the family. We are happy to accommodate you for an alternative period and hope you will understand the situation that necessitates this unfortunate step.
>
> Cordiali saluti
> Signora F. Bambieri

'Bad luck number three,' her gran's voice intoned cheerfully.

'Well, actually, Gran,' Gina argued, trying to smile, 'it's good luck really because now we won't lose our deposit and Evie can't blame me.'

As if she'd been listening in, Gina's mobile rang and Evie's name popped up. Eve Beeston, her best friend since age eleven, was a highly successful divorce lawyer who had resisted marriage on the grounds that, in her experience, so many ended up in acrimonious argument. Ironically, Gina had often tried to persuade her that most marriages were perfectly happy.

'Gina, guess what?' Evie asked. 'You remember Ruth O'Halloran?'

'Of course I remember Ruth,' replied Gina. 'How is she?' Gina pictured the hearty large-framed Ruth, their third musketeer at school right up to sixth form, last seen when she'd come up to town to get a Geri Spice haircut for her wedding, which neither of them dared to tell her made her look more like Ron Weasley. 'How lovely to hear from her.'

'She wants you to go and stay.'

'In Southdown?' demanded Gina, stunned. Southdown was the sleepy seaside town where they'd all grown up together, which Gina and Evie had wanted to leave as soon as possible. Through their eighteen-year-old eyes Southdown had represented narrow values and limited aspirations. London was the place to be! To their astonishment, Ruth had married at nineteen and happily settled there.

'Why on earth does she want me to stay with her?' Gina enquired. 'I haven't seen her for years!'

'She's got some job she wants you to take on,' continued Evie. 'It's to do with antiques. Sounds barmy to me, but I told her I'd let you know. Typical of Ruth to have lost your phone number. Anyway, you can't go, as I explained to her, because we're off to Sicily! And not a moment too soon—'

'Evie, about that—' Gina attempted to interrupt her with the bad news.

'You know what it's like with holidays . . .' Evie bulldozed on. 'You don't even think about them, then you wake up feeling like you'll die if you don't have one. That was me this morning! This last divorce has done for me. How people who say they loved each other can behave like hyenas descending on a wildebeest is beyond me. I really need a break.'

'Evie,' Gina tried again to interrupt her. 'About Sicily—'

'Can't talk now,' Evie replied. 'Due back in court. Just wanted to warn you about Ruth.'

Any hope of telling her about Mark and asking her advice was dashed as Evie rang off with a cheery, 'Catch up soon. Byee . . .' And she was gone, leaving Gina to wonder what on earth this job in Southdown could be.

Before she did anything else she had to talk to their accountant about how much money Mark had removed from their business and what it meant for their financial future.

Not long after they were married they had started the company selling and valuing antiques and built themselves quite a reputation as the people to go to if you needed the contents of a stately home valued or your granny had started hiding her jewellery in the salad crisper and you needed someone canny and tactful to sort it out. Gina had thought of the name Whitehall Valuations, which gave the company the ring of governmental authority while in fact the Whitehall referred to was the road where they lived, a row of Victorian villas off one of the main arteries out of London. Now a lot of their antique trading was done online.

After the call with Evie, Gina steeled herself to get in touch with their accountant.

'Andrew . . .' she greeted him hesitantly.

'Gina!' he replied instantly. 'I'm so glad you've called. What the hell is Mark up to? Doesn't he realize he's put you on the verge of bankruptcy?'

Gina felt her stomach tighten and had to battle a bout of nausea. 'How much has he taken exactly?'

The sum the accountant told her was devastating.

'Oh God, Andrew, I had no idea it was that much! I've been trying to get it out of him, but he's never given any sign there was any problem.' They had two business accounts. One for everyday costs, which she managed, and another for their major outlays, which Mark took care of. 'Is there anything I can do to save the company?' she asked anxiously, trying to stifle the desperation she was feeling and think straight.

'Shut down these accounts and stop Mark having access to the money! Is there any way you could find yourself a job and live off your earnings for now? And Gina . . .' There was something in his tone of faint embarrassment that put Gina on her mettle. 'You could sell the house and think about downsizing.' He hesitated a moment then barrelled on. 'I mean, you do live in a big house and the area's become quite desirable. The estate agents call it the Whitehall Quarter.'

Gina had to admit he was right. Victorian houses with big gardens, in the catchment area for a highly rated school and handy for the tube, were what agents called 'highly sought after'. Funnily enough, Gina had noticed how popular it had become with actors. She kept seeing faces she recognized from TV dramas in the local greengrocer. It could be quite embarrassing, because without realizing it you found yourself smiling at them as if you knew them. She'd even said hello to one woman and tried to work out how they knew each other until the woman had put her out of her misery and replied. 'Actually, I don't think we've met but I'm on TV.'

Letters and flyers from local estate agents were forever coming through the door, and even the occasional hand-written one announcing that the writer *really wanted to live in the road and if they were thinking of selling we could both save on fees and do it privately.*

Yes, they probably could sell the house extremely easily. But where would they find to live that was half as nice? And how would the girls feel about their family home being sold?

She realized Andrew had asked her something. 'By the way, I assume the house is in both your names?'

With a jolt of relief Gina remembered that the house was in fact in her name. She'd thought it strange at the time when Mark had suggested it a few years ago. He'd given her some complicated explanation and it wasn't until recently she'd realized he was scared about his gambling debts and that the bookies might come after him and take the house away.

'OK,' she replied, still feeling dazed, 'I'll think about it.'

It was only as she was driving home that she remembered the call from Evie. Something about Ruth having a job she wanted her to do – in Southdown of all places. What on earth could it be?

Her thoughts were interrupted by the car phone ringing. It was her younger daughter, Sadie. Strange. Sadie never called, insisting that phoning was for old people. She only texted or WhatsApped. Her older daughter Lisa was the one who usually rang to chat.

'Mum,' for once Sadie's confident tones, which Gina admired and envied, sounded very wobbly. 'What on earth's Dad up to? I've been messaging and phoning with absolutely zero response. He hasn't done a bunk with Doris, has he?'

In spite of her anxiety Gina had to laugh. Doris, who

supervised the warehouse where they kept their stock, was over seventy with uncompromising short grey hair.

'I don't think Dad is Doris's type.' Gina attempted a joke which unsurprisingly fell flat. 'Look, I'll get him to ring you as soon as I find him. Better not chat while driving. Bye darling.'

Once she was back in her own home, Gina stared at her reflection in the hall mirror. There were shadows under her eyes and her face was pinched with anxiety. People often told her what a good-looking woman she was with her arresting eyes that curved slightly upwards and her chiselled cheekbones, accentuated by the line of her stylish haircut, still almost black with only a stray grey hair. She had the look of a Slav from the Steppes, they teased, rather than coming from generations of solid citizens in Southdown.

She was still standing there when the door opened and her husband Mark slipped into the house. He was reading an official-looking letter, which so absorbed his attention that he almost didn't see her.

'Gina!' he blurted, as if his wife was the last person he'd expected to see in their own front hall. 'I thought you were at the warehouse.'

'I just got in,' she replied. 'What's in the letter?'

'Oh, it's just one of those silly scam letters pretending to be important.' He attempted one of his boyish grins and shook his thick curly hair, which he always kept slightly too long, in a gesture Gina recognized as another tool in his arsenal of charm.

She grabbed the letter out of his hands. It was from a firm of bailiffs, threatening to come round if he didn't meet one of his gambling debts.

'Mark, stop lying to me! I've just been talking to Andrew. He says I should close the business accounts down.'

'Bloody typical!' he accused, his eyes blazing, in a tone that combined resentment with a kind of suppressed loathing. 'Going behind my back! Just like you always did with the girls. Always undermining my authority.'

Gina almost had to laugh. 'What authority did you ever have? You were always off at some racecourse or other while I brought them up.'

'What about the good times?'

'You mean the times you won and took us all out to some expensive restaurant when the girls just wanted a takeaway and to watch some silly telly on the sofa with you?'

'You always had to put me down, didn't you Gina?'

Gina looked at him levelly. 'No, Mark. I tried to cover for you and keep running the business. I even told myself you had qualities I didn't have, and that was part of our success.'

'Oh, yes, you're such a saint, aren't you?' he flashed back. 'Sweet, patient Saint Georgina!'

'Well, Saint Georgina's coming to the end of her patience,' Gina replied caustically. 'We're going to pay the debts as best we can. I'm sure these companies are realistic and will recognize something's better than nothing.'

'No, they're not, they're sharks!' Mark threw back at her. 'And you're going to throw me to them!' His voice was full of hate.

'Not if you go to Gamblers Anonymous and we tell them so!'

His answer was a laugh so scathing that it chilled her to the bone.

Gina almost went towards him to try and reason, and finally she saw the truth. There was no vestige of the man she'd once known and loved in this sad and angry figure.

'Mark,' she announced, a break in her voice, 'we can't go on like this.'

'Too bloody right,' he replied. 'I've lived with your holier than thou sanctity for too long. I'm leaving right now. I can't think why I stayed with you so long. Except for the girls, of course.'

He ran upstairs and she could hear him opening cupboards and drawers and throwing things into a bag.

It was the end of her twenty-eight year marriage. Her grandmother was right. Back luck did indeed come in threes. When he came back downstairs he refused to even look at her.

'Mark, where are you going? The girls will need to know.'

'I'll tell them as soon as I find somewhere. Goodbye, Gina.' He slammed the door behind him and walked off down the street.

Gina felt as if some malevolent god had turned her to stone. She wanted to cry. To scream. Yet nothing happened. And then the phone rang and because she thought it might be one of her daughters she made herself answer it.

'Gina, hello! I hope you don't mind me contacting you out of the blue? Evie gave me your number.'

It was Ruth.

And somehow the spell of desperate paralysis was broken and she felt as if she were herself again. Ruth suited the role of good fairy.

'As a matter of fact, I was going to ring you soon,' Gina replied, relief flooding through her. 'How's life in sunny Southdown?'

'Well, er . . . sunny!' laughed Ruth. 'It's awful to celebrate climate change and of course we must cut back on greenhouse gases, but it's turned Southdown into St Tropez! A hundred solid days of sunshine last summer and it's started brilliantly this year too. You'd hardly think it was the same place we grew up in!'

Gina thought of all the damp summers of her childhood spent sheltering from the rain in bus shelters and bandstands, and the August Bank Holiday carnival procession that was regularly cancelled due to summer deluges, and laughed. 'Too right! Doesn't sound like the Southdown I knew at all. So, what's this job you've got for me?'

'Do you remember Rookery Manor?'

'That amazing medieval place on the way to the Downs?'

'That's the one.'

Gina smiled at the memory. How many times had she and her friends made up stories about the owner while they were out walking? Miss Havisham from *Great Expectations* still wearing her wedding dress, fifty years after being jilted? An eccentric rock star seeking privacy? A witch? The place had certainly stirred the imagination.

'A lovely old lady called Maudie lives there,' Ruth continued. 'I'm friends with her great-niece, Lucy. The whole house is stuffed with antiques and Lucy suspects some of them are disappearing. You know, small things no one might notice. She's heard about your antiques business and she wants you to go and stay as a sort of companion and while you're there do a valuation and keep an eye open about what's going on.'

Gina's first instinct was to refuse. It sounded like one of the Famous Five mysteries she'd adored as a child. Strange shenanigans in lonely manor houses. At least Rookery Manor wasn't on a clifftop. 'What does Maudie think of the idea?' she asked.

'Maudie adores company apparently,' replied Ruth. 'Lucy's sure she'd love it.'

'What about the rest of the family?'

'I'm afraid I don't know the answer to that.'

'But surely if stuff's disappearing it's a matter for the police?' suggested Gina.

'That's what I thought,' seconded Ruth, 'but Lucy's adamant the family would absolutely loathe that.'

Andrew the accountant's words that she should and get a job rang in her head. The offer seemed heaven-sent. But shouldn't she be staying and comforting the girls? How would they react when they knew their father had left?

Then again, it wasn't as if she'd be out of reach in Southdown. It was only an hour and a quarter by train, simple for her to dash back if they needed her, and they could easily reach her by mobile. And if she wanted to save the business, following Andrew's advice might be her only option.

'Oh Gina,' Ruthie's effervescent enthusiasm bubbled over in her voice. 'I can't tell you how glad I'd be if you came! It'd be just like old times! Do you remember how we used to hide in the airing cupboard at Wolsey and share all our secrets?'

The memory of those innocent times suddenly over-whelmed Gina – when their deepest secrets were about boys they fancied, and how they would die of misery if the boys didn't fancy them back.

And she knew she had to tell someone.

'The thing is, Ruthie, I really need to come. Mark's just left and he's taken a lot of money out of the company. I'm about to talk to the girls, and I haven't even dared tell Evie yet. She's never liked Mark and I'm sure she'll say it's all for the best!'

'And that isn't what you want to hear right now.' Ruthie's comforting tone was a balm to Gina's drooping spirits. 'I can't wait to have you here and give you the biggest hug you can imagine. And Gina . . .'

'Yes?' Gina replied, feeling her depression lifting with Ruthie's reply.

'We'll have a bloody good time too. I promise!'

Two

'What do you mean, the hotel has cancelled our holiday?' Evie protested, waving her brimming glass of Pinot Grigio in outrage, when Gina told her next day. They were enjoying the April sunshine outside a wine bar in Lamb's Conduit Street. 'I've been fantasizing about it non-stop!'

'There's been a death in the family. Italians take death very seriously. And family.'

'And I take holidays very seriously!' fumed Evie. She took in Gina's shocked expression and laughed. 'It's OK, I'm not as selfish a cow as I seem. I was decimated when my Gran died. I just needed to let off a bit of steam. We'd better get out our diaries and rearrange.'

'Can we leave it for a little while?'

'This isn't to do with Ruth's offer, is it?' Evie asked suspiciously. You're not actually considering going? I mean,' Evie pronounced loudly, 'moving in with an old dear in a medieval manor as a sort of lady's companion! It's like something out of Jane Austen!'

'Well actually,' grinned Gina, 'more Miss Marple!'

'If Miss Marple had any sense, she'd stay away from Southdown,' replied Evie. 'Far too dull. Don't you remember

12

what it was like when we were growing up? Everyone was ancient. Shops closed on Sundays, not to mention early closing on Wednesday afternoons, and the tide seemed to be permanently out! No wonder we couldn't wait to leave!'

'Ruth says it's got much better,' Gina noted that Evie was drinking impressively fast – the current divorce case must a stressful one. As usual they were attracting a lot of interest. With her shiny copper bob and flashing green eyes, Evie was always the centre of attention in legal circles. There was a kind of electric energy she gave off that always seemed to draw the eye.

Gina studied her friend over her glass. Evie was quite a conundrum. Terrifying as an opponent in court, yet generous and fun with those she loved. And steadfastly single. Gina couldn't recall even one serious romance. Evie's career really did seem to have put her off men and marriage. Which was a pity because she was very attractive and adored her many godchildren.

'She would say that, wouldn't she?' replied Evie sarcastically. 'She stayed there and married that Robin and had God knows how many children.'

'*That Robin*, as you call him, is very nice and Ruth sounds very happy.' Gina had to hold onto herself at the thought of Ruth's happy marriage. She'd been building up to tell Evie about Mark and ask her advice, but now that she was sitting across a table from her she found that she didn't want to. It would make it too real, too final. Evie had never liked Mark and would probably tell her it was a blessing in disguise, something she wasn't ready to hear.

'Listen to you,' teased Evie. 'You'd better watch it or you'll be moving back there permanently!'

'Of course I won't,' protested Gina. 'But lots of people are. City life's got so expensive, and now that people are working from home, places like Southdown are suddenly in vogue.' To take her mind off Mark, Gina had spent last night doing some research into her home town. 'Londoners are moving there in droves. Look at this.' She held up a property supplement from *The Times* and read an extract, putting on her best posh estate agent voice: '*Attracted by the nearby seaside and the charming cobbled streets and artistic atmosphere of its old town, Southdown is becoming highly sought after by families seeking a calmer and cheaper way of life.*'

'Charming old town, my arse!' Evie refilled their glasses. 'A few old warehouses and fishing huts turned into second-hand shops!'

'Come on, Evie.' Gina guessed her friend's objection had nothing to do with the burgeoning attractions of Southdown; it was the prospect of losing her best friend and wine bar buddy, even for a few weeks, that bothered her. 'I'd only go for a while. You could come down and rediscover the joys of Southdown at the weekend.'

Evie looked at her as if she had completely lost her mind. 'Not going to happen. I come out in hives if I'm more than a couple of miles from Piccadilly.'

'What about Mauritius and Jamaica and jolly old Sri Lanka?' Gina started to giggle. Evie was famed for her luxurious and exotic winter breaks.

'That's different,' pronounced Evie pompously. 'Those places need the tourists.'

'Well, who knows,' Gina teased her. 'Maybe Southdown does too.'

On the tube home she thought hard about Ruth's offer. She'd only been back to her hometown a couple of times since her parents died twelve years ago, and one of those visits had been with her brother Neil, to clear her parents' house. How different their attitudes had been to that task! Her brother had wanted to simply junk the lot.

'Mum and Dad never had any taste,' Neil had shrugged, leafing through the Yellow Pages for house clearance companies.

'Maybe they couldn't afford any,' Gina had gently reminded him. 'They saved all their money to send you and me to private school.'

'They should have saved their money. Minor public schools are worse than state schools.' She'd looked at her brother then, wondering when he'd become such a crashing snob. Besides, she'd liked her school. Wolsey Hall had been small and eccentric, and it was there she'd met both Evie and Ruth.

Her brother had wanted virtually nothing from the house, but Gina couldn't resist taking a few pictures she remembered from her childhood, a pair of clocks that didn't work because her parents couldn't afford to have them mended, and some of the artwork from Lisa's GCSEs which her mother had insisted on keeping. At the last minute she'd added a box of keepsakes her mother had hoarded over the years: old school reports, postcards Gina had sent from ski-trips or her brother from rugby tours, invitations to special occasions. Finally she'd slipped in a couple of photo albums with attempts at funny inscriptions like *Gina does it again!* beneath a picture of a fat baby version of herself in a frilly dress taking a tumble on the lawn.

She closed her eyes, overcome with emotion. Her parents' life had been so much simpler than her own. The idea of Dad, who worked as a middle manager for the same company all his life, turning into a secret gambler who removed large sums from their joint account was unimaginable. Her father had always been the steady, reliable type. Of course, he lacked Mark's raffish charm, but look where that had got Gina.

Damn you, Mark! Where the hell are you? she wondered. He'd ignored all her messages and calls. Maybe it was time to accept that their marriage really was over. Trust had to be at the root of a relationship, and she certainly couldn't trust Mark. She would help him all she could for her daughters' sake, but that would be it.

It was only a five-minute walk from the tube to her home. It came as a shock to find her husband was standing outside the door about to put his key in the lock. With his curly brown hair and hazel eyes, he looked so like her elder daughter, Sadie, that she had to take a deep breath to keep herself under control.

Gina stopped dead, paralysed by conflicting emotions. What if he had changed his mind? Would she take him back?'

'Gina, hi.' Was that a rare note of apology in Mark's voice? 'I thought you'd like to know. I've decided to get help.'

'Mark,' there was no doubt now in her response. 'That's absolutely wonderful.'

'The thing is,' he continued, avoiding her eyes. 'I haven't been entirely honest with you. Three months ago I met someone else. At the races, for God's sake. She used to be a bit of a gambler herself and she's making it a condition of us staying together that I get treatment, and I've agreed. I'm sorry, Gina, but I want a divorce.'

Gina stood frozen, the front door half open. *You bastard!* she wanted to scream at her husband, remembering the numerous times she'd tried to persuade him to go for treatment herself. And yet for this new woman he was prepared to do it with virtually no argument! The pain was almost too much to bear.

For the sake of her dignity, she kept her emotions in check. 'You'd better leave then,' she replied coolly. 'You can expect to hear from my lawyer. And good luck to your new partner – I suspect she's going to need it.'

She stepped inside the front door and slammed it before he could follow her.

There was no longer any question about whether to take the job in Southdown. She was desperate to leave right away. If Mark could start a whole new life, then so could she.

The moment she heard him drive away she got out her phone and rang Ruth.

'Ruthie, hello. It's Gina. About the job. How soon can I start?'

'I'll call Lucy, but I don't see why you shouldn't come as soon as you like.' Ruthie replied with her usual gutsy enthusiasm. 'I'll book you somewhere and you can come down and get reacquainted with Southdown for a day or two first.'

'That sounds great, thank you.'

She really ought to ring Evie and ask her advice about Mark, but she still didn't feel ready to face it. Maybe she'd do it tomorrow after she'd told the girls. For now she had to face the moment every woman dreaded – breaking the news to her beloved daughters that their parents' marriage was over.

She wandered restlessly round the house where they had lived for most of their married life. Everything was so familiar. The comfortable sofa where they'd all squeezed in to watch silly films together; the photos of the girls through all their stages of growing up; the huge kitchen table where so many friends had shared meals with them. It had seemed a happy house until she'd begun to suspect her husband's behaviour was becoming secretive. The irony was, she'd suspected an affair, not a growing obsession with betting.

* * *

'This is nice, us having a proper family supper,' Sadie commented when she and Lisa came round the next day in answer to Gina's summons. She was helping her mother lay the table in the kitchen. The French windows to the garden were open to let in the cool evening air. 'Pity it takes Dad buggering off to get us together,' she added sarcastically.

'Sadie, don't . . .' Lisa was much softer than her sister and knew that Sadie only sounded so harsh because she was hurt. But so was her mother. They all were. 'Is there any news?' she asked gently.

'I'm afraid there is.' Gina steeled herself for Sadie's reaction. 'He's asked for a divorce. He's met someone else. I'm so sorry.'

'Why are *you* sorry?' demanded Sadie angrily.

'I don't want you being hurt by it.'

'Oh I'm quite tough,' Sadie asserted, while Lisa slipped her arm round her mother. 'It's not someone my age, is it?' Sadie demanded. 'We're not going to hear the patter of tiny half-siblings?'

'I'm afraid I don't know the details.' She knew Sadie's harshness came partly from self-protection.

'Are you OK, Mum?' Lisa asked.

'I've been better,' Gina admitted before mentally pulling herself up. She needed to be strong for their sake, not have them feel the need to look after her when they had their own pain to deal with.

'Would you like me or Sadie to come and stay for a while?'

'It wouldn't be a problem,' Sadie endorsed. 'I know I'm a trial, but I do love you.'

'Oh girls,' Gina put her arms round them both, feeling unbearably touched. 'I'll be fine, but the offer means the world to me.'

'That was a result,' grinned Sadie. 'All the credit and none of the faff of moving back home at our age!'

'Are you sure, Mum?' Lisa insisted.

'I know this'll surprise you, but I've had a job offer.'

'What kind of job?' Sadie asked, stunned that anyone would think of employing her ageing technical innocent of a mother.

'To live with an old lady in a medieval manor and value all her antiques.'

'Sounds like something out of Dickens,' laughed Lisa.

'Or Roald Dahl,' said Sadie. 'In which case the old lady is going to turn out to be like Miss Trunchbull and be absolutely terrifying.'

Gina laughed at how different this was to her own idea of Maudie. 'And the funny thing is, it's in Southdown where I grew up.'

'I used to love staying with Gran,' Lisa reminisced. 'She used to let us get away with murder, didn't she, Sadie? Coca-Cola and chocolate cake for breakfast, remember?'

Sadie laughed. 'It was a great house for kids. Do you remember that trampoline in the garden? No net or anything boring about it. I nearly broke my ankle.'

'That's brilliant about the job, Mum,' said Lisa. 'Except that I thought you hated Southdown? All those stories about the tide always being out and the shops closed!'

'Apparently it's changed a lot. It's very hip now, though they can't have done much about the tide,' Gina conceded.

'God knows what it's like if you think it's hip,' snorted Sadie. 'When are you going?'

'Tomorrow. That is, as long as you're all right.'

'We're fine,' reassured Lisa. 'I'm glad you've got something to look forward to.'

'Absolutely,' agreed Sadie. 'Though personally I couldn't

think of anything worse than having to go to some old-fashioned seaside town full of wrinklies on walking frames. Now where's that bottle of wine I bought?'

The drive to Southdown, into her past, seemed almost over-whelming. She had left her childhood home so full of dreams that she would come to the city and discover a new way of living, and of course find love and then everything would be happy ever after.

How naive had she been?

A sign above her reminded that TIREDNESS COSTS LIVES. Did sadness as well, she wondered, pulling in at a Costa Drive-Thru and ordering a triple espresso. It wouldn't do much for the heartache but would make sure she stayed awake and give her the chance to open any messages. The first was from her daughter Lisa.

> Darling Mum
> Dad phoned and told us. We're all right so don't worry. And remember we're here for you.

That somehow was too much. Her espresso was suddenly flavoured with salt from non-stop tears.

'I'm not going to let this ruin my life,' she announced out loud, taking the man in a Porsche parked next to her by surprise. She couldn't resist making a rude gesture at him, adding, 'Sorry, mate. That's for all men, not just you.'

The tears turned to laughter as she made a vow that she was going to get through this. She kept laughing as Porsche Man drove away from this dangerous lunatic. Or possibly feminist, which was probably much the same in his book.

* * *

'Come on, kids, into the car or you'll be late for school!' Ruth chivvied her grandchildren who were currently living with them, along with their parents, Ruth's daughter Leigh and her husband Wilf, until the leak in their roof was fixed.

For the sake of her long-suffering husband, Ruth had pretended to moan when they all moved back in but secretly she loved it. Robin had been looking forward to having some Me Time; planning holidays in the motor home, spending more hours in the garden. But nothing made Ruth happier than having her family round her. She couldn't begin to imagine living alone like Evie. It would be complete torture for her. Ruth was a person who thrived on company.

It was certainly a bit crowded in their small terraced house near the seafront, with seven people shoe-horned into three bedrooms. Especially with only one bathroom. Robin had got so irritated he'd drawn up a timetable, and if you missed your slot, too bad. Thank heavens there was at least a down-stairs loo!

Ruth, on the other hand, was in her element. At almost six feet, with broad shoulders, and long awkward limbs, she'd been nicknamed Big Ruth at school. Her mother had called her a *hobbledehoy*, the Celtic name for a great clumsy oaf. Ruth had accepted it all calmly. Calm was what Ruth did best. The idea of being pretty or popular was so off her radar that she'd learned to take pleasure in helping other people and the habit had stuck. And the people she most enjoyed helping were her family, or anyone she felt she could be really useful to.

That was why she'd wanted to help out her friend Lucy with her great-aunt Maud at Rookery Manor.

'Shall we order pizza tonight?' she suggested to Robin. 'I mean, with Gina coming, it's an awful lot of people to cook for!'

'Your friend's not staying here, is she?' Robin wouldn't put it past his wife to invite her friend to sleep on the sofa with a rug even though they had more people in the house than the old woman who lived in the shoe.

'Where would she sleep?' Ruth laughed. 'Under the stairs like Harry Potter? I booked her into that posh pub on the seafront.'

'The one with the stall outside selling crab claws?' Robin enquired.

'It's gone upmarket,' Ruth pointed out. 'They're lobster claws these days. In rolls with mayonnaise.'

'Now that is posh,' Robin replied. 'I remember when it used to be cod and chips.'

'Southdown's getting trendy.' Ruth prodded his generous tummy. 'Full of what they call DFLs – Down From Londons. Hadn't you noticed?'

'They haven't penetrated the hallowed ground of the Baker's Arms.' Robin smiled at the thought of his favourite pub.

'Hardly surprising. Spit and sawdust on the floor and old Alf monopolizing the dartboard isn't exactly fodder for Instagram.'

'And thank God for it.'

'You wait,' threatened Ruth, laughing, 'another year and it'll be all Farrow & Ball and quails' egg omelettes.'

Robin shuddered, then put his arms round his wife and squeezed her affectionately. 'I hope it doesn't get too trendy for the likes of us.'

'Speak for yourself, fatty.' She twirled so that her long skirt billowed around her, and the bright colours of her paisley top, purchased in Oxfam to disguise her spreading midriff, lit up in the sunlight. 'I'm bang on trend. I'm not second-hand, I'm upcycled!'

* * *

Even with her stop for coffee, Gina found she was making such good progress she was going to be early, so five miles from Southdown she decided to take the scenic route instead. She turned down a small country lane. It was a glorious morning with only a few fluffy clouds high in the clear blue sky and the sun so bright she had to shade her eyes. The kind of day England did best.

A moment later the car was out of the bright sunshine and into a deep tunnel of shade created by the trees lining the hedgerows. It was almost as if they were throwing their arms round her in welcome. Gina smiled at her own extravagance.

The thought of Mark's announcement invaded the peace of the morning, making her feel sick and shaky. Why did she mind so much? Her husband had never protected her. He was a gambler. He had taken their money and left them. But it was still the death of a dream of happy families shared by almost every woman.

She tried to push the thought out of her mind and look around her. The sight of a giant chalk figure carved into the side of the downs was so vast and unexpected that she just had to pull in and study it. A memory faintly stirred in her. The Long Man, a vast nude figure holding two staves, thought to date from the Iron Age. Gina giggled, remembering when she was about ten some naughty students from the local tech had added a giant willy using football-pitch marker during Freshers' Week.

To her right the landscape opened up almost as far as the blunt snout of a distant hill which she faintly recalled as Beale Beacon. Further down the quiet valley she passed through a pretty village and onwards towards the sea. The road turned left here, climbing upwards. To the right she caught sight of the dramatic snake-like meanders of the river valley. Surely they'd come here with Miss Smith, the geography teacher, to study oxbow lakes for GCSE?

A sign to the right read the Seven Sisters and Beachy Head. Looking at her watch, Gina decided she had time to take this detour down memory lane. Ten minutes later she pulled into a National Trust car park and found herself staring at one of the most famous of all English national landmarks – the white cliffs that had formed the backdrop to countless paintings, calendars, fashion shoots and ad campaigns, the image that stood almost as shorthand for the nation itself.

Staring out to sea, Gina thought how strange that children don't see beauty as adults do. She had grown up near sights like this and they'd struck her simply as days out or school trips. Standing here today she felt unbearably moved by it.

The sound of an ice-cream van, a much more real reminder of her childhood, made her remember why she was here and she turned back to the car, fighting the temptation to buy a 99. Did they even still make them, she wondered. As she started to reverse, a father with two small children approached the van and turned back moments later clutching a cone filled with ice cream and topped with a chocolate flake. Clearly, 99s had held their own. Gina found herself laughing out loud. Some things never changed – except the price.

'You're a lovely girl, Lucy,' the Honourable Maud Tyler reassured her great-niece, 'but the last thing I want is to be bothered with an old lady's companion. Mrs B and I are perfectly fine here on our own!'

Maudie smiled with calm and self-assured certainty. She was a beautiful woman, even in her eighties, in her well-cut black dress with her long ice-white hair swept up into a sophisticated chignon, recreated every Friday by a visiting hairdresser from Southdown and protected at night by sleeping in a hairnet.

'Gina isn't a lady's companion,' announced Lucy firmly. 'She's an expert in antiques. She runs her own successful business in London, and she's also a good friend of Ruth – you remember Ruth, the tall one with lots of children who lives on the seafront.'

'And why would I want an expert in antiques to stay? Apart from to work out how much all my precious possessions are worth when I die? Really, Lucy, you sound as bad as Rosa and Awful Ambrose, forever trying to get me to insure every last thing in the house. Possessions are to be enjoyed not valued.'

Lucy smiled at the reference to her bossy older sister and her pompous husband. She decided to try another tack.

'Ruth says you'd be doing Gina a favour,' she added, hoping Ruth wouldn't kill her for disclosing private information, but she understood the way her great-aunt's mind worked. 'Her husband's a gambler and he's just buggered off with most of their money.'

'Is he indeed?' Maudie seemed to grow almost misty-eyed. 'When I was young I had a lover who almost broke the bank at the Casino in Menton. He was addicted to gambling and I was addicted to him. Franck, his name was if I remember it right. Perhaps I will let your friend stay after all. It might be amusing to swap stories.'

Lucy didn't think Gina would be at all amused by gambling reminiscences, but at least her aunt seemed to be coming round to the idea of letting her come. Lucy wondered for a moment how her older sister Rosa would take Gina's arrival.

Badly, no doubt. Maudie was right about Rosa and Ambrose. They were always putting their oar in where it wasn't welcome. Rosa was a naturally autocratic personality and she'd married a man who was even worse than she was. Both of them felt the manor ought to go to them when Maudie died. And Susan, her middle sister, was the kind who wouldn't say boo to a goose and had sensibly moved to the Lake District.

Lucy decided to leave now while she still had the advantage.

'Bye for now, Maudie. Shall I get Mrs B to bring some tea in for you?'

Maudie consulted an elegant gold watch and sighed. 'I suppose it's a little early for my Gin & It. Tell her just to wave the teabag at the water. You have to watch her or she brings the kind of tea even a builder wouldn't drink.'

'I will.' Lucy bent down to kiss her, breathing in the pungent waves of Estée Lauder's Youth Dew which hadn't changed since she was a child. 'I always associate that perfume with you, Maudie.'

'You know it puts off mosquitoes?' Maudie smiled. 'And we need that here in summer. It comes of being in a valley. Funny how the Italians build on hilltops and we go for valleys.' Maudie put her feet up on a stool and settled down to watch *Countryfile* on iPlayer. Even though she lived bang in the middle of the countryside she preferred to watch it on the TV, preferably with a large aperitif, rather than go out and about. That way you didn't get your feet muddy.

Gina, meanwhile, was arriving at the Jolly Sailor on Southdown seafront.

The room she'd been allocated was obviously one of the best, with a bay window and balcony looking out towards the sea. It was cheerful and clean with en suite facilities just big enough to contain a bath rather than the usual shower, which Gina had requested with the idea of relaxing in it with a nice chilled glass of something white.

She put her bag down on the bed and decided to go out for a walk. Plenty of time before she was due to head for Ruth's house where she would be meeting Lucy, the old lady's niece.

It was glorious out. The sun was still shining in a cloudless blue sky. One of those spring days that felt hot enough for midsummer. The beach was scattered with young mothers and small children, come for a paddle or to build sandcastles on the patches of sand left by the receding tide. For a brief moment Gina thought about putting on her swimsuit, before reminding herself she was here to work. And anyway, the water would be freezing.

She turned down a narrow street into the heart of the old town and found it had changed beyond recognition since she'd last been here. Small hip cafes offering freshly ground coffee and avocado on sourdough toast were dotted between smart boutiques and interior design emporia. Gina smiled to herself. In the Southdown where she'd grown up, no one would have even known what an avocado was. She stopped outside an inviting window, enticingly decorated with Indian scarves, Moroccan beads and silk shirts in jewel-like patterns and felt tempted to go in and try one on, before reminding herself that no matter how much she needed cheering up, she was broke, and the money she was spending on the room at the pub was already pushing her budget to its limits.

She stopped at the end of the street and found herself even more astonished at how much the place had altered. In her childhood there had been only the usual bakers, greengrocers and sweet shops, plus a few of the well-known chain stores. She could still remember her excitement when City Girl boutique opened, bringing hip and desirable clothes. Finally, the exciting world of Swinging London had penetrated dull and suburban Southdown!

Walking around the Southdown of today Gina could see why Londoners might be attracted by this new slightly raffish atmosphere. Moving here must feel like coming on holiday all year round.

She thought of Evie, hard at work on steering yet another divorce case through the courts. Evie would be shocked that Gina could be even a little seduced by Southdown. She turned back towards the beach and found herself a picturesque spot with the sea sparkling behind her and held up her phone to take a selfie.

'Can I be of any assistance?' enquired a total stranger. He was standing in the shade and she could hardly make out his features, except that he was tall with broad shoulders and had a deep voice that seemed to have a laugh in it. 'At our age I find photographs are more flattering taken at a distance.'

Gina's first reaction was indignation. How did this man think he knew how old she was anyway?

'I'm fine, thank you,' she replied curtly.

His reply was a shrug and a laugh. 'Enjoy your stay,' he grinned before turning and walking away.

Gina stared at his receding back. There was something faintly familiar about the man that almost prompted her to call out after him, but if she'd got it wrong it would look as if she were trying to pick him up, and she assumed, from very little evidence, that the stranger's ego didn't need any stoking.

Irritated, she added the message: Greetings from Sunny Southdown and sent it to Evie.

It did nothing to improve her mood when she got an almost instant reply reminding her that some people were working.

Didn't Evie remember that this was work too?

On that note she quickly bought a bottle of wine to take with her and headed for Ruth's.

Knowing that most people didn't live in the habitual chaos natural to the O'Halloran family, Ruth had made a big effort to tidy up.

Of her five children, only one still lived at home, but with the temporary addition of Leigh, Wilf and their little ones plus their dog, wittily named Fido, it was hard to keep any order at all.

At least she'd got the dishwasher stacked and the floor space more or less cleared.

Gina found the house with no difficulty, but it was a different matter with the doorbell. It didn't seem to work no matter how hard she pressed it and she ended up knocking loudly.

'Gina, so glad you're here, darling girl!' Ruth folded her into a tight bear hug, while tactfully making no mention of the situation with Mark. 'It's going to be so great to have you back in Southdown! Luckily for you the brood are out at the moment. They're back for supper though, so you won't mind having Domino's? Clever Robin found they have a three-for-two offer!'

Gina followed her hostess into the living room. Sometimes Gina and Evie, sitting over a glass of chilled Sauvignon, would pride themselves on having worn well for their age, but Ruth, staggeringly, had hardly changed at all. You could put her in the largest possible school pinafore dress, add a shirt and tie, pull her unruly auburn hair into a plait and she would

29

look exactly the same as she had done at Wolsey Hall all those years ago.

In fact, Gina noted, Ruth's dress sense hadn't evolved much from those days either. She had graduated from a school pinafore to a tubular dress in stretchy jersey which, Gina would learn, she possessed in six different colours and wore in rotation. Comfort definitely won over style in Ruth's universe.

'I really am glad you've come!' Gina could tell from the large dose of understanding in Ruth's tone that she was happy to lend a sympathetic ear.

Gina's first instinct was to play it down. She didn't want people feeling sorry for her, even Ruthie. Besides, she had to admit there was so much warmth emanating from Ruth that you almost felt you could wrap yourself in it, like an old fur coat, and forget about everything bad.

'Fido!' Ruth bellowed. A large furry dog jumped off the sofa and abased itself at their feet. 'Sorry. He's not allowed on the furniture.'

Fido looked up at them appealingly as if to say, *Not while you're looking, anyway.*

'Let's sit down while the coast's clear and I'll fill you in about the job. Robin!!!' she bellowed at maximum volume. 'Can you get us a drink, love?'

'Beer or wine?'

Gina judged this was probably a beer household. She'd leave the good wine she'd brought for them to enjoy alone. 'Beer would be lovely, as long as it's lager.'

'I'll have a glass of that Macon Villages Gina brought,' Ruth announced knowledgeably. 'Louis Jadot's always worth drinking.'

So much for jumping to conclusions, thought Gina, enviously eyeing Ruth's large glass of white wine.

'So,' Gina sipped her not-quite-cold lager, trying not to make a face, 'tell me about the set-up at the manor.'

'My friend Lucy is the youngest of three sisters,' Ruth explained. 'Rosa's the eldest, bossy as they come, the type who runs the Neighbourhood Watch and acts as if she's chair of ICI. Susan in the middle's a mouse, and Lucy's lovely. I suppose I would say that, since she's my friend. Anyway, their great-aunt Maud lives in Rookery Manor with a cleaner and gardener in the cottage nearby. Of course, they're all wondering what's going to happen when the old lady goes, who'll get the house and all the stuff in it – some of it very valuable apparently.' Ruth sipped her wine. 'The thing is, the cleaner told Lucy she thinks some things are going missing. Small stuff you wouldn't notice mainly. But she's worried about it. Hence the invitation to you. So, what do you think?'

Gina twirled the beer in her glass thoughtfully. 'I'm not sure, Ruthie. I've never done anything that involved things disappearing. It sounds more like a matter for the authorities.' *On the other hand*, she thought but didn't add, *I really need the money.*

'Lucy suggested to Rosa that they call in the cops and guess what? One hundred per cent denial. She thinks the cleaner's imagining it and her aunt will get upset. Besides,' she grinned at Gina, 'bad publicity like that wouldn't go down with her country friends.'

A loud knock on the door told them that Lucy had arrived on the doorstep. Gina suppressed a grin. She'd also found the bell wasn't working.

'Lucy, come in!' Ruth administered another bear hug, giving Gina the chance to look at the new arrival before being introduced. She was a tall, elegant woman, probably in her forties but with the kind of polish that made her seem younger. In marked contrast to their hostess, she looked like a woman who took care of herself – probably with regular gym and spa visits plus an expensive hairdresser. Despite their different images, the warmth between them seemed real.

'This is my very old and dear friend Gina. Gina, meet Lucy. I've been filling Gina in a little about the background to the manor.'

'Thank you,' Lucy acknowledged with a smile. She had a wide, generous mouth, noted Gina. 'Quite a tricky situation, isn't it?'

'Yes. It must be very difficult for you to know what to do.'

'That's why I was so relieved when Ruth suggested you. The fact you have your own valuation business makes absolute sense of why you should be there for a while, besides, Maudie will love the company. She always says she's quite happy in that great place with Mrs B and her husband, but she must get lonely sometimes. She loves TV, mind you, and has totally embraced the internet. Susan thinks she may even be trying internet dating! At eighty-one!'

Maudie certainly sounded an engaging character, decided Gina.

'How about the rest of your family?' she asked Lucy. 'Have you told them that you've asked me to come?'

Lucy shrugged, looking embarrassed, then added, with a streak of irritation hardening her attractive face, 'No I haven't, because my older sister Rosa would veto it. She acts like she owns the place already and is always working on Maudie to leave it to her. "I'm the only one who appreciates its place in history," is the line she peddles. Bollocks! She's the only one who's enough of a social climber to want the cachet of being lady of the manor. Maudie always refuses to even hold the church fete there. God has plenty of alternatives, she says, and she doesn't want his followers trampling her tulips. She held it there once and caught some old dear pinching a cutting from her darling Savoy Hotel roses. The old dear had brought a pair of tiny scissors and a little plastic bag which she kept under her hat. I was quite impressed but Maudie said that was it, no more "fete worse than death" on her watch!'

The evening passed pleasantly. Gina, who hadn't eaten take-away pizza for years, laughed as she realized what she'd been missing and the warmth of the O'Halloran household made her feel a little sad. This was what family life ought to be like.

Lucy offered her a lift back to the pub around ten, insisting that she'd been careful with what she'd drunk. 'I do hope you'll get on with Maudie. She's my favourite relative and she's led a very exciting life. She's lived all over the world. Cyprus, Egypt and Syria too, before the war obviously, and has fascinating stories about it.'

'Was there ever a Mr Maudie?'

'He died ages ago. Yet she never seems lonely. Anyway, do let me know how you get on. She's expecting you at eleven. Mrs B will have your room all ready.'

'Thank you, I will,' Gina smiled. They had arrived at the Jolly Sailor, which seemed to be the centre of Southdown social life. In fact, was that the man who had offered to take her photograph standing at the bar?

She surprised herself by feeling a momentary flash of attraction. But what kind of man propped up the bar in his local on a Tuesday night? Great choice, Gina: swap a gambler for a drinker. She firmly resisted making his further acquaintance in favour of an early night.

* * *

Maeve Haran

Next morning Gina set off deliberately early to meet Maudie so that she could take stock of her surroundings. The road to Rookery Manor snaked through the back of the old town, past a maze of suburban streets, then upwards in a sweeping curve and onto the main road across the downs. Gina glanced back and was impressed at how beautiful the view was down to the sea.

The road kept going for another couple of miles till she encountered a church next to a lily pond. She found a car park hidden away for use of the parishioners and decided to leave her car here and walk for a while before heading for the manor.

It was a perfect morning with the sky burnished almost to cobalt blue. Gina headed up across the scrubby downlands, home to thousands of Southdown sheep and their lambs who were frolicking together in the sunshine.

From here she could smell rather than see the sea. Yet there was also that little jolt of excitement you always felt when you knew that over the next hump the blue expanses of the English Channel would be spread beneath you. The few small trees up here were bent over sideways from the wind, like old men who could only walk by leaning on sticks.

She stood still for a moment, entranced. There it was. The sound she could remember so well from childhood walks. A skylark. Invisible and high in the sky, its unique melody still audible as it swooped and turned high above its nest in the rough grass. As a child, Gina used to lie here for hours in the turf and listen. It had been her guilty secret. Pupils at school would laugh at her if they knew and call her a weirdo.

Glancing around first to make sure no walkers were approaching, she lay down and closed her eyes. For a moment she was a child again, not old enough to make choices of her own. Like falling for Mark, knowing there was an element of danger in him she couldn't identify or explain but was drawn to. Why couldn't she have fallen for some nice safe boy instead? How different her life would be now. Then she remembered her lovely daughters Sadie and Lisa, who wouldn't have existed, and made herself get to her feet. Thoughts like that were stupid and useless.

She crossed over the last few tussocks and there it was: the vast expanse of turquoise sea, lighter towards the shore with darker patches where hidden rockpools lay beneath. The extraordinary thing was how empty the entire landscape was. There was virtually no one on the horizon but a man and his dog in the far distance. In a busy overcrowded island like this it seemed a small miracle.

Glancing down at her watch, Gina realized it was time she got a move on to Rookery Manor. She was surprised how well she remembered the path. Straight ahead to the triangulation point right at the edge of the cliff, marked by a structure in stone and steel next to the dizzying drop down to the sea, turn left along the clifftop, then as the path dipped down a small flint bridleway became visible to the right between high hedgerows which she knew led back to the car park.

Just before eleven she found herself in the tiny hamlet of Rookery: a small scattering of cottages dominated by the impressive Elizabethan manor house, built of rust-coloured brick in a herringbone pattern, with stone mullions and high barley twist chimneys. It was a startlingly impressive building to find in this tiny fold of the downs, only moments from the sea yet hidden away rather than proudly proclaiming its existence. Perhaps its first owners had not wanted to draw attention to themselves.

As Gina raised her arm to tug the enormous bell pull that hung from the impressive front porch she felt an unfamiliar shiver of doubt. Was this a place she wanted to spend weeks or even months trying to find the answer to the mystery of the disappearing objects?

Before she'd had a chance to pull the rope, the huge front door opened and a smiling Lucy ushered her in. 'Hello, Gina. Perfect timing. Maudie and I were just about to have a coffee. Come and meet her then I'll show you round.' She stood back to let Gina pass into a large hall panelled with intricate linen-fold carving and wide, almost black ceiling beams.

'Quite something, aren't they?' Lucy followed her gaze. 'They're made from the hulls of those little ships they sailed round the world in.' Gina looked up, trying to picture fragile craft like Drake's *Golden Hind* voyaging across wild tumultuous oceans, imagining at any moment they might fall off the edge of the earth.

Lucy led Gina through an arched door into a dark passage that opened into a sunny drawing room. It was so full of exquisite objects that Gina almost let out a gasp. From the slender-legged Regency cabinets to the polished mahogany console tables, every possible surface was covered with gorgeous decorative artefacts: rare Chinese vases; gilt candelabra featuring nymphs in diaphanous robes; delicately painted porcelain birds, which Gina knew at a glance would have the raised anchor of the Chelsea pottery on their base; a tiny silver object, which she recognized as a highly collectable Georgian cinnamon grater; and beneath them all the seductive pale green of an Aubusson carpet. But the star of the show was undoubtedly the striped Empire daybed with its gilded lion's paw feet. Gina smiled, remembering the quote from the racy Mrs Patrick Campbell about the deep peace of the marriage bed after the hurly-burly of the chaise longue and wondered if Maudie had entertained any lovers on it.

'Maudie loves collecting,' Lucy interrupted her thoughts. 'And now she's got the whole of the internet to choose from, things can get a bit out of hand.'

'Are you trying to imply I have a problem, Lucy dear?' asked a voice which appeared to be coming down from the heavens.

Lucy's reply was to giggle. 'What are you doing up in the gallery, Maudie?'

Gina had been so dazzled by the variety of antiques that she hadn't noticed the minstrel's gallery that hung dramatically over the far end of the large room. Even more dramatic was the gallery's sole occupant. The Hon. Maudie Tyler was dressed in black as usual with her white hair swept up into its immaculate French pleat. To Gina she seemed so elegant and stylish that to speculate about her age seemed somehow irrelevant.

'I thought I'd get a good look at you before we were introduced. Appallingly rude, I know. But one of the few benefits of age is pleasing yourself.' With a decidedly royal air, she began to descend the carved oak staircase. Gina tried not to stare but found herself fascinated all the same. Beneath the sophisticated hairstyle, Maudie had soft skin and blue eyes with an engaging expression which, despite their twinkle, also possessed a remarkable shrewdness. Maudie might be old, but Gina suspected not much got past her.

'Maudie,' Lucy embraced her great-aunt affectionately. 'May I present Gina Greenhills, Ruthie's friend from London.'

'Hello Gina, if I may call you that,' replied Maudie. 'And how was London when you left it? Any nightingales singing in Berkeley Square? No, of course not. Not that I expect they ever did. I do miss the Savoy though. My husband and I used to stay there, and they'd always put a vase of Savoy Hotel roses in the room, specially for me. That's why I grow them in the garden. Lucy dear, go and see if any of them are out yet – the pale pink scented ones – and put some in Gina's room.'

Lucy dutifully went to look for secateurs. Clearly, when Maudie asked you to do something, you did it.

'Now, Gina dear, sorry about my little ruse to get Lucy into the garden,' Maudie continued as she led her to the grand-looking daybed and elegantly sat down. 'There was something I wanted to say to you. I know why she's invited you and it's all complete nonsense. Mrs B probably broke the ornaments and didn't want to admit it. She's a great one for doing that. I'm happy for you to come because I'd enjoy the company and for you to do the valuation. But I'd like you to remember one thing: if you stay with me it will be to enjoy yourself. It's famously beautiful round here, and when it heats up you're only ten minutes from the beach. Lucy tells me you were supposed to be going on holiday to Sicily?'

Gina nodded.

'Taormina! Siracusa! Palermo!' Maudie declaimed theatrically, closing her eyes as if lost in memory. 'I love them all. Well, *Signora* Greenhills, if you stay with me it will be to enjoy an English holiday. Is that clear?'

When Lucy returned with a small bunch of fragrant roses, she found Gina and Maudie in gales of giggles. It was clear, if nothing else, they were going to enjoy each other's company.

'So,' Maudie announced in a tone few would have argued with, 'bring in your things and unpack, Gina dear. I want you to feel at home. The weatherman says we're in for a heatwave, and there's nowhere on earth more pleasant when the sun shines than this corner of England. People go on about Cornwall, but it's so bloody *far*! Southdown is an easy drive from town and there are plenty of beaches with hardly anyone on them. I'll grant you it's pebbles rather than sand, but that means the water is extra clear. When I was younger I can remember no greater pleasure than swimming at high tide and I'll expect you to do the same!' Her smile softened the command. 'I'd like to know if it still feels as divine as it did back then.'

'I'd be more than happy to report back,' replied Gina, stifling a giggle at the unusual request from her new employer. 'I love swimming. My friends think I'm crazy because I sometimes swim in the Serpentine in the middle of winter!'

'You're definitely my kind of girl,' pronounced Maudie. 'One last thing, dearest Lucy, and then you can scoot off home. Have you told Rosa and Ambrose about this little scheme of yours?'

'Not really, no,' replied Lucy, trying not to look furtive and failing. 'I don't see why Rosa should be a self-appointed guardian of you and the manor.'

'I couldn't agree more, dear, but Rosa may think otherwise.' Her smile held a hint of engaging malice. 'And Ambrose will no doubt scent a conspiracy to deprive them of some unspecified rights.'

'Then they're going to have to jolly well lump it!' insisted Lucy.

As she went out to the car to get her suitcase, Gina couldn't help wondering what she was in for. Was she making the mistake of jumping into the middle of a family feud as well?

Well, too bad, Maudie's depiction of an English holiday was too tempting to resist. If she couldn't have Sicily she could at least have the sunny South coast of England instead.

And the best thing was that the sunshine and the task ahead would not only keep her busy but also take her mind off her own painful situation.

Three

Gina opened the boot of her car to get out her bag and start unpacking. The room she'd been given was at the back of the house, with a vast canopied four-poster bed that looked like a room in itself. She couldn't wait to climb into it later.

She was hunting for the pair of sensible walking shoes she'd brought when she noticed the cardboard box of souvenirs from her childhood that her mother had saved. She remembered now that she'd meant to sort through it while she was here, since she was back in Southdown – throw away the rubbish and only keep the things of real emotional significance. She tucked it under her arm and began to wheel her bag towards the house.

On the question of the valuation, she would do what she usually did when she was called in. Start by discreetly photographing all the valuables in the house on her phone so there was a visual record of everything, then transfer them to a file on her laptop. And tomorrow she'd have a chat with Mrs B, the cleaner and housekeeper, about what she thought had disappeared and whether, by any remote chance, there were photographs of any of the missing objects.

As she closed the boot she noticed that the garage doors were open and there was a large Mercedes estate car parked inside. Even though from the number plate and the model it was obviously an old vehicle, it was the cleanest car she'd ever seen. Every bit of the pale gold paintwork and chrome wheel hubs sparkled in the afternoon sunshine as if the car were brand new.

'Amazin', ain't it?' growled a voice behind her.

Gina turned to find an old man dressed entirely in forest green from head to toe, including a forest green beanie hat, which made it hard to tell him apart from the greenery behind him. This had to be Mr B, the husband of the cleaner/housekeeper, who looked after the garden. 'The old lady takes it to that car wash in Southdown twice a week, inside and out. Bloomin' bonkers, I call it. I've told her I can do it here with my power hose, but she won't have any of it.'

'Maybe the car's her pride and joy,' suggested Gina. 'Or she likes driving into Southdown.'

'Then why don't she have a cup of tea or meet a friend like a normal pensioner would, instead of getting the car cleaned when it don't need it?'

Part of the answer, of course, was that Maudie was in no way a normal pensioner, and perhaps the sparkling Mercedes was one of her ways of showing it.

'And she always goes to the same place: Mad Mike's. Won't take it anywhere else. Weird, Mrs B and I think it is.'

Gina shrugged. She was beginning to feel that maybe Mr and Mrs B might be part of the problem rather than the disappearing antiques. The image of the sinister housekeeper Mrs Danvers from Daphne du Maurier's *Rebecca* slipped into her mind and she had to smile. The rotund and determinedly cheerful Mrs B might be an interfering busybody, but she didn't strike Gina as someone with evil intent. All the same it must be annoying for Maudie to be so closely watched.

Who knows, maybe Maudie had a soft spot for Mad Mike. After all, Lucy had said they thought she might be up for online dating!

She bid Mr B goodbye and headed for the house.

Once upstairs in her room, she had to admit there was more evidence of kindness than sinister manipulation. The canopied bed had been turned down, a pile of fresh towels left on top and a single bloom placed in a bud vase on the other side of the bed from the roses Lucy had picked. A larger bunch of flowers graced the fireside, next to a cosy-looking armchair. In an alcove by the window Gina spotted a kettle, tea-making things plus a tin which she guessed contained biscuits. There was also a note in spidery writing stating *fresh milk will be outside your door later.*

Gina sighed. It felt like she was staying in a lush boutique hotel. It was a long time since anyone had made a fuss of her. She'd have to keep reminding herself why she was here.

In fact, now would be the perfect time to approach the housekeeper since Maudie had announced she herself always had a nap at three. 'Like the Spanish, such sensible people,' Maudie had confided. 'Makes me bright as a button to watch my favourite television – without it I'd nod off during the nine o'clock news.' Despite being considerably younger, Gina had to confess to the same problem, and she smiled in sympathy.

She finished unpacking quickly, impressed that for once there were enough hangers in the wardrobe, and went to the kitchen to look for the housekeeper.

'Hello, Mrs B,' Gina greeted her. 'By the way, what does the B stand for?'

'Browning,' the housekeeper replied, 'like the poet.'

'Perhaps I could call you Mrs Browning?'

Mrs B was dressed in sludgy brown, the kind of colour Farrow and Ball would probably have called Slurry, with a bright red apron on top and matching red baseball cap pulled so far down over her face that it appeared like a beak. It struck Gina that the housekeeper was like a little robin: cheery and friendly on the surface, but capable of being surprisingly savage when the situation demanded.

'So, Mrs Browning,' Gina made sure she used her full name. 'What exactly has disappeared from the manor?'

'A place for everything and everything in its place is my motto, and that's how I know what's gone,' chirped Mrs B. 'Would you like me to show you?'

'An excellent idea,' agreed Gina.

Mrs B led the way into the treasure-packed drawing room, where decorative objects vied for every inch of visible space. She stopped at a black lacquer console table. 'There!' she pointed. 'There used to be a glass scent bottle. Double ended, it was. Used to make me think of a little rolling pin with silver knobs on. And over there' – she grabbed Gina's arm in her enthusiasm – 'on the mantelshelf, there was a little Bible, bound in leather. Belonged to a soldier, and he'd known he'd probably be killed so he inscribed it to his darling wife. Made me cry every time I read it.' She scanned the room with narrowed eyes, looking for suspicious spaces. 'Oh yes, the little man . . .' This time she led Gina to an alcove near the door to the kitchen. 'He was on the wall there. Like that one,' she pointed to a tiny portrait, no more than two inches high, framed in gold with a small loop on the top. A miniature, Gina decided, obviously quite early. She knew a little about these as she'd once collected them herself. 'He was better than that one,' continued Mrs B, 'so real you almost expected him

43

to speak. Mrs Tyler said he'd have been in a locket, sent to some great lady to show her the man her father had picked for her to marry. The royals always did it, she said, and Henry VIII got right cross when the picture of Anne of Cleves didn't look anything like her! Called her a Flanders Mare!' Mrs B burst into laughter at this oafish royal response.

'Excuse me, Mrs Browning,' interrupted a voice so glacial it could have frozen the pipes on the central heating. 'But who exactly is this person you're showing round my great-aunt's home?'

'Mrs Winstanley, I didn't see you there!' Mrs B's cheery robin persona dissolved in the face of the new arrival. The newcomer's type would have been instantly recognizable in an Indian hill station during the colonial era but seemed out of place a hundred years later in sunny Sussex. 'I'm not sure if you know . . .' she tailed off, unsure how best to describe Gina.

'Georgina Greenhills.' Gina offered a brisk handshake. 'But do call me Gina. I'm actually here at your sister Lucy's invitation. I run an antiques business that specializes in valuations. She asked me to come and take a look at your great-aunt's absolutely fascinating house and assess the contents.'

'Ambrose!' shrieked the new arrival.

A small, startlingly neat man appeared from behind her, wearing an immaculate pinstripe suit. His thick grey hair was cut with almost military precision to match his eyebrows, with a small, equally neat moustache grazing the top of his lip. 'What is it now, Rosa?' he enquired in a voice bristling with irritation. His temper was obviously not subject to the same level of control as his hair and wardrobe. 'I'm looking for a book in the library!'

'Did you know anything about this?' she nodded rudely towards Gina.

'About what, my dear? You'll have to make yourself clearer.'

'Mrs Greenhills here,' Rosa replied. 'She's come to value the antiques. Surely it ought to be Sotheby's or Christie's? Or at least Waddington's?' Gina recognized the name of the local firm of auctioneers. 'I mean,' she added in a distinctly audible whisper, 'what do we know about her anyway?'

Gina studied Ambrose, wondering whether his response would be as rude as his wife's outburst.

Every inch of Ambrose looked offended. His bearing became even more military. His hair looked stiffer. Even his eyebrows had taken on a straighter line. 'I agree with you, my dear, the whole thing is highly irregular.'

'As a matter of fact,' interrupted a voice behind them, 'Mrs Greenhills is well known in her field. And as you know, Ambrose, I am highly irregular too.' Maudie at her most *grande dame* had entered the fray. 'So it's hardly surprising she and I are getting on like a house on fire, though I have never understood why houses being on fire should denote good relations.'

'You've lost me there,' Ambrose shook his head.

'Excellent,' replied Maudie. 'Suffice it to say that Mrs Greenhills is staying with me for a while. She will assess the value of the contents of the manor—'

'If you had listened to me an insurance assessor would have done that years ago,' he huffed.

'Then you should be glad it's being done now. I have also invited her to enjoy herself while she's here.' She opened the French windows in a dramatic gesture. 'Look at the weather! Completely gorgeous. Gina, finish up here as soon as you can and go down to Sheldon Gap and swim. It's high tide in half an hour. Then you can come back and tell me all about it over a delicious cocktail. And don't look at me like that, Rosa, you should be doing the same! Why live in one of the most beautiful landscapes on God's earth and never enjoy it? You should go swimming too!'

Rosa wrinkled her nose in disgust and patted her unattractive perm. 'I don't like sea swimming,' she announced.

'Maudie, have you finally taken leave of your senses?' demanded Ambrose.

'No, Ambrose, I believe I've just found them,' she replied. 'In fact, Gina, if you don't mind an old dear accompanying you, perhaps I could come too?'

'I'd be delighted,' said Gina, and with that they gave a parting nod to the outraged pair and made their exit.

Ten minutes later they were in Maudie's old Mercedes, heading for the beach. 'Oh dear,' commented Maudie, not sounding at all sorry, 'that was naughty of me, but they do take over so!'

'I suppose they were surprised to find me examining the china,' Gina offered diplomatically.

'I know they view the manor as virtually theirs,' Maudie tutted, swerving to avoid a gatepost while Gina held on to the side, trying not to think of the late Prince Philip and the hazard of older drivers, 'but I am still very much alive!'

A couple of miles later they turned off onto a narrow track through sloping fields dotted with sheep. The sight triggered a memory in Gina, of being brought to a farm nearby to feed the newborn lambs. A group of hikers appeared on the horizon. As an official area of Outstanding Natural Beauty, it attracted walkers in their thousands. Gina leaned back, grateful she was in a car, even one driven by Maudie, so that she could take in the full drama of the landscape.

Before long they arrived at a car park not far from the cliff's edge. Maudie surprised her by instantly accessing the right app and paying for the parking on her phone. Once out of the car, the scene in front of them literally took Gina's breath away. To the right stretched the Seven Sisters. Below, the pebble beach lay encircled peacefully in the arms of the bay, with a turquoise sea beyond. Up and down the beach little knots of swimmers and sunbathers were taking advantage of the early sunshine.

The silence, apart from the gentle lapping of waves and the occasional raucous cry of a young seagull, was intense and soothing. It might not be Sicily but it had a spellbinding charm of its own.

'What's the name of the red and white lighthouse?' Gina asked Maudie, her hand over her eyes as she stared out to sea.

'That's Wellhaven,' Maudie replied. 'It may look peaceful but that was the famous wreckers' lighthouse. It would lure ships into the bay and they'd founder on the rocks hidden out there, then everyone from Southdown would rush out and help themselves.'

Gina shuddered despite the heat at the thought of such deliberate cruelty.

'It seems bad, I know, but this is smugglers' country. It made people tough.'

'Thank God that's in the past,' said Gina.

Maudie shook her head. 'Nowadays they just find different things to smuggle. But let's have our swim and think of happier things. Have you got your sea shoes? Everyone wants sandy beaches but pebbles make the sea much clearer. It's hell though without shoes.'

'Only these.' She produced a pair of plimsolls so old and worn that they looked as if they'd been bought when she was in primary school. 'I found them in my mum's cellar. I knew they'd come in useful.'

'Good for you!' congratulated Maudie. 'I hate this cult of throwing everything away.'

A vision of the manor where beautiful antiques were crowded on top of every conceivable surface came to Gina and she smiled. And then the thought of the missing objects intruded. The reason she had come here. Tomorrow she must start investigating those properly.

They both ran down the beach towards the beckoning sea. Despite her age, Maudie was extraordinarily lithe and slender in her black swimsuit, the silver French pleat tucked neatly into a flowery bathing cap. 'You're wonderful, Maudie!' Gina laughed. 'You put me to shame!'

Maudie glanced at Gina's bright swimsuit with its palate of jewel-like greens and blues. 'You're not so bad yourself!' she winked. 'If your husband's gone and left you, he must be blind, deaf and dumb!'

Gina followed her, smiling to herself. So Lucy had told her about Mark. Maybe that was for the best.

As they plunged into the gentle blue waves a group of women in bathing caps like Maudie's rounded the bay and ran shrieking into the sea next to them. 'Hello!' shouted the woman nearest to them. 'We're the Southdown Sirens! We swim all year round and bring good luck to these shores!'

'There you are,' Maudie grinned at Gina. 'Maybe you'd better join them. I expect you could do with some good luck at the moment.'

'Not by swimming all year in freezing temperatures,' Gina replied. 'Besides, the good luck was in coming to work for you!'

At least, she certainly hoped so.

* * *

'Why don't we pop into town for something to eat?' Maudie enquired as they got back into the car after the swim. 'Come on,' she insisted as Gina hesitated, wondering if she ought to be doing something useful instead. 'What did I say about you having an English holiday? The Langdon Arms on Southdown seafront may not be Sicily, but their calamari is excellent!'

Ten minutes later they were sitting at a picnic bench outside the pub, watching the happy tourists queuing up for the big wheel or screaming as they came down the somewhat sedate rollercoaster. Beyond was a vista of tall narrow buildings made out of black-painted wood. 'I'd forgotten how historic Southdown is, with all the fishermen's huts,' said Gina. 'Remind me why they're that shape?'

'I think it was to dry their nets,' replied Maudie. 'They'd hang them up inside. And that chain on the beach . . .' She pointed to a heavy chain attached to a large pulley. 'That's to pull up the fishing boats because there's no harbour here. Any more fishing facts I can supply?' she laughed.

'I should know all that myself since I grew up here,' Gina admitted, 'but I probably thought it was too boring.'

'That's called being young. The same as one's attitude to men. The first rule of being young is that you never like anyone who likes you.'

Gina giggled. How true that was. You always fell for the tricky ones. Like Mark.

She looked away, overwhelmed by the thought of her future, of the effect on the girls, of all she had to do. *You're doing what your accountant told you to do to save the business*, she reminded herself sternly. *One step at a time.*

'There are always good things in life,' Maudie interrupted her thoughts. 'Here comes your calamari. I always tell myself, no matter how shit life gets, you can always enjoy a good meal.'

Gina buried her face in her hands, overcome by laughter. Maudie certainly was a law unto herself.

And she was right. The calamari – not the usual frozen hoops thrown into batter – were the type you got in Spain. *Chiprones*: baby squid in crunchy tempura, and they were utterly delicious.

'Here you are, madame,' announced the server as she put down the plate. 'Would you like a glass of chilled Picpoul with that?'

'Pinch me,' Gina whispered to Maudie, remembering the limited choice of her childhood, when sophistication had meant a glass of Babycham. 'I can't really be in Southdown!'

'Southdown's changed.' Maudie replied, gazing into the distance as if thinking of something too painful to mention. 'And not always for the better, I'm afraid.'

Gina, unsure whether she should ask what Maudie meant or change the subject, was spared by the arrival of a group of men in bright tropical shirts, coloured sunglasses and hats festooned with faux flowers. 'We're the Southdown Morris Men,' explained the nearest, pressing a flyer into her hand and winking as if he'd taken a shine to her. 'Only we prefer to play Bruce Springsteen and Bob Dylan to English folk songs!'

'That sounds very modern,' Maudie laughed.

'That's Southdown!' he grinned back. 'We like to combine the best of the old with the best of the new.'

'I can't argue with that,' smiled Gina.

'Come and watch us then,' the morris man persisted, 'we'll be performing outside this very public house. Every evening this week at six. I might even buy you a drink as an incentive!'

'Come on, Colin,' shouted his mate. 'Stop harassing the punters. Even if they are very attractive!'

'You seem to have made a hit there,' whispered Maudie.

'You have to draw the line somewhere,' replied Gina, all the same feeling cheered by the compliments, 'and I think for me it might be morris dancers!'

On the way home, Maudie turned right instead of taking the road back to the manor. 'Do you mind if we just nip into the car wash? I like to keep the car looking nice.'

Gina glanced up at a large sign announcing MAD MIKE'S MODERN CAR WASH. Interesting. It was the one Mr B had said she was obsessed with.

As they drove in, Gina experienced the usual pang of middle-class guilt, knowing you wanted your car to look good, but realizing the workers in the car wash were probably being both exploited and underpaid.

A tired-looking young man came and began to spray the outside, before he was joined by two others, armed with microfibre mitts of soapy water, who attacked the body of the car. Meanwhile, Maudie craned her neck as if she were looking for someone. Perhaps it was Mad Mike.

If so, she was in luck because a heavy-set balding man in a tight T-shirt which demonstrated, should anyone be interested, that his bulk was made up of muscles rather than fat, appeared and began bellowing at someone. The three men working on their car avoided his gaze and concentrated on their work, casting the occasional nervous glance at one other as they applied themselves at double speed.

'Nasty bully,' murmured Maudie softly, her eyes scouring the forecourt, clearly on the lookout for someone else.

As soon as the car was rinsed clean, dried and the wheels painted with tyre shine, the young man gestured that they should move on to the polishing area. Gina noted with interest that this was staffed by tired-looking women. But there was one young woman who stood out. She was tall, dark-haired and exceptionally striking. Not only that, there was a grace about her movements that marked her out and made the setting of a car wash doubly remarkable. Maudie's eyes fixed on her throughout. At the end they exchanged a brief smile. The rest of the women threw all their cloths, clean or dirty, into a large vat. But this girl stood folding her clean ones into a neat pile, stroking them as if they were beautiful articles of great value. Suddenly she jumped as Mad Mike shouted at her and the carefully assembled pile fell to the ground. Maudie would have leapt out of the car had the girl not subtly shaken her head in silent communication.

'Do you know her, Maudie?' Gina enquired.

'A little,' Maudie replied, her face looking troubled. 'Her name's Jasmin. She's from Damascus. My husband worked for the British Cultural Commission there for many years and it's a place we came to love.'

Gina couldn't help feeling intrigued, but there was something about Maudie's manner that didn't encourage further questioning.

As it happened, it was Jasmin who took the payment. As she handed over her cash, Maudie slipped a fiver into the girl's hand. 'A tip. For you,' she added firmly, only to find that the boss had witnessed the transaction. In a flash, Mad Mike came across and removed the money from her hand and put it in the staff tin. 'Thank you, madame,' he announced ironically. 'The staff will much appreciate it.'

'If they ever get to see it,' Maudie mumbled, putting her foot down as if to achieve maximum distance between herself and the manager of the car wash.

Gina looked out of the window and said nothing. It was obvious that Jasmin mattered to Maudie. Perhaps it was her beauty, the strangeness of her setting, or perhaps she simply brought back happy memories of Damascus. Intrigued, Gina longed to know more.

When they got back, Gina went up to her room. The cardboard box caught her eye and she sat down with it on the four-poster bed and spread out the contents. As she'd remembered, they were mostly small everyday things. Postcards from French exchanges, certificates for swimming widths and lengths, a report or two, all laboriously handwritten, a photo of her brother winning a tennis tournament age twelve, the small mementoes of ordinary lives. She was touched that her mother, who came from a generation that didn't believe in giving praise, had seen them as meaningful and kept them.

At the bottom of the box was a smart invitation, the kind that rarely fell on their humble doormat. It was made of stiff white card and the lettering was embossed not simply printed, which was significant in those class-ridden times. The memory came back to her of her mother running her finger along the print of any invitation to see if it were printed or embossed, which denoted a grand party.

Mr and Mrs Stephen Napier invite Georgina to the 21st birthday of their son, Daniel, at the Grand Hotel, Southdown. Drinks 6 p.m., Dinner 8. Carriages at midnight.

A moment of hilarity at the thought of any carriages arriving in the 1980s was interrupted by the beep of her phone. It was Evie.

'Right,' her friend stated in a businesslike tone, 'I've known you since we were six, and after all this time I know when there's something you're not telling me. It can't be the holiday because I was the one who really wanted to go, so what is it?'

Gina knew she'd been burying her head in the sand. Or perhaps burying her head in Southdown. She took a deep breath. 'It's Mark. He wants a divorce. He's met someone else who says he's got to give up the gambling, and also, it seems, me.'

'I'm sorry, Gina, but you know what I think of Mark,' replied her friend gently. 'In my opinion, it's an excellent thing.' She paused, realizing this might not be the most tactful answer. 'Sorry for being blunt, but you know me. I realize it probably doesn't feel that way to you, certainly not at the moment. Do you want me to take it on? Free advice honestly given and all that. My view is, if you're really sure it's over, file for a divorce first. You don't even need grounds any more if the marriage has broken down, though any court would have accepted Mark's gambling as unreasonable behaviour. Just tell me when to get going.'

'Thanks, Evie, I appreciate it,' Gina replied, trying not to feel overwhelmed at how fast things were moving.

'How have the girls taken it?' asked Evie.

'Sadie seems OK,' Gina replied, 'but I'm not so sure about Lisa. I think she's really hurt.'

'And how about you?'

'I'm all right. To be honest, I haven't really faced it yet.' She shook herself. She mustn't get bitter. Bitter only hurt you. She decided to change the subject so she had more time to think. 'Evie, do you remember someone called Daniel Napier?'

'Haven't the foggiest. Who is he?'

'Well, that's the thing. I don't know. I found an invite to his twenty-first that my mum had kept. She obviously thought it was significant.'

'Not Danny from dancing school?' suggested Evie.

Gina thought about it then grinned. 'Danny from dancing school! You could be right. God, I hated that place.'

'We all hated that place. What sixteen-year-old kid wants to learn bloody ballroom dancing? We wanted to be out at the disco – not learning the sodding cha-cha-cha! But our parents were stuck in that middle-class rut of wanting us to mix with the right people!'

'I'd gone to college by the time this invite came,' Gina admitted. 'Thinking I was so sophisticated and cool and had left the Daniel Napiers of this world way behind. I don't think I even bothered to answer.'

'Don't worry. Your mother probably did,' Evie supplied. 'Miss Georgina Greenhills thanks Mr & Mrs Napier for their kind invitation to their son Daniel's twenty-first and is sorry to refuse because she's turned into a stuck-up snob who thinks she's hipper and more switched on than you, you benighted suburban nobodies.'

Gina laughed so much she started to choke. 'What was he like, this Daniel Napier?'

'Hmm. Sweet and shy, I seem to remember,' Evie replied. 'Not at all one of the bad boys we found attractive. He used to wear a midnight blue velvet jacket.'

'I loved velvet jackets!' Gina reminisced. 'Martin Amis wore one and look dead cool.'

'That's because he was dead cool. Unlike your Danny. His was two sizes too big. Like a kid's blazer on his first day at school.'

'He's not my Danny,' Gina protested.

'Maybe you'd have done better if he had been. Sorry. That was below the belt. Look, I'd better go. Duty calls. Have fun in dear dreary old Southdown. Maybe you'll bump into Danny Napier.'

'I very much doubt it,' said Gina.

'I wonder what he's like now,' Evie speculated. 'Best not to get your hopes up though: he's bound to be married.'

'Evie,' Gina replied, trying not to sound irritated, 'I am not looking for another man.'

'Not till after the divorce at any rate.'

'Not ever.' There it was. That word. Divorce. Bandied about as if it was perfectly normal. Merely an inconvenience. But it felt worse than that to Gina. Much worse than that.

Maybe staying in sunny Southdown would lift her spirits. She really, really hoped so.

Four

The best way to follow up on the missing objects, Gina decided, was to go and see if they'd made an appearance at the local auction house, Waddington's.

She checked with her contact there and discovered that the next auction was the following day. She made up an excuse for Maudie, who was proposing they make the most of the glorious weather and head for the beach again, and drove to Greenfield, where the auction was being held, in time to look round before the bidding began. She was feeling more upbeat and in control having talked about the situation with her daughters. She'd also looked at their own company website last night to discover a couple of their valuable items had been sold. That was encouraging. She decided to call Doris and see if there was anything she needed.

'Doris dearest, heroine and bedrock of Whitehall Valuations, how are things going without me?'

'Not too bad,' replied Doris in her usual phlegmatic manner. 'Good, actually. We sold two hideous G-Plan sofas I would personally have enjoyed burning for their execrable design.'

'I hope you didn't tell the customer that,' teased Gina.

'I could do with some more stock, truth be told. Especially Eames-type chairs. Maybe Kim Kardashian's been parking her expensive bum on one or something. Anyway, they're all the rage for some reason.'

'I'll keep my eye out,' promised Gina. 'Quite good hunting down here, I suspect.' She hesitated for a fraction of a second. 'Any sign of Mark?'

'Silent as the grave.'

'Not even to do with the business?'

There was a short silence. Gina could picture Doris deciding whether to give Gina a frank opinion about her husband and restraining herself. 'Do you want me to forward your post?'

'Anything interesting?'

'A mass of estate agents wanting you to know they've sold a house in your very desirable road. Oh, and a handwritten one from someone who wants to buy your beautiful house direct and cut the vultures out.'

'Could you scan that one and send it to me?' Gina requested.

There was an uneasy pause. Doris rarely mentioned emotion, which Gina greatly appreciated. 'Are you OK, Gina love?'

'More than OK, Doris. Partly thanks to you. You and my good friends Evie and Ruth.'

'Good. Friendship is the bedrock of everything, I've found.'

'Thanks, Doris. I really couldn't get by without you.'

'Glad to be of help. And don't forget the chairs.'

Maybe things were looking up.

Although Waddington's didn't have the prestige of a Christie's or Sotheby's it was still a big player, and attracted buyers from a wide area and even some from London. Auctions were always exciting occasions, full of exotic characters, although with the popularity of online and telephone bidding some of the most fascinating no longer turned up in person. But there was still an air of excitement. Had someone discovered an Old Master in the loft which hadn't been recognized by the seller or the auction house? The biggest success Gina had chalked up was a Chagall drawing which most people dismissed as hideous, but when authenticated by the right expert had sparked a bidding war that produced half of their profits for that year.

As the bidding today began on a large oil painting, Gina could feel the charge in the room grow, and it struck her that it was a lot like the atmosphere in a casino. Perhaps it was this that had led Mark to keep looking for the big win off duty as well.

After two hours they broke for lunch and Gina was able to approach her contact, Gavin Miers, a portly balding man in his sixties who mistook an inappropriate sense of humour for charm.

'Gina!' he smiled broadly. 'Good to see you in the flesh! All this phone and internet nonsense is good for business but it isn't exciting like the old days when it all happened in the room! How's Mark – or shouldn't I ask?' Rumour obviously travelled fast in the antiques world, probably because his celebrated charm made Mark a well-known character. 'Tell me, what can I do for you?'

'I just wondered if you'd had any double-ended scent bottles in lately?'

'Silver stoppered? They're very popular. We have quite a selection, would you like to see?'

'I'll have a browse through the showroom.' Gina cast her mind back for a more hard-to-come-by item from Mrs B's list. 'I'm also on the lookout for a sixteenth-century miniature of a young man, very high quality. The kind that were sent to prospective brides and bridegrooms.'

'Nicholas Hilliard-style? I'd remember that, but sorry no dice on that one.'

'Or a First World War Bible with a romantic inscription?'

Gavin shook his head. 'Best thing would be to look through our online catalogues. My memory isn't what it was.' He winked roguishly. 'Though I do recall you like a white wine now and then. Come next door to the Dog and Parrot?'

Since he'd obviously heard about the split between her and Mark, Gina sensed Gavin was about to get unprofessionally intimate, but she had one more question to ask, and suspected he'd be more forthcoming in less public surroundings. Reluctantly she agreed to join him.

'Right,' Gina eyed the enormous glass of wine Gavin had bought her and decided she'd stick to one sip, 'if you wanted to offload small decorative antiques with no questions asked, where would you go?'

'Hayward's in Eastcliff,' he replied without a second thought, at the same time slipping his hand on to her knee. 'Huge shop, and Billy Hayward's none too fussy. What is all this anyway? It's not another of these TV programmes about antiques? They're bloody everywhere. Irritating too – they make the punters feel their rubbish is actually valuable!' He leaned towards her and smiled, revealing yellow stained teeth, with the suspicion of tobacco on his breath. 'I've always thought you were an attractive girl, Gina . . .'

'Thank you, Gavin, you've been really helpful.' Gina stood up.

'You haven't even started your drink,' he protested with barely concealed irritation.

Gina picked up her bag and somehow knocked over the wine so that it fell in a dramatic cascade over his trousers and shoes. 'So sorry,' she apologized. 'Just remembered. Mustn't drink and drive. Thanks for your help, Gavin.'

How could men be so bloody transparent? Gina mused angrily. Did they really think because you'd split from your husband you were available to any sleazebag who bought you a glass? She turned up the music on her radio only to find Carole King singing 'It's Too Late' about her own breakup. You had to laugh or cry, and Gina chose to laugh. In fact she laughed so loudly that the other motorists all gave her a wide birth. But all those laughter gurus were right.

It did make you feel better.

The sun was still blazing, so she decided to go to the beach and see if Maudie was at her usual spot. What glorious weather they were having so early in the season. Each day dawned with a tempting pink glow that turned into Mediterranean blue skies and temperatures in the low to mid twenties. Bliss.

Naturally, Maudie had her own beach hut painted pale grey, with pink window and door frames, and a lattice screen inside that protected her from the sun and gave the impression of being more Kashmir than Southdown. Maudie lay behind it on a day bed covered in bright cushions sipping mint tea with a group of admiring grey-haired ladies sitting round her, like acolytes worshipping a goddess.

'Have you brought your swimming things?' Maudie enquired. 'Don't worry if not. I always have spares in that box over there.' She pointed to a painted pirate's chest. Gina opened it to discover a wonderful array of swimsuits dating from the 1950s just like her mother had worn, all with curvy sun tops and little skirts. Gina selected a pretty coloured one plus a towel. 'Suncream's on the ledge there,' Maudie pointed out.

'Thanks, Maudie, that's perfect.' Gina left the group to continue dissecting the juiciest gossip in Southdown and headed towards the sea.

Maeve Haran

She slipped on the costume, using the tried and trusted British method of wrapping the towel round herself and hoping for the best as she stripped off underneath it. Then she sat down on the warm pebbles. It was almost five o'clock, and the bright afternoon light was dissolving into the gentle glow of early evening, with a touch of sea mist, or sea fret, as the locals called it. Next to her two young boys were blowing up a kayak. A little way off the shoreline she could just distinguish a paddleboarder illuminated like a Japanese cut-out against the shimmering golden pathway of the setting sun, with a little dog standing on the board next to him, obviously as practised as his owner at this new sport.

Grateful for the loan of Maudie's sea shoes, she ran down the beach and flung herself joyously into the water, which was so deep at high tide that in three steps she was already out of her depth. Gina turned onto her back and let herself be held up by the water, her hair trailing round her shoulders, while at the water's edge small children shouted with delight as their parents kept vigil further up the beach. With the golden shimmering light around her, Gina felt an unexpected happiness. Perhaps it was a link to this place, or the nurturing power of nature, but she no longer felt powerless and rejected.

Remembering the mantra that Evie said she should use at yoga she asserted: 'I am Georgina Greenhills, and I love myself. I am beautiful. My spirit is unique. There is only one me.' But not being the mantra type she couldn't help thinking something completely different. 'I am Mary Poppins. Practically perfect in every way.' And she started to laugh so much the salt water got up her nose and she had to retire, still laughing, to her towel on the beach.

She lay back to let her skin dry in the last rays of the sun, closing her eyes as she felt the power of its warming rays.

Maybe she'd even get a tan. It might not be Sicily, but to her great surprise her old hometown was turning out to be a lot better than she'd expected.

By the time she'd got dressed and headed for the beach hut she discovered that mint tea had been replaced by Pimm's.

'Here you are, Gina dear,' Maudie insisted. 'And I ought to tell you, tomorrow night's my turn to host everyone for bridge. I do hope you'll join us.'

This was a step too far for Gina. She associated bridge, like bowls, with a stage of life she hadn't yet reached. Eager not to offend, she groped wildly for a good excuse and remembered the invitation to the Langdon Arms. This was only slightly better, but who knew if Southdown was capable of surprising her again.

'Actually, Maudie, I'd planned to go and watch the morris dancing.'

'Good idea,' Maudie replied instantly. 'You don't want to spend an evening with a bunch of old bags. Especially when one of the morris men took a fancy to you.'

As she changed into clothes suitable to sit outside a pub the next evening, Gina found herself thinking about Dancing Danny and the unanswered invitation. What a stuck-up little cow she'd been to not even bother to answer, especially when, from what Evie said, he sounded like the kind of tender-hearted boy who would have been hurt.

She riffled through her mother's cardboard box until she found the invitation. The address for RSVPs was 21 Southdown Crescent. As far as she recalled, that was a grand row of Georgian houses near the seafront. Not far, in fact, from the Langdon Arms. Maybe she'd leave a little early and achieve the twin purpose of missing Maudie's early birds and checking out if, by any remote chance, Danny still lived there.

Since she'd already had a glass of Pimm's and would no doubt order some wine during the evening's entertainment, she went into town by the bus that stopped at the end of the lane to the manor. Google Maps confirmed that her memory was correct. She got off the bus at Southdown Crescent and began to walk down its elegant curve. The houses, she noted, were surprisingly large for Southdown, built perhaps by rich merchants who aspired to dizzy social heights. By now a number of them were rather run-down, and some had been turned into flats.

Gina was feeling quite nervous as she approached twenty-one. To her disappointment it, too, had been divided into apartments and five different bells greeted her.

She decided to ring the ground-floor one first. After a long wait a hip-looking young man wearing earplugs appeared. She had to shout her request twice before he deigned to take them out.

'I'm looking for an old friend who used to live in this house,' Gina volunteered. 'His name's Daniel Napier.'

'Sorry,' he'd already started to put the plugs back in, 'never heard of him. But I've only been here six months.'

The next two bells resulted in no reply, and the top-floor apartment owner was clearly eager to get back to the TV programme Gina could hear blaring in the background. 'Sorry,' he shouted, 'can't help. You could try the lady round the back.'

'Thanks,' Gina made her way down the narrow side alley. If she hadn't been told there was another flat here, she wouldn't have guessed.

'Hello,' a white-haired lady greeted her hopefully before she'd had a chance to ring the bell. She was holding a broom and sweeping the back path, even though it looked immaculately tidy. 'Are you looking for me?'

'Actually, I'm looking for someone who used to live here. Daniel Napier. His family owned the house when I was growing up.'

'Sorry, can't help.' She was already losing interest in Gina and going back to sweeping. 'I suppose you could try the agents, Boyd & Mackinnon. Their number's up the front.'

'Thanks so much,' said Gina, fighting a sense of disappointment. Silly to think he'd still be here. She'd write down the agents' number, but she wasn't sure she'd pursue it.

Why are you trying to find Daniel anyway? she asked herself as she began to walk in the direction of the seafront. Was it nostalgia, or was she hoping to find more than lost antiques while she was here?

One of the benefits of small towns like Southdown was that nothing was too far away. Five minutes later she was standing on the busy prom, looking across at the pier where she'd enjoyed spending her pocket money in the arcade on that tantalizing and infuriating claw device like a mini crane with a hook on the end which just might pick up the teddy or fluffy white rabbit and award it to you, but virtually always dropped it again and left you with nothing.

Gina smiled to herself at the memory of when she was little and how scared she'd been of falling through the wooden slats on the pier; the reality was that life held quite different, un-imagined dangers. Pushing the thought from her mind, she closed her eyes and felt the delightful sun on her face. The heatwave was persisting and the beach was as crowded as August, with parents and children who'd dashed down after school. Everywhere were the happy sounds of friends chatting and children shouting lustily in the waves.

She decided to give in to the temptation of a home-made salted caramel cone made by a place called Holy Cow and concluded that ice cream was another thing that was wildly better now than when she was growing up. In her own childhood the acme of the exotic was a Neapolitan wafer, with the pink, white and brown layers tasting equally of nothing. This, on the other hand, was the food of the gods.

She passed the big wheel, another innovation, and peeped in the window of the new gallery of modern art. No wonder Londoners were finding Southdown an attractive place to live.

The ten tables in front of the Langdon Arms were filling up fast. The Southdown Morris Men were assembling in a large open space right on the corner, where passing motorists were tooting either encouragement, or possibly derision, at this curious survivor of medieval mumming. With a nod to tradition they had swapped their tropical shirts for the traditional all-white outfits decorated with coloured sashes, bells tied to their knees and straw hats decked with fake flowers. As their accompanist tuned up they brandished their sticks and grinned at the audience, who had lined up their drinks and were well into the holiday spirit.

Gina fought her way to the bar and bought a glass of wine which she carried to a discreet seat where she hoped to be able to enjoy the occasion without attracting the attention of the show-off in the tropical shirt who had encouraged her to attend.

They began with a novel interpretation of Bob Dylan's 'Blowin' in the Wind', which, perhaps because it too was in the folk tradition, lent itself surprisingly well to the addition of bells and clashed sticks.

The follow-up was 'Lay Lady Lay', one of her favourite Dylan songs, and Gina leaned back against the wall to listen to the haunting tune with its accompanying words of longing and love, just as the sun began to set over the sea behind them.

'Enjoying morris dancing?' interrupted an unfamiliar voice. 'Next you'll be joining the National Trust and taking up gardening.'

Gina's eyes snapped open to find herself looking at the stranger from the other day who'd told her that selfies were unflattering at her age and had offered to take it for her. What bloody cheek!

'Excuse me,' she flashed angrily, 'are you trying to imply I've got nothing to fill up my empty life?'

He stood there, over six feet of him, dressed in execrable faded blue jeans and a denim shirt, mercifully not showing any chest hair, considering her, as though he found her highly entertaining. 'You're far too elegant to have an empty life,' he replied, with an ironic twinkle behind the flattering words.

Again Gina felt that flash of familiarity and was about to ask his name when a blonde dashed out of the crowd and grabbed him.

'There you are!' she announced, pulling him towards the pub entrance. 'The table's ready. I was wondering where the hell you'd got to.'

She gave Gina a swift assessing look which Gina remembered from teenage parties in instances where you'd chat someone up only to find their girlfriend appearing and angrily taking possession.

'Nice to encounter you again,' he smiled ruefully, before he disappeared in the swarm of onlookers just as the morris men took a break and the cheeky wearer of the tropical shirt descended on her. 'Couldn't resist my charms, eh?' he demanded cockily.

The stranger in the double denim paused at the pub entrance and shot her a wry look, eyebrows raised. No doubt he thought she was a desperate older woman out on the prowl.

'You don't happen to know who that man is?' she asked the morris man.

'What, that old geezer?' he replied, offended. 'If that's your type I'm definitely too young for you.'

'As a matter of fact,' Gina downed the last of her wine, 'I was just leaving. But I loved the act. In fact, I'd love a request.' She hoped blue jeans could still hear her.

'What's that?'

'Bob Dylan's "Forever Young",' she announced with her most attractive smile.

'I'll see what I can do,' he smirked back at her.

She was just leaving when she felt a tap on her shoulder. 'Gina! How brilliant. Come and join us, we're on the way to the cinema.' It was Ruth and Robin and a group of their friends off to see a French film at the new cinema that used to be a bus station.

Southdown had definitely changed for the better.

'Why don't you ask that friend you mentioned who grew up in Southdown too – Eve, was it? – down for the weekend?' Maudie asked next morning at breakfast. 'It must be lonely stuck out here with me.'

'You're wonderful company, Maudie,' Gina replied truthfully, admiring the painted silk kimono Maudie was wearing for breakfast. 'But I'd love to, if you're sure you don't mind. She'd be staggered to see how much it's changed.'

'There was certainly plenty of scope,' laughed Maudie. 'I found it as dull as you did. That's why I was so glad when my husband was posted to Cyprus and Egypt and finally Damascus. I loved that best, and it breaks my heart to think of that poor city now. The people were so friendly and helpful everywhere. My husband was so busy he couldn't look at anything of course, but he had a colleague who showed me round instead. His name was Fahad. It's Arabic for lynx.' She turned her face towards the window as if she could escape through it into the past. Her whole face somehow softened and became younger. 'He took me round all the palaces with their courtyards and fountains, the famous mosque and the ancient ruins. My husband was so pleased that because of Fahad I wasn't lonely.' She shook her head as if to banish the memory. 'Back to your friend. By all means ask her.'

Whether Evie would agree to come was another matter.

Despite another day of glorious heatwave beckoning her to the beach, Gina reminded herself sternly why she was here. She made an appointment with the antique shop her contact at Waddington's auctions had suggested.

Hayward's Antiques was a fascinating set-up right on the edge of the downs, housed in some dilapidated old farm buildings. Following the old business maxim that to stay viable you should offer 'something to see, something to buy and something to eat', that was exactly what they did. For the 'something to see' they had a duck pond and small petting farm which attracted the after-school mums desperate for a cup of tea and a gossip with their friends, while the children bounced up and down in a small soft play area. The cafe itself had become quite a destination, with its antique-strewn décor and menu of Eggs Benedict or avocado on sourdough toast, plus scones and home-made cakes in the afternoon. It had also somehow scrounged a licence and was able to supply the mummy market with the glasses of white wine that kept the tables filled.

And then there were the antiques. Two members of staff were in evidence. The owner, sixtyish, affecting a goatee and beret, as if his shop were on the Left Bank rather than the outskirts of a small provincial English town. His female colleague, or possibly wife, was masterminding the cafe as well as the shop and doing a good job of looking harassed, as well she might, since a group of mums had just arrived with rampant small children who were racing round the room like so many tiny bulls in a china shop.

After being offered a seat on a Lloyd Loom chair which, somewhat disconcertingly, she suspected was actually a discreet commode for people who couldn't make it to the loo, Gina began to describe the missing objects, wondering at the same time why her contact at Waddington's had directed her here. She'd been hoping to find a Fagin's lair full of stolen goods, but this seemed anything but.

The only response she could detect was faint boredom as she produced her inadequate sketch of the double-ended scent bottle. 'We get quite a lot of those,' remarked the man in the beret. 'Old ladies like collecting them, but none are in at the moment.' The Bible with the romantic inscription aroused a faint flicker of interest. 'Things like that can do surprisingly well at auction. I'd have remembered that. Sue?' he addressed the harassed-looking woman. 'Do you recall anything like that coming in?'

Before Sue could reply there was a crash followed by a wail from the cafe area. She was up out of her seat trying to placate a group of angry mums blaming her that their toddlers had pulled a Victorian jug and washbowl from the dresser where it was being displayed.

By the time Sue returned, Gina had picked up her handbag and was saying her goodbyes, having given up. She'd shown the owner an image on her phone of a similar miniature to the one that had gone. But he had simply shrugged and glanced at his watch.

'Thanks for your help,' offered Gina him, trying not to feel discouraged.

She had reached the car park before she realized she'd forgotten her phone and turned to find Sue running after her, holding it. Suddenly she stopped. 'Oh,' she chirped, sounding quite excited at the photograph of the miniature. 'Is that one of the things you're looking for? We did have one like that come in a couple of months ago. I noticed it because I'd seen one very much like it – in the Queen's Gallery at Buckingham Palace! I went up on a day trip. The one I saw was of Queen Elizabeth I's lover, the Earl of Essex.'

'Why the hell didn't you tell me all this!' snapped Beret Man, who had obviously followed her. Given the mix of irritation and condescension in his tone, he had to be her husband.

'I did,' Sue replied, standing her ground. 'You said we weren't interested, it wasn't the sort of thing we handle.'

'I would have been interested if you'd filled me in about the one in the Queen's Gallery.'

Men trying to put the blame on women, as usual, Gina noted, but with a feeling of rising excitement. 'So where did it come from, this miniature?'

'That was the odd thing,' Sue replied defensively, 'it was all a bit cloak and dagger. I found a package in our postbox round the front there.' She indicated a wooden box attached to the five-bar gate that led into the farm building complex. It had a note saying if we were interested in any of the things we should name a price and put it back in the postbox, so I said no thanks, but thanks for showing us.'

'Why the hell!' exploded her husband. 'It sounds as if this might have been a real find. We could have outdone Philip Mould in finding Old Masters in the junk shop!'

'It was what you told me to do,' countered his wife, finally discovering some spirit. 'It was all too dodgy anyway. It was obviously stolen, if you ask me. And any buyer or auction house would need to know its history, where it came from, or they wouldn't touch it.'

'Rubbish!' he muttered. 'There are ways round that.'

'And you'd certainly know them!' she accused.

Gina chose that moment to quietly leave them to it. At least she'd found out how careful whoever took the things was being in order to hide their identity. And also that the miniature was potentially extremely valuable. Had the thief known that, or was it a lucky accident?

'What, me come to Southdown for a relaxing weekend?' Evie snorted. 'Since there's nothing I'd want to do there it'd certainly be relaxing, if by relaxing you mean deeply dull!'

'Evie,' protested Gina laughingly, 'it's changed. I promise you. We'll have calamari and chilled Picpoul on the beach, and there's a clothes shop even you might find something you like in.'

'Hang on.' Evie's voice took on a note of suspicion. 'You're not going native, are you? Like Stockholm syndrome, where the victim starts empathizing with her captors. Wake up, you're a Londoner!'

'I'm not asking you to move here,' said Gina. 'Just come for two days. We might even be able to swim if the heatwave holds.'

'*Swim*,' Evie repeated in horrified accents, 'I don't even swim in Sri Lanka!'

'That's because the current's too strong and you're frightened of sharks. There aren't any sharks in Southdown. Though I did see a seal the other day. Oh, and a paddleboarding dog.'

'That settles it. You've lost your mind. How could a dog paddleboard?'

'It was with its owner.' Gina was on the verge of conceding that the invitation was a mistake when Evie capitulated. 'OK then, I'll come. Just to make sure you're not being brain-washed by Moonies into embracing the suburban lifestyle.'

'Oh, Evie, that's brilliant. I'll tell Ruth. We can have a girls' night out!'

'I can't wait. Where exactly? The fish and chip shop near the Dome or the fake Irish pub near the station? That was particularly choice.'

'I'll find somewhere, don't worry!' Gina assured, though she wasn't quite sure what would be up to Evie's big city standards. Hopefully Ruth would know.

When she woke the next morning there was a text from Evie awaiting her. *Arriving next Saturday. 10.05. Will you meet?*

Gina found herself smiling. Decisiveness had been a hallmark of Evie's character even when they were kids. It had been Evie who had decided what they would all do, where they would go, and Ruth and Gina who tagged along. It was also one of the reasons she was so successful in her career. Whether the decision was right or wrong, Evie never dithered. So having decided she'd come and give her old hometown another look, she was wasting no time in making the arrangements.

Gina leaned back on her pillows with their lovely crisp white covers. It was very kind of Maudie to let her invite her friend. She thought about yesterday's visit to the antique shop again and who had taken the objects and whether she should advise that they involve the police. Yet Lucy had insisted the family was against that, including Maudie herself. But Maudie's suggestion that it was just Mrs B covering up her own clumsiness didn't hold water, given that someone was trying to sell the stuff, even if they were doing it very discreetly. Would Mrs B be up to that? And if so, why had she tipped Lucy off about the thefts? The whole thing was unpleasant and uncomfortable. Gina decided the most useful contribution she could make was to get on with cataloguing and valuing the remaining antiques so that if any further objects went missing they would at least have a pictorial record.

She jumped out of bed with renewed energy and pulled open her curtains. Another glorious day. The garden was a sea of blue forget-me-nots with pale pink, purple and yellow tulips mixed together like a spring bouquet hand-tied by nature. A lone pheasant proudly strutted across the lawn, its colourful feathers catching the morning sun, knowing it was safe from hunters for months yet, and wonderfully exotic in this safe domestic setting. She knew how it felt. Despite the disappearing objects, Rookery Manor had a feeling of solidity, of being rooted in time, which was enhanced by Maudie's generosity and warm personality.

After a hurried breakfast, Gina got down to work, photographing and cataloguing. Then she took a coffee up to her room. On Monday she would begin the task of getting the objects valued by her many and varied contacts in the antiques and art worlds, and approach auction houses or galleries that she knew had particular expertise.

Despite Maudie's kind suggestion she should treat her stay as a holiday, Gina felt better after a week's hard work at her laptop, so that by the weekend she felt entitled to concentrate on Evie's visit.

Except that when she went to start her car to pick up her friend she found the battery had gone flat. 'Don't worry,' Maudie insisted. 'Phone the AA and we'll leave Mr B to deal with them, while I take you to the station to pick up your friend. It'll be all sorted by the time you get back.'

Gina smiled at Maudie's blithe optimism and decided to borrow a bit for herself.

'That would be wonderful!'

So it turned out that Evie had a welcome party waiting for

her outside the station, consisting of Gina in her slacks and shirt, plus Maudie, white hair swept up into its usual elegant chignon, wearing a dramatic black jacket with a giant shawl collar, leaning against the bonnet of a large and very shiny Mercedes station wagon.

'I'm disappointed you haven't got me a bouquet,' smiled Evie. 'With a reception committee like this I feel like a diva!'

'Evie, this is the Honourable Maudie Tyler. Maudie, this is my very good friend Eve Beeston.'

'Gina!' Maudie shook her head. 'For goodness' sake. Your friend can't be bothered with silly titles.'

'Indeed I can,' replied Evie instantly. 'As a lawyer I live in a world of Lord Justice This and Lady Justice That. I'm very honoured to meet an Honourable.'

'The feeling's mutual,' Maudie agreed. 'I've been hearing lots about you from Gina. And you hail from these parts too?'

'Indeed. Though I haven't been back for a very long time.'

'Your parents aren't still here then?'

'Dead. Ages ago.'

'Probably died of boredom,' Maudie replied with an impish smile. 'That's why I was grateful to live abroad a lot. But things have got better.'

'Maudie, I can see you're the gal for me,' Evie shook her hand enthusiastically. 'Do you know the painting by Walter Sickert called *Boredom*? It's of an old man smoking a cigar and his wife looking as if she might die of dullness. That was Southdown for me, but Gina insists it outdoes St Trop in sophistication these days.'

'Evie,' tutted Gina, trying not to giggle, 'you always exaggerate.'

'That's why I'm good at divorce settlements,' Evie flashed back, then wished she hadn't when she saw the cloud cross Gina's face. How bloody tactless.

75

'Come on, then,' Maudie sensed the change in atmosphere and opened the car door. 'Let's head back to the manor and you can unpack.'

They were approaching the crossroads where there was a left turn up towards the manor when they stopped at a traffic light next to Mad Mike's Car Wash. 'Oh, look,' Maudie announced, 'no queue. You girls won't mind if I nip in here?'

There was no evidence of Mad Mike today, except in the anxious looks one of the men kept casting behind him. The women were tougher, brandishing their wet sponges with hardened impassive faces.

'It must be tough, working in a car wash,' murmured Gina, glancing round to see if the beautiful dark-haired girl was here. 'They must dread sunny weekends when so many people bring their cars in.'

'Probably brought here illegally,' said Evie, shaking her head in disgust. 'The immigration rules in this country are so byzantine it's a wonder anyone gets a visa.'

Gina glanced at her, surprised. She hadn't seen this side of her friend before.

'Utter bastards!' Maudie seconded in such a passionate voice that they both fell silent.

The car passed on from the soaping to the polishing section and Gina spotted the girl. She had been standing alone, building the cloths into a neat pile as she had when Gina had noticed her the other day.

The team of polishers moved in on the car like a swarm of insects. The dark-haired girl was on the passenger side and Gina was struck again by the inappropriateness of her setting. Instinctively you felt this girl shouldn't be here in a Southdown car wash.

76

Maudie rolled down the window and handed over £10 for a £6 job and told them to keep the change.

'That's generous,' commented Evie.

Maudie shrugged, watching the girl go back to her endless task of folding cloths. 'They work so hard, poor things.'

She turned on the car radio and Mozart suddenly filled the air. 'Time for something beautiful!' announced Maudie as they drove the last couple of miles listening to the music and thinking their own thoughts.

Mrs B had prepared Evie a lovely sunny room under the eaves, with sloping ceilings and a fire burning in the grate even though it was blazing outside.

'I always like a fire for guests arriving,' insisted Mrs B. 'Makes sure there's no damp in the air.'

Evie sat down on the bed and almost toppled backwards the mattress was so soft. 'I'll feel like the princess and the pea,' she announced. 'But then, staying here is like a fairy tale anyway. Do you remember all the stories we used to make up about this place?'

'Yes, and all of them scary, when actually it isn't scary at all. Maudie's the kindest, most generous host you could imagine.' The memory of the stolen things made her pause a moment, wondering if she should tell Evie.

'By the way,' Evie's words broke in on her thoughts. 'Did you see how Maudie was staring at that girl at the car wash? With a kind of desperate longing? And then she switched the music on as if to make herself stop and be upbeat. It was really noticeable.'

Gina looked out of the window. It did make sense. Maybe this was the key to Maudie's obsession with the car wash.

For a moment she wondered what she'd taken on. Her first reaction had been that she'd walked in on a family feud, but with the disappearing antiques, the overprotective house-keeper and now this – even though it seemed so peaceful – it was also a house of mysteries.

'Fancy a trip down memory lane once you're unpacked?' Gina suggested.

'Why else do you think I've given up my candlelit yoga class? Of course I do!'

'Right. See you downstairs in ten.'

Gina slipped back to her own room for a moment. Why hadn't she talked more to Evie about the divorce? Had she unconsciously changed her mind? Did she secretly want Mark back?

She sat down on the bed, remembering all the anxiety about why he was always out, dreading the mood swings that came with a good or bad day at the racetrack. They had a long history together, and two daughters, but wasn't a lot of that history based on a cover-up, that her husband had a habit that ruled his life, that mattered more to him than his family? And now he had someone else. Someone who had made him finally admit he had a problem – the very thing she had tried to do for years. Somehow that hurt more than anything else.

Yes, she wanted a divorce.

'Let's start with our houses,' Gina suggested.

'All right,' Evie shrugged. 'Me first, I suppose, as I'm on the way.'

They drove down Forest Road, passing a large detached bungalow. 'Except that my mum would never call it that,' recalled Evie. 'She religiously referred to it as a cottage and grew roses round the door to prove it!'

Evie, as Gina knew, was the only child of affluent elderly parents.

'I was a miracle baby,' Evie announced, staring at the house while showing no inclination to get out of the car. 'My parents had been trying for twenty years. My mother was forty-three, when forty-three was practically senile. They even went to Lourdes to pray and then – wham! – the fertility angel flew over and Mum got pregnant. People made jokes about the milkman. It couldn't have been through sex, as sex was never mentioned in our house – along with a lot of other things. Love. Fun. Enjoyment. I was such a precious baby she turned over-protectiveness into an art form. Once Dad died, she would have preferred me never to leave the house again.'

It was a strange atmosphere for such a successful, exuberant person like Evie to emerge from. 'I took after Naughty Auntie Vi, apparently. She spent a lifetime outraging her family, became an alcoholic and then decided when she was really ill she wanted to be looked after by nuns. When she knew it was the end she called over the reverend mother. And guess what her dying words were?'

Gina shook her head.

'"I bet you've never slept with a helicopter pilot."'

They both collapsed in giggles.

'And then Mum's best friend, Mrs Roberts, got divorced,' continued Evie, still looking pained at the memory. 'I remember it so well. It rocked Mum's world. They didn't know anyone else who was divorced. And people were so awful to the poor woman. My mother had to actually meet her in secret in that cafe by the petrol station. She took me once as cover. I'll never forget how angry I was, even at age twelve, at how narrow and disapproving people could be. I think that was what made me want to be a divorce lawyer, so I could help women like that poor Mrs Roberts.'

'And you have!' Gina gave her friend a hug, moved that Evie had never told her this before. Maybe it was because of her own situation. At least things were beginning to get better at last.

Gina's family home was next. A small, detached house in a row of six built near a green. 'We were firmly lower middle class and we knew it. So, it was a big step getting a detached house. It meant we were moving up and joining the middle class. It was the pinnacle of my mum's dream!'

It would have been hard to explain to her daughters, mused Gina, just how much class mattered when they were growing up in Southdown. Success was defined by whether you managed to claw your way into 'the professions', by which they meant becoming a doctor, lawyer, accountant, architect or possibly dentist. Her brother Neil managed the feat by becoming an engineer, but choosing to work in antiques like Gina was labelled by her father as 'one step up from the tinker who comes round sharpening knives'.

But everything changed when she met Mark, who could charm the birds off the trees, and certainly charmed Gina's parents. Suddenly, being an antique dealer was viewed as interesting and even exciting. Her dad actually started looking out for finds in junk shops and showed them off proudly to Mark.

It was a very ordinary family, but Gina had always found something comforting in that. It was secure and reliable. Always there for her.

It was Ruth who had the warmest family life. The Donnellan clan, another Irish family like the one she married into, was numerous, noisy and continually in each other's houses. Evie claimed she couldn't bear it, but Gina admired the happy, relaxed atmosphere, with a pot of tea brewing away non-stop, and problems being shared instead of hidden away as a source of shame. Lucky Ruth.

They drove on to a narrow little street hidden in the heart of the old town where there was a wonderful second-hand bookshop piled up to the rafters with used paperbacks, a record shop which seemed to be still flourishing and a small cafe with a side entrance.

'Viva Roma!' purred Evie. 'Our very own Italian cafe, club house, dating centre and absolute hub of our teenage universe!'

'I know,' seconded Gina. 'I often used to tell my daughters that they might have Costa and Nero but we had our own one-off, original place to meet. They didn't get it, of course.'

Viva Roma was the cafe where their friends gathered every Saturday morning, plus as many after-school nights as they could get away with. It was their home from home.

'Do you remember that huge Gaggia coffee machine?'

'And the posters of Italian pop stars none of us had heard of?'

They closed their eyes, transported back to being sixteen, with the world still ahead of them.

'Come on,' Gina announced finally. 'Back on the road. We're meeting Ruth later, remember.'

They got back in the car and set off for the next location on their sentimental journey: the pub where their favourite group played every Saturday night, with one of their school friends' older brothers as the singer. To their delight there was a space right outside.

'What was he called?' Gina enquired as they got out. 'How could I forget? I was in love with that boy for a whole year even though he never even looked at me!'

'Pouting Pete!' Evie announced.

'And what was their theme tune? The one they always sang?' Gina screwed up her face in an effort to remember.

81

'Gina!' replied Evie, mock-shocked. '"La Bamba"! You can't have forgotten!'

It all came back to Gina, and she began to dance down the street singing: 'Bamba, bamba . . . bamba, bamba!'

Suddenly a deep voice took up the chorus from somewhere behind them;

'Yo no soy marinero,
Yo no soy marinero,
Ay, arriba, arriba!'

A tall and attractive man wearing a Panama hat stepped out of the shadows, smiling broadly. 'Eve Beeston, you haven't changed a bit!'

'I hope I bloody have!' protested Evie. 'I was three stone overweight with the worst haircut since Donald Trump.'

'Stuart Nixon,' announced the newcomer. 'I was in the year above.'

He doffed his hat in a mock-theatrical gesture and Gina registered a shock. He was almost completely bald! And yet with his humorous manner and attractive smile, he still managed to look years younger.

'I remember you,' replied Evie. 'You were captain of the football team, as well as being really good at chess.'

'I like to think I was something of a Renaissance fifteen-year-old,' he replied, cutting the boastful statement with a self-deprecating grin.

'You were!' Evie endorsed. Gina watched in wonder as her friend's fearsome courtroom manner dissolved into feminine fluttering. 'Well, at least I thought so.' She seemed to wake up and come back to the present. 'So, what are you up to now?'

'I'm an estate agent.' Another engaging grin. 'I gather we come somewhere between car salesmen and bailiffs in the public perception of villains.'

'Don't worry,' Evie laughed girlishly. 'Lawyers are probably even more unpopular than you are!'

'How about a drink to celebrate bumping into you both after all these years?' Stuart suggested, gesturing to the pub behind them, 'After all, I feel we ought to discover if they still play "La Bamba"!'

In fact, the pub bore no relation to the beery and jolly place it had been in their teenage years.

'There used to be a jukebox in that corner,' Gina pointed out.

'And a dartboard over there!' Evie indicated. 'And the stage was round the back there,' she added. 'Just room for Pouting Pete, two guitars, the drummer and an enormous amp.'

'Which sounded truly dreadful,' agreed Gina, laughing.

'So,' Stuart leaned on the bar. 'What can I get you? In fact, why don't we have some lunch?'

'Aren't you supposed to be at work?' Evie enquired, still smiling away.

'I'm the boss. I tell other people off for taking long lunch hours. The food here's supposed to be quite good as a matter of fact.'

They shared a plate of Turkish-inspired mezze with a glass of fresh, crisp rosé.

'Southdown's turning out to be a revelation,' marvelled Evie.

'I could show you plenty of other examples,' agreed Stuart. 'The Modern Art Gallery. The new French place on the end of the pier. The gelateria in the Dome cinema . . . How long are you staying?'

'Just the weekend.'

'That's a pity,' his tone was light with the right shade of

genuine regret. Gina found herself wondering if he was nice or clever. It was of course possible to be both.

'London's not exactly the end of the earth,' teased Evie, looking at him sideways so that Gina had to try not to giggle at this new and unsuspected version of her friend.

Gina could have sworn he was going to ask them what they were doing tonight, but that perhaps he decided it might seem over the top.

'Well,' he turned to them both outside the pub after they'd finished lunch, 'what a delightful coincidence this has been. And if you're planning to come again, let me know.' He handed them each a card. 'You don't even have to buy a property!'

'Get you!' Gina teased as soon as Stuart was out of hearing. 'That was an Eve Beeston I've never seen before!'

'Haven't you ever heard of the many faces of Eve?' Evie grinned. 'That was another one!'

'Well, it certainly made an impression on Stuart Nixon!'

Five

_____

'This is turning into a real adventure,' announced Evie when they got back to Rookery Manor. 'Not only do I get to stay in the spooky old house I used to fantasize about but we bump into Sexy Stu from the upper sixth who I frankly had quite a crush on!' Since there was no sign of Maudie, they were heading for the kitchen to ask Mrs B if she knew when Maudie would be back. 'Obviously our next task is to look for Dancing Danny!'

Before Gina could admit that she'd already started, they heard raised voices and came to a halt, not wanting to intrude.

'What do you mean, she's got a friend staying?' Rosa was demanding angrily. 'Good God, does she think the manor's a hotel? She's not on holiday, she's supposed to be assessing our antiques!'

Gina waited, her hand on Evie's arm, noting that possessive pronoun about the contents of the house.

'I can't think what Lucy was up to, taking her on without even consulting the rest of us,' Rosa carped on.

'Oh, they're no trouble,' Mrs B's tone suggested she didn't like the woman any more than Gina did. 'Mrs Tyler may seem the life and soul, but she gets lonely out here.'

'That's exactly why we've been suggesting she moves into a nice flat with other people around,' huffed Rosa.

But Mrs B stood her ground. 'Gina's been good company for her,' she continued, 'and the new one's a hoot. Posh as all get out, even though she's supposed to come from Southdown. A lawyer or some such.'

Evie tried to suppress a giggle while Gina pushed her back towards the hall. 'What an old cow. We've got one just like her on the bench. Lady Justice Blah. Bite the bullet and smarm her with charm, that's what I do, and it works every time.'

They were about to go upstairs when they heard the sound of Maudie arriving.

'Come on,' Evie suggested. 'Let's go and greet our hostess before that old bat in the kitchen gets to her.'

Maudie had just got out of the car and stood leaning on it, looking at her feet, showing none of her usual fizzy gaiety.

'I wish I knew what was worrying her so much,' Gina whispered.

'Best way is to ask,' Evie strode forward. 'Hello, Maudie,' she greeted her in the reassuring tone she used on clients, 'is something troubling you? Sometimes I've found in my career it's best to get it out in the open.'

'Oh, hello,' Maudie sighed. 'I'd hoped to get some news and it's taken a lot longer to come through than I expected. Oh well.'

'Would it help to talk about it?'

Maudie seemed almost to wake from a dream. 'No, thank you very much for the offer, but I don't think that's a good idea. I need to think this one out for myself.'

'Fine,' said Evie. 'Well, you've always got Gina here if you need some moral support.'

'Ah, there you are, Maudie dear,' Rosa's strident tones cut across their conversation. 'Do you think I could have a word inside?'

The tiniest smile quivered over Maudie's features. 'I know someone I won't be confiding in,' she murmured so that only Evie and Gina could hear.

By mutual agreement they slipped up to Gina's bedroom. 'The weather's gorgeous and you've only got one more day, so let's make the most of it,' announced Gina.

'If you mean swim in the English Channel, I'm sorry, but there are limits,' protested Evie.

'I was thinking of my secret find. A country hotel with its own pool.'

'Indoor or outdoor?' demanded Evie.

'Outdoor of course. But they have sun loungers and very good rosé. We could have a swim and sunbathe before meeting Ruth later.'

'Say no more, I'll get my things.'

Half an hour later they were stretched out on sunbeds in their swimsuits, the promised rosé on a small wooden table, contemplating the Hockney-blue pool. The other side of the picket fence, sheep looked satisfyingly picturesque as they nibbled peacefully away.

'It makes me think of that music by Bach,' Evie sighed happily. 'Where sheep shall safely graze.'

'Ooh I didn't know you were cultured,' teased Gina.

'I'm not,' replied Evie shamelessly. 'Some bloke got me wrong and took me to the Albert Hall. Now, about Dancing Danny . . .'

'As a matter of fact,' Gina admitted, 'I did go round and check out the address on the invitation.'

'You sly old thing. And . . . ?'

'It's been turned into flats. None of the tenants had heard of a Daniel Napier.'

'What a drag!'

'Though one old lady suggested I contact the managing agents.'

'Which you haven't done.'

'Well, I have been a bit busy,' Gina reminded her. 'Taking a lot of pictures and getting expert advice on some of the paintings as well as Maudie's more recherché objects, approaching auction houses in London. There is a certain expertise in what I do, you know,' she added wryly. 'Even if Rosa doesn't appreciate it.'

'Why does your Maudie put up with her? She seems a spirited lady.'

'Rosa and her horrible husband are the only family members who really want the manor. Lucy's very well set up anyway, and the other sister isn't the lady-of-the-manor type.'

'And Rosa reckons she is,' concluded Evie.

'With knobs on.'

'Can't Maudie give it to the nation or something?' asked Evie.

'Ruth told me she looked into it, but the house has to be of national importance, and apparently you need to give them money for the upkeep as well, and Maudie hasn't got a bean. So it'll almost certainly go to Rosa and Awful Ambrose. That's why they're so protective of it and view me as a bad fairy who's come to make trouble for them.'

'The label rather suits you!' Evie stretched out blissfully, feeling the hot sun on her skin. 'Come on, Bad Fairy, keep the rosé coming!'

Gina filled up Evie's glass before diving into the blue depths of the pool. Since it was early in the year and the season hadn't really started, they had the pool to themselves. The deep blue silence was somehow healing, like a meditation that shut out thoughts of loss and failure, and whether she should have done things differently.

By the time she put her head back above the water, her mind had cleansed itself of negative thoughts, at least for the moment, and she felt brave enough to ask Evie the question she'd been putting off.

'Have you heard back from Mark about the divorce?'

'He's appointed a fancy firm of lawyers but they haven't responded yet. If they don't in the next couple of days, I'll contact them.'

'I wonder how he's paying for them. He told me he was flat broke.'

'All husbands tell their wives they're flat broke. Especially the rich ones. I spend most of my time looking for the money. Of course, it's possible she's paying. Do you know anything about her?'

'No,' Gina turned her head away. 'And I'd rather keep it that way.'

'Gina . . .' There was something about Evie's tone that made her look at her friend. 'Unless you can afford to buy Mark out, you'll probably have to sell the London house and split the proceeds.'

'Andrew, our accountant, said I should do that anyway. As a matter of fact, Doris forwarded me a letter from someone who wants to buy it. Maybe it's an actor. The road's got very popular with actors. It's as if they all flock together like parrots. I keep thinking I know them and say hello, then realize I've just seen them on the telly,' said Gina brightly, trying to hide her panic at all this possible upheaval. 'Maybe it makes sense to move away from a house full of reminders of Mark. Every time I open a bloody cupboard a memory seems to jump out at me,' she commented wryly. 'Not sure how the girls would take it,' she added.

'Why don't you talk it over with them?' suggested Evie. 'There might be a lot of advantages to moving somewhere smaller.'

At this, Gina burst out laughing. 'That's exactly what Rosa keeps telling Maudie!'

'Thanks very much,' Evie pretended to flounce. 'At least I have your best interests at heart, which I suspect is more than Rosa does with Maudie!'

Ruth had chosen a noisy Italian restaurant of the old-fashioned family-run kind where the chef stuck to the tried and true like chicken cacciatore, spaghetti carbonara and melanzane parmigiana, and cooked it deliciously.

Gina ordered gnocchi, which she'd forgotten how much she liked. Evie threw calorie-counting to the winds and went for the carbonara, and Ruth and Robin shared a vast pizza. With everything washed down with a rough but surprisingly tasty red wine, they were all soon laughing as if there hadn't been a yawning twenty-year gap in their friendship. But then maybe, mused Gina, that was what real friendship was like.

'Come on then, Gina,' Ruth gently elbowed her. 'How's it going up at the manor? Have you found out who's been nicking Maudie's knick-knacks?'

Evie shot her a look. 'I thought you were just doing a valuation.'

Gina shrugged. 'I didn't mention it because I haven't made any progress. Some valuable items have been disappearing from Rookery Manor and Maudie's great-niece Lucy wanted me to look into it. Unless it was a sneak thief, there's only eight possible suspects including Mr and Mrs B, but they were the ones who raised the alarm . . .'

'Could be a clever double bluff,' suggested Ruth's husband, Robin.

'Any of the three sisters: Rosa, Susan or Lucy,' added Ruth.

'Or their husbands,' Evie reminded. 'My money's on Awful Ambrose.'

'But wouldn't that be counterproductive if he thinks they're going to inherit it anyway?' asked Robin.

'They might want to get someone into trouble to make sure the manor definitely came to them,' said Evie.

'And then of course, there's Maudie herself,' added Gina.

'But what would be the point of stealing from yourself? Unless you were going to claim on insurance?' added Robin.

'There's no suggestion of that.'

'Then why, if she wanted the money, wouldn't Maudie just go ahead and sell the stuff? After all, it's her own property,' enquired Ruth.

'I did find an antique dealer who'd been offered some of the items but it was all done anonymously.'

'And nothing else has gone?' asked Evie.

Gina shook her head. 'Not that I know of.'

'And there's another mystery,' Evie announced with relish. 'I'm sure there's some connection between Maudie and the girl in the car wash.'

'Good God,' Ruth looked appalled. 'I had no idea what I was getting you into!'

'Well I think it's all rather exciting,' Evie insisted, draining her glass.

'That's because you're well out of it in London,' admonished Ruth.

'Not at all. A lot of my job involves solving mysteries.

Mostly about hidden money. Gina, you need to sit down and really think about it.'

'You don't think it's dangerous, do you?' Ruth asked, paling.

'Of course not,' replied Gina. 'Can you see Rosa with a revolver? She's more WI than MI5!'

The next day, after they'd been for a walk, shared a cocktail with Maudie and been floored by the delights of one of Mrs B's Sunday roasts, Gina dropped Evie at the station.

'The most extraordinary thing,' Evie confessed, looking stunned, 'is that I have actually enjoyed myself. Can that be true?'

'It means you need to come back soon,' suggested Gina. 'To avoid shocking Rosa, you could stay at the Jolly Sailor,' she went on. 'It's a very nice pub. I stayed there on the first night.'

'And we've got to find Dancing Danny, of course,' Evie grinned as she climbed onto the train. 'I expect that's why I don't want to leave.'

'So your enjoyment's got nothing to do with Sexy Stu from the Upper Sixth?' shouted Gina as the train departed.

To avoid disturbing Maudie, Gina only intruded into the antique-stuffed drawing room while she was out. She could do the rest – research, follow-up, estimate – from her laptop in the bedroom. This morning, though, she needed to take a closer look at one of Maudie's prize possessions – a vast family portrait which Maudie believed was the work of Joshua Reynolds. It had many of the right hallmarks – a highly romantic sylvan setting, unusual tenderness in the portrayal of the smiling children – but no signature. Maudie always said she was grateful as, if it were signed, she would have to keep it in a bank vault instead of enjoying its uninsured beauty, but Gina's instinct told her that it was genuine and would probably be worth millions if a signature could be detected.

On the way it was a much less showy artwork that caught her eye. A small, brightly coloured drawing of a dancing nymph and satyr, accompanied by a naked creature playing a pipe which, in Gina's view, had all the attributes of Marc Chagall. It strongly reminded her of the similar one sold through her own company that had proved extremely profitable. She knew from the research she'd done back then that a large number of Chagall's works were unsigned, and many of those that were tended to be forgeries, since a signed work was worth ten times more than one that is unsigned.

Gina had to laugh when she looked online at the variety of fake Chagall signatures. Fortunately, there was a research centre in Holland that specialized in authenticating his work, so Gina photographed the drawing to send it off to them. She would be fascinated to hear what they had to say.

She was embarrassed at how little she had known of Chagall's work before one came into her possession. Like most people, when she thought of Chagall it was of ghostly figures in the sky, amazing colours and lots of strange animal imagery. If she were truthful, she might have echoed the immortal words of Cher in the romcom *Moonstruck*, when faced with a huge Chagall mural at the Lincoln Center in New York: 'Kinda gaudy, isn't it?'

But now, as she discovered more about him, she was stunned at the range of his work, and his extraordinary diligence in cataloguing almost everything he created. It should be much easier to find out if this were genuine than with a Picasso or a Matisse.

She would print off the photograph, plus all the information, and send it to Holland. Since this would involve a trip to the local post office, which was down by the seafront, she might as well go for a swim while she was down there.

* * *

As usual, there was something about swimming in deep water that helped Gina put her problems into perspective. The sea was so deep and blue and vast. The pull of the waves, controlled by the gravitational force of the moon, made you feel like a tiny speck on the face of the earth.

It was up to her to try and be a happy speck.

Laughing at herself, she came to a decision. She'd go to the managing agent today and set about finding Dancing Danny. She wasn't sure why this had become so important to her, but somehow it had.

Boyd & Mackinnon, Property Management, was based in the prime location of Sea Street a few hundred yards away.

Gina attempted to dry her hair, wishing she had dressed a bit smarter instead of the shorts and flip-flops she'd worn for the beach. This was ridiculous. She was only going to see some agents, for goodness' sake! She plucked up her courage and marched in. 'Hello,' she greeted the girl behind the desk. 'I'm trying to get in touch with an old friend whose family owned 21 Southdown Crescent. It's been turned into flats now and they're managed by you. My friend's name is Daniel Napier.'

'Right,' replied the girl, looking a little flustered. 'I'll see what I can do. If you'd like to sit down?'

'I'll deal with this, Tracy,' interrupted an assertive female voice. Out of the back office a super-thin blonde magically materialized wearing a geometric dress Gina had tried on in Maje and decided she couldn't afford. It was the same woman who'd grabbed the man in denim just when Gina was asking who he was!

'I'm Rebecca Boyd,' she introduced herself in the manner of the Princess Royal accepting another wilted posy. 'And you are . . . ?'

'Georgina Greenhills.'

'Good morning, Mrs Greenhills, how may I help you?'

'Ms not Mrs,' replied Gina firmly, lifting her head to uphold the honour of the women who had fought so hard not to be defined by their husbands. 'Ms Gina Greenhills.'

'I'm sorry, Ms Greenhills,' the sarcasm in her voice so obvious that Gina wanted to slap her, 'but we can't possibly give out information like that for reasons of—'

'Data protection,' supplied Gina, repressing an equally sarcastic smile and thinking how useful this defence was to people who didn't want to help you anyway. 'I understand. But if you could simply convey to Mr Napier that I wanted to get in touch?'

'I really don't think that's within our remit. I suggest you try some other method to look for your friend.'

'Thank you so much,' Gina replied. 'You've been most unhelpful. I mean helpful,' she instantly corrected herself, thinking what a bitch the woman was.

The whole idea was stupid anyway. It was funny, when your life disappeared down a rabbit hole, you started to behave like the Mad Hatter in response. It was high time to recover her sanity.

She got into her car and drove off, deciding to forget all about Dancing Danny. After all, she had plenty to do at the manor, and even if Maudie kept insisting she should treat it as a holiday, she wasn't going to forget her real purpose here. She might not be getting very far with the disappearing objects, but she was at least making good progress with the valuation.

Fortunately, the valuation work was not only fascinating but absorbing as well. Hours would pass with her happily cataloguing the items, taking photographs and hunting through recent auction prices to see if there was anything similar to get an idea of the current worth. Half of her expertise was in the contacts she'd made over the years so that, when necessary, she could call someone at Sotheby's or Christie's, as well as the big auction houses in Paris or Rome, and they would not only take her call but be actively helpful.

She was studying a huge chandelier consisting of five gilded *putti*, the fat cherubs so beloved by Italian rococo artists, each holding a candle-shaped light bulb, and wondering how to get a sense of the value of so unfashionable an object when Maudie arrived in the room.

'There you are! I was wondering if you were back. Enough work for one day. Come and join me on the terrace for an after-work cocktail.'

The idea of the sunny terrace with its pots of red and pink geraniums was a tempting thought, but Gina felt a tinge of guilt at stopping work at five o'clock.

'We can talk about my antiques, if you like,' Maudie tempted.

'If you give me a guided tour of your garden statues,' replied Gina. 'Otherwise I'll think I'm skiving.'

'Dear girl, you must rid yourself of this protestant work ethic. Hedonism's so much easier to live with. I'll see you in ten minutes.'

Gina had hardly opened the French windows to the garden before Maudie descended on her, pressing a large G&T, bursting with fresh limes, into her hand.

'Come on then, you asked for it!'

Maudie led her down six steps to a sunken garden where a row of marble statues stood out white against the greenery in the tender sunlight of early evening. 'As you see, I have a weakness for statues of Aphrodite, or Venus, as the Romans insisted on calling her. Here is a bathing Venus,' she pointed to a life-size statue, uselessly holding a flimsy cloth to protect her modesty. 'That one's reclining on a couch – holding the golden apple awarded to her for being more beautiful than Hera or Athena. I love her smug smile, even though they call it the Apple of Discord because it's the thing that starts the Trojan War.'

They walked further into the green depths of the garden.

'There's the Venus de Milo – a copy, obviously, and not one of my favourites. Frankly I always thought her a tad over-weight,' Maudie grinned.

At the last statue in the row, she stopped and bowed her head in reverence. 'This is the one I like most of all. The Crouching Venus – there's one in the British Museum. Look how lifelike she is, kneeling down with her arms delicately disguising her charms from anyone daring to take a peek. You could almost touch the skin and expect it to be warm!' Maudie placed an arm round the statue as if it were a living being. 'I'd have enjoyed being Venus,' she sighed. 'She was very naughty, you know, always having affairs with gods as well as unfortunate mortals, who never came out of it well. She had lots of fun. I see you more as the goddess Hera – trying to keep her husband Zeus on the straight and narrow. She made one nymph burst into flames when Zeus showed her his willy, and poor Echo had to repeat everything she heard for eternity.'

'And you think that's like me!' Gina laughed out loud. 'I wish I had the nerve to copy her. I'd turn Mark into the god of sex who couldn't get it up, and this new woman into a nymphomaniac who couldn't get enough of it!'

'Come on, fetch us another cocktail and we'll watch the sun go down. Not over Mount Olympus but beautiful Beale Beacon.'

Maudie led them back up to the sun-filled terrace, sighing with pleasure at the beauty of the afternoon and the gorgeous eccentricity of owning four different Venuses. The phone in her handbag rang, and though she didn't answer it, she saw the name of the caller and her expression lost its carefree happiness.

'You sit there,' Gina pulled out a comfortable-looking lounger, 'I'll get the drinks. What would you like?'

'Same again, please dear,' replied Maudie. 'And not one of those thimblefuls of gin Mrs B always gives me!'

Maudie kept her drinks in an old-fashioned drinks cabinet at the far end of the drawing room, which ran across most of the back of the house. Gina had just located the bottle of Bombay Sapphire when she heard low voices emanating from the kitchen, first a man's then, listening hard, she detected a woman's as well. The gadflies were back to torment them!

'She's a lonely old woman, and this Gina is taking blatant advantage of her!' Rosa announced in a whisper, but even a whisper from Rosa could be heard on the other side of a large room. 'I mean, what are they doing out there drinking together? Call this working!'

'I mean, Mrs B,' Ambrose had his plain man-only-doing-his-duty face on, 'how long does she actually spend doing this valuation?'

Mrs B then made the mistake of trying to answer.

'None!' interrupted Rosa. 'Because she's always off to the beach with one of those so-called *friends*. What if she's in league with some two-a-penny dealer round here who'll tell Maudie her stuff is worthless and then they both buy it and flog it?'

'But, Rosa, love, you've always said we ought to get the stuff valued,' pointed out Ambrose with unexpected good sense.

'Yes, but not by her!'

Gina was tempted to materialize and defend herself, but there was really no point with Rosa. Very quietly she dropped a slice of lime into the gin and tonic, picked up the glass and made her way back to the relative safety of the terrace.

It was early evening and all around her the office was beginning to empty. Evie sat looking out at the square outside her window. It was bursting with roses – pale pink, yellow, apricot, dark red. Funny, she'd never really noticed them before. Work had always been her priority, and she never paid much attention to her surroundings. The only advantages she had appreciated about the location of the office were its proximity to good transport and the fact that it was useful being so near barristers and the courts. The grandness of the office building didn't hurt with their more distinguished clients either.

But for some reason, tonight it was memories of childhood evenings that kept coming back to her: the smell of newly mown grass after her father had cut the lawn and the joy of running through the sprinkler. Pushing herself up and down on her swing listening to the birds begin their night-time chorus.

She hadn't thought about any of this stuff for years. Probably going back to Southdown had stirred up the memories more than she'd suspected. Or perhaps she was simply missing Gina's company. When you were single, your girlfriends were your support group and your lifeline, even for someone as successful as she was. And maybe she ought to admit that, selfishly, Mark's habit of always being on a racecourse had meant that Gina had been more available than most of her married friends. Should she have said something to her?

She only hoped that Mark hadn't managed to wreck the business and their finances before he met the other woman and left. And it was Evie's job, and indeed pleasure, to make sure Gina got as much as possible of what was left.

She knew that Gina was feeling both stupid and like a failure at the moment – the usual effect of divorce, in her experience, no matter how much of a loser the man was – but at least Gina had her daughters Sadie and Lisa. What did she herself have apart from a healthy bank balance and a house in Hampstead?

One of these days, Evie told herself, you ought to do something that really makes a difference. 'Good heavens,' she stood up, starting to pack up her stuff, 'what's this maudlin meandering about? Time I headed for the wine bar and had a large glass of Pinot. I must be getting soft in my old age!'

Casks wine bar was a cavernous underground space that claimed to be the oldest in London. It consisted of one area where every single centimetre was covered in maps and dark oil paintings leading to a series of low arches, straight out Dickens, lit only by candles and extremely popular for assignations.

Evie sat down, suddenly self-conscious of being alone. This was ridiculous, she told herself, she never felt like this. Confidence in herself had carried her through the patriarchal, and certainly archaic, world of the law. She'd not only broken through glass ceilings, she had ignored them – and won. Her name was both respected and feared.

She looked around for the server – Dutch courage was called for – and found herself looking straight into the humorous grey eyes of the man sitting opposite. Who just happened to be Stuart Nixon.

'Fancy meeting you here, as the common parlance has it,' he commented, with the beginnings of a smile. 'What a coincidence.'

'Coincidence, my arse,' replied Evie pithily. 'Since I come here most days to detox. This is practically my office.'

'I know,' the smile grew. 'I asked at your reception. They said I might find you here.'

'Bollocks,' insisted Evie, surveying him with all the trust of a fly confronting a spider, 'they wouldn't tell you!'

'They would if they thought I had an important document you needed for tomorrow's case.' He put a finger in front of his lips. 'Too important to email. You know how easily things get hacked. We had quite a long chat about the evils of scams.'

'Stuart Nixon, you are one step from a criminal!'

'I had no idea I was so glamorous. To think I thought I was a boring estate agent.'

'So, why did you go to these extraordinary lengths rather than the more conventional route of calling me?'

Before he could reply, a giggling couple materialized out of the darkness. 'Excuse me, but are you using both those tables? Only we booked that one for seven thirty.'

Evie grinned and gestured to the seat opposite her. 'I suppose you'd better join me.' She turned round and waved assertively to the server, more the old Evie this time, a person no one could ignore.

'A large Pinot please,' she ordered.

'And you, sir?'

'I think we'd better make it a bottle, don't you?'

'Good idea. Then you can explain why you lied to my receptionist and lurked here waiting for me.'

'Hardly lurked.' He looked around at the various couples in the candlelit darkness. 'Though it does seem to be the place for assignations.'

'Is that what we're having? An assignation?' A sudden panic

gripped her that he probably had a perfectly nice wife and kids waiting in Southdown.

'An assignation sounds very Victorian novelish,' he replied. 'Something forbidden.'

'Then how would you describe it?'

'I was in London for a meeting. I thought it'd be great to see you.'

'Since marriage is my business,' Evie announced, very matter of fact, 'I think we'd better get something straight. What exactly is your marital status?'

'We *are* moving along fast,' he replied wryly. 'Happily divorced, if such a thing is possible.'

'I very much doubt it,' Evie shrugged. 'But maybe you can convince me.'

'We both changed and agreed that our marriage was over fifteen years ago. No one else was involved.'

'That would help,' Evie conceded. 'Any children?'

'I'm not your client, Ms Beeston,' he raised a quizzical eyebrow. 'But yes, two daughters. Grown up now. Well balanced. Hopefully not too scarred by the experience.'

'I'm sorry. I didn't mean to sound like the Spanish Inquisition.' They both laughed, remembering the Monty Python sketch at the exact same moment, just as the bottle arrived.

'Time we had a bloody drink,' Evie decreed.

'I couldn't agree more.' He filled both their glasses with a nice healthy slug, much to Evie's approval. 'A toast. To non-forbidden assignations.'

Evie clinked her glass against his, enjoying something she rarely let herself experience. A moment of excited optimism, untinged by her usual scathing cynicism. Her work had led her not to trust the males of the species.

Maybe it was time to give men another chance.

Six

_____

'Gina!' shouted a voice from the seashore. 'I thought it was you! Wait a minute, I'm coming in!'

Gina's peaceful after-work swim wasn't going to be so peaceful after all. The unmistakable sight of Ruth O'Halloran running down the beach in a swimsuit, that looked as if she had owned it since school days, had stopped the conversation between the after-school mums, the sunbathing pensioners, and the eccentric dog walkers alike.

'Gorgeous, isn't it?' she enquired on arrival.

'Er . . .' Gina thought she meant the swimsuit and was saved from giving an opinion by the realization that Ruth was referring to the water.

'Yes,' agreed Gina. 'It's an incredible colour today. Somewhere between aquamarine and lapis lazuli. And so cool! I hate it when you're in Turkey or Greece and you get in the water and it's the temperature of a warm bath! I find this perfect.' It was strange how, in her memory of Southdown the tide was almost permanently out, and yet during this visit it seemed to be the opposite.

It couldn't really have changed, of course. It must all be a matter of perception. She had been focusing on the negative. And maybe age changed what one appreciated.

Today there was plenty to be positive about. It had rained in the night and left the air with that extraordinary crystalline brightness that followed heavy downpours. If she looked hard enough she could even see the faint outline of the French cliffs.

'How's life up at Rookery Manor?' Ruth asked cheerily.

'Fine. It's going well.' Gina hesitated, then made up her mind to say something. 'I've overheard Rosa and her husband talking about me a couple of times, though. They really resent me being here and seem to think I'm taking advantage of Maudie by going to the beach when it's Maudie who keeps telling me to go!'

'I wouldn't worry about them. They think they own the place already, that's all. But Maudie's still pretty lively.'

'Is she really going to leave it to them?'

Ruth flipped over onto her side, making Gina think of a large friendly seal.

'Lucy and her husband aren't the type to want to live in Rookery Manor. They like minimalist architecture. You haven't been to their place yet, have you? It's the barest house I've ever seen. An art deco penthouse in the middle of town with incredible sea views. They've only just finished doing it up. And when I asked Lucy's husband if he was happy with it, do you know what he said?'

Gina shook her head.

'"Next time I wouldn't have the light switches!" So you can see they wouldn't exactly want the temple to maximalism Maudie's created.' She grinned. 'Or the risk of taking on a twelfth-century manor. Lucy's husband made his pile in insurance and won't get out of bed unless he can claim for it.'

'And what about the other daughter?'

'She'd never dare stand up to Rosa.'

'Mrs B says she and Ambrose are quite broke and they'll probably sell off the good stuff.'

'Is there any good stuff? Maudie always says there isn't.'

'I think so. Though I am getting second opinions.'

'And what about the disappearing objects? No more gone?'

'No, but I still think it's a matter for the police.'

'Ain't gonna happen. Lucy's a strong girl but she doesn't want to start a family feud.'

'I'm beginning to get cold,' Gina admitted. 'I think I'll go in and dry off.'

'I might just head round the bay. I hate exercise, but swimming seems more of a pleasure than a chore.'

Gina made her way up the beach and laid on a towel, feeling the life-enhancing rays dry off her skin. She propped herself on one elbow and watched Ruth's progress. Gina liked to stay in her depth or not far out of it, but Ruth had no such qualms. She struck out for the horizon then turned towards the first of the Seven Sisters before heading back into the shore.

'You're quite a swimmer,' congratulated Gina as she plopped down beside her.

'It's one activity where my blubber's actually useful!' Ruth laughed.

Gina had to admit, she rather envied Ruth's freedom from either fashion sense or vanity. How liberating would it be not to care what anyone thought of you? She tried not to think of her own fragile self-confidence and willed herself to be more like Ruth.

As if sensing her friend's sudden vulnerability, Ruth put down her towel. 'Let's go and do something fun! Eat toffee apples and ride the big wheel on the seafront, or visit the famous smugglers' caves. Haven't done that since I was a child. They're really amazing!'

'Sounds interesting!' Gina allowed herself to be pulled along in the wake of Ruth's enthusiasm. 'I don't think I've ever been to the caves.'

'The caves it is! We'll probably have them to ourselves since all the kids are still at school.'

They drove into the town centre, parked in one of the car parks on the seafront and walked towards the funicular that took you right up the cliff face to the caves' entrance at the top.

'This is fun already!' Gina laughed as the funicular creaked its way upwards at an impressive angle.

They came out into an area of green that ran right along the clifftops and made for the entrance. After handing over their money in the brightly lit pay station they were in for a shock. The light completely disappeared and they were standing in a small cave in total darkness. Ahead of them an arched passageway opened up. Candles flickered in more than twenty niches that had been carved into the rock along its entire length, creating the atmosphere of a medieval monastery.

'It's called the Monk's Walk,' whispered Ruth.

'Quite creepy,' shivered Gina. 'You half expect a headless figure to appear at any moment!'

'Let's go on. There's a whole acre of caverns to see,' announced Ruth, who had picked up a leaflet at the pay station.

Next they found themselves in a large dimly-lit cave. In one corner were two life-size figures of smugglers hiding a stash of tobacco inside a book. A sign above informed them that tobacco that was worth £100 in Belgium would bring £1,000 in England because of the heavy taxation imposed by the king to pay for a war.

'It reminds me of the Kipling rhyme we all learned as children,' Gina whispered. 'How did it go?'

Ruth stood to attention and began to declaim:

> 'Five and twenty ponies
> Trotting through the dark
> Brandy for the Parson
> Baccy for the Clerk
> Laces for a lady
> Letters for a spy
> And watch the wall, my darling,
> While the Gentlemen go by.'

'You've got an amazing memory!' marvelled Gina.

'Actually, it's all written there above your head!' Ruth pointed upwards.

They giggled as they left the spookily convincing atmosphere of the first cave and passed through a passageway into another, this one dominated by a vast pagan statue.

'Popular for Satanic rites, it says here,' Ruth announced prosaically. 'Personally, I'd stick to smuggling.'

Their laughter was interrupted by a muffled voice at the other end of the cavern.

Carved into the rock was a reconstructed prison cell. Behind bars was a disconcertingly realistic figure of a young man.

'God, he's lifelike,' whispered Ruth. 'He looks like my son when he was younger.'

Suddenly the figure shouted, 'Help me! I didn't do it!' and rattled the bars in desperation.

Ruth and Gina clung to each other for a moment. Something

that might have been almost comic in the midst of crowds and bright lights was chilling when the space around you was empty and echoing.

Next to it was another tableau of the same young man hanging from a noose, his lifelike young face contorted in the agony of death.

They turned round and Gina gasped. Another figure, heavy-set and threatening, glowered at them through narrowed eyes.

'Jesus,' blurted Ruth. 'I didn't see that one.'

To their horror, it spoke. 'Afternoon, ladies. Interesting place, isn't it?'

Gina felt her breath quicken. It was Mad Mike from the car wash. What the hell was he doing here? The thought floated into her mind that he might have been following them. Ridiculous as it was, she felt unnerved at the prospect.

'Are you all right?' Ruth asked as they climbed the steps back into the open air.

'Glad to be out of there, I must admit,' confessed Gina.

'Yes, there's spooky and scary spooky, and that was scary spooky,' admitted Ruth. 'And what was that thug Mike Marshall doing in there? He doesn't strike me as the tourist type.'

'I was thinking that myself,' Gina agreed. 'Those figures are altogether too realistic!'

Ruth hugged her goodbye. 'I'm so glad you're back,' she smiled, 'even if it's only for a while. We were all too close to lose touch.'

'I'm enjoying myself much more than I ought to be, given I'm here to work.'

'I'm sure Maudie would be very happy about that.'

There was no sign of either Maudie or Mrs B when she got back to the manor. Feeling relieved to have a little time to herself, Gina made herself a cup of tea and took it up to her room.

She opened the door to a pleasing aroma of beeswax and lavender furniture polish that harked back to her childhood. Mrs B had obviously been tidying the room. Her own home in London rarely achieved such heights of housewifery.

Mrs B was so thorough that even the inside of the wardrobe had been dusted. To do so, she had removed the cardboard box of souvenirs from her mother's house and forgotten to put it back.

Gina began to look idly through it. Under a couple of school reports she came across the letter from Danny, which must have been in with the invitation. *Dear Gina*, it read. *If you can face a second meeting since those glorious days of dancing classes, do come to my twenty-first. You'll probably be back at university but I really hope you can make it.*

There was something about the tone of restrained hope that touched her heart and made her wish she had at least answered the invitation herself and not left it to her mother to send the kind of offhand reply Evie suggested.

Gina's phone suddenly beeped and made her jump. She went to get it, glad her daughters weren't here to laugh at her. They found her generation's distrust of technology a hoot.

It was a response from the Chagall research unit in Holland requesting more information. Could she remove the work and see what, if anything, was on the back? On first inspection, the message asserted, the work looked genuine.

Before going to do as they asked, Gina searched for recent saleroom prices for similar works. It wasn't like finding an oil painting, which would be worth millions, but the lithograph would certainly fetch a fair sum if it could be authenticated. Between £10,000 and £12,000 seemed a reasonable estimate.

She slipped quietly down to the drawing room to take the artwork down and check the information.

Except that she couldn't. The empty space told its own shocking story.

Someone had got there before her. The flute-playing faun and the brightly coloured couple were no longer in their frame on the wall, they had completely disappeared.

Seven

'Mrs Browning, can I have a word?' Gina asked.

Mrs B, up to her elbows in flour, looked up suspiciously. 'I'm a bit busy at the moment, can it wait?'

'I'm afraid not. Do you know where the small picture that was in the drawing room, between the bookcase and the windows, has gone?'

'You mean the one with that pagan creature playing the flute with his pecker out?' Mrs B enquired. 'In the bin, hopefully. Best place for it.'

Gina ignored this opinion on the work of one of the modern era's most celebrated artists. 'But you didn't put it there, I imagine?'

'Of course not. Wouldn't want to touch it, the nasty thing.'

'Thank you. Is Mrs Tyler about?'

'Gone to get the car cleaned.'

'Thank you. Has she been long?'

'About an hour.'

Gina went back up to her room, torn between waiting for Maudie to ask her about the missing lithograph or whether she should contact Lucy to urge that this time they involve the police no matter what Rosa thought of the idea.

It was another hour till she heard Maudie speeding up the rutted driveway and went down to greet her. She found her seated quietly with the engine switched off, a curious Madonna-like expression lighting up her features.

'Hello, Gina dear, can I help you?'

'Maudie, the Chagall lithograph of the couple with the pipe-playing faun, do you know where it's got to?'

A brief look of confusion clouded her soft features. 'The thing is, Gina dear, sometimes I can't remember if I've done something or not. But yes, I think I took that into the auction-eers for them to have a look. I saw a similar one in the roundup of saleroom prices in *Country Life* and was quite surprised at how much it went for.'

'I see,' replied Gina, not entirely convinced. Maudie usually claimed to be so uninterested in the value of her possessions. 'It's just that I approached a gallery in Holland that specializes in Chagall authentication and they want a few more facts.'

'That was clever of you.' A sudden look of panic flashed across her face. 'You won't tell Rosa, will you? That I can't remember?'

'Of course I won't.' Realizing she wasn't going to get any further with Maudie, Gina decided to go into town and have a word with Ruth. She was a friend of Lucy, after all, and of the family, as well as the person who'd got her the job in the first place. Maybe she'd have more idea of what Gina should do next.

Since it was a lovely day she decided to park in the centre of town and walk around for a while to clarify her thoughts. The job offer couldn't have come at a better time, providing an escape from a horrible situation with Mark and the chance to earn money as well, but now that she knew the participants in the drama it was making her very uncomfortable. For example, was Maudie telling the truth about taking the Chagall in to the auctioneers? Her manner had seemed decidedly odd. But if it had been stolen, then who by? An outside thief was very unlikely to strike twice, and that meant it had to be one of the family or staff.

She wandered through the town, not noticing the hip cafes, art galleries, and even a vast graffiti of the Birth of Venus, the joke being that this particular version was surrounded not by blue water but ice and snow – presumably as a protest against climate change. The tatty old cinema had reopened with plush double seats and tables for your glasses of wine, with a programme aimed at the leisured over-sixties who still believed that going to the cinema was better than sitting at home and streaming.

In the centre of town, bang outside Marks and Spencer, there was a tiny dancefloor where an elegant grey-haired couple were dancing a rather steamy tango.

Gina found herself gazing at them, admiring the way their steps matched so flawlessly. She wondered if they had taken up dancing as a joint interest, and a flash of guilt clouded her consciousness. Instead of letting Mark go off on his own to the races, should she have tried to persuade him to do some-thing together, or at the very least have gone with him?

All at once she felt blindsided by the thought of this new woman and had to stop and fight back the tears. How could she have the power to get him to change where Gina had failed?

The couple who seemed so in tune with each other were finishing their tango. All around passers-by stopped to clap.

As Gina willed herself to stop living in the past, she felt an arm slip round her waist and she was propelled firmly towards the dancefloor before she could gather her wits to protest.

'Come on, you can remember the cha-cha.' She found herself looking up into the laughing blue eyes of the denim-clad stranger who had stopped her taking a selfie and greeted her the other night at the Langdon Arms before he was swept determinedly away.

'Just follow me,' he counselled. 'And don't worry, I'm no Anton du Beke, but I think I can remember the steps. Side-close-side, then back, triple step, swing the hips, one two three cha-cha-cha!'

Silently they glided backwards straight into Gina's memory of the ballroom at the Grand Hotel, rented by the hour by the feisty Mrs Francis, a single mother in the days when single mothers were called divorcees.

'You're Danny from dancing school,' she half accused as they came to a halt, greeted by a surprising round of applause. 'I knew there was something familiar about you!'

'I'm injured to hear that,' was the sardonic reply. 'I thought I'd changed beyond recognition from that gawky kid who could never think of anything to say.'

'You've certainly got the gift of the gab now!' agreed Gina.

'Well hello, Ms Georgina Greenhills,' he persisted before she realized he was still holding her. 'How've you been all these years. I hear you've been looking for me?'

'I came across a letter from you inviting me to your twenty-first with your address on it,' she replied, trying to sound more nonchalant than she felt. 'I wanted to know if I'd answered it.'

'You didn't. Of course you didn't. But then I didn't expect you to. I was used to adoring pretty girls from afar.'

'You were always very kind to me,' admitted Gina. 'Pretty was the last thing I felt. My mother always used to call me a gawking great thing. That's why she made me go to Mrs Francis. So that nice boys might dance with me.'

'And like most girls you preferred the bad boys,' he reminded her.

'I remember your velvet jacket.'

'God, that thing, I thought I was being so smooth. A Southdown James Bond.'

She blushed, suddenly remembering his limp handshake, and what Ruth had said *that* meant.

'Now what are you thinking?' he asked, watching her curiously. 'Clearly something I'm not going to live down easily!'

'Oh, nothing. So, what have you been doing all these years?'

'I'm a boring businessman. I think I heard you were in antiques?'

She nodded. 'Husband and children, no doubt?' he enquired.

'Two daughters, Sadie and Lisa. But it's all got a bit complicated lately.'

'It often does,' he replied sympathetically, and to her great relief didn't push her any further.

'You?'

'Widowed. My wife Janey died ten years ago. Look, I have to run now, but why not get together and talk about old times?'

'I'd like that.' She wrote down her phone number and handed it to him.

As if he'd somehow guessed what she'd been thinking earlier, Daniel held out a hand and shook hers. His handshake certainly wasn't limp now.

As she walked from the centre of town to Ruth's house she found herself smiling. There was one phone call she couldn't resist making. 'Evie! You're not going to believe it. I've found Dancing Danny!'

'Oh the excitement!' Gina could hear a wave of murmuring in the background and realized Evie was probably in one of the Inns of Court at some do, stuffed with ancient lawyers. 'Was it through the managing agent?'

'Absolutely not. She was a right cow. There's a tiny dance-floor outside M&S and I was watching this couple do the tango when someone swept me off my feet and started doing the cha-cha!'

'And is there a Mrs Dancing Danny?' Evie instantly enquired.

'Evie! Honestly!'

'Go on, Gina, don't tell me that didn't run through your mind when you were doing your paso doble!'

'I don't think you do a paso doble in cha-cha.'

'Stop splitting hairs. You know what I mean.'

'As a matter of fact, he's been widowed for ten years.'

'And still single. Does he look like Shrek or something?'

Gina giggled. 'He's quite nice looking, actually.'

'Gina,' Evie announced instantly, 'this settles it. I'll be down on Friday. Tell Maudie I'm happy to stay in the pub you mentioned. In fact, I think I'd prefer it. I don't really like staying in other people's houses. I'm too much of a spinster, set in my ways.'

Gina could think of no one less like a spinster than Evie but, given Rosa and Ambrose's critical attitude, it would probably make more sense. Besides, the disappearance of the Chagall did change things.

It suddenly struck Gina that she could simply go and check with the local auctioneers and find out if Maudie had been telling the truth.

Ruth was looking after her grandchildren when Gina arrived, and delightful though they were, this did rather limit the conversation.

'I was just wondering what you thought I should do about the Chagall going missing?' Gina enquired.

Ruth attempted to put the boisterous two-year-old down on the sofa next to her. 'Tell Lucy, for a start. She hired you to look into to it, so honour bound she ought to be kept in the picture, if you'll pardon the pun.'

'Even if it turns out to be one of the family members who's doing the stealing?'

'Do you get the feeling Maudie is worried about burglars? I mean, it can't be pleasant having all these things disappear.' Ruth ignored all attempts made at pulling her hair and put her attention back to grandchild number two. 'Maybe it's Rosa and Awful Ambrose trying to scare her out. They're always leaving McCarthy & Stone brochures all over the place – you know, those posh sheltered housing developments – and trying to persuade her to move into a flat somewhere in town.'

Gina giggled. 'I can't see them resorting to burglary to do it.'

'They would if they could get away with it, I bet,' insisted Ruth.

For a moment, Gina was tempted to tell her about dancing with Daniel, but decided against it; she wasn't sure why. Ruth might well know him and Gina realized she didn't want to hear all the local gossip. If she was here for a while, she'd find out for herself what she thought of him.

'OK, why don't you fix a meeting with Lucy and I'll suss out the auction house.'

'Ooh,' Ruth gave in to the increasingly shrill demands of her grandson, 'isn't it exciting! I feel like a private detective!'

Gina was grateful that, after her last encounter, her contact at Waddington's, Gavin, was busy doing valuations for their upcoming auction, since he would probably have told her to get lost. Instead, she was offered their newest intern, who made up in enthusiasm what she lacked in experience.

'Did you say a Chagall?' she enquired. 'I love Chagall! All those brides and grooms floating in the sky. I'd put them on my wedding invitation if I was getting married. I'm sorry Gavin's busy, but if a lithograph was left with us – especially one by a famous artist – we would definitely have a record of it.' She turned to her screen and tapped away. 'Do you know when it would have been brought in, roughly?'

'Yes.' Gina thought back to when she'd last looked at it. 'It would have been last Wednesday or Thursday, the fifteenth or sixteenth.'

The girl went back to her register.

'Sorry, absolutely zero for those dates.'

'Thanks for checking.'

Hoping the sea air might clear her head, Gina decided to walk along the promenade for a while rather than dash straight back to the manor. Above her seagulls wheeled crazily, calling out to each other with their harsh raucous cries. Something eventful must have happened in their airborne world. Near the shore a small crowd seemed to have gathered, perhaps connected to the wild cries of the gulls. She hoped it wasn't something sinister. But no, she could see from the smiling faces and happy chatter that it couldn't be.

And then she saw the cause of all the excitement. A seal, its black shiny head bobbing up and down in the water only a short distance out. Sensing he had an audience, he wheeled and flipped exuberantly as if he were the star of the show at a sea life centre, while his admirers laughed with delight and captured his antics on their phones.

'Amazing, isn't it? Bet you don't get this sort of thing up in town!' Gina turned to find Sexy Stu standing behind her on the beach, looking as incongruous in his smart suit and Gucci loafers as a vicar at a Hell's Angels reunion.

'They think he's escaped from a seal sanctuary in Norfolk. He's quite a hero round here, a kind of aquatic Clyde Barrow.'

'Pity there's no Bonnie to keep him company,' replied Gina.

'A male needs his mate?' he enquired wryly. 'Speaking of which, when is your friend Evie next visiting us poor suburbanites?'

'This weekend,' replied Gina, taken aback by his overt interest but deciding it was rather attractive that he wasn't playing games.

'You should tell her about the aquatic magic she's missing.'

'Not sure it's up Evie's street.'

'Maybe she's not such a hardened Londoner as you imagine.'

Gina smiled. Good luck to him if that was what he thought.

'We have a lot of them, you know – Down From London types. They tell me you get to a point in life when the city loses its charm. The friendliness of a small place is suddenly attractive.'

'Yes, I can see that,' Gina agreed. She had been feeling it herself but wasn't sure it applied to Evie.

'By the way,' he hesitated, not quite sure what her reaction would be. 'Your old house has just come on the market. The current owners have done some really interesting work on it and I wondered if you'd like to have a look?'

As she walked back to look for her car, Gina was aware of how mixed her feelings were about seeing round her childhood home. In one way she'd be fascinated, but in another she feared that the security and normality of where she'd grown up might overwhelm her in her current fragile state. Her mother and father had been ordinary people leading an ordinary life. In those times people expected less of each other in marriage – if the man earned a reasonable living and the woman made a respectable job of bringing up the children, the marriage was seen as a success. They didn't expect each other to be either soulmates who would truly understand you or sexual athletes who would provide endless variety in the bedroom.

Perhaps she should make the most of having Evie here and look round it together. Evie adored all those property programmes and talked of Kirstie and Phil as if they were old friends. She'd kill Gina if she gave up this chance. Besides, it would be a good way of getting her together with Sexy Stu again, since he was so obviously intrigued by her.

'I know it must be very frustrating for you,' Lucy apologized to Gina when they met a few days later at Ruthie's, 'but I don't think you should do anything about it yet.' She shook her head in bewilderment. 'Though what I don't get is why Maudie should tell you she took it into the auctioneer if she didn't.'

'Maybe she's getting dementia,' suggested Ruth cheerfully. 'My mother-in-law's the same. She tells you she went shopping yesterday and then you find her fridge is absolutely bare when she'll swear blind she filled it. It drives Robin spare.'

'For God's sake don't suggest there's anything wrong with her to Rosa,' Lucy insisted, looking worried. 'They'd have her in a care home in five minutes flat. And not one of those posh ones either. Oh dear, maybe I shouldn't have started all this. I didn't realize it was going to be so complicated.'

'That's families for you,' Ruth contributed somewhat tactlessly. 'Full of things they'd rather you didn't know.'

'But the valuation's going well at least?' Lucy enquired hopefully.

'Very well,' reassured Gina. She decided this wasn't the moment to raise her concerns that Maudie had an obsession with the girl in the car wash. Lucy was already worried enough and beginning to wish she'd never lifted this particular family stone.

'Of course I'd *love* to come and see your old house!' Evie ignored the expensive client sitting opposite to take Gina's call. 'Say yes to Stu and I'll definitely be down at the weekend. In fact, could you book me into the pub?'

Gina envied her friend's decisiveness but then Evie had the personality to carry it off. *Come on, Gina,* she told herself sternly, *you used to be confident too. Maybe not on the Evie scale but enough to run a successful business. It's this situation with bloody Mark and this new woman that's temporarily done for it. Try and live in the present like the yoga teacher told you.*

And there were aspects of the present that were very enjoyable. Like going for lonely rambles along the spectacular coast, as she was today. She stopped for a moment to stand and take in the whole panorama of the coastline from the lighthouse that stood guard over the town to the almost-turquoise sea. And it wasn't only the beach that was tempting, but the green and fertile farmland that surrounded it. The hedgerows were alive with wildlife, skylarks soared. It was like being in your very own episode of *Springwatch*.

In the distance rustic barns built of the local stone with harmonious russet rooves dotted the landscape, giving way to the spires of small parish churches. It was a view that had hardly changed in centuries. She stood and breathed in, letting the peace and timelessness calm her troubled mind.

Inland from the cliffs a stream meandered peacefully, adorned with yellow lilies and the odd early damsel fly. Gina looked around. There was absolutely no one in sight, even though this was the busiest corner of a busy country.

On a sudden impulse, Gina slipped down to the bank and began to take off her clothes. She didn't even have a towel with her, but what the hell. It was like an irresistible pagan urge. She wanted to wash off the worries of the past and feel herself emerging fresh, new and confident.

The bank was muddy with no obvious way to get in. With a yell of joy she jumped and let the clear waters close over her, flowing over her bare breasts and between her naked thighs. It was a release so complete it was close to orgasm.

At the very top of the nearby lighthouse Daniel Napier was inspecting the place as a local volunteer. He trained his binoculars on Gina and laughed with delight. He had been watching her off and on since she'd left the car park – not in a creepy way, more as a guardian angel, he told himself with a laugh, and mainly because of the surprise at her being there at all.

Jumping in the river would do her good, he decided, just as taking to the dancefloor had done. He had sensed her pent-up anxiety then and wished he could think of ways to help her get over it.

It looked as if she was finding some on her own.

Evie packed up early on Friday, to the astonishment of her assistant who was used to seeing her working long after everyone else had left, and often taking work briefs on to her favourite wine bar. Today Evie seemed to be in a holiday mood, ribbing the clerk who came round with the post and not even pouring the usual venom on her clients' unpleasant husbands.

'Are you going to a party?' the girl ventured.

'Just off for the weekend to see a friend.'

'How lovely. Where to?' enquired her assistant, expecting the answer to be Rome or Venice, or at the very least Soho House in the Cotswolds.

'Southdown.'

Southdown? the girl had to fight the urge to ask: *Isn't that full of old people?* She went back to her desk, grateful she was going to a hen do where everyone would be under thirty.

Evie merely smiled and went on packing her work bag.

Gina had been worrying that the Jolly Sailor, in its busy seafront position, would be too noisy and pubby, but Evie declared that it was perfect. She liked to be in the centre of things and the sound of other people revelling through the night on the seafront was like a lullaby to her, she insisted.

'Why don't you come for breakfast?' Evie suggested. 'It looks terrific. No avocado on sourdough in sight. Just good old bacon and eggs and toasted white. Terrific!'

Gina smiled. The wonderful thing about old friends was that even when you thought you knew them almost as well as you knew yourself, they could still surprise you.

'I'll be there tomorrow, bright and early,' she promised.

'Ten o'clock will do fine,' replied Evie firmly. 'What time are we seeing the house?'

'Not till midday, so lots of time for bacon and eggs.'

'And is Sexy Stu showing us?'

Gina giggled. 'I have no idea, but given the questions he was asking about when you were coming, I suspect he will.'

'I was only wondering whether to go for the full vamp or a bit of suburban subtlety?'

'Oh, subtlety always wins with me,' replied Gina, dying to see Evie's version of suburban subtlety.

It turned out to be a slightly fitted ribbed dress in an eye-catching chrome yellow, teamed with a silk scarf to disguise any slight suggestion of crepey neck. Evie's long slim legs in almost invisible tights and high heels gave it more than a hint of sexiness.

'Very suitable,' congratulated Gina, who was wearing her usual loose trousers with a silk top in a pretty shade of peach.

Evie looked her over. She picked up her glass of orange juice and held it up. 'To us. We don't look too bad for a couple of old broads!'

Gina's family home was halfway between the golf course and the seafront, one of a group of six that looked out onto a small area of green.

'I remember moving here,' Gina reminisced. A detached house! It was a dream come true for my parents. To them it was a big rung up the social ladder but to us it just meant it was miles to the bus stop. Can you believe I used to go to school on my own from the age of four.'

A smart open-top BMW overtook them.

'That must be Sexy Stu,' remarked Gina.

'Never trust a salesman with a smart car,' Evie pronounced, as they walked towards the house. 'It means they're charging you too much.'

'A little harsh, don't you think?' laughed Stuart, having emerged from his car and walked silently across the grass. 'I was left some money and decided to indulge myself.'

'By a grateful client?' asked Evie.

'By my father,' Stuart corrected, with a twinkle in his eye that undercut the sternness of his tone. 'My grateful clients stick to a bottle of champagne.'

'I don't suppose you have many from what one hears about estate agents,' replied Evie.

'You'd be surprised,' responded Stuart, who had clearly decided not to rise to Evie's deliberate provocation. 'Despite our bad image we do manage to be helpful occasionally. You'd be astonished how often I end up as a shoulder to cry on after deaths and divorces.'

'I'm sure you do,' replied Evie crisply. 'Especially if they're attractive. After all, women in that situation are so vulnerable they'd probably turn to the dustman. Believe me, in my job I'm forever telling them they need to think for themselves and not depend on the wrong people to make up their minds for them.'

Gina looked at her friend in astonishment. She'd hardly ever heard Evie being so rude. Was this another tactic? she wondered.

A quick glance at Stuart told her that, far from being offended, he was actually enjoying himself!

'I'll bear that in mind,' he replied with a straight face. 'Now, perhaps you'd like to look round the house?'

'Are the owners here?' asked Gina, beginning to have reservations as they approached the front door of her family home.

Stuart shook his head. 'They're out making final arrangements. They're moving to America. Apparently, the vendor's had the kind of career opportunity you can't refuse. That's why this house is such a good deal. They need someone to buy it quickly.'

'Now that,' Evie smiled, 'is the oldest sales pitch in the book! You show people around and they feel they have to buy it now or someone else will! What nonsense.'

'Except,' Stuart replied, looking remarkably unruffled, 'it's 100 per cent true. This house is an amazing buy. Wait till you see all the work they've done on it.'

'Hang on,' Gina interrupted, feeling like Alice down the rabbit hole again. 'This is hardly a sales pitch. I'm only looking round for old times' sake so I can see what's happened to my childhood bedroom.'

'Let's go and look then.' Stuart held out the key to the

front door. 'Just say if you want to leave. Looking round family homes can be overwhelming.'

'She can always cast herself onto your strong shoulder,' interjected Evie rudely.

Until she went inside the front door, Gina would have felt he was exaggerating. She'd really come, so she told herself, because then she could describe it all to her brother Neil – not that he'd be interested.

But seeing the transformation had an extraordinary effect. Gone was the chilly front parlour, reserved for visitors who rarely visited, the tiny kitchen with its small New World cooker, the pantry, the larder and even the lounge. It had been transformed into one huge light space with comfortable squashy sofas down one end opposite a giant TV screen, an island down the centre of an entirely new farmhouse-style kitchen and, if that wasn't enough, a glass extension had been added to house a long dining table and another sofa at the far end. And all illuminated by clever lighting which made the whole seem cosy and enticing despite its huge dimensions.

'Wow!' was all Gina could think of to say, realizing in that moment how much she loved the new look and how much her mother would have hated it.

'Come and see this,' Stuart grinned. 'There's a hidden laundry room with one of those wooden hanging racks to dry your clothes in an eco-friendly way.'

'Now that,' Gina marvelled, 'is something even my mother would approve of! Although she'd probably still insist there's nothing to beat drying clothes outside even if it does make your garden look like something in a Stanley Spencer painting!' She turned to her friend. 'What do you think of it so far?'

'I'm stunned,' Evie replied. 'Would it be mean to say that your house was never exactly cosy?'

'That's very polite of you. In fact it was freezing and so tidy that I always felt Mum was just waiting for me to go so she could straighten the cushions.' She looked around again. 'Can we see upstairs?'

The first floor was, if anything, more extraordinary. Her own bedroom, the tiniest in the house, made for a baby, not a music-loving sixteen-year-old whose hobby was collecting clothes and junk from charity shops, had been extended by borrowing from the large bathroom next door and fitting built-in wardrobes to maximize the space, which they had decorated with hip non-matching handles.

But the seriously gobsmacking revelation was her parents' bedroom. In the era when she'd grown up, people used the bedroom simply for sleeping. But with the addition of a French bed and a comfortable chair in the window, plus a luxurious en suite bathroom, the room seemed like something from a smart boutique hotel where you'd be tempted to stay all day.

Evie looked longingly at the bed. 'If I was sleeping in something like that I'd have parties from my bed like Louis XIV at Versailles!'

And indeed, the large bed with its carved headboard and silk hangings had more than a faint suggestion of a Parisian brothel. Nothing could have been more different to the repressed sexual attitude that had characterized her parents' marriage. Sex must have happened to produce her and Neil, but she suspected the two occasions would have been repeated as rarely as possible.

'You haven't seen the best bit yet,' offered Stuart.

'There's more?' asked Gina, already unable to recognize her childhood in these rooms.

At the far end of the bedroom there was a hidden corridor

with a small staircase. They climbed up to the roof space and stopped in amazement. A huge room had been created up here, with windows either side of a double bed. The views were stupendous. Right down to the sea from one skylight, and to the green, lush heights of the downs from the other.

'Now that is something,' admitted Evie. 'What a view! From the sublime to the necessary, I don't suppose there's a bathroom up here?'

'Tucked just behind there,' Stuart pointed. 'It's a shower room with basin and loo rather than a bathroom, but then the younger generation prefer showers to baths anyway.'

'I wouldn't put a bloody teenager in here,' protested Evie. 'Much too good for them. I was a right slob at that age. My bedroom looked like a pigsty. That is, if pigs wore twenty-seven pairs of three-inch stilettos.'

Stuart grinned. 'I'm sure you're exaggerating.'

'You'd be surprised. And I had a penchant for thongs. I used to hang them along the bedstead.'

'Pigs in thongs,' Stuart marvelled, still managing to keep a straight face. 'Now that's an image to treasure.'

'How much is it?' Evie insisted, while Gina stared out at the equally transformed garden.

The sum Stuart named almost made Evie choke. 'It must be more than that!'

'You're used to London prices. Southdown is cheap and this house is even cheaper. They need a quick sale. They leave for the US in two weeks.'

As they went back downstairs, Gina tried to picture her mother in these magically transformed surroundings and failed dismally. With a little spurt of guilt, Gina realized she was glad.

Evie was staring out of the loft windows when she turned

to Stuart. 'Could you give us ten minutes, Stuart. I want a quick chat with Gina.'

Evie had been remembering her vow to herself to do something good. It didn't come easily, especially in this case when it meant a loss to herself.

Gina wasn't just her wine bar buddy but best friend, and probably her only confidante. She needed to think about Gina's future. Gina hadn't faced the reality yet, but the stark truth was that although Evie could make sure she didn't get saddled with Mark's debts, when their divorce finally came through, unless Gina could find the money to buy her husband out, they would have to sell their house. And once the mortgage was repaid and the money divided between them there would probably only be enough for Gina to buy a small London flat, maybe not even big enough to have Sadie and Lisa to stay.

Unless she bought her old family home here in Southdown.

Eight

'Right, Gina love,' Evie, her voice suddenly serious, propelled her friend towards the bed with the incredible views and they both sat down. 'You're going to have a fit when I suggest this, but hear me out.'

'You think I should buy it, don't you?' replied Gina instantly.

Evie looked at her in surprise. 'I do. The thing is, when the rich get divorced, it's easy. The wife can stay in the marital home and they simply adjust their assets so he gets more, but when your house is the only asset it's much tougher. Could you afford to buy Mark out?'

Gina sighed and looked out of the window. 'As I think I told you, my accountant already advised me that it would make good sense to sell the house.'

Sudden images of happy family days at their London home flooded into her mind. Sadie and Lisa running through the sprinkler in their large back garden, frosty mornings when both girls climbed into their big double bed, the arrival of a puppy which somehow made the family complete. But all that was firmly in the past. She had to create a new future for herself in a house where even opening a cupboard door wouldn't result in memories flooding out and trapping her. 'As a matter of fact, Doris told me lots of estate agents have been inundating us with flyers encouraging us to sell. We even had a proper hand-written one in posh writing saying how much they liked our house! Doris sent it to me. You'd think Whitehall Avenue was the Garden of Eden. But surely I wouldn't get a loan before I sold in London?'

'In his quiet way Stuart Nixon strikes me as a bit of an operator,' Evie announced with a sly smile. 'He'll find you a way of doing it, I'm sure.'

'With an unsold house as collateral?' Gina shook her head. 'You have to be joking!'

'With me guaranteeing the bridging loan they might,' smiled Evie.

'You'd do that?' Gina asked, feeling both embarrassed but also deeply touched.

'It'd be a pleasure,' replied Evie squeezing her hand affectionately. 'I've got no kids to spoil; best friends are the next best thing. More important is whether you'd want to do it. You never liked Southdown much. But I suspect you've changed your mind about that, haven't you?'

'Funny, isn't it?' agreed Gina. 'I came here expecting to loathe it, only to find I really like the place. We used to laugh at all the old dears on the seafront and maybe I'm about to become one of them!'

Evie considered her friend. Gina had hardly a grey hair in her smart chestnut bob, her skin was unlined and even though she had created a uniform for herself of wide-leg trousers and silk tops, she wore them with an air of style and chic. 'Much as I don't want to admit it,' conceded Evie, 'I can see you being happy here. What about Sadie and Lisa?'

131

Maeve Haran

'I don't think they really mind where I am. They're way off having children. In fact, they'd probably like me here in a house by the sea where they could park them when they do! There's just one condition . . .'

'What's that?' asked Evie, intrigued.

'I'm not sleeping in my parents' bedroom!' Gina insisted.

'Just as well you've got the lovely loft then,' Evie replied. 'Shall we go down and make Stuart an offer?'

Gina, who had been feeling as if she were still down the rabbit hole, finally began to see the light. She got up off the bed and hugged her friend. 'Absolutely! Let's go and do it now, before anyone else does!'

Stuart was waiting at the bottom of the stairs.

'Have you come to any conclusion?'

'I'd like to make an offer!' Gina announced, more certain than ever she was doing the right thing.

'Congratulations.' Stuart nodded. He looked at Evie: 'You're thinking, "He would say that, wouldn't he?" But speaking as a friend, I think you're making a very wise decision. Houses as good as this don't come up often, and certainly not at this price. What exactly is your offer?'

Gina announced that they'd offer the asking price.

'Can I give you a word of advice? Offer slightly less.'

Gina looked puzzled. 'What Machiavellian strategy is this?' enquired Evie. 'I wouldn't want you selling *my* house.'

'The thing is,' Stuart explained, 'you're almost the first to see it, and if you offer the asking price, the vendors are going to think, "Oh my God, we must have underpriced it!" It's only human nature, but you'll probably end up paying more.'

'So, what would you recommend?'

'You won't mention this to the vendors?' Stuart looked from one to the other. 'Scout's honour?'

132

'I was a Brownie, actually,' Evie announced.

'I'm not sure I can cope with that thought,' laughed Stuart, 'especially after the pigs in thongs. Brownie's honour then?'

'Brownie's honour,' conceded Evie.

'How about a little bit under?' he suggested. 'Then, if they don't accept it, you've got room to negotiate.'

'Fine,' agreed Evie. 'Now all we need is your best mortgage broker and a shit-hot conveyancing lawyer to get it all through double quick.'

'You're not doing it yourself then?' enquired Stuart, barely suppressing a grin. 'I'd heard you were a legal superwoman!'

'Divorce only, dahling. I'll make sure Mark doesn't screw Gina financially, but houses aren't my thing. Oh,' she added as if it were an insignificant detail, 'and I'm happy to guarantee a bridging loan.'

Stuart looked serious. 'That's very generous.'

'What are friends for?' Evie asked lightly.

'I'm not sure most people's friends would go that far, even if they could afford it. You could end up being liable for the whole cost.'

'Well, lucky me!' Evie shrugged. 'If the house is as good value as you keep insisting, I might sell it at a profit. In fact, it could be a whole new career opportunity! I can see myself becoming a property millionaire easy peasy.'

'That's just what I was thinking myself.' For the briefest of moments his eyes held hers.

'Let's go to that nice pub I'm staying at and celebrate!' Evie suggested after they'd said goodbye to Stuart.

On an early summer's day like this one, the area in front of the Jolly Sailor was packed with hopeful sunbathers having a lunchtime drink before they headed for the beach.

The promenade itself was even busier, with the ice-cream van doing a roaring trade.

'You must try their mojito ice lolly before you go back to town,' Gina insisted.

'Mojitos! Forget the lollies. Let's have a jug of the real thing,' Evie signalled for the bar person. 'Just the thing to mark your house offer. Did I tell you, at one of those ghastly school reunions, Miss Smith – do you remember her? She taught us geography – leaned over to me and whispered, "Eve, can I give you some advice?" I thought it was going to be about North Sea drift or some such thing. And do you know what she said?'

Gina had learned that no answer was actually needed.

'"Three mojitos and go for it!" Miss Smith with greasy brown hair giving me sex tips! I ask you!'

'And have you taken it?'

The jug of mojitos arrived at that moment.

Evie looked around her. 'I might. Who knows? When the right moment arises. So, are you really happy about making the offer? No second thoughts?'

'None whatever. And do you know, it's quite nice to have a man looking out for me. Even if he is your man.'

'*My* man?' repeated Evie incredulously.

'You can't fool me,' insisted Gina bravely. 'The URST between you two could practically light up Southdown!'

'What the hell is URST?' demanded Evie angrily.

'And you, a divorce lawyer too. Unresolved Sexual Tension!'

Behind them, a flurry of whispers broke into tangible words.

'Really, Ambrose, do you think she does *any* work?' and then, louder. 'Hello, Gina, glad you're enjoying your holiday in our little town.'

'Have you ever heard of weekends, Mrs Winstanley?' Evie flashed back.

'In the antique world,' Rosa replied pompously, 'as much happens at the weekend, if not more, than in the week. Is your valuation going to be ready soon?'

To Evie and Gina's relief, Rosa got up to pay, with Awful Ambrose in tow.

'I really don't like that woman,' Evie announced in her most penetrating courtroom tones.

'Neither does Maudie, as far as I can tell.'

'Then why is she leaving them the manor?'

'Because there's no one else. None of the others want it.'

'I'd turn it into a dog's home rather than leave it to those two,' declared Evie.

'Maybe Maudie will adopt an orphan and leave the whole thing to them instead.'

As they sipped their mojitos in the sunshine neither Evie nor Gina had the slightest idea how prophetic these words might turn out to be.

'Gina! Evie!' They were walking back along the seafront when Ruth, draped with grandchildren, wearing her current charity shop find of a Bedouin wedding dress, appeared from behind the ice-cream van. 'I didn't know you were down, Evie. You can't keep away from sunny Southdown, I bet! What are you both doing later? Come round to mine for potluck supper!'

Since they didn't have firm plans, and Ruth's joyous exuberance was hard to resist, they agreed, though Evie insisted they stop off and buy a posh ready meal to bring 'to save Ruth the trouble of having to cook for two unexpected guests', but really to make sure they got something easy and delicious instead of one of Ruth's haphazard dishes that probably wouldn't appear till 10 p.m.

The sunshine was so glorious that Gina suggested a swim on the way home.

'But I haven't got my swimming things!' protested Evie.

'Don't worry, since I've been here I've learned to always keep a towel in the car, and I've found this secret swimming spot where no one can see you.'

'In the sea? At this time of year? You must be crazy!'

'No, the river.'

'Actually skinny dip, you mean?' asked Evie.

'Absolutely!'

'I haven't done that since I was sixteen and slender,' protested Evie.

'I won't look if you don't,' promised Gina as they turned down a small lane off the main road back to the manor.

They parked where the lane widened to allow tractors to pass, climbed over a stile and began to walk across the fields, scattering sheep as they did so, until they came to the secluded spot where Gina had done her wild swimming before.

'I hope the farmer doesn't come and shoot us,' said Evie nervously.

'Don't worry, I've actually never seen a soul down here,' Gina reassured.

'Do you come often then?'

'When the pagan spirit moves me,' grinned Gina, and started to run.

All around them was the countryside at its blazing early summer best. Young green shoots of corn waved in the slight breeze, the golden horizon defined by a deep blue sky dotted with cumulus clouds like ice creams in the air. In the corner of the far field stood a wooden shepherd's hut, apparently unoccupied. 'I've always wanted to spend the night in one of those,' Gina sighed as she slowed down. 'So romantic.'

'You really are turning into a country girl,' Evie replied. 'Give me the Ritz every time. For romance I prefer room service and an en suite bathroom.'

'Here we are, just across that last field. The river is hidden by that line of bushes.'

'Through all that mud?' Evie winced as they got to the water's edge.

'It is a bit muddy as you get in,' admitted Gina, removing her clothes as she spoke. 'You have to be brave and launch yourself in. Damn, I've forgotten my hair tie. Oh well, I'll just use my knickers!' She gaily started to twist her bikini briefs into a rope and tied her hair up with them.

'I'm seeing a whole new side of you!' laughed Evie.

'And not just a side,' agreed Gina, removing her bra and starting to slide, naked, through the thick brown mud.

A few moments later she was out in the middle of the stream. 'Come on, it's absolutely delicious.' She looked around at the peaceful empty countryside. 'It's like they must have felt at the beginning of the world!'

Looking nervously behind her, Evie followed in Gina's path into the cool brown water. 'Gosh, it's really deep,' she paddled out to the centre of the stream, 'can't believe I'm actually doing this!'

'It must be high tide,' Gina pointed out. 'It flows into the sea a couple of miles away. Look at those waterlilies!'

On the far side of the stream a big drift of yellow water lilies shaded themselves under the branch of a weeping willow and beyond them the tall pink spokes of loosestrife.

'What's that pretty purple flower next to the water lilies? Why are you laughing?'

'Because you won't believe the name!' Gina laughed. 'It's called Venus's Looking Glass!'

137

Evie made for the bank and examined the delicate spikes of purple wildflower. 'I could fancy myself as Venus,' she laughed. 'At least she had a good time. Better than poor old Eve, blamed for all the ills of mankind. My mum clearly chose the wrong name for me.' She closed her eyes, taking in the sunshine and utter peace of the place.

'Hello girls,' a voice rang out through the silent afternoon. 'Having a walk on the wild side?'

From beyond the line of bushes a red setter came into view, with Daniel Napier holding on to the lead.

'Well, manifestly,' Evie replied, trying to regain her dignity by hiding behind the reeds, 'we are not walking but swimming.'

'Merely a figure of speech,' Daniel appeared to be finding the whole thing extremely funny.

'I didn't know you had a dog,' commented Gina, making sure not too much of her was showing.

'He belongs to my friend. The farmer whose land you're on. As a matter of fact, I saw you coming down here the other day.'

'Oh my God. Talk about biblical!' protested Evie. 'It's Susanna and the Elders!'

'Except for the fact that I didn't watch,' laughed Daniel. 'Not my kind of thing, spying on naked women. But I did want to be sure you were OK. And now that I know you are, I shall take Rufus here on his way. Enjoy yourselves. And don't frighten the cattle or they may chase you.'

Without a further word he disappeared into the bushes and out of sight.

'Well I never,' Gina announced. 'First you can't find him and then he's popping up all over the place.'

Evie eyed her speculatively. 'Yes. I wonder why that is.'

* * *

On the drive back to the manor they passed the car wash that Maudie used so obsessively. There seemed to be some kind of row in progress, so Evie suggested Gina slow the car so they could see what was going on.

'The extra money was for her, not you!' a high-pitched woman's voice could be heard above the sounds of the jets of water cleaning the other cars.

'Oh my God, it's Maudie,' said Gina. 'We'd better stop and see if we can help.'

Mike Marshall, the man Gina had last seen in the Southdown caves, was leaning aggressively towards Maudie, muscles standing out in his already red face, as she tried to wrest a five-pound note from his powerful hand, while his assorted workers looked on. The tired-looking blondes Gina had noticed the other day continued to polish and wipe impassively, as if there were nothing usual in outbreaks of near-violence. The shift leader was clearly buttoning his lip, and several bewildered and scared-looking men tried to look as unobtrusive as possible, but their eyes, wide with anxiety, gave them away.

Beyond the group, half hidden by the giant roller that dried off the vehicles, the young woman Maudie was so taken with was managing to stand apart, her eyes focused beyond them all, as if she had developed the knack of imagining herself to be somewhere completely different.

'Excuse me, sir!' Evie strode onto the scene in smart London lawyer mode. 'How dare you treat a defenceless elderly lady like that! What's going on here, Maudie?'

'I'm trying to leave a tip for Jasmin and this pig is pocketing it!' insisted Maudie, tears of suppressed anger making her eyes water so that two black runnels of mascara ran down her beautifully made-up cheeks.

'All tips are shared equally,' stated Mike, glaring round at his staff to prevent any challenges.

Basic practice had taught Evie that intimidated witnesses rarely gave accurate testimony, so she didn't ask if this were true, though she suspected, looking at his barely contained aggression, that the tips went straight to Mike and nobody argued.

'And you call her a defenceless old lady?' he jeered. 'Then you don't know her very well!'

'I am not old!' countered Maudie.

'And certainly not defenceless!' jibed Mike.

'Evie,' Gina interrupted. 'You go back with Maudie and we'll talk about this back at the manor.'

But Mike couldn't resist one last shot. 'You think because you're rich, living in that crazy old house, you can treat people however you want!' he almost spat.

'The funny thing is,' Maudie remarked as they got into the car. 'He thinks I'm rolling in it and I haven't got a bean! Everything I've got goes on running the manor and employing Mr and Mrs B. I'd never tell them, but Rosa and Awful Ambrose are absolutely right. It's madness living there alone, but I love the place, and the last thing I want to do is move to a nice flat on the seafront!'

'What do you actually live on, if it isn't an intrusive question?' enquired Evie.

'I don't mind at all, dear,' replied Maudie as she turned off the main road into the lane without even looking. 'I had a tiny inheritance, and I still get a small pension from my husband's days working abroad. My grandmother left me some jewellery but it was far too grand for my lifestyle, so I've sold that off bit by bit. Her tiara paid for the new roof!'

'I guess you'd call that posh upcycling!' Gina hesitated before going on. 'Maudie . . . If you dislike the owner so much, why do you keep going to that car wash?'

They were just pulling into the manor's driveway. 'Because of Jasmin, of course,' she insisted with quiet dignity as they drove into the garage.

'Who is Jasmin?' asked Evie. As a lawyer, she didn't want to over-prompt, but something about the dark, contained space of the garage might well lead to more intimate revelations than their usual setting.

'You must have noticed her!' Maudie announced passionately. 'She's like a ruby in the dust!'

'Is that what upsets you so much?' Evie enquired gently. 'That she's too refined to be working in a car wash?'

'Not just that!' Maudie exploded as if she couldn't keep it to herself any longer. 'She reminds me of someone. Someone I knew very well.' Her voice softened into melting tenderness. 'I can't get it out of my mind. The likeness is haunting me. I just know they have to be related!'

'Have you tried talking to the girl?'

'Once,' Maudie conceded almost reluctantly. 'But she's too frightened.'

'Of that lump Mike?' asked Evie. 'I didn't exactly take to him myself.'

'I've been making enquiries,' said Maudie. 'In Damascus. The trouble is, nothing is working there because of the war.'

'That sounds intriguing,' Gina agreed. 'And if you find she is related to your friend, what then?'

'I don't know.' Maudie shook her head, her confidence deserting her. 'That will be up to her.'

Evie felt suddenly moved that Maudie, who she knew so little, had shared an obviously important revelation. 'Well, if there's anything I can do to help in London, I'll do my best,' Evie offered. 'A lot of my job is about finding things out!'

'Thank you.' Maudie hugged her as they got out of the car. 'I knew I liked you from the first, a feisty girl like you! Maybe we're destined to be sisters under the skin.'

'Maudie,' Evie smiled, 'I'd like nothing better!'

Nine

'Have you heard?' Ruth demanded excitedly as she ladled out the boeuf bourguignon Gina and Evie had supplied, charmingly still in its foil container, 'there's a new car wash opening in Harpers' car park!'

'I can't wait!' replied Evie sarcastically. 'To think, Gina, you'll be moving to a town where the opening of a new car wash is the news event of the year! I do hope I've given you the right advice to buy the house and stay here.'

'Gina!' gushed Ruth, waving the ladle with so much enthusiasm it threatened to soak them all in red wine gravy, 'You're not buying a house! That's absolutely fabbydoo! Where is it?'

'As a matter of fact, it's the house I grew up in,' replied Gina shyly, 'done up so it's unrecognizable by a couple who're off to the States. And the price is almost irresistible. I've actually made an offer!' she added, excitement seeping into her voice. 'But it's a bit complicated, so I'm not counting my chickens.' She turned to Evie. 'I don't suppose you've heard anything from Stuart yet about finding a loan?'

'Give the man a break. You only asked him yesterday!'

'I know,' conceded Gina. 'It's only that I'm getting so excited!'

'Well, I'm seeing him tomorrow before I go back to town where people talk about art and theatre rather than new car washes.'

'All right, Ms Snootypants City Lawyer!' Ruth poured them all large glasses of questionable red to go with the casserole. 'For your information, this isn't any old car wash. It's called Desperate Dan's Ethical Car Wash and they're promising to pay all their workers fairly so we don't have to feel guilty about using it!'

'I must admit,' Evie conceded, 'that is quite interesting. I wonder what the delightful Mr Marshall's going to make of that?'

'I wonder how on earth they're funding it,' Gina added. 'Unless it's a wheeze of Harpers to drum up business or some kind of charitable venture. I know, maybe Maudie's Jasmin could go and work there instead!'

'Who's Jasmin?' Ruth enquired, taking a large gulp of wine.

'Maudie's obsessed with this girl who works in Mad Mike's,' explained Gina. 'She's convinced the girl's related to someone she knew ages ago in Damascus.'

'Sounds like we're in for an interesting summer, one way or another.' Ruth rubbed her hands. 'Now, seeing as you brought your own main course, I have actually made us a panettone bread and butter pudding. It's Nigella's recipe so I had to do a lot of pouting and pushing my chest out.' She gave them a display which left them both almost in tears of laughter. 'And here it is!'

Evie took a small mouthful. 'It's absolutely delicious!' she conceded. The spices really come through with the sultanas and the sort of brioche taste. Mmm . . . It's really nice.'

'Thank you,' Ruth bowed. 'I'm glad the pouting paid off.' She turned to Gina. 'How's the antiques business going on without you?'

'Better than I expected. Thank God, like so many things, a lot of it has gone online. People make a choice from our website and wonderful Doris organizes delivery. Not many people actually come and look in person these days. So it's been bubbling away perfectly well even though I'm down here.'

'Weird, isn't it,' commented Ruth. 'Looking for antiques used to be such a fun hobby! There are two flea markets in Southdown and you nearly always find something you don't need in one of them!' She gestured round her living room, which was more than testimony to this fact. Strange objects, from ancient petrol pump lights to art deco glassware; Victorian biscuit tins to a fringed Bohemian shawl draped over a table lamp; Clarice Cliff china, ranged along a wooden shelf next to three globes of varying sizes; the whole lit by an enormous glass chandelier, which on further inspection could have done with a good polish.

'I know my style's a bit . . .'

'Eccentric?' supplied Evie helpfully.

'Individual,' corrected Ruth, smiling round at her diverse possessions. 'Anyway, back to you Gina. It's such good news you're thinking of coming back here.'

'It all depends on whether I can get a loan quickly enough,' she glanced nervously at Evie, who was studying her phone.

'That was Stuart,' she looked up, rather too smugly, in Gina's view. 'He's invited me to lunch as well.'

'That's nice,' Gina commented with a slight edge of sarcasm.

'Except that it's to talk about your loan situation,' Evie corrected.

'Anyone for a sip of my home-made limoncello?' tempted Ruth.

'Did this require pouting too?' smiled Gina.

'Nah,' quipped Ruth. 'This one's Jamie Oliver. Just a lot of dropped vowels and a cheeky grin.' She gave them a demonstration. 'Oh, and taking all my clothes off. After all, he used to be called the Naked Chef.'

As soon as she got back to the manor, Gina checked her messages to see if Mark had responded to her suggestion that they sell. As the house was in her name, she wasn't sure if she needed his agreement, but he'd certainly argue he was entitled to half, whatever the documents said. Probably communicating with her made him feel guilty and that was why he hadn't replied. That would be so Mark. Yes, was the response. He would be agreeable as long as the price was right, and she should get valuations from three estate agents. Thank heavens for wonderful Doris to help her set them up!

Stuart had nominated a pub in the old town to meet Evie, between the row of imposing black fishermen's huts and the cobbled street that wound up past a string of antique shops to the famous church that stood over the town, allegedly protecting those in peril on the seas.

As she walked up the hill, Evie stopped to read the notice explaining its history.

'It didn't do much of a job making the fishermen holy,' commented a voice behind her. 'Once the harbour silted up, they happily turned to wrecking instead. Not a very Christian activity.'

Evie turned to find Stuart was reading the notice too.

'I thought it was smuggling they went in for round here,' she enquired. 'Brandy for the Parson, Baccy for the Clerk and all that?'

'They were happy to turn their hand to both. Southdown's history is not an entirely edifying one.'

'Weren't you ever tempted to leave it and move to London?' asked Evie.

'Where the real crooks are?' The warmth of Stuart's smile undercut his cynicism. 'I prefer being a big fish in a small pool. Besides, my kids are here and, believe it or not, I quite like them.'

'How extraordinary,' she teased, surveying him as they walked together. In contrast to his sleek working clothes, as weekend wear he was sporting an outfit that, to London eyes, looked ultra conservative and old-fashioned: check shirt, beige chinos and red tie, topped off with a tweed cap. On the other hand, he wore them with a jauntiness that defied easy categorisation.

'Are you making sartorial judgements by any chance?' he challenged.

'I was just thinking that your father and even grandfather probably dressed exactly the way you are today.'

'You're out there,' Stuart challenged. 'My father was a natty City gent. Bowler hat, rolled umbrella, buttonhole, seven fifteen to Charing Cross, the lot. Probably why I never wanted to work in London. That's *my* idea of modern slavery. I suppose I should be grateful you're not commenting on my hair!'

He doffed the cap with all the flirtatious chivalry of a Walter Raleigh, revealing his bald pate, glinting in the sun.

To her surprise, Evie found herself wanting to reach out her hand and stroke it.

'Morning Stuart!' a man with his dog called out. 'Nice morning for it.'

Stuart waved back, to Evie's frustration not stopping to ask what 'it' was.

A few minutes later they reached the pub.

'Hi Stu,' called out one of the other patrons as they sat down at their table.

'Wotcha, Bill,' Stuart replied.

'My, we are popular,' commented Evie, reaching for the menu.

'It goes with the territory in a small town. I imagine you either like it or hate it.'

'And which do you?'

'Actually, I quite like it. You, I imagine would hate it.'

'Got it in one!' agreed Evie.

'The usual is it, Stuart?' enquired the smiling server as she showed them to a table.

'Oh dear, I *am* unmasked as a man of regular habits,' replied Stuart. 'Yes, thank you Dottie. Rare roast beef – and don't forget the Yorkshire!'

'Stuart,' the young woman shook her head. 'Do we ever? We give Yorkshires with everything here. Even the roast pork!'

'Have you felt the temperature outside?' Evie asked, amazed. 'It must be mid-twenties at least.'

'Twenty-four,' Stuart confirmed. 'My watch tells me.'

'I'll have the sea bass, thank you,' announced Evie.

'Chips or salad?' Dottie enquired.

'Salad please.'

'Down from London are you?' the girl winked at Stuart. The locals knew better than to pass on the best chips in Southdown. 'What would you like to drink? White wine, is it?'

'Alas, thus I am unmasked as well,' Evie admitted. 'Chilean Sauvignon if you have it.'

'What about you, Stu? Run Wild IPA?'

'After a pint of that and roast beef aren't you going to be prostrate in front of the telly?' teased Evie.

'It's non-alcoholic. I usually play football on Sunday afternoons.'

'Five-a-side?'

'Very good.'

'Even a hard-bitten career woman like me has godchildren.'

'Since you've asked me one or two, can I ask you a personal question?' Stuart enquired, his eyes on hers.

'Fire away, m'lud.'

'Why have you never married, or even, as far as I can tell, lived with anyone?'

'Good question, opposing counsel. My professional career has led me to believe that the male sex is not generally trustworthy.'

'My professional career,' he replied with a hint of mischief in his eyes, 'might well endorse that. But in defence of my sex, I have to plead that there are exceptions.'

'And are you one of them?'

'You would have to ask my ex-wife that. I do try to protect the interests of women, especially when they are forced to sell the family home at a time that is not beneficial to them.'

'How do you do that?'

'I persuade their spouse that to sell now would be a disaster, and suggest that it's far better to leave their ex-wife in the home until the market recovers. I have developed many and various arguments to do this. The husbands are tempted not to believe me, but I do have an excellent reputation in the town.'

'Very good.' Although her tone was measured, Evie found herself genuinely impressed.

'Not really. My father left when I was ten and we suffered a lot of financial hardship. If I can, I try to soften the blow.'

'Speaking of softening the blow. We'd better get round to Gina's loan.'

'All sorted. Well, provisionally so at least.' He reached into what she had thought was a sports bag and produced a document. 'See what you think. I'd say it was a pretty good deal. They will need to see a valuation of the London house and proof of ownership. A note from you explaining the divorce situation wouldn't go amiss. Your contribution was crucial, of course. You're a good friend.' The warmth of his smile was irresistible.

'When you're someone who – as you so acutely pointed out – doesn't have a husband or partner, friends become very important, and Gina is a very good friend.'

'She's lucky to have you.'

'As I am to have her.'

'I think she'll be happy here,' Evie said finally. 'Under different circumstances, I might be myself.'

Good God, Evie, she mentally corrected herself, *what the hell are you saying?*

'Maudie,' have you heard the hot news?' Gina enquired as she and Maudie sat down to breakfast next day.

'What's that, dear?' enquired Maudie, far more focused on doing the crossword in the *Southdown Gazette*.

'There's going to be a new car wash opening in Harpers' car park soon, and they're promising to pay all their workers a reasonable wage!'

'A new car wash!' Maudie dropped the newspaper. 'Do you know who's behind it? Are they trustworthy?'

Gina laughed. 'It's going to be called Desperate Dan's Ethical Car Wash – to annoy Mad Mike, I assume. With a name like that they'd better be honest, or they'll find themselves in a lot of trouble.'

'But who is this Dan person?'

'No idea,' Gina shrugged. 'He may not even exist.'

Maudie started to wring her hands anxiously, literally took a deep breath and stood up. 'I am going to make sure Jasmin knows about this, and if she will insist on working in a car wash then she should move somewhere where she is at least paid properly. Away from that horrible Mike Marshall.'

'Have you managed to talk to her again?' enquired Gina.

'A couple of times, briefly. My fear is that this Mike person has some kind of hold on her. She seems really frightened of him.'

Gina didn't quite know if it was appropriate, but she gave Maudie a reassuring hug. 'At least she has you on her side, Maudie.'

'Yes. But I'm just one old lady.'

'Do you want me to try and find out more about this new place. If they've started hiring for instance?'

'Gina, dear, that would be absolutely wonderful. How lucky I am that you came into my life.'

'I'll go into town and ask later on.'

It was another perfect day. May had turned into blazing June and the shops near the seafront were hanging up rubber rings, air beds shaped like sea monsters and plastic buckets and spades. There was a seaside smell of fresh doughnuts and tangy salt air. People seemed extra happy in the sunshine. Most Southdowners wanted to get their daily tasks accomplished quickly so that they could head for the beach. With English weather, everyone had learned to enjoy it while they could, but this summer was proving an exception, with every day as blessed as the one before.

Gina made herself ignore the lure of the sunshine and concentrate. *Where would I start if I was a journalist chasing a story?* she asked herself as she drove into town and parked in Harpers' car park.

Harpers was an upmarket supermarket chain, with a good reputation; probably pricier than its rivals but with quality rather than quantity as its watchword. The idea of an ethical car wash fitted neatly with its company profile. She should probably talk to their PR department.

She could see the construction at the far end of the tarmac and decided to go and ask the builders as well. It might be quicker than getting involved with all the red tape.

They smiled cheerfully at Gina, happy to down tools for a moment in the heat and take a slug from their water bottles. The car wash and coffee stall were almost finished, they announced with pride, but they knew nothing about when it would actually open and when the hiring would start.

She went into the store and looked around for a manager. The general manager turned out to be tied up and the assistant claimed to have no more idea than the builders.

Her next stop was the local paper. After a twenty-minute wait a grumpy-looking young woman appeared and grudgingly asked Gina what she wanted to know. Her whole body language seemed to say: *Why don't you just buy the bloody paper and leave us overworked hacks alone!*

But when Gina explained about the car wash, her attitude transformed into suppressed excitement. It became immediately obvious to Gina that the reporter had had no suspicion about the story and could tell that, for the paper's readership, it would be an absolute cracker.

Unfortunately she had no idea about who was running it or when they would be hiring.

'Look,' Gina got out her pad and wrote down her phone number, 'since I've given you the story, could you at least let me know when and how they're hiring?'

The reporter nodded, though Gina had little faith that she would bother.

'Thanks a lot,' Gina reiterated. 'It would be really useful if you could.'

Feeling frustrated, she sat on the seafront with a coffee, surrounded by memories of coming to this exact spot after school for a pre-homework swim, the thought suddenly struck her: how had their friend Ruthie known about this story even before the local paper?

As usual, Ruth wasn't answering calls or texts, so Gina decided to drop round.

'Gina! What a lovely surprise,' Ruth answered the door in a colourful kimono and wellington boots.

She took in Gina's stunned expression. 'I was taking some stuff that shouldn't be in the kitchen out to the garden shed. It can be muddy out there.'

'In this weather?'

'To be honest I couldn't be bothered to find my flip-flops.' She gestured to the pile of coats, shoes and assorted school paraphernalia on the floor behind her. 'Anyway, what can I do you for?'

'I was wondering how you knew about the car wash? I've been trying to find out more about it for Maudie. She really wants Jasmin to try and get a job there, but even the local paper didn't know. I rather think it'll be on the front page now. I hope that doesn't matter?'

'No idea,' Ruth shrugged. 'Robin overheard someone talking about it in the Jolly Sailor, that's all. But I tell you what, the next day the barmaid – oops , we're not supposed to say that any more,' she corrected herself, not looking at all apologetic, 'was telling everyone that the place was a really new idea – part funded by local people who liked hand car washes but worried about the people who worked at them.'

'I think I'd better go and see this famous bar person. You don't know her name by any chance?'

'Robin might, but unfortunately it's not his local. He was only in there because the Baker's Arms is having some work done. I'll give him a ring, shall I, and see?'

Unlike his colourful spouse, Robin answered almost immediately. 'Right. OK. Daisy? Dawn? I know it was something beginning with D. I know – Dottie. I remember thinking it suited her because—'

'Right, darling, that's lovely, see you tonight,' cut in Ruth before Robin could explain the full extent of Dottie's dottiness. Did you get that?' she asked Gina, with a grin. 'Dottie.'

Gina thanked her and headed off for the Jolly Sailor.

Of course Dottie wasn't in today, supplied the bar person on duty unhelpfully. And, no, they couldn't give Gina her number.

'Chasing after female bar staff? That's very gender fluid of you,' a voice teasingly remarked from the end of the bar.

Gina turned to find Daniel Napier nursing a pint of the local bitter.

'It's for my employer Maudie up at Rookery Manor,' replied Gina, trying not to giggle. 'She wants to find out about whether they're hiring for this new car wash.'

'Rather advanced in years for the work, surely?' quipped Daniel.

'It's not for her, idiot! She has a young friend who already works at the other one, and she wants her to get away from there.'

'And Mr Marshall's being difficult about it?' The laugh had gone from his voice. 'I'm afraid that's because a lot of his staff are in debt to the people who got them here. And if they're not he makes them sign unenforceable contracts which scare the shit out of them.'

'Oh my God,' Gina paled. 'You mean they were smuggled?'

'Some of them, certainly. Southdown has a bit of a dark history. Wrecking and smuggling are nothing new.'

'But not people! That's the worst kind there is. Even worse than drugs,' insisted Gina.

'Absolutely,' Daniel agreed. 'That's why this new place will give assistance from a refugee charity to anyone who needs it. It can't actually employ people without a visa, but they will help people get one and support them while they try. And as soon as they can the car wash will try and employ them with proper decent working conditions, as its name implies.'

Gina stared at him, a sudden revelation dawning on her. She'd never heard her old dancing school partner speak with so much fire and passion. 'Oh my God!' she announced to the entire pub. 'I should have guessed from your name. It's you! You're Desperate Dan!'

Daniel rewarded her with a sphinx-like smile. 'I'm sorry, Ms Greenhills, but I couldn't possibly comment.'

Ten

'You're not serious!' Ruthie burst out when Gina rushed straight round to her house to break the news. 'You actually think Danny from dancing is Desperate Dan of the Ethical Car Wash!'

Gina nodded enthusiastically.

'Blow me! I always thought he was a good egg, the way he'd dance with you all those years ago when no one else would—'

'Excuse me,' protested Gina, 'but I did have a few partners.'

'But you were more interested in Flashy Trev with the red MG! And Danny still remembered to ask you to his twenty-first. Aww, that's so nice.'

'Oh God,' confessed Gina. 'Liking a boy for his flashy confidence and his red sports car! You're so stupid when you're young!'

Ruthie didn't say that Gina had made the same mistake again with Mark, but clearly Gina was thinking it herself. She sighed, trying to push the thought away.

Ruthie, still in her kimono and wellies, offered to make them both a cup of coffee. Gina thought her own kitchen was untidy, but it wasn't in the same class as this one. All the pans from last night's dinner stood soaking by the sink, which was already crammed with dishes, on which the leftovers were shrivelling in the hot sun and attracting the attention of a number of flies, to which Ruthie seemed entirely impervious.

'Daniel Napier,' Ruthie repeated. 'It makes a lot of sense. He's a good guy. Always getting involved with local charities and using his money to help people. It's certainly going to cause a sensation in Southdown when it gets around. I suppose he must have kept it quiet so far in case that Mike Marshall tried to put a spanner in the works. Can't wait to tell Robin. I'll call him now.'

But to her disappointment her husband already knew. 'Haven't you seen today's *Gazette*? It's on the front page. They've really gone big with it. LOCAL HERO OPENS ETHICAL CAR WASH!'

Gina felt a frisson of guilt that she'd been the *Gazette*'s source. She hoped the front-page story wasn't going to be a problem for Daniel. Or would he enjoy being described as a local hero?

On her way back to her car, she picked up a copy of the paper. It had a huge picture of Daniel on the front page. She had to congratulate the photographer. They had caught that wry, self-deprecating, yet entirely charming smile of his, which Gina wished she could have noticed when she was younger.

As she drove back to the manor, Gina thought about what a dark horse Daniel Napier was. He must have taken on a huge task in getting the funding to open a car wash, let alone an 'ethical' one: negotiating with Harpers, constructing the right building plus coffee van, with whatever licences were involved, and then finding the appropriate staff to work in it while knowing there could be reprisals from the unpleasant Mad Mike Marshall. She shuddered for a moment remembering the frightened look in the eyes of some of his employees. A nasty bit of work, Mike Marshall. And of course, there was the problem of Jasmin.

Still, this was Southdown, not downtown Chicago. Crime was almost unknown. The most exciting bit of news here was a cat stuck up a tree being rescued by the fire brigade or a duck family trotting down the main road on their way to the duck pond.

As soon as she got back, Mrs B jumped on her with the alarming news that Maudie was 'in a bit of a pother'.

Gina hurried up the wooden stairs, through the minstrel's gallery with its carved oak panelling, and knocked on Maudie's door.

Maudie sat at her dressing table with her long white hair down round her shoulders instead of in its habitual stylish French pleat. Her face was pale and there were dark circles under her eyes. And she was still in her dressing gown even though it was midday.

'Oh hello, Gina dear,' she almost whispered, with no sign of her usual sparkle.

Gina decided the discovery she'd made this morning might cheer her up. 'Maudie, I have to tell you the most amazing thing. Desperate Dan of the new car wash is actually Daniel Napier – Evie and I knew him from dancing school!' It struck Gina that she hadn't told Evie the news about Daniel yet.

'I know Daniel Napier,' Maudie brightened a little. 'He was involved in business projects with my husband. Gerald said he was a man of principle.' The old Maudie peeped out for a moment. 'Not always useful in business, of course! But Gerald liked him.'

'He told me they're hiring through an agency in town. That means your Jasmin could go and have a look.'

To Gina's surprise, instead of looking pleased and relieved as she'd expected, Maudie's face fell.

'Thank you, dear. That's very helpful of you,' she managed to reply, but there was no enthusiasm in her voice.

'Why don't I go and choose you a dress for today?' Gina offered with a smile. 'Something bright to cheer you up!'

'No thank you,' Maudie shook her head. 'I'm not in the mood for bright. I'll be all right. You go and get on with life. Go to the beach. Have a swim!'

Gina went to her room instead. She couldn't desert Maudie when she was like this. Perhaps she was upset that the news she'd been hoping so desperately to hear still hadn't come through.

It was just like Maudie to tell her to make the most of the weather and head for the beach, but today she needed to work. First, she had to ring Evie and tell her about Daniel.

Naturally, Evie was tied up, so she texted her instead: *Hot News in Southdown!*

She opened her laptop and scrolled through the online catalogue from one of the big auction houses hoping to find items that were a match for the few remaining pieces so she could complete her valuation. She especially wanted to see what price Victorian overmantel mirrors were going for in London. Maudie had a very large and attractive one in carved giltwood and gesso in her drawing room, with vines draped down its fluted columns, and Gina was eager to see the guide price for similar examples. She was delighted that a far less elegant version was on offer at £1,000–£1,200. Given that the big auction houses covered themselves by estimating a sale price lower than the one they hoped to get, this was good news.

There was also a very pretty Empire bergère chair just like the one in Maudie's bedroom, in carved fruitwood, dated *c*.1840 going for £750. She added both these sums to her valuation.

She glanced out of the window and noticed with relief that Maudie had got dressed and gone outside. Though her chignon lacked some of its usual stylishness, the fact she had put her hair up suggested she was making an effort to engage with life again.

A message arrived from Evie saying that she was in court with a difficult case so they should talk later. *Can't wait to hear*, it concluded.

Before she went down and had a chat with Maudie, Gina decided to have a quick check on a well-respected art website for news of Chagall prints like theirs.

She spooled through pages of offers, remembering again what a very prolific artist he was, then stopped.

There it was. The same Chagall image that had disappeared from downstairs. But the thing was, it wasn't just similar to theirs. It *was* theirs, with the same reference number. What's more, it had the certificate of authentication from the Chagall research institute that she had been trying to get.

And it had been sold for for an impressive asking price. Not a fortune but a very good price for a lithograph.

But who was it who had pocketed the money?

Gina was tempted to confront Maudie with her discovery and press for answers, but the old lady had made it clear that she wanted the matter dropped and, since the house and its contents were hers to dispose of as she wished, what option was there but to respect that?

Not everyone had Gina's compunction.

When she made her way downstairs, even before she got to the drawing room, she could hear raised voices. She softly opened the door to find Rosa, her face alight with triumph like some latter-day Boadicea, leaning over Maudie, who was sitting with her hands over her face.

'Maudie,' Rosa was loudly insisting, 'face facts! Who else could have sold it but that so-called valuer of Lucy's? It's obvious she knows as much about antiques as Mrs B. In fact, Mrs B probably knows more, because at least she cleans them!'

Maudie continued to sit still as a statue, her face hidden behind her hands. 'If you want proof,' Ambrose intervened, as if pulling a masterstroke, 'it was a Ms Gina Greenhills who got in touch with the Chagall experts to get it authenticated. Why do you think she'd do that, if not to make sure she'd get the best price for it?'

Gina could see Maudie's eyes peering through a chink in her hands, imploring her to come to the rescue.

'Don't you remember, Maudie?' Gina intervened with all the confidence she could muster. 'You told me you'd taken the Chagall into the auction house in town. They must have gone ahead and sold it for you.'

Instead of expressing relief that a valuable object had not after all been stolen, Rosa and Ambrose looked more like a pair of bloodhounds who'd had a juicy bone wrested from their slavering jaws.

Of course, Gina knew perfectly well that the local auctioneers had never had the Chagall, which meant that Maudie was either covering for the person who had sold it, or that she had sold it herself.

As soon as Rosa and Ambrose had taken themselves grumpily off, Gina sat down beside Maudie on the sofa.

'I know this is a difficult question, and you don't have to answer if you don't want to, but did you take the Chagall to be auctioned?'

161

Maudie sighed and looked away, then seemed to come to a decision.

'I'm not sure,' she admitted. 'I took it off the wall but after that I can't remember. It was for Jasmin, you see.' She grasped Gina's hand and held it in a surprisingly strong grip for such a birdlike figure. 'The poor child came here with no one to look after her, without a penny to her name, and got this job with that horrible, horrible man. She was staying in a hostel and one of the others told her about the car wash. A lot of them do it, and of course they have no rights, so Mr Marshall knows he's safe to exploit them. He's especially got it in for Jasmin because she fought back when he tried to force himself on her. I wanted her to have some money so she could leave.'

'And the other things that went missing?'

'They're upstairs. Hidden in the eaves.' She attempted a small smile. 'I suppose I could always say a magpie took them.'

'A magpie with very good taste to carry off a miniature by Isaac Oliver,' replied Gina.

'I told you, Gina dear, I don't have any money! They're my personal bank account. Stored away, just in case. I'd like Jasmin to have a place of her own.' Her eyes looked imploringly at Gina. 'Or even come and live here, if she'd agree.'

'Have you had any more news about her from Damascus?'

'That's why I'm so upset. I'd really expected to know by now, but the area where she grew up is in ruins. Fortunately, her grandmother took her away when she was quite young, and she missed the worst of it. It used to be such a beautiful place.' Her eyes misted over at the memory.

'Especially if you see it with the right person?' Gina asked gently.

'Gina!' Maudie gripped her hand again. 'You understand!'

'I think I can guess. There was someone there you loved?'

Maudie nodded. 'Someone who wasn't my husband,' she admitted in such a soft voice Gina could hardly hear what she said.

'And you had to give him up?'

'It was a bit more complicated than that,' Maudie replied haltingly. 'I had his baby. A daughter. Morals among the British out there were pretty lax, but falling for a "native", as the local tabbies would brand it . . . well, that broke all the rules. I couldn't even pretend she was my husband's, so I had to give my little girl away.' Tears began to flow down Maudie's cheeks like the bursting of a long-defended dam.

'And you think Jasmin might be related to you?'

'She's so like him, Gina! Her eyes could almost be his eyes!' Maudie hid her face in her hands. 'Of course it may be an old lady's fancy.'

'But you want to help her anyway.'

'I don't want to, I must!' Maudie insisted passionately.

'Then we'd better get her away from Mike Marshall.'

'We have to, Gina – there's no telling what that man is capable of!'

Eleven

The next morning at half past ten, Gina sat anxiously in the coffee shop opposite the employment agency where she'd heard they would be doing the hiring, waiting for Jasmin. The girl hadn't wanted to meet her anywhere near her workplace and this cafe seemed suitably anonymous.

At five to eleven Jasmin arrived still wearing her working clothes. She would have been hailed as striking anywhere, with her tall frame, glossy black hair, glowing skin and wonderful bone structure, but in applying for a job at a car wash in Southdown she made you think of Cinderella banished to the kitchen by the Ugly Sisters. Surely she could get a better job than this? But according to Maudie, it was what she wanted to do.

The interview went very well, despite Jasmin's obvious nervousness, particularly when asked to outline her previous experience. Gina was surprised that they should go through such an official process for so menial a job, but the new business was obviously intent on doing things properly.

'It's quite a set-up, isn't it?' Gina commented to the interviewer.

'Like nothing I've ever come across,' the woman agreed. 'The owner is investing an awful lot of money and effort into this venture.'

Gina nodded, seriously impressed.

After the interview she suggested they go for a coffee, but as they stepped out of the premises they found Mike Marshall barring their way. 'Look here, Jasmin, or whatever your name is,' he snarled, looming over the girl threateningly, 'you've got a contract with me and I mean to enforce it. You can't just walk out and join this shower!'

Jasmin tried to look haughty, but Gina could feel the hand that had grabbed hers tremble.

'Excuse me, Mr Marshall,' Gina announced, trying to sound more confident than she felt, 'but I very much doubt that's true – and we will certainly be taking legal advice to find out.'

'I know you,' he accused, 'you're always hanging around with that meddling old lady. I've had to have words with you before.'

Wiping the spittle that accompanied his words from her face, Gina replied icily, 'She's an old friend of mine, Mr Marshall. Not that it's any business of yours.'

'Which makes one wonder what you're doing hanging around here?' They all turned to find Daniel Napier calmly surveying the scene, with a sardonic look in his eye, as if Mike were a joke rather than a threat.

'My, you do turn up out of the blue, Daniel,' murmured Gina, at the same time feeling deeply grateful.

'Only when I think I might be useful,' he shrugged. 'Now, Mr Marshall. With respect, you know that's a load of bollocks. If this young lady worked for an investment bank you might have a point, but a car wash? Do me a favour.'

He turned his back on Mike and faced the two women. 'May I offer you a lift somewhere? I'm sure Mr Marshall will want to go and urgently consult his lawyer on this fine legal point.'

Gina put her arm round Maudie's protégé, who looked as if she might collapse at any moment. 'Come on, Jasmin, let's take Daniel up on his kind offer.'

Daniel nodded to Mike with exaggerated politeness, and the little group headed off.

'I'd better go back to the hostel,' Jasmin whispered, still looking shaken.

'I've got a better idea,' said Gina. 'Why not come up to Rookery Manor? I know Maudie would love to see you again.'

Jasmin paused on the pavement, looking undecided.

Understanding the girl's hesitation and need for reassurance at such a big step, Gina added that Maudie had told her all about Jasmin's wonderful grandmother.

Turning to Daniel, conscious that she was making rather a habit of relying on his support, Gina asked, 'Are you sure you don't mind giving us a lift?'

'I'd be delighted,' agreed Daniel at once.

'Maudie says her husband did business with you years ago,' she told him as they made their way to his car. 'Apparently you're a man of principle.'

Daniel bowed and grinned at the same time.

'Not always an asset in business, according to Maudie!' Gina teased.

'I'll bear it in mind,' he shook his head, laughing.

Daniel's car turned out to be a Saab.

'You know,' Gina laughed, 'if I'd had to guess your car, I might well have come up with this.'

'Solid, dull and reliable, you mean?' he enquired.

'Not dull. Different. Image conscious but not someone who runs with the crowd. A lot of architects have them. Antique dealers too. And the kind of men who open ethical car washes.'

'What do you think of the idea, by the way?' he asked.

'Does it matter?' she challenged.

'Yes.' He looked her directly in the eye. 'I rather think it does.'

'OK,' she acknowledged, aware of a frisson of excitement that he cared so much what she thought. 'I think it's highly admirable.'

'It'll all be worth it then.'

'Daniel Napier!' laughed Gina. 'I never know if you're joking!'

He opened the car door for her. 'Maybe you need to get to know me better then.'

Before she could reply, he closed the door, which was just as well because she didn't know what to say.

They drove through the back streets of Southdown, higher and higher up towards the downs and down into the valley where the manor house nestled among its beds of pink roses, hollyhocks and bright rhododendrons. Jasmin opened her window and leaned out. 'What magical place is this? It is like a fairy tale in the storybook I read as a little girl!'

'It's called Rookery Manor,' explained Gina. 'It's the home of the lady who's been trying to get you to a better situation.'

'The lady with the white hair on top of her head like an English ice cream? She is Maudie?'

'Exactly that! You describe her so well. She lived in Damascus a long time ago and feels . . .'

Gina stopped. Perhaps it was for Maudie to tell the girl what she thought appropriate.

As if she instinctively knew they were coming, Maudie was standing at the door when they drew up and she rushed out to meet them.

'Jasmin! My dear girl.' She clasped Jasmin's hands tightly. 'Have you managed to leave that awful man?'

Jasmin nodded.

'The thing is, Maudie,' Gina began 'Jasmin feels she should move out of the hostel because so many people who work at the car wash live there.'

'Of course. Jasmin, my dear, could you possibly consider staying here for a while?' Maudie offered eagerly. 'Just until things settle down for you? I mean, I would love you to stay as long as you like – I would be most happy – but you may not want to be buried out here with an old lady for company!'

Jasmin looked all around her. 'It would be like living in a storybook!' she replied with a choke in her voice.

'My dear girl, I'm so glad!' Gina could sense Maudie restraining herself from folding the girl into her arms and perhaps scaring the life out of her at the same time. 'I can't tell you how welcome you are!'

'And, Maudie,' announced Gina, 'I've got another surprise for you. This is Daniel Napier, one-time business associate of your husband's, I understand.'

'Hello, Daniel! What an absolute delight! Let's see if Mrs B can summon up any celebratory cake – or at least some biscuits!'

Ten minutes later they were all sitting in the antique-filled drawing room, with its French windows open to the sunny garden, sipping tea.

As they were talking, Jasmin's gaze, Maudie noticed, kept straining over her head to the open doors.

'Would you like to see round the garden, dear?' asked Maudie gently.

'Please! My family had such a beautiful garden once.'

Jasmin put her cup down and followed Maudie outside. She stood for a moment breathing in the scent of the herbs and flowers.

'You have Damascus roses!' She pointed to the small pink flowers, her voice ringing with emotion.

'They're my favourite rose of all and give off such a gorgeous scent,' replied Maudie gently. 'They remind me of living in Damascus and the wonderful time we had there.'

'You really lived there!' Jasmin's eyes glowed with a dark fire. 'I would love to come and stay with you. Is there a bus into the town from here? So that I can get my things?'

Maudie looked momentarily nonplussed. 'We'll ask Mrs B.'

Mrs B, who'd come to clear away the tea things in the hope of finding out what was going on, called over her shoulder: 'Of course there is, Mrs Tyler. Bottom of the lane. Five minutes' walk away.'

'Would you like me to come and help you get your things?' Gina offered.

'I'll take her, if you like,' suggested Daniel. 'We could go now if you wanted to?' he asked Jasmin.

'Thank you,' she replied gratefully. 'If it is not too much trouble?'

'Of course not. I'd be delighted. Might be as well if I accompanied you, just in case your delightful employer is hanging around.'

'Yes, I had not thought of that. I will be grateful to be so far away.'

'That's fixed then, dear. Mrs B and I will get your room ready,' Maudie said eagerly.

They watched as Daniel and Jasmin disappeared down the drive.

'He's very dashing, isn't he, your Daniel,' Maudie commented wistfully, as if remembering her own dashing beaux from the past.

'Dashing?' replied Gina. 'Not the word I'd choose. And he certainly isn't mine.'

'What word would you use, dear?'

'Kind? Honourable?' It struck Gina as she described Daniel that these were exactly the qualities she had said she wanted after Mark had turned out to be so unreliable. But there was more to it than that. She couldn't help admiring someone who was a successful businessman putting in so much time and effort for a venture like this. He could have simply given a donation; instead, he'd rolled up his sleeves and got stuck in. Even if those sleeves did remind her of Rick Parfitt from Status Quo.

Remembering that in all the excitement she hadn't told Evie about who was behind the new car wash she ran up to her bedroom.

Evie was always hard to get hold of, but on this occasion, Gina struck lucky. 'That hot news from Southdown in my message yesterday, Evie! You're never going to guess!'

'Daniel Napier is Desperate Dan from the car wash!'

'How the hell did you know?' demanded Gina, flabbergasted, and slightly annoyed that her big reveal had fallen flat. Surely Evie hadn't become a *Southdown Gazette* subscriber.

'It was something Stuart said,' replied Evie, delighted at being ahead of Gina with the goss. 'About Daniel raising funds for some do-gooding venture that was going to cause a big splash. I didn't put two and two together at first, then I thought about the car wash and it struck me it'd be just like Daniel to take on Mad Mike. Haven't you noticed, there's something protective about him? This is protectiveness on

170

a bigger scale – of people who usually get exploited and can't do a thing about it. I think it's rather noble, actually. And of course,' she smiled down the phone, 'there is a clue in the name!' Feeling a fool for not having worked it out sooner, Gina was grateful when another call came through and Evie had to go.

But moments later Evie was back on the line.

'That was Stuart calling about the house. Not only is the loan sorted but the sellers are asking if you would be ready to exchange contracts next week?'

A sudden rush of fear overtook Gina. It was all happening so frighteningly fast! Was she doing the right thing? But here in Southdown, in a house that was such good value, surely she could build a life without Mark, and even be able to afford it?

What would her daughters think, though? Gina had to admit she'd put off telling them until it was a *fait accompli*. *And why shouldn't I?* she told herself, stiffening her sinews. *I love them to bits, but it's my life, and I have the right to choose where I want to live!*

Downstairs she could hear Mrs B getting Jasmin's room ready and an idea struck her. She slipped into the garden and picked a bunch of the pale pink roses with their evocative aroma of sun-warmed fruit and put them in a vase by Jasmin's bedside, just as Lucy had done for her what felt like an eternity ago.

'Can I help?' she asked Mrs B, who stood behind the bed, boot-faced, shaking out a duvet as if it had personally offended her.

'I'm already behind with the lunch and now Mrs Tyler airily says, "Could you get a room ready?"' Mrs B huffed.

'I could take over,' Gina offered. 'If it's all right with you.'

Mrs B struggled for a moment, torn between the pleasure of moaning about being put upon and handing over the work to someone else. Then the delicious scent of beef wafted up, reminding her of her other duties. The beef won.

'I'm used to running my own home,' continued Gina, 'and when you're staying with someone else you actually rather miss it!'

'Fine. Only, if Mrs Tyler complains about something, you'll have to say you offered to take over.'

'Of course.' As it happened, she did quite like making beds. That moment when you smoothed the duvet cover out without a crease gave her an odd satisfaction. It's funny how being domestic was considered little short of slavery to her liberal hippyish generation and now, thanks to social media, giving the house a good clean and enjoying the results was all the thing.

The sound of a car in the drive announced Jasmin's return. Gina hurried through the minstrel's gallery and down the panelled staircase to the hall. Jasmin stood by Daniel's car with a small backpack holding her pathetically few possessions. Gina hoped she wouldn't be too proud to let Maudie buy her some nice new things.

'Thank you so much, Mr Napier. For everything you have done for me.' A small smile lit up the sadness of her features. 'I always seem to be leaving.'

'An absolute pleasure,' he replied gently. 'Hello, Gina.'

'I don't think Maudie heard the car or she'd be here to greet you too. I'll take you to your room then go and find her. It seems to be thank you again, Daniel.'

'It's not necessary,' he shrugged.

Her room was on the same floor as Gina's, looking out over the flower-filled gardens.

Jasmin gazed around the room, fighting back tears. 'It is beautiful. Thank you!'

At that moment Maudie appeared behind them, her cheeks pink with pleasure. 'Jasmin, dear, so glad you're here.' She caught sight of the vase of roses on the bedside table. 'Who put those there?'

'I did,' Gina replied.

Jasmin leaned down and breathed in the scent. 'One day I will show you how to make my grandmother's special tea with their leaves!'

Gina glimpsed the sudden pain in Maudie's eyes at the word 'grandmother' and hoped she wasn't in for a disappointment. What if the news came back that Jasmin and she were not related? Maudie would be devastated. Although it was possible just getting to know each other and enjoying each other's company would turn out to be enough. Gina fervently hoped so.

Beneath her feisty facade, Maudie was a lonely old lady, even if she would be the last to admit it.

To her surprise, Daniel was still downstairs when she left Maudie and Jasmin.

'Maudie asked me to stay for a drink, but I think she may have forgotten,' he smiled.

'Would you like one?' offered Gina. 'It's a choice between Gin & It or Martini vermouth, I'm afraid. Maudie's tastes are stuck in the Fifties.'

'I love the drinks trolley,' Daniel indicated the gilt and Formica creation, loaded with various brightly coloured bottles. 'My parents had one the same. But where's the pineapple stuck with bits of cheddar like a wounded hedgehog? It was my job to pass it round at cocktail parties.'

'Do people still have cocktail parties, I wonder? I love a

margarita as much as the next person, but they don't exactly fit into real life, do they?'

'I would be delighted to corrupt you with a margarita!' Daniel bowed playfully. 'Actually, they do a very good one in the Jolly Sailor. They have a barman who did a course in mixology.'

'Is that a word?'

'Ms Greenhills, I'm shocked. And you a DFL too,' he tutted. 'We get used to you lot coming down and patronizing us, so I'm delighted the boot is on the other foot for once. Mixology is the science of mixing cocktails. Come and try him out on a cocktail challenge. He claims he can mix anything you name.'

Even Sex on the Beach? Gina almost asked, then stopped herself. What was she up to?

'I'm a bit busy here at the manor,' she pleaded, nervous of where this was going. She wasn't even divorced yet, and if you were going to live in a small town you couldn't jump into things only to find yourself regretting them. And what was his relationship with the fearsome Rebecca Boyd?

'Of course,' he replied with a twinkle. 'You were always a serious girl, even at ballroom dancing.'

She watched him climb into his car, trying not to imagine sharing a margarita with him – or even a mojito, she smiled to herself – on the sunny seafront. Instead, she forced herself to think about whether she should include all the dusty treasures in the attic as part of her overall valuation.

It was amazing how quickly things could happen when everyone wanted them to and you had effective people involved. Stuart was dealing with the private buyer in London and Doris had arranged for three local estate agents to provide valuations. The buyer had even made an offer, though Stuart thought it too low.

Exchanging contracts on the new house turned out to be a low-key affair. Stuart had recommended some very efficient local solicitors and Gina didn't even have to leave Rookery Manor but was able to add her name by a miraculous process called Docusign.

'Brilliant, isn't it?' Evie congratulated. 'And I hear your vendors are asking if you can complete in a couple of weeks.'

It was time to break the news to her daughters.

'You're actually buying back Gran's old house?' Sadie's voice rose in astonished outrage that her mother would do such a thing without consulting her. 'In Southdown? As a holiday home, you mean?'

'Not necessarily,' Gina replied, reminding herself that this was *her* life. 'The London house would have had to be sold anyway when the divorce came through, and then the mortgage would have to be paid off and the proceeds split with your father. If I'd bought in London, the best I could have afforded was a one-bedroom flat. This way I get a much better lifestyle and there's room for you both to come and stay.'

'In *Southdown*?' Sadie repeated in the withering tones of a born Londoner. Though Gina had to admit a short while ago she would have felt the same.

'It really is quite nice here,' Gina reassured.

'But it's full of old biddies!' protested Sadie.

'I'm flattered you don't think I'm one of them,' replied their mother.

'I suppose you will be before long.'

'Thanks for that!'

'Actually,' Sadie conceded generously, 'you look pretty good for your age. In fact, I'm rather hoping I've got your genes.'

Gina glanced in the mirror and caught her laughing face. She was looking much more relaxed lately. Her shiny bob still had no touch of grey and she wasn't going to give in to it if it tried to appear. Her ski-jump cheekbones were still her most notable feature. In fact the lines only appeared when she laughed, and she was pretty happy to settle for that.

Lisa was more positive. 'How exciting, Mum! I loved that house! We had such good times there when we were little.'

'You both need to come and see the house as it is now. You'll hardly recognize it, it's so stylish.'

'I hope it isn't all minimalist, is it?' enquired Lisa anxiously. 'I'm not sure I'd like that. It was such a homey place, even if Gran was manically tidy.'

'Don't worry,' replied Gina, laughing, 'I'll get my friend Ruthie to give us some style advice. She'll make it untidy before you can say Marie Kondo.'

They were both giggling away when Lisa suddenly got serious. 'Mum, I ought to tell you. Dad's been in touch.'

Gina felt her chest tighten involuntarily. 'That's good,' she made herself reply. She realized she actually meant it. When your husband first leaves you, the woman part of you is furiously angry and you hope your children never want to see him again. Then the mother part kicks in and you want what is best for them, and that would mean getting on with their father.

'The thing is . . .' Lisa hesitated, wondering whether to go on or not. 'He says he's not happy in his new relationship . . .'

Twelve

Gina stood holding the phone and staring out of the window for what seemed like hours. What did it mean that Mark wasn't happy? Would he want to stop the divorce? He couldn't imagine he could walk back into her life?

She messaged Evie to ask her what the possible ramifications were, feeling slightly dizzy and clammy-handed. Mark had probably found himself having to make some actual sacrifices for the first time in his life. Presumably he couldn't go to his beloved race meetings any more. Horse racing, whether in reality or online, had taken up most of her husband's life. Far more than his family had.

'Don't worry,' came the almost instant reply from Evie. 'You're the one who's doing the divorcing. It would be very difficult to oppose it at this stage.'

She found herself wondering again if she could have done anything more to help him and stopped herself. He wasn't a child. In fact, he had neglected their children to indulge his addiction. Why did women feel so much guiltier than men? It was this tendency that some men exploited and made women feel that everything was their fault.

Well, she wasn't falling for it.

She decided to go and see how Jasmin was settling in, but as she passed the kitchen she heard hushed voices and paused to listen.

Rosa and Awful Ambrose had ambushed Mrs B again and were pumping her for information.

'This immigrant girl, where did she come from?' demanded Rosa. 'And why is Maudie so obsessed with her?'

'She worked in that car wash in Abbot Street,' replied Mrs B, entering into the fray with relish. 'Mad Mike's, they call it. Mrs Tyler couldn't keep away. Up and down, she was, like a bride's nightie.'

'Really Mrs B,' Rosa commented, torn between prudishness and the need to know more. 'I hardly think that's a suitable analogy.'

'What's an analogy when it's at home?' enquired Mrs B.

Gina, listening from the pantry, almost got the giggles.

'But what's she doing here?' persisted Ambrose.

'Mrs Tyler asked her to stay,' replied Mrs B. 'That nice Mr Napier dropped her off with her things. She didn't want to stay in the hostel no more because she'd left Mad Mike's. I think she thought he might come after her. He's a nasty sort, that Mike Marshall.'

'What's the woman talking about?' demanded Ambrose. 'Why on earth should Maudie have anything to do with a girl in a car wash? I didn't even think there *were* any women working in car washes.'

'You're behind the times, dear,' Rosa corrected him. 'There are plenty.'

'I suppose it is a low-skill job,' he conceded generously.

Thanks, Ambrose, thought Gina. *Ever the champion of women's equality.*

'None of that explains why she's here,' continued Rosa. 'I bet she came up with some sob story and sold it to Maudie. Maudie's such a soft touch. It's why I don't think she should be living alone.'

'She doesn't live alone,' interrupted Mrs B. 'Mr B and I are here.'

'In the gardener's cottage,' Rosa insisted. 'She's technically alone. She'd be much better off in a nice flat, as I keep telling her. She could have a concierge.'

'But that would put me and Mr B out of a job, wouldn't it, Mrs Winstanley?' Mrs B enquired, raising an eyebrow.

Rosa exchanged a silent look with her husband, implying that this would be part of the attraction.

'How do we know it isn't worse than taking advantage,' Ambrose intervened darkly. 'I mean, she might be a con artist. A lot of these immigrants just pretend to be refugees to get the benefits.'

'Good luck to them with *our* council,' commented Mrs B witheringly.

'Anyway, I don't think it's appropriate for her to be living here among all these valuable antiques.'

A slim, dark figure appeared from the terrace wearing simple white jeans and a white T-shirt that probably came from Primark, though on her they looked as good as anything Bond Street had to offer. She could obviously sense the waves of hostility emanating from Rosa and Ambrose and stopped where she was standing.

'Good morning, my name is Jasmin,' she announced, turning to the pair with a shy smile. 'You are probably wondering who I am. I am from Syria. My father was a professor of English at the university, but he and my mother died a long time ago and I lived with my grandmother, who took me away from all the fighting. Before she died she arranged that I should I come to this country because it is one of the most liberal in the world. I would like to take a glass of iced water up to Mrs Tyler now, please? She is feeling the heat a little.'

Mrs B fussed around finding a glass and a slice of lemon and finally handed it over.

'What a nerve!' murmured Rosa. 'Pretending to look after Maudie!'

'And if you ask me, her English is suspiciously good,' seconded Ambrose.

Gina could resist no longer. She didn't know which of the two was more appalling than the other. 'Well,' she commented as calmly as possible, 'she did say her father was a professor of English.'

Since they already saw Gina herself as a suspicious interloper, they ignored her completely.

It was quite a relief when Stuart phoned to say that now completion had taken place she could move out of Rookery Manor and into her new, or rather, old home. Jasmin was looking after Maudie and seemed instinctively to know how to handle Mr and Mrs B so that they welcomed her arrival instead of viewing it as an intrusion. Unlike Rosa and Awful Ambrose, who remained as suspicious of Jasmin as if she were an international jewel thief.

With her bone structure she did look a bit like Audrey Hepburn in *How to Steal a Million*, Gina admitted with a slight stab of envy, though the best thing about Jasmin was that she seemed entirely unaware of her startling beauty.

The date fixed for moving in was the following Friday. There was very little to move since, by mutual consent, the vendors were leaving her everything for the moment as they were moving into a furnished apartment. That meant Gina, to her considerable relief, wouldn't be trying to sell an empty house in London if nothing came of the offer she'd received, since agents always said it was easier to sell a house if it was furnished. Once she did sell and wanted to move in her own furniture, the vendors had agreed to put their stuff in storage till they knew exactly what was happening in the US. It was a great idea, as in the short term it saved them both on storage. The wonderful Doris supervised the removal at the other end after numerous exchanges of photos of everything from her father's whisky decanter to a strapless bra that had fallen down the back of the wardrobe. Gina smiled, remembering the occasion she'd worn it under a new dress to a smart party and actually felt rather beautiful and sexy. Mark and she had also had lengthy and sometimes acrimonious negotiations over who got what. Thank God the dog was dead or she could see them ending up in court over who got custody. Whereas he seemed remarkably disinterested in what was happening with his own daughters.

On the day of moving, when Gina finished packing the car, Maudie got quite tearful. 'What a lovely time we had, my dear! I was so lucky to have you here.'

'Thank you, Maudie,' replied Gina, giving Maudie an affectionate hug. 'I really enjoyed it too. And I'll only be down the road, so we can still have fun.'

She was touched to see Mr & Mrs B and Jasmin join Maudie to wave her goodbye. As she glanced back a final time she saw that Maudie was gazing at Jasmin with something close to adoration, and wondered how those searches were going on back in Syria.

When she arrived at 9 Downview Crescent she was stunned to find Evie waiting for her holding a bunch of keys and some moving-in flowers.

'Ah ha. I see you've got the keys from Sexy Stu,' Gina pointed out. 'Of course the fact that he's the agent had nothing whatsoever to do with your decision to come and surprise me! And naturally he knows you're staying for a while? At least, I hope you are?'

'The whole weekend if you'll have me,' Evie announced, trying to keep a straight face. 'Stuart has asked me to go paddleboarding tomorrow.'

They both laughed out loud at the idea of Evie, who rarely got off her sunbed at the most luxurious of pools, donning a wetsuit and facing the probability of looking absolutely ridiculous falling off a paddleboard. She really must be attracted to Stuart to go through that, Gina decided.

Evie handed Gina the keys so that she would be the first to open her own front door. Gina took a deep breath, feeling herself caught up in a maelstrom of emotions: apprehension that moving to her hometown might not be the right step, relief that whatever its emotional significance, this was a beautiful house she could actually afford, tempered by a sudden rush of failure that she had not made the dream of happy family life come true.

Sensing her friend's turmoil, Evie attempted to make her laugh a little. 'I thought I'd take the day off and carry you over the threshold,' she offered, attempting to pick Gina up.

'I think that's the role of the bridegroom and I've had enough of them,' replied Gina with an attempt at a smile. 'And speaking of bridegrooms,' she said, remembering the news about his state of mind. 'Still no word from Mark's lawyers? No attempts to slow things down or put spanners in the works of our divorce?'

'Not a thing. And as I said, it'd be difficult given how far you've got.'

'Phew,' Gina breathed as she turned the key. 'He must have pulled himself together. It's very kind of you to come and support me. And as you never take time off work I'm doubly honoured, especially as I know how much you charge by the hour – and I'm sure Stuart would be if he had any inkling.'

'You're making me sound like a prostitute!' protested Evie.

'Yes,' teased Gina. 'But a very expensive one!'

'When's the removal van coming from London?' enquired Evie.

'First thing tomorrow. It's only a small one. Since you're here, I wanted to say how much I've appreciated your support. I wouldn't have done it if it weren't for you making me braver.' She knew Evie hated being thanked but persevered all the same. 'I won't dwell, don't worry, but thank you!'

'That's quite enough of that,' replied Evie. 'Now where's the corkscrew?'

Once inside, Gina looked around her, remembering that the old hall had gone and you stepped straight into a dramatic open-plan kitchen-diner.

'My dad would have got lost in this space. He was a burrow person, happiest in small dark places like a rabbit. He'd have been off to the shed in no time!'

'Except that they've turned the shed into a work-at-home studio!' reminded Evie.

'I wonder what Mum would have made of having an island?' Gina stroked the marble-effect quartz worktop. 'A sink in the middle! She would have worried where the water went to!'

'Tell you what, Gina,' Evie announced decisively. 'You're going to have to stop thinking of it as their house and realize it's yours!'

Evie followed Gina upstairs. 'The big question is, which room is going to be your bedroom?'

'I told you. I'm certainly not sleeping in my parents' bedroom!' insisted Gina. 'Even though it's got an en suite bathroom rather than Dad using a pot hidden under the bed—'

'He didn't!' Evie interrupted, appalled.

'They all did in that generation. They'd think we're very namby-pamby with our roll-top baths in the bedroom.' They went up the small staircase to the dramatic new loft conversion.

'This would be the room for me!' announced Evie. 'Look at those views!'

It was indeed spectacular with its vista to both the downs and the sea.

Gina looked around at the tasteful room with its carved wooden bedstead and matching smart bedside tables and decided she agreed with Evie. But she would change one of the bedside tables for the one her mum had rescued from a junk shop, painted white with added gold plastic Louis Quatorze handles in an early outbreak of upcyling. Every time she opened its drawer she thought of her mother. It was in tiny ways like this that a person lived on for you.

Memory isn't on a gravestone, Gina often thought, it's recalling a stupid saying of your dad's, or your gran telling you to tuck a fiver down in your bra for an emergency taxi in case you got your handbag stolen, or an upcycled bedside table made by your mum.

'Oh, I forgot!' Evie delved into her enormous shoulder bag and produced a bottle of champagne in its own cooling jacket. 'I brought you this. Congratulations! Let's go down and open it.'

On the ground floor they slid open the huge glass French window the vendors had added and sat down with their champagne on the sunlit patio.

'To staying in Southdown!' Evie clinked Gina's glass. 'God, I can't believe I'm saying that. And now,' she turned the spotlight of her attention on Gina. 'What news of Dancing Danny?'

'If you mean romantically, absolutely zero.' To her surprise, Gina was aware of a slight jolt of disappointment. 'Of course he must be very busy with the car wash. Jasmin says it's opening soon. But it must have been pretty complicated to get the financing together. Mad Mike wasn't fussy where his workers came from so he could pay them shit wages and they wouldn't dare complain. Daniel has been negotiating with the authorities about how to make the new one work fairly.'

'He's quite an operator for a lad with a limp handshake, that Danny,' commented Evie.

'Shut up, Evie!' Gina found herself feeling quite angry on his behalf. 'That was thirty years ago!'

'Only joking! My, you do care, don't you?'

'He seems like a very kind bloke that's all.'

'And you swore that after charming but unreliable Mark, kind was what you wanted now, as I recall?'

Gina stood up. 'Well kind isn't on the menu at the moment, thank you very much!'

Evie put on her new swimsuit and surveyed herself in the mirror. It was pale green Lycra with a plunging neckline, possibly not the ideal design for paddleboarding but the only one-piece she had. At least she looked good it in it. The colour suited her red hair. Why the hell had she agreed to do it anyway? She hated looking ridiculous. As a woman in what was still largely a man's world, she liked to be better informed than her male colleagues, so no one could ever put her at a disadvantage. She knew paddleboarding was supposed to be enjoyable, but it just reminded her of when her mother made her join the tennis club in Southdown 'to have fun and meet nice people'. She'd even made Evie a tennis dress the spit of Billie Jean King's. The only trouble was Evie couldn't get the ball over the net and looked doubly silly because of The Dress.

She'd arranged to meet Stuart by the Martello Tower near the beach. As a child she'd had no curiosity about this large round structure but as an adult she was fascinated to read that it had been built in the days of Napoleon, when this whole coastline was terrified of invasion.

'Pity Josephine didn't have you as her lawyer – she'd have done a damn sight better out of Boney when she got dumped for a younger woman.' Stuart must have got there early and was leaning on the wall about six feet away, waiting for her.

'That's the story of most of my clients,' Evie laughed. 'The richer and more powerful the man, the younger the woman!'

'Mind you,' Stuart parried, 'she did lie on her marriage certificate and pretend to be four years younger!'

'That's market forces for you,' Evie countered with spirit. 'Life's stacked against women all the way. Youth and beauty in exchange for money and power. The old story hasn't changed as much as you'd think. Among the rich at least.'

'I can see why you have such a fierce reputation!' Stuart twinkled.

'Pure sexism. I've got red hair and I fight for women, ergo it's dangerous to approach me.'

'Fortunately I'm not scared, or I wouldn't offer to teach you paddleboarding.'

'Promise you haven't been hired by an angry husband to maroon me beyond the distant horizon.'

'Scouts honour. Though it does happen. The coastguards are always having to rescue stranded paddleboarders!'

'Now he tells me . . .' she protested.

'Too late. I've hired you a board. It's waiting on the beach.'

She followed him across the hot pebbles, picking her way past enthusiastic beachgoers with brightly coloured pop-up tents to shelter from the sun, giving the whole place the feel of a summer rock festival now the season was properly underway. As she negotiated the steep bank to the sea, Evie was grateful she'd put on proper surfing shoes or she'd have been squeaking in pain. There was no sand until the water's edge. But the sea did look inviting, she had to admit.

Almost navy out at the horizon, it softened like tie-dyed silk into turquoise, then pale green breaking along the shore-line in tiny waves, all under a bright blue sky and framed by the famous outline of the Seven Sisters. English summer at its beautiful best. It was days like this that made you wonder why anyone went abroad when they had so much beauty on their own doorstep.

'Right,' Stuart lifted up a paddleboard by the small handle in the centre, 'this is where you pick it up. You carry it to the water and attach it to your ankle with this bracelet, so that if you fall off it can't float away from you. The currents round here are very powerful. And this' – he reached into his backpack and produced a hideous padded life jacket – 'is what you have to wear even if you are a successful woman who makes up her own mind.'

Dutifully, if not willingly, Evie put it on. They both stood looking out at the dozens of paddleboarders coasting up and down. 'I had no idea it was so popular,' said Evie. 'No one seems to be swimming any more.'

'Yes,' Stuart agreed. 'It's definitely the new big thing.'

'Oh my God, look at that!' Evie pointed to a paddleboarder cruising past with his dog happily standing on the back just as Gina had described. 'I suppose having four legs gives you more balance.'

'You're absolutely right,' laughed Stuart. 'Which is why' – he took her hand and led her towards the water – 'you need to get onto all fours before you stand up! Kneel down, keep steady till you've got your balance and remember to keep your eyes firmly on something fixed like that buoy out there.'

Evie glanced round, hoping no one was watching, and tried to climb on. Fortunately for her dignity, the sea was quite calm. 'Excellent,' congratulated Stuart. 'Now put your paddle flat and press your knuckles down on it and raise yourself up one leg at a time.'

'This is harder work than City Gym!' complained Evie.

'It gets easier with practice,' he reassured. 'Now, knees bent, and paddle out, three strokes to one side then three the other. And remember, start upwind and come back with the wind behind you. That's how a lot of boarders get into trouble. They shoot off with the wind behind them and are too tired to get back against it.'

'I'm not planning on going out of my depth,' insisted Evie. 'And anyway, which way is upwind?'

Stuart laughed and pointed to the flag flapping over the ice-cream stall. 'That way.'

To her delight, following Stuart's advice, Evie managed to not only stay upright but, once she began paddling, to start moving swiftly through the water. Soon she found herself quite far out, zipping over the waves like one of Neptune's daughters – that is, if they had to wear hideous life jackets.

'How the hell do I turn this thing round?' She began to panic. But Stuart, back on the shore watching out for her, began to mime pulling the paddle behind her like a rudder, and paddling fast on just one side. Feeling thrilled with herself at mastering a new skill, she headed for the shore. Ahead of her, two young women, both tall and striking in their black wetsuits, arrived on the beach shouldering what looked like large backpacks and began to chat to Stuart. Evie, still some way out, was piqued to see them all laughing together and felt a stab of disappointment. Was Stuart one of those men who couldn't resist the lure of younger women?

Whether it was due to these new arrivals or not, Evie made a sudden beeline for the shore, came in much too fast so that her board collided with the hidden banking of the shingle, and promptly fell off.

Still spluttering, her hair plastered all over her face, and for all she knew her mascara creating attractive black runnels down her cheeks, she climbed awkwardly up the beach.

'Eve,' Stuart greeted her warmly, 'what good timing. Come and meet Maddy and Jessica, my two daughters.'

At any other time Evie would have probably laughed at herself, but she felt at exactly the kind of disadvantage she spent her life avoiding. Further up the beach she caught sight of a sign proclaiming Ladies Toilet.

'If you don't mind, I'll just go and get changed quickly.' She grabbed her things and headed towards the Martello Tower, feeling two sets of critical eyes charting her progress.

Glancing in the fly-blown mirror, she decided she looked like a creature from the bottom of the deep and instantly set about some emergency repairs to her appearance.

Dragging the brush-comb combi through her hair that had come in her first-class courtesy pack with Thai Airlines, carefully dabbing her eyes with wet wipes and adding a slash of confidence-boosting Chanel Rouge lipstick, she felt ready to face Stuart's grown-up daughters.

'Well, that was fun,' she announced back on the beach with what she hoped was a warm and engaging smile. 'Are those tents you're unpacking?'

Maddy and Jessica's response was to stop unpacking their giant backpacks and burst out laughing.

'The girls are ace boarders,' Stuart explained with a shy grin. 'These monstrosities they carry round on their backs are blow-up paddleboards! Come on, girls, give us a demo!'

'Cover your eyes for two minutes then,' insisted Jessica. 'Or better still, go and buy an ice cream and come back in five.'

'Come on then, Evie.' He took her gently by the arm. 'Let me guess what you'd like: salted caramel with maybe a scoop of passion fruit?'

'The combination sounds horrible but probably a fair assessment of my taste. How about you? Dark chocolate with a little lemon sorbet?'

'How did you know?' Stuart asked delightedly. 'That would be my perfect choice.'

'Tell me about the girls. Do they live with you?'

'Hardly, at their age. They live in Brighton, or London-by-the-sea as people like to think of it.'

'Hence the paddleboarding. And what do they do?'

'Maddy is in PR, or Comms as they seem to call it these days, and Jessica works in Children's Services. They're great girls.'

Evie couldn't help smiling at the ring of pride in his voice. How interesting to be the father of girls. She wondered how it changed a man.

It all sounded so normal. Happy families. So different from the ones she encountered in her work. She had to remind herself that happy families did exist. Lots of them. And yet Stuart and his wife were divorced, which made it even more impressive.

'So how did you manage it? The successful divorce?' she asked as he handed over the salted caramel cone, unfortunately without passion fruit this time.

'It was a long time ago,' Stuart replied. 'We both tried very hard to make it work. There was no one else involved. I think that was probably key. We had drifted apart, as the Relate cliché goes.'

'Congratulations. I don't see a lot of goodwill between spouses in my line of work,' Evie shrugged.

'I hope you haven't let it prejudice you too much,' he replied with a smile as melting as her caramel cone. 'People can like and respect each other, you know.'

'So I'm finding out,' she smiled back. 'Right, let's inspect the paddleboard parade.'

Maddy and Jessica, in their sleek black wetsuits, stood next to their sleek black paddleboards, looking like characters from an action-adventure movie.

'Wow,' commented Evie. 'I am impressed.'

'See you in half an hour, Dad,' said Jessica as they headed for the sea.

Stuart produced two low beach chairs from his car. Evie looked around. Half the occupants of the beach had the same dinky little seat. 'You're well equipped, I see.'

'I come down whenever I can in summer, work permitting.'

'That explains the tan.' She'd noticed how brown he was, and how natural it looked the first time they'd met again. I was wondering if it was fake.'

'Thank you!' he replied, mock outraged.

'Mine is,' confessed Evie. 'But I do it myself. I don't have time to go to one of those spray tan places. And they only make you look like a contestant on *Love Island* anyway.'

'How on earth do you do your back?' he asked, fascinated.

'Ah ha. I have patented the Eve Beeston single woman

application technique. A loo brush – new obviously – with kitchen roll over it, attached by a scrunchie. To which I apply the fake tan.'

'What is a scrunchie?'

'And you the father of girls!' Evie pretended to be shocked. 'One of those elastic things that keeps your hair up.'

'Not a problem of mine!' With a laugh he indicated his bald head. 'Doesn't the stuff leave streaks though?'

'Yes, but it's still better than being the colour of a plucked chicken,' replied Evie with her usual candour.

'I think I prefer the image of you in thongs!' he teased.

'Whatever gets you to sleep . . . dirty old man!' Evie realized she was flirting again. Well, why not?

'I suppose you'll be going back tonight?' The question felt like that icy feeling when you open the freezer.

'Work calls. Look, the girls are coming back in, I think.'

Unlike Evie, neither fell off their paddleboards but glided elegantly in and climbed off as if they were stepping from a yacht in the harbour at Marbella.

'Did you see me deal with the backwash from the ferry, Dad?' asked Maddy. 'It was huge . . . Like a mini tidal wave!'

Evie noted how much his good opinion mattered to her.

'I think Dad had better things to do,' commented Jessica with a touch of acid in her tone. She unzipped her wetsuit with the panache of a Bond girl and sat down next to Evie. 'Dad says you're a hotshot lawyer.'

Evie shrugged, wondering what was coming next.

'You must be very impressive, to have got that successful.' There was something about her voice that told Evie this wasn't a compliment. 'Don't you ever want to use your skills for the greater good – like climate change, or refugees, or even child abuse?'

'Jessica,' interrupted Stuart, 'that sounded very aggressive. Eve's our guest.'

'*Your* guest,' corrected Jessica, which Evie divined was the nub of the problem. Jessica didn't like Evie because she suspected her beloved father of being interested in this tough, career-obsessed stranger from another world.

'Don't worry, Stuart,' Evie replied. 'It's a fair question. Yes, Jessica, I do sometimes wonder if I could do more. But there are different ways of helping people that are equally important, you know.' Jessica might feel different if she'd heard some of the pain that was daily poured into Evie's sympathetic ear. But then, Evie reminded herself, you had to make allowances for youth, and she quite liked the girl for her combative attitude.

'Well, if you ever do more than wonder what you could do to be useful, message me. I can put you in touch with any number of worthy causes who could really use your skills!'

Evie watched them walk away, gilded in all the certainty of youth. Compromise and reality hadn't yet reared their heads, at least in Jessica's world.

What none of them could have guessed was that Evie's legal skills would be needed sooner than any of them anticipated.

Gina opened the built-in wardrobe in the magnificent loft conversion and hung her clothes on the hangers she'd found in her parents' old mahogany one. This item, she suspected, had been kept by the new owners to use as the vintage touch that can make a minimalist room look quirky and fun.

The hangers were a bit of social history in themselves: small children's ones from Hubbard's, the local department store which had closed down years ago, black plastic ones from M&S and some proper gents' outfitter-style hangers from her father's tailor. The thought of all the different clothes that had been hung on them made Gina want to cry. Moving back into her parents' house had made her feel unexpectedly vulnerable, a failure somehow alone in a world of couples, with no partner to discuss whether or not this move back home was a good idea. Not that Mark had been much use at talking about things that mattered, but at least he was there.

She looked at her watch, wondering where the time had gone. Evie would be coming back any moment to get her stuff before heading home. Funny how Evie never seemed to feel alone and vulnerable. Evie was Superwoman: strong, capable, totally independent.

She would have been astonished to learn that Superwoman was, at that very moment, walking up the hill from the beach, wishing that it wasn't Sunday night, with the week ahead snapping at her, and feeling, for the first time she could remember, dubious about her life in London. It must be something to do with Jessica and her scathing tone, implying she was wasting her talents. *Come on*, she told herself, *you love your job! And it's extremely useful!*

Of course she did, and she had a particularly busy week ahead. London was her home. The artistic capital of the world. What had Southdown got to offer apart from a slightly scruffy old town and a charming estate agent?

Gina was already standing with the door open when she walked up the front path. 'How was the paddleboarding? Did you manage to stay upright?'

'Most of the time,' laughed Evie. 'But I did have a very good teacher.'

'You're obviously going to have to come all summer and hone your skills,' Gina teased. 'Do they do paddleboarding at the Olympics?'

'Now I'm doing it they will.'

Evie stayed for a quick cup of tea and waved goodbye. When she'd gone, Gina sat at the new island and caught up with that week's turnover on her antiques business. They weren't making a fortune by any means, but enough to pay the thankfully very reasonable rent on the warehouse and Doris's equally reasonable salary plus a little bit of profit.

After the remains of some spag bol she'd made for lunch yesterday, and a mediocre TV film, she headed up for bed. The one thing she'd said to herself when she'd bought the house was that she wouldn't move into her parents' bedroom.

Anyway, the loft was far bigger and more colourful.

Halfway through the night she sat up, overwhelmed by a wave of loneliness, feeling like a loser and a failure again. She had let the dream of a happy family run away from her, perhaps through bad luck, perhaps through choosing someone who could never deliver or fully participate in it. She had failed her children. She had lost at life.

The powerful desire to be in her parents' room came over her, to feel the warmth of their protection as she had when she was a child. She half crawled down the new stairs and into the bed on the floor below and pulled up the duvet. Suddenly remembering the box of stuff Doris had sent on ahead, she riffled through it till she found a pair of large curtains which reminded her of her childhood. They featured that reassuring cliché *The Strawberry Thief* by William Morris. Tomorrow, before the van arrived, she would move her things down from upstairs and hang them properly. For tonight she pulled the curtains over the duvet like a bedspread and fell into a deep and comforting sleep.

* * *

Next morning Gina woke feeling that something extraordinary had happened.

The sensation of being a loser who had failed at marriage had miraculously lifted and instead she felt that she was being given a new start. With so much of their antiques business happening online she could do it at least as easily from here, and premises would be cheaper too. She might even be able to extend the garage and store her stock there. She could make sure there was a role for Doris too, though one or two hints from the doughty Doris had implied she was pretty keen to retire and had only stayed on because Gina had been so badly let down by Mark.

The valuation of Maudie's possessions was virtually complete and she would soon be free to get on with her new life.

By the time the furniture van arrived she was feeling full of energy. Ruthie came to help and by early afternoon it was all done and she decided to go into town and celebrate.

It was another of those glorious days when you just had to be outside. The sky was so blue you needed an impressionist painter to capture it – Monet or even Van Gogh. It sparkled like sapphires on the horizon without even the suggestion of a cloud along the whole skyline. A light breeze made it the perfect temperature and Gina wished she'd brought her swimsuit. Maybe she'd have an evening swim later. That was the beauty of living here – there was no hurry. It would all be waiting for her. Walking past the cafe at the entrance to the pier, she couldn't resist buying herself a freshly made doughnut. She had no sooner closed her eyes and was savouring the hot delicious sweetness which took her straight back to her childhood when a voice penetrated her daydream.

'I like a woman with sugar all over her nose. She's obviously prepared to experience life to the full!'

Gina opened her eyes to find Daniel Napier standing inches away. Involuntarily she stepped back.

'I'm not quite sure how to take that,' said Gina.

'As a compliment. Shall I brush it off?'

'No thanks, I can do it,' she replied, feeling she must look stupid covered in sugar.

It was too late. His hand was already moving towards her upper lip.

She reached up and grasped it. There was no trace of that limp feeling that had put her off him all those years ago. This hand knew what it was doing.

Gina! she admonished herself severely. The truth was, she had felt a sudden stirring of the senses that shocked her. She wasn't even divorced yet! And this was Dancing Danny, someone she had never remotely fancied.

Daniel laughed, watching her, as if he could read every thought in her head.

'I have to go,' Gina announced firmly.

'Of course you do,' was Daniel's reply. 'But next time you feel like buying a doughnut, do invite me.'

Gina walked off quickly in the other direction, her thoughts in a whirl, and disappeared into the nearest antique shop to look for more stock for Doris.

'It's so wonderful having you here, dear child,' Maudie assured Jasmin with a tear in her eye. 'Living alone is frankly boring when you're old.' She wasn't going to admit to the word lonely and invite the girl's pity. That wasn't her style. 'Having a young face about the place is such a pleasure!'

'You need an interest perhaps,' Jasmin smiled back.

'Like golf, you mean? Or bell ringing? That's what most old ladies go for. Or knitting. Or charity coffee mornings. I'm no good at any of that. But I do like people.'

'You should have paying guests,' suggested Jasmin enthusiastically. 'A long time ago, long before the war, my aunt had a big house and she did that. They needed the extra money. My aunt put her children through school thanks to the guests! And not only that, she really enjoyed all the different people and their stories. It gave her a new interest. How many bedrooms do you have here?'

Maudie wrinkled her nose. 'Eight, I think.'

Jasmin laughed out loud. 'I love that you don't know!'

'Well, I don't use many of them, as you can imagine. I like the idea a lot, but I'm not sure Mrs B could cope. She's almost as old as me! And I couldn't afford more help. To be honest, dear girl, the manor is very expensive to run as it is.'

'Perhaps if you would let me help?' asked Jasmin shyly. 'I learned all the skills from my aunt. And if I was doing that I wouldn't need to work at the car wash.' She hesitated, realizing she might be going too fast for Maudie. 'I'm sorry, I tend to let my enthusiasm lead me, how do you say it, down the garden path?'

'No, no dear, you're not going down the garden path. I love the idea of having people to stay. I used to be a great hostess in my time.'

'Shall I do some research for you? I'm sure there would be a lot online.'

'Of course, the wonderful internet. Indeed, why don't you ask Mr Google what he thinks of the idea?'

Jasmin began to laugh and laugh.

'Have I said something amusing?' Maudie enquired.

'What on earth's going on here?' Rosa's disapproving face appeared round the door.

'We were just having a laugh,' replied Maudie. 'You should do it more yourself. To what do I owe the honour, by the way?'

'Wednesday's the day we go into town together.'

'Do we?' Maudie asked absently.

Jasmin noted the fury tinged with jealousy flash across this woman's face, before she disguised it with a small, forced smile.

'We'd better get along then,' Maudie took Jasmin's hand. 'You talk to Mr Google, dear, and we'll catch up later.'

'What on earth was all that about?' Rosa asked, trying to suppress her resentment as they walked to the car.

'Oh, we've got a little project we're hatching – it'll probably come to nothing. And, Rosa dear . . .'

'Yes?' Rosa replied suspiciously.

'You must watch this distrust of people. First Mrs Greenhills, and now Jasmin. If you always distrust people, you'll end up being narrow and bitter, and you wouldn't want that, would you?'

'It's because I've got your best interests at heart,' Rosa insisted firmly. 'You're a vulnerable old lady, Maudie. It's just that you won't admit it.'

Thirteen

Next morning Gina made herself a cup of tea and got back under the William Morris curtains. The feeling of optimism was still there. The sun was shining and this was the first day in her new home with all her favourite pieces of furniture around her. She threw back the covers and did a little dance of joy. Today she'd hang the curtains properly. She sipped her tea, grateful her mother had taught her to use a sewing machine. When she'd told her daughters that her own mother had made all their clothes, they'd looked at her as if she were telling them a fairy tale. Cinderella, perhaps, or Sleeping Beauty, so far away did it seem from their own lives. Why make anything when you could buy it so cheaply in Primark? They had felt sorry for their mother, wearing home-made clothes when all her friends' were shop bought.

As soon as she was dressed, she slipped out to the garage where the old foot-pedalled Singer sewing machine had been kept. There'd been so much to clear from the house after her parents died that she and her brother had forgotten all about the pile of stuff in the corner of the garage until they were back in London. Not that there was the slightest hope it would still be there.

To her delight she discovered the sewing machine under a tarpaulin in the darkest corner. She could imagine the recently departed couple arguing over whether to throw it out and deciding to keep it for the intricate iron legs, which she'd seen featured in interiors magazines, repurposed as a vintage desk or kitchen table supports.

Dragging it back to the house was hard work as it seemed to weigh a ton, and she mentally cursed Mark for buggering off and leaving her to drag heavy sewing machines around alone. It looked out of place in the spanking new kitchen, but she found an empty corner of the sitting room and set to giving it a good clean and oiling the mechanism with WD-40.

First she needed to measure the curtains compared to the size of the bedroom window. As she'd expected, they turned out to be twenty centimetres too small. Damn! Looking round, Gina realized it hadn't just been the need to feel at home that had impelled her to drag the curtains over the bed. The understated décor of the room didn't suit her personality. She longed for some colour. So what about cutting out panels of the Morris pattern, which famously featured a speckled thrush stealing a bright red strawberry against a background of intertwined green plants and a deep blue night sky, and inserting them into lush velvet of the same colour?

If she'd been in London she'd have gone straight to lovely John Lewis, but the department store in Southdown had shut down years ago. She remembered the retail park at the fringe of the town where there was a home furnishings store and set out for it at once, not wanting to lose the first real sense she'd had of making the house her own. The strawberry-thieving thrush would have understood implicitly, Gina decided.

To her disappointment there was only one fabric that was halfway suitable. The colour was a near enough match, but it wasn't the true silk velvet she would have wanted. Still, it meant she could do it today and she had to admit, it was remarkably good value, so she took the plunge and bought five metres. As she was making her way to the checkout she remembered to pick up sewing cotton and curtain hooks. She had pins and fabric shears in her sewing basket, and the needle in the machine had seemed fine. If she'd got home and found she didn't have those, her creative impulse would no doubt dry up like an old yogurt, leaving her feeling frustrated and a failure at even the simplest task.

Instead, she made a coffee and lost herself in the satisfying art of upcycling. She was rewarded by finishing the new curtains as dusk was falling. She wasted no time in hanging them and stood back to admire her handiwork.

As a reward she poured herself a glass of wine and – feeling like she was at a state unveiling – pulled them closed for the first time. She had to laugh when she found she was clapping her own achievement. But why not? They looked wonderful.

Back downstairs she popped a Marks and Spencer's fish pie into the brand-new oven, topped up her wine and flopped onto the sofa, TV remote in hand. Flipping through the channels, she tried not to be one of those old grouches who moaned that there were 'a hundred channels and still nothing to watch' and settled on *Gogglebox*.

The delicious aroma of cheesy fish told her supper was ready and she ate it on her knee with some slightly aged salad leaves.

Halfway through the programme she felt the familiar anger welling up at finding herself alone. And then she noticed something. The reason *Gogglebox* was so entertaining was not only because it reviewed the week's television but also because of the people they'd chosen to review it. And they weren't all couples. There were couples, admittedly, but also a brother and sister, a father and his two sons, two giggly sisters, a lively family and – her personal favourite – two wonderful old ladies who'd been friends for years. Having fun, she told herself firmly, didn't have to always involve having a partner.

She tidied up the kitchen and went up to bed with a cup of mint tea. This was how you coped with being alone, she decided, through creating small habits. Looking forward to a warm bed, a good book, admiring the stylish curtains you'd made yourself! They were the small pins that held up the large thing called Life.

As she put down her book and leaned over to turn off the bedside light the sudden memory of Daniel Napier brushing sugar off her top lip came back to her and she found she was smiling. So much for her new philosophy of surviving the single life!

She had almost fallen asleep when her phone, charging on a shelf by the window, beeped.

She shuffled sleepily over and found herself wide awake.

It was a message from Mark asking to speak to her urgently.

Jasmin spent all morning sitting in front of Maudie's ageing PC. The sight of it had made her laugh at first but, in fact, it worked perfectly well.

Rather than go with one of the big letting agencies, it seemed simpler to register with the local tourist one, which got very good reviews, since Maudie was only considering renting out one room to begin with. Jasmin wondered what the interfering relatives would make of it, feeling grateful for once that she didn't have any of her own.

Tears blurred her eyes. What a stupid, crazy thought. If she'd had any relatives left to take care of her she wouldn't be here, worrying if she would be allowed to stay, wearing herself out with the menial labour of the car wash. Worse, working for a bully who would do her harm if he could. How lucky she had been that Maudie had taken such an interest in her, even though she had not understood why, and had eventually helped her leave that awful place. Maudie was lonely, sensed Jasmin, and that was why she thought having guests would appeal to her. There was also something about Maudie that reminded Jasmin of her own grandmother. That liveliness of spirit and refusal to be conventional for the sake of others. Maybe that was why she felt so safe here with her.

Stop it, Jasmin, she told herself. *Your grandmother always said you imagine things instead of living in the real world.* But then her experience of the real world so far had not been a very encouraging one.

In the morning Gina tidied the kitchen, checked on the company website, and messaged Doris about a delivery, feeling guilty that she hadn't yet sourced Doris's most recent request for more stock.

She was about to put the bins out before she admitted to herself she was avoiding replying to Mark's message.

What the hell did he want? She sat down staring at her cup of coffee. What if he was going to say that leaving was all a mistake and he wanted them to get back together? Would she ever consider taking him back?

Stop stop stop . . . it was probably something to do with selling the house, or him wanting more money from the business. If she'd learned anything during their marriage it was that Mark always came first with Mark.

The doorbell buzzed and she jumped up, grateful for an interruption.

In an unconscious gesture she tidied her hair in the hall mirror. It struck her that she was doing the same thing her mother had always done when she was nervous, though the mirror had been an old-fashioned gilt affair rather than the snazzy new one left by the departing owners. Gina began to laugh, and was still laughing when she opened the door to find the husband she was in the process of divorcing standing on her doorstep.

'You look pretty,' were his first words, accompanied by his most charming smile. 'I haven't seen you laugh like that for a long time.'

Gina stiffened. 'I haven't had a lot to laugh at,' she replied, not smiling back. This was classic Mark. Believing charm could conquer all. Even her.

'Can I come in? I couldn't believe it when Lisa told me you'd moved back here. You despised it so much.'

Gina stood back to let him pass. 'It's changed, and so have I. This house came up incredibly cheaply. If I'd stayed in London, I wouldn't be able to afford much.'

Mark looked around the kitchen. 'Someone's done a nice job.'

'Yes. I remembered it had always been a happy house.'

'Unlike ours, you mean.'

Gina looked him in the eye. 'Yes, Mark. Unlike ours. You left for someone else, if you recall. And even when you were there, your family never mattered to you compared to the excitement of betting on horses.'

'That's all changed now.'

'So what happened with the woman you left us for?'

His expression changed as if she'd shown poor taste in raising the topic. 'She turned out to be a control freak.'

'You mean she made you stick to what you'd agreed?'

'Don't be hard, Gina.' He took a step towards her. 'You were never hard.'

'Maybe I've had to toughen up,' she announced, moving to the safety of the other side of the island. 'Why are you here, Mark?'

He gave her a searching look, a look she recognized. It was the expression of someone who wanted to keep their options open. The new woman was giving him a hard time, and without apology or admission he had come to see how the land lay with Gina. She almost wanted to laugh. If he had come to sincerely apologize, to say how sorry he was for wrecking their marriage, would she have wavered and been tempted to believe the bullshit, for all the wrong reasons?

Before she had the chance to say anything the doorbell rang again. She saw the look of irritation, quickly suppressed, that crossed her husband's face.

'Probably only Amazon or something. They'll leave it on the doorstep – just ignore them,' insisted Mark tetchily. She recognized the controlling tone and was grateful she no longer had it in her life.

'Except that I haven't ordered anything from Amazon.'

She walked across the hall and opened the front door.

Daniel Napier stood on the doorstep holding a brown paper bag. 'Doughnuts,' he explained with the half-laughing expression she was coming to recognize. 'I was seeing a client on the seafront and I walked past the stall. For some reason I thought of you.'

Mark materialized and stood behind her with a possessive air. 'Aren't you going to introduce me?' he enquired, his voice dripping with irony. He reached out and took the bag from

Daniel's hands. 'These smell great. One thing to recommend Southdown, at least. I'm Mark, by the way, Gina's husband.'

'Daniel . . .' Gina started to explain.

'It's OK, no need,' Daniel shook his head, avoiding her eyes so that she wouldn't see the hurt in his. 'Sorry I intruded. I should have called first. Enjoy the doughnuts.' He turned and walked quickly back to his car.

'So who's Doughnut Boy?' Mark asked sarcastically. 'You don't waste much time, I must say.'

'You left me, Mark. Remember? And I'd appreciate it if you didn't turn up uninvited. I'm sure there are things we'll need to discuss, but we can do it on the phone or in London.'

'How's the business going?' he enquired as if he were asking about train times. She could hardly believe he had the nerve.

'If you bothered to look at the website, you'd see for yourself!' she snapped. 'Though it would look a lot healthier if you replaced the money you removed. You could start by getting Doris some more stock. She can let you know what's selling.' The buying had been Mark's role, using his raffish charm to good use for once. Gina ran the rest of the business. What happened to the company would be part of the divorce settlement, she assumed, and he'd better not bloody well expect to get half!

'I'll see what I can do. How about the Brighton Marina boot fair? That was always good for us. And Gina . . . about the divorce . . .'

Gina felt a rising sense of panic. The girls had said his relationship wasn't working.

'I'd rather discuss that through our lawyers,' Gina interrupted, avoiding his eyes. 'But for now I'm calling you a cab. You can eat your doughnut on the train.'

'When did you get so tough, Gina?' He attempted a disarming smile.

'I'm not,' she replied with unusual firmness as she hustled him out of the front door. 'But believe me, I'm trying to learn.'

After he'd gone, Gina sat staring at her uneaten doughnut. Mark had managed to kill off all the pleasure and fun it represented. Whatever she thought of Daniel Napier, he had obviously revised his opinion of her. Anything she did to disabuse him would seem fake. From now on he was going to see her as someone with a husband she still had a relationship with. Worse, that she hadn't even been honest enough to tell him so.

Twenty minutes later, in the reassuring familiarity of his office, Daniel began to recover from feeling quite so devastated and start to deal with the day's challenges. It wasn't long now till the new car wash was due to open and he was still struggling with the final stages of setting up the company and organizing the opening ceremony with both the bigwigs from Harpers supermarket and the town hall.

He'd had the idea for an ethical car wash years ago, but it had taken all his organizing and business acumen to actually get it off the ground. Raising the money had been easier than he'd expected – perhaps because everyone loved hand car washes and, equally, everyone shared the slight feeling of unease at where the employees came from and how they were treated. Consequently, a lot of people were eager to support a venture that put the two together.

'I see you're working far too hard, as usual,' a teasing voice accused. He looked up from his screen to find Rebecca Boyd holding a box from Gail's Bakery and had to smile bitterly at the irony of Rebecca bringing him pastries when he'd just handed a bag of doughnuts over to a man who described himself as Georgina Greenhills' husband.

'Thanks, Rebecca.' He knew she wanted their relationship to deepen and, until Gina's arrival in Southdown, he might have felt the same.

When Gina had come back to her hometown, he had expected to greet her simply as an old friend. Instead, he'd found that she evoked all the feelings in him she had done as a teenager. Overwhelming attraction tempered with a desire to shield and protect her. And until the appearance of her husband, he had thought that she was drawn to him almost as strongly as he was to her. When he had held her in his arms and danced the cha-cha, it had been as if the years that separated them had melted away like mist in sunshine. He had been almost on the point of taking the biggest risk he'd allowed himself for years and telling her.

And then he'd rung her doorbell and found her husband with his arm round her.

He could still feel the pain as he attempted to smile at Rebecca.

'I think I have a pretty good understanding of you, Daniel Napier,' she announced, sitting provocatively on the edge of his desk so that the slit in her long skirt revealed inches of brown thigh. 'You've been getting yourself tangled up with your old girlfriend, haven't you? But sex with an ex is always dangerous territory. Forwards not back is always better.'

'As a matter of fact we never had sex. Times were more innocent then.'

'That's the secret then.' Rebecca revealed another half inch of thigh. 'You want to know what it would be like. A disappointment, that's what. As I say, I've been making a study of you. You're brave and she's too soft. You need someone whose courage matches yours.' The dark eyes which contrasted so effectively with her blonde hair bored into his.

'I bought you a croissant by the way.' Without another word, she removed it from a brown paper bag and held it to his mouth and, since he could hardly do otherwise, he took a bite.

'Come on, Gina dear,' Maudie called out as she rang Gina's doorbell later that morning. 'Don't you remember, we're going swimming!'

She put her head out of the window and called down to Maudie. 'Oops, sorry, Maudie, I forgot!' The sudden arrival of Mark and then Daniel had pushed their arrangement to the back of her mind. She quickly hunted for her costume, grabbed a towel and stuffed them into her backpack with a pair of sea shoes and a hair tie. Minutes later she was opening her front door.

'I didn't expect you in the morning,' she greeted the sprightly old lady.

'Best time of the day, dear. The mornings are like life – beautiful and full of possibilities. It's only later that clouds arrive and spoil everything.'

They climbed into Maudie's smart station wagon which, Gina tried not to smile, was no longer as shiny clean now that Jasmin had left Mad Mike's. 'Jasmin not coming?' she asked.

'To be honest, she thinks we're crazy swimming in the sea at all. She's putting it down to English eccentricity.'

'Any more news from Damascus?'

Maudie's face closed up. 'No, nothing. And I was so hopeful. Oh well, it's enough to have her with me. That girl is an absolute ray of sunshine.'

'I'm so glad for you, Maudie.'

'She's looking into the idea of paying guests at the manor.

Her aunt had them and found them very rewarding. Dear girl, she knows how I like having people around. And of course it would bring in some money. That's how her auntie put her children through school, Jasmin says.'

Maybe then you wouldn't need to hide antiques in the roof, Gina thought, but didn't say.

They had reached the back of Southdown and Maudie turned left instead of right to the usual swimming area. Gina wondered if she'd forgotten the way. 'Aren't we going to the Martello Tower, Maudie?' she enquired tactfully.

Maudie shook her head and smiled mysteriously. 'No, I've got a little surprise for you.'

Gina sat up, trying to stop herself imagining Daniel Napier, wearing nothing but that wry smile of his, waiting for her with a bag of doughnuts. *Stop it, Gina,* she told herself firmly. *That's not the kind of surprise Maudie means!*

Round the next corner the scene almost took her breath away. The empty beach stretched out towards a sea so calm and pellucid it seemed carved from mother-of-pearl. At the horizon it melted into a pale blue sky, with a line of grey lifting joyously into sunlit clouds which really did look like candy floss. As they parked she noticed a group of people, mainly women and mostly nearer Maudie's age than hers, standing near the water's edge. Gina recognized them as the group of swimmers they'd met the other day.

As they approached gingerly along the treacherous shingle a flowery bathing cap separated itself from the crowd.

'Maudie Tyler, well I'm blowed!' its owner greeted them.

'Hello Christine – meet my friend Gina Greenhills.'

'Hello, Gina. Welcome to the Southdown Sirens!'

Gina had to fight the impulse to laugh. As far as she remembered from her classical education, sirens were beautiful, dangerous creatures who lured sailors to their death with their mysterious songs. She had never felt like less like a beautiful, dangerous creature in her life.

'Welcome to the Sirens! We swim all year round, even Christmas Day. I hope you're going to join us?'

Gina felt a sudden surge of affection for Southdown and for this doughty group of ladies who ignored the elements and took to the water for the fun of it, even though in the freezing cold and rain, fun must seem the last thing on offer. 'Thank you, Christine, I'd be honoured,' she replied.

Laughing away her sense of failure at life and love, Gina ran gaily towards the pearly sea and threw herself in. To think she'd despised her hometown for most of her life and yet it was still capable of surprising her.

Moving back here, she decided, was the best decision she could have made.

Two hours later, her hair sticky and salty, and her skin tingling from the refreshing seawater, she found the real surprise waiting on her doorstep. Her daughters Sadie and Lisa.

'It's locked!' complained Sadie. 'Gran used to leave the key on a hook next to it.'

'Different times,' replied Gina. 'Besides, you'd stick me in a care home if I left the front door unlocked.'

'True,' conceded Sadie with a rueful smile. 'We would!'

'We brought something special for you,' interrupted Lisa.

'It's not a dog?' Gina replied nervously. 'Everyone keeps telling me I should get one. They're the number one husband replacement, apparently.'

'Mum,' said Sadie in her most holier-than-thou tone. 'Would we foist a dog on you without making sure you wanted one?'

Gina suppressed the response on the tip of her tongue,

which was a resounding *Yes*. A lot of people seemed to think dogs were the answer to everything.

Sadie stepped sideways to reveal the biggest bunch of flowers Gina had ever seen.

'They're wonderful!' breathed Gina.

And they were. And she loved that they'd chosen them themselves rather than trusting to the anonymity of Interflora.

'Well, let's see what you've done to the place!' insisted Sadie.

Gina opened the front door, pausing only to put the flowers into the sink to soak, none of her usual vases being big enough, and showed them round.

'It's amazing, Mum,' congratulated Sadie when they got back to the sitting room.

Gina, who'd expected at least one sarky comment smiled delightedly. 'You really like it?'

'It's so cosy that it reminds me how basic it was before.'

'Different times again.'

'Bags the top room,' insisted Sadie, sounding as if she were bagging the front seat of the car aged six.

'That's not fair,' Lisa responded. 'Just because you're older.'

Gina put her arms round them both. 'The sweet sound of bickering! How I've missed it! Now, what do you want to do? Go out and explore Southdown or stay in and have pizza and watch a silly movie?'

'Pizza!' they both chorused.

'And I choose the movie!' added Lisa.

Eve Beeston might be known as a force to be reckoned with, but few of her colleagues would recognize her as she sat in the shade of Embankment Gardens, surrounded by beds of English roses watching the peaceful scene unfolding. It was a Saturday and extremely hot. To Evie this meant slipping on a shift dress and hiding behind large sunglasses in case she was spotted by any legal colleagues to whom Saturdays were just another working day. To be honest, that was usually her too. But to most of the young people around her, perhaps without gardens or balconies of their own, it meant the freedom to strip off into shorts and bikinis. In fact, today the gardens looked more like a beach resort than a retreat for tourists and workers to sit and have their sandwiches among the birds, fitness addicts and the occasional rough sleeper. From her bench she could see Cleopatra's Needle, the London Eye, and even glimpse the statue of Robert Burns, though what he'd make of being surrounded by almost naked youth, who knew. Given his weakness for love, he might actually be quite happy. There was even a bit of history in the stone watergate which in Elizabethan times had been right on the water's edge, before the famous engineer Bazalgette had built the Victoria Embankment.

This was the London she loved, Evie told herself. Theatres and culture on your doorstep, young people who'd flocked here to make their fortunes, like modern Dick Whittingtons, and yet green spaces too. So what the hell was the matter with her? One face among all the happy revellers around her kept insistently making an appearance.

He was tall, bald and smiling. His attraction wasn't the obvious kind that hit you the moment he walked into a room. In fact, apart from his height, you might not notice him. He certainly wasn't Sexy Stu of the sixth form any longer. And though she wouldn't exactly kick him out of bed if she got the chance, it was, Evie decided, his personality that shone through. A gentleness spiked with a nice dry wit.

'Bloody man,' she shook her head as if trying to free herself of his persistent image, 'you've ruined London for me, and I could have sworn there was no man on God's earth who could do that.' She was a city girl through and through. Until now. But what the hell was she going to do about it?

Although she hadn't the slightest suspicion, the answer was about to present itself.

After she'd dropped the girls at the station next morning, Gina headed for the main shopping street in the old town, remembering she'd promised Maudie to pick up something to read.

Maudie didn't believe in internet shopping, preferring to patronize charity shops or Southdown's second-hand bookshop, which claimed to have more paperbacks than any other shop in the country. It was just possible to ease your way in the front door, past a literal maze of bookshelves, each packed so tightly it was a struggle to remove anything when you decided to buy it. Usually, Gina didn't make it much further than Crime Fiction, partly because it was nearest the door and also because it was her favourite genre. From Sherlock Holmes to Poirot and onwards via P.D. James and Ian Rankin to *Killing Eve*, she loved them all.

She had just picked up an old American thriller with a bloodthirsty cover of a young woman being strangled by a dangerous-looking middle-aged man when she realized someone was talking to her.

'She probably had it coming,' stated the voice, its owner concealed behind the next row of bookshelves. 'People who stick their noses in ought to be careful. You're friends with that interfering old lady who lives in the manor, aren't you?'

An unpleasant, angry face appeared who Gina instantly recognized as Mike from the car wash. 'She shouldn't be taking people in when she doesn't know anything about them. Who's to say her new friend isn't illegal? I would watch

215

it, if I were her. The authorities might be interested in that girl's case. You can tell her that with my compliments.' He threw down the book he was holding and left the shop, pursued by the ancient and extremely angry owner.

'Charming type,' commented the bookshop owner when he returned, so out of breath he looked as if he might expire himself. 'Are you OK? I wouldn't let him worry you – I've seen his type before. All mouth and no trousers. They get off on making people scared of them.'

Gina certainly hoped the owner was right.

Fourteen

Maudie and Jasmin were sitting on the terrace enjoying the sunshine when Gina got back. 'I was just showing Jasmin round my garden,' Maudie greeted her. 'The dear girl loves flowers, and of course the gardens have all gone in the part of the city where she lived. And they used to be so beautiful.' She stared into the herbaceous border, almost as if she were back there herself as a young woman, being shown round by the man who became her lover and whose child she bore.

Gina realized how difficult that would have been in those less liberal times.

'My favourites are these tall ones, what do you call them?' enquired Jasmin.

'Hollyhocks,' smiled Maudie. 'Though the churchwarden told me they ought to be "holyhocks" because the first seeds were brought back here from the Crusades.'

'Ah, yes. I remember you told me. They used to grow in the streets at home. And jasmine too. That's why I am called after it.' The familiar sadness Maudie was coming to recognize descended on the girl. 'And you talk of the Crusades!' she flashed back. 'Why do there always have to be wars?'

It was a question that had been asked so many times over the centuries. *Greed*, thought Maudie, *religion, nationalism, good and bad, and sometimes freedom,* but she made no attempt to answer. Instead she opened her arms and Jasmin buried herself in the old lady's powdery embrace.

It struck Gina that she had never seen Maudie so happy. Whether the connection with this girl was real or simply wishful thinking, it clearly filled a need in an old woman who had given away her baby and had no further children to replace the loss. A loss she had probably buried for the sake of self-preservation until she had seen Jasmin folding cloths as if they were made of precious silk.

It was just as well, she thought privately, that the ghastly Rosa and Ambrose had not noticed how well they were getting on. They had already been wary of Gina becoming close to Maudie, but what would they make of the deep feeling that was blossoming between a lonely old woman and the girl she had plucked from a car wash?

'Perhaps you could persuade Jasmin to join the Southdown Sirens?' laughed Gina in an attempt to lighten the mood.

'She wouldn't want to waste her time with a lot of old ladies, would you dear?' replied Maudie.

'I like old ladies,' insisted Jasmin. 'My grandmother was my best friend and ally. They are all gone now, apart from me, but it was my grandmother who made me leave. She said there were good people here, and now I know she was right.' She smiled at Maudie and Gina. 'To think I am here in this beautiful place.'

'Your grandmother sounds a wonderful woman, Jasmin,' acknowledged Maudie gently. 'I would like to have known her.'

'You remind me of her sometimes. You are very different, of course, but you share the capacity to love. That is a very great gift, not given to everyone. I think she would have recognized it in you. Can you wait a moment? I have something to make for you that she loved!'

Jasmin ran back towards the house past the roses and hollyhocks, the bright red geum and the nodding blue delphiniums of high summer. Soon they would be past their best with autumn beckoning.

'She's right, Maudie,' Gina agreed. 'It is a wonderful place.'

'More wonderful now that Jasmin is here,' she sighed. 'I wonder what she's making?'

Five minutes later the girl reappeared carrying a tray bearing a teapot and three cups. Beside it was a beautiful glass jar full of what looked like pink rose petals.

'It is called Zhourat Shamia,' she announced, putting the tray on the table beside them. 'People call it Sham. There are different recipes but my grandmother's is made of rose petals, mixed with chamomile, marshmallow flower, lemon verbena, with thyme and rosemary. I picked them all the other day from your garden. It was my grandmother's favourite drink and she showed me how to make it when I was a little girl, but you can also buy it in the souk or the big market at home. It is famous to soothe and calm. And my grandmother said it was very good for you if you cannot . . .' Comically, Jasmin pretended to squat with a pained expression on her face.

Laughing, Maudie took a sip. 'Delicious! I applaud your grandmother – especially about a cure for constipation!'

As they sat peacefully in the beauty of an English garden, Gina remembered Mike Marshall's voice threatening to make trouble for Jasmin. He was just a bully, she told herself. And he no longer had any power over Jasmin now she no longer worked for him.

* * *

219

'So, girls,' Stuart bravely asked his daughters when they came round to cook him supper, 'what did you think of Eve? Impressive, isn't she?'

'She's obviously very successful at what she does,' his older daughter Maddy replied carefully, avoiding the eye of her more hard-line younger sister, Jessica.

'And you're obviously very taken with her, Dad,' Jessica pointed out. 'Maybe a long-distance relationship suits you. You don't have to really commit if the other person's always sixty miles away. Everything feels special. You haven't got to cope with the dull every day.'

'I can't quite imagine her living here,' Stuart conceded. 'And I don't think I could face moving to London. Too anonymous. I like being somewhere where I know people and they know me.'

'I worry she's too tough for you,' persisted Jessica. 'You're such a softie. She'll have you for breakfast.'

'Isn't that rather a crude expression from a young person such as yourself?' replied her father. 'You mean she'll use me sexually?'

'*Dad!*' replied Jessica, shocked.

'And, after all, you had your pick of the casserole ladies,' Maddy changed the subject diplomatically.

'Who on earth are the casserole ladies?' he enquired.

'You know,' Maddy laughed. 'After you and Mum split, all the women who turned up with nice comforting casseroles, saying how awful it must be for you to be alone so here's a nice mac'n'cheese to pop in your oven.'

'You mean they weren't genuine?' enquired Stuart, puzzled.

'Da-ad!' chorused both his daughters spontaneously.

'Oh God, men are such innocents,' shrugged Jessica, with the accrued wisdom of her twenty-nine years. 'They were moving in on an attractive, suddenly-single man.'

'But Wendy next door wouldn't have done that,' protested Stuart. 'She was Mum's best friend!'

Maddy and Jessica exchanged knowing looks. 'Wanna bet? This Eve's certainly a lot brighter than they were, but hasn't it occurred to you that maybe she's *too* successful? I mean, heaven knows what she earns! She could probably buy your agency and still have change left over for a few tropical holidays!'

Stuart sipped his glass of beer. He'd never been in a relationship quite this complicated. Perhaps he was too much of an innocent, as Jess had said, to get more involved with Eve. And anyway, back in London she was probably feeling much the same thing.

In fact, Stuart couldn't have been more wrong. What Evie was actually asking herself was why, after all these years of distrusting men, she thought Stuart was any different. But somehow she did. Maybe it was because he hadn't rushed straight into another relationship when his wife left, as most men would have done. Perhaps it was seeing how well he got on with his daughters. Or even the look in his eyes. Smiling but direct. A genuine warmth. He was a kind man, and frankly she could do with a bit of that. She had become too cynical over the years. And she rather liked his bald head. One of her favourite judges, a good man like Stuart, had the habit of removing his full-bottomed wig at pivotal moments during cases he was hearing and polishing his head with a cloth. In fact, several times she had been tempted to drop a kiss on it. Stuart's, not the judge's, of course . . .

She was interrupted from her musings by a phone call from Gina.

'Hello, stranger,' Evie greeted her. 'Can't tell you how I'm missing you! I know, you're calling to say that life in

Southdown is ineffably dull and you've decided to move back to the old smoke!'

Gina giggled. 'Afraid not. Actually, it's lovely here. I'm sitting in a cafe and I can see a line of people from old ladies to school kids wending their way down to the beach. It's another glorious day in this glorious summer.'

'Stop!' Evie commanded. 'It's bad enough not having you here without hearing what a wonderful new life you're having!' She paused. 'Are you though?'

'It's very pleasant. But nothing's perfect. Which is why I'm ringing you. That bully Mike's said something about reporting Jasmin to the authorities. And I thought, ah ha, my best friend's a lawyer – so I'm ringing you. The thing is, Evie, Jasmin's so happy here and so is Maudie.'

'You really care about these people, don't you?' Evie enquired.

'Yes. Maybe it's the small-town thing. You get involved with other people's problems. No man is an island and all that.'

'I'm perfectly happy being an island,' Evie replied. 'In fact I've always prided myself on it. Besides, I'm not an immigration lawyer. I know fuck all about immigration.'

As she said it, the thought of Stuart's feisty daughter, burning with white-hot enthusiasm for good causes, asking whether she ever felt the need to use her skills to help the world, made an unwelcome return like a wasp in a summer tea garden. Faced with the unfamiliar sensation of guilt, she almost found herself offering to get involved.

Fortunately Gina's next revelation stopped her in her tracks.

'Evie . . . Mark turned up yesterday.'

'Mark? Your about to be ex-husband?'

'The very one,' Gina tried to joke but found the memory too painful.

'What did he want?

'To see where the land lay. The new woman's being tough with him and he wanted to find out if I was a soft alternative.'

'I hope you made him see you weren't.'

'I've got hard apparently. Sad, isn't it?'

'Absolutely bloody brilliant,' congratulated Evie. 'And about time. So you sent him packing?'

'I told him I only wanted to communicate through the lawyers.'

'Good for you. His is so expensive you won't be hearing much.'

Gina smiled, then remembered what had happened next. 'The really annoying thing was, Daniel Napier arrived with a bag of doughnuts while he was there.'

'And you think he got the wrong impression?'

'Mark made sure he did.'

'He really is a charmer. Well, you'll have to find a way of disabusing him, won't you?'

After Gina rang off Evie decided to go into her office. It would be empty on a Sunday. She made a coffee, opened her laptop and searched for the legal rules to help Jasmin.

It was going to be a long afternoon.

'It's high time we started planning the Grand Opening of Desperate Dan's. Assuming you want to make a big splash, that is.' Rebecca perched on the bar stool opposite Daniel in the Jolly Sailor. 'Sorry,' she added, with a provocative smile, 'no pun intended.'

She got out her phone and began to make a list. 'You'll need the bigwigs at the council, and from Harpers of course,' Rebecca insisted, 'plus the local paper and radio, but I'm pretty sure this could make a national story, certainly on social media. You're doing something important here, Daniel.'

Daniel was conscious of mixed feelings at how quickly she had begun to take over. It might be quite useful if she helped organize the opening, leaving him to sort out the remaining practical issues, but his instinct was to do it quietly and not make a big fuss. 'Look, Rebecca, I'm sorry to disappoint you, but I really don't want this to turn into some media circus. Mr Marshall's going to be unhappy enough as it is, without shoving it down his throat with some tactless newspaper head-lines. Let's keep it low-key, shall we? We'll need to invite all the donors, large and small. We could set up a tent next to the coffee van and have all the drinks handed out from there. And I suppose we'd better get some Southdown celebrity to declare it open, if such a person exists.' He thought for a moment, then produced that surprisingly boyish grin. 'I know – how about Maudie Tyler, the old lady from Rookery Manor? Everyone knows her and she'll certainly look the part.'

At the next table Ruthie's husband Robin was eavesdrop-ping on their conversation with interest, both for the news that the car wash would soon be opening and even more that the pushy blonde from the managing agents was seriously moving in on Daniel Napier. Pity. He was pretty sure that Ruthie's mate Gina really liked the man. Ruthie had been watching the progress of the relationship with glee, delighted that Gina would not only be living here but had fallen for someone local to seal the deal. In fact she'd been going round grinning about it for days.

Robin took a long look at this man who seemed to have two attractive women competing for him. It certainly wasn't his fashion sense, unless double denim was an unexpected aphrodisiac. It might be his hair, which was outrageously luxuriant. Or his habit of looking at you directly, then smiling as he glanced away, as if he'd found you charming and funny. Yes, he could see the appeal and unconsciously found himself rooting for Gina. But where was she? Ruthie had better get her back on the scene or this Rebecca would get her claws in too deep to let go. And wasn't it rather unfortunate to suggest the one person to open it who would most annoy Mike Marshall?

Stuart Nixon had to admit to himself that he had never felt so uncertain in his life. Over the years he'd had relationships with a number of women but no one had taken his world and shaken it like a snowstorm paperweight as Eve Beeston had done.

But if there was one thing he had learned about her, it was that she was a committed city girl. Her career required her to be. The sense of community offered by a small town might appeal to him, but to her it would be suffocating. He had thought and thought about this and come to no conclusion. Until this week when an email had arrived from an old colleague announcing that an estate agency in Croydon was looking for a new partner. A large and busy suburb on the outskirts of London wasn't exactly his dream but it was only twenty minutes from the centre and from Evie.

He decided to at least go and see it. He certainly wouldn't mention anything to his daughters. This was just an exploratory trip. He might well hate Croydon, or the other partners in the agency.

Stuart climbed into his open-topped BMW and smiled, remembering Evie's comment that you shouldn't trust a professional with an expensive car as it probably meant they'd overcharge you. What an outrageous girl she was. And then the memory of teaching her to paddleboard, his arms holding hers, his skin on her skin, flooded out any other memory.

Maddy and Jessica had come along moments later and he'd had to pretend everything was normal. But would it ever be normal again?

After an hour's drive he emerged from an underpass into a different world. Office block after office block, a wall of glass that seemed to go on for miles, making him think of the vast urban sprawl of New York, but without the sense of glamour and excitement. These nondescript suburbs held no appeal for him at all.

As he sat in traffic, glad that he'd allowed plenty of time to get to his meeting, his gaze was attracted by an enormous white structure with a long queue outside. As he looked up, wondering what it was, a smartly dressed woman in a sculptured black suit and high heels emerged. To his delight and amazement, he realized it was Evie.

She saw him at the same time and leaned down to the level of his open window. 'Not stalking me by any chance, are you? That's a crime, you know.'

As with her little dig about his expensive car, she undercut the words with a mischievous grin.

'As a matter of fact, I'm here for a meeting,' Stuart replied.

'Have you got time to give me a lift to the station? It'll only take five minutes.'

She began to fold her long legs into the passenger side before he had the chance to refuse.

'What brings you to the joys of commuterland?' enquired Stuart. 'I wouldn't have thought it was your patch.'

'Jasmin,' she announced gaily. 'That delightful building,' she indicated the enormous white structure that had caught Stuart's eye 'is where all the decisions are made as to whether people can stay or go. I've been talking to a charming inspector and he's finally agreed to see her. It's been very hard work

226

persuading him, so I'm exceptionally glad and relieved. What did you say your meeting was about?'

'A business opportunity. A firm here needs a new partner.'

'But wouldn't that mean moving here from Southdown?' she asked incredulously. 'I thought you loved it there, where every third person says "Morning Stu"?'

'I couldn't live in London,' he replied bluntly, his eyes on hers, 'but this is near enough.'

'But why would you want to?'

'Why do you think?' he replied, opening her door. 'You'd better run. I'm already late.'

Evie climbed out of the car and watched as he did a U-turn and drove off, her breath suspended in her throat. Could he possibly mean what she thought he meant?

Fifteen

'Gina darling, can I come and stay for a couple of nights?'

'Evie!' Gina almost squeaked. 'Of course you can. I can't think of anything nicer. I knew you'd feel the pull of the old hometown again soon!'

'Well, it's less the old hometown and more that I need to take Jasmin and her passport to see a lovely Home Office inspector in Croydon.'

Gina restrained herself from asking if that was the only reason for her friend's sudden visit. 'Evie, that's so kind of you. I thought you said you didn't do that kind of law.'

'I'm making an exception,' announced Evie. 'It took a bit of a prod from the younger generation but I think I've mastered basic principles. Tell you what, though: give me divorce any day! You know where you are with that.' Realizing this might not be the most tactful observation, she added: 'Any more developments with Mark? I haven't heard anything, but as far as I know it's all progressing fine.'

'No, nothing since his sudden appearance,' Evie replied. 'I assume he's gone back to the dominatrix, this woman who can make him do whatever he says. I never could, that's for sure. I wonder if she has an actual whip to crack. So when will I see you?'

'Tomorrow morning,' Evie replied. 'I'm sorry it's such short notice, but appointments with inspectors are like hens' teeth! It's a miracle we've got one so soon. Don't bother to meet me – I'll grab a cab.'

Next day, Gina had barely finished putting welcome flowers next to the bed in the loft conversion when the bell rang and Evie stood on the doorstep with a bottle of fizz and an enormous bunch of flowers.

'Ooh,' Gina greeted her with a hug and took the flowers. 'I won't say you shouldn't have bothered because I'm extremely glad you did. Here, I'll take your case. Now come and see where you're sleeping.' She led her up the new stairs to the bedroom at the top of the house.

'It's sensational,' asserted Evie, staring out at the wonderful views. 'But I thought this was going to be your room? You wouldn't sleep in your parents' room for love or money.'

'That's what I thought,' Gina admitted, a shade embarrassed, 'but I was wrong. I'm really enjoying it.' She didn't want to explain the sudden emotional release she'd felt on moving in, because she thought it might sound strange, but she was thrilled the feeling had lasted. In her brain she called it Southdown syndrome – and it had nothing to do with sympathizing with your captors. Evie would laugh at her if she admitted it, but living here was making her happy. Now that she'd virtually finished the valuation she was free to visit auction houses or antiques markets to replenish Whitehall Valuations' stock, or take an hour or two off to do what she wanted. She'd spent yesterday happily painting a crappy old chest of drawers the colour of a pigeon's breast, and after that she'd changed the handles for some hip non-matching ones. The result made her happy every time she passed it.

They drove up to Rookery Manor together to talk to Jasmin. The girl's reaction was a humbling one.

'No! I won't go!' Jasmin insisted desperately when Evie told her about the meeting. 'How do I know if I go to this head-quarters of officials I'll ever be seen again?' she sobbed. 'I don't trust officials. Please Eve, I don't want to go!'

'Jasmin, this is England,' Evie gently reassured. 'People don't just disappear. That's why your grandmother wanted you to come here, remember?'

Jasmin looked a little comforted but remained convinced she would be going into the lion's den.

'Besides, I'll be with you all the time.'

Jasmin flung herself into Evie's arms. 'Oh, that's all right then! I'll be safe with you.'

Evie surprised herself with a sudden wave of tenderness for the girl. There was so much Jasmin had kept to herself since she'd been here and yet a remark like that had such a wealth of meaning in it.

'So, how have you been getting on at the manor?' Evie asked her, deciding it would be best to change the subject to some-thing easier till Jasmin felt better.

The answer was in her seraphic smile. 'I love it! Maudie and I have been preparing the rooms for the guests she wants to invite. Paying guests! Of course it is complicated looking into insurance and things, especially as Maudie doesn't believe in it! But she is sure this is the best idea we can think of to cover the costs of running such a big house.' She turned towards Evie with a serious expression. 'Maudie, she does not want to move to a comfortable flat with a concierge as those people keep pressing her to! She wants to stay here with Mr and Mrs B looking after her, but they have to be paid.'

The comment prodded Gina's conscience. She had completed the valuation of the entire contents of the manor but had not yet decided when would be the best time to present her findings to Maudie and Lucy. The considerable and surprising value of her belongings would present a problem for Maudie because Rosa and Ambrose would no doubt insist that she insure them for their full value, and then there'd be the installation of alarms, window locks and all the other paraphernalia necessary to guard valuable possessions. Maudie would loathe it, and there was no way she could afford the outlay without selling off some of her most precious objects. And then there was the question of the missing items.

The valuation, she suspected, was a bomb waiting to go off.

Maudie arrived in the room dressed in an elaborate kimono, and made a fuss of embracing them both.

'Come on, Jasmin,' Evie suggested. 'Let's you and me go up to your room where it's nice and quiet and have a chat about the meeting.'

Jasmin looked anxiously at Maudie. 'But will you be needing me, do you think, Maudie?'

'Of course not, dear. It's far more important that you and Evie talk about your meeting. She's a big-time lawyer, you know. We're very lucky to have her.'

'But how will I pay her?' blurted Jasmin, looking stricken, like some young doe that scented the hunter.

Maudie's pink cheeks, which would have graced a woman forty years younger, glowed, and her eyes took on their usual characteristic twinkle. 'I think Eve is eager to help mankind,' she teased. 'Aren't you dear?'

Evie let out a booming laugh. 'Well, let's hope mankind appreciates it! Now you'd better change into some smart clothes, Jasmin. Do you have anything black? That always seems to work.'

At this, Jasmin looked nervous again, but Gina took her arm and they went up to her room where they found a pair of black slacks and a white T-shirt. There was a knock on the door and Maudie appeared with a simple black blazer probably designed by Chanel herself, knowing Maudie.

'I'll get the car and drop you and Evie off to catch the train,' offered Gina, deciding that would be less scary for Jasmin than going in a taxi.

At Southdown station she waved them both goodbye, hoping passionately for a positive outcome.

Gina had been wrong in thinking that Rosa and Ambrose hadn't noticed Maudie's obvious delight in Jasmin's company.

'You were right about Maudie skipping round like a spring lamb since that girl came on the scene,' Rosa commented bitterly.

'Before that Greenhills woman arrived, the old girl was seriously considering the purpose-built flat on the seafront I mentioned,' seconded Ambrose. 'And what's happened to the bloody valuation of the house contents? She's probably on the beach again!' His voice rose with a brooding resentment, as if Gina were to blame for all their ills, real or imagined. 'I don't think we should waste any more time. Let's go and demand she bloody well produces it!'

'Quite right! Interfering bloody woman,' Rosa's tone endorsed her husband's intense dislike. 'And then we can finally get rid of her!'

* * *

On her return from dropping Evie and Jasmin at the station, Gina found the Winstanleys' mud-caked Honda Civic carelessly parked in the driveway. She could hear the raised voices from halfway up the drive. Then Mrs B scuttled out, looking even more like a robin than ever, only this time it was an angry robin defending its nest against dangerous predators.

'It's that Mr and Mrs Winstanley again,' she whispered loudly. 'They never leave poor Mrs Tyler alone! This time it's you they've got in their sights, dear. That's why I came out to warn you. On the warpath, they are. Saying everyone takes advantage of her – you, Jasmin, probably me and Mr B and all! Where's this famous valuation you were hired to produce, they want to know. They're saying they knew you weren't up to it and were probably hoping no one would ask now that you've moved out. What a pair of slimy slugs, nibbling away at good things until they ruin them! You go up there, Gina dear, and sort them out!'

'Good morning, everyone,' Gina adopted the tone of a brisk district nurse as she greeted Maudie, Rosa and Ambrose, all gathered in the panelled drawing room, drinking tea, as the British always do in a crisis.

'Gina, dear, I'm glad you're here,' Maudie greeted her. Without Jasmin at her side she seemed suddenly older and more vulnerable. Gina could have happily killed this pair for taking advantage of that and picking a fight.

'We both feel Mrs Tyler is being exploited,' began Ambrose officiously, using his military bearing to try and intimidate Gina. 'This girl Jasmin . . . I mean, what exactly do we know about her?'

'I understand you also want to hear the valuation I have been working on. Well, of course my client is actually Lucy and, though I would be perfectly happy to reveal the valuation, I do feel she needs to be consulted first.'

'Your client, indeed!' snapped Rosa. 'As I've said before, how dare Lucy bring in someone from outside without consulting us?'

'Sorry, I'm confused here,' Gina replied, being careful to keep her tone neutral. 'Isn't it a bit late in the day for that comment? I thought you wanted to hear what the manor's antiques were worth?'

'Of course we do,' Rosa announced piously. 'For Maudie's sake. And who is behind these not inconsiderable thefts? Indeed, Ambrose and I have discussed whether, despite my very natural distaste for the idea, since you appear to have got nowhere, it might be time to involve the police.'

'Of course, if Mrs Tyler agrees,' Gina replied, itching to slap the woman.

'But I do not agree,' insisted Maudie loudly and with spirit, recovering herself in the face of their unpleasant officiousness. 'I do not choose to become the object of police and press interest, like some meretricious storyline in *Downton Abbey*! I can see it now. "Mystery at the Manor: who is to blame for serial burglaries?" If Lucy agrees, I will however agree to including you all in hearing the valuation. Now, take yourselves off, please, before I change my mind.'

As Rosa and Ambrose headed back down the drive, Gina could hear a distinct snort from the direction of the kitchen, and concluded that Mrs B had been quietly eavesdropping, as usual.

'Sometimes I don't think I can bear to leave the Manor to that pair!' Maudie poured herself another cup of tea. As she turned, Gina was shocked at the sight of Maudie's face, suddenly as old and lined as an African mask. 'Gina, what if it came out after all this time that it was me who took the missing items?'

Gina sat down next to her. 'Do you think we should tell Lucy the truth? That you've kept the missing things to help Jasmin? My instinct is she's trustworthy and would probably understand.'

'I wish Lucy wanted to live here. It's important to me that the heritage goes on.'

Gina pictured Lucy's pared-down penthouse with its few carefully chosen objects, its air of being almost a gallery of modern art. She glanced around at Maudie's wildly over-crowded sitting room, where china figurines competed with gilded candlesticks, jade ornaments and scent bottles adorned with flowers and birds were on every surface and elaborate fans of French pastoral scenes, Japanned coffee pots and a silver and mother-of-pearl loving cup crowded out every surface, while beyond them every inch of wall was packed with yet another gilt-framed painting.

Gina took her hand and smiled. 'To be honest, Maudie, I don't think there's much chance of that.'

There was still no sign of Evie's return, so Gina left her a note that she was going for a quick swim near the Martello Tower. The encounter with Rosa and Ambrose had left her so wound up that she desperately needed half an hour of peace.

She took the car and headed out into the blazing heat of the best English summer anyone could remember for years. It would have to change some time, but not before they enjoyed a week or two more of glorious sunshine according to the weatherman. The corn in the fields behind them stood out intensely yellow against the deep blue of the sky almost like a child's drawing.

Gina was grateful to find what seemed to be the last space in a long snake of parked cars opposite the beach. Resisting the lure of a salted caramel cone as she walked past the ice-cream shack, she caught sight of Ruthie wearing what her mother would have called a muumuu, a cross between a dress and a skirt, in a dazzling red, yellow and blue fabric.

'Gina!' Ruthie greeted her gaily. 'Just the person I wanted to see. Are you going for a swim? Mind if I come?'

Gina, who had been looking forward to a head-clearing session lying on her back looking up at the sky, recognized *force majeure* when she saw it, and smiled her agreement.

Ruthie turned out to have her costume conveniently underneath the muumuu. 'They're brilliant for putting on your cozzie,' Ruthie confided. 'Like wearing your own changing tent!'

A crueller critic might have replied that that was exactly what Ruthie looked like. Gina glanced round at the beach. Everyone was watching the sea so she quickly slipped off her silk blouse and replaced it with a bikini top.

'Wow!' commented Ruthie in a piercing tone. 'What great tits you've got!'

Gina dipped down to remove her pants from under her towel and slipped on her bikini bottom. 'And don't tell me I've got a great bum!' she giggled.

'Bums are tougher,' replied Ruthie giving the matter some serious thought. 'They're all Kim Kardashian-shaped these days. Even I might be in the running!'

They headed for the water, which was deep and clear as gin. 'I love high tide,' announced Gina. 'And the water's just the right temperature; cool rather than warm. Cool makes you feel cleaner.'

'So how are you finding it now you've actually moved in?' enquired Ruthie. 'Have you changed the house much?'

After making the curtains, there hadn't been much to do except to paint the bedroom her favourite restful green and put up her most treasured paintings. To her delight, she'd even found some cushions in town that perfectly coordinated with the colours she'd chosen.

'Loving it,' replied Gina. That wonderful feeling of security the night she changed to her parents' room had lasted and was still growing. 'I'm amazed at how much of my old life I can carry on with here and yet go to the beach as well! If everyone's feeling like me, no one will need to go to cities again!'

'And what about Daniel Napier? How does he fit into your new life?'

Gina coughed and took in a mouthful of seawater. Fortunately, they were within their depth, and Ruthie began to bang her heartily on the back.

'The thing is, Robin overheard something in the pub you ought to know.'

'Robin always seems to be overhearing things in pubs,' Gina replied with an uncharacteristic frostiness. She wasn't sure she was ready for another emotional revelation so soon after having to deal with Rosa and Ambrose.

'It's that pushy woman Rebecca Boyd. Blonde hair, long legs, your average nightmare. Robin says she was making a real bid for Daniel, and if Robin noticed it, you can bet it was about as subtle as a sledgehammer.'

'Look, Ruthie, it's very kind of you both to look out for me, but I think it's too soon for any relationship. After all, I'm not even divorced yet.'

'You're scared!' accused Ruthie.

'Terrified!' admitted Gina.

Ruthie gave her a damp hug. 'It's not surprising. You've been badly hurt. But Daniel's one of the good ones. Don't let Rebecca bloody Boyd carry him off like some award for effective management just because you're not sure you're ready for a relationship! She's got a shocking reputation for pinching other people's men. By the time you *are* ready he'll have been frogmarched down the aisle by Ms bloody Boyd, you can take it from me! So what are you going to do about it?'

'I'll have a think,' agreed Gina.

'Not good enough,' insisted Ruthie. 'You should be marshalling your assets!'

By now they had made their way back to the beach and started to get dressed. 'And may I say,' Ruthie continued relentlessly, 'Rebecca Boyd may have legs up to her armpits, but you have the best tits in Southdown, and all you do is hide them under upmarket bin liners.' She plucked at Gina's silk top derisively.

'Excuse me,' argued Gina, 'but that bin liner cost me a hundred quid.'

'Forget about the price. I'll take you shopping and find you something that makes the most of your assets!'

Grateful to get away from the tsunami that was Ruthie, Gina opened her front door and felt the familiar leap of the spirits that told her she was home. She threw down her swimming bag in the cosily untidy hall and went to see what there was in the fridge to cook for supper. Two slices of fresh salmon beamed up at her, ready for the salmon teriyaki she'd planned if Evie was staying. She glanced at her watch, anxious that it was getting late and there was still no sign of Evie, and no communication to explain the delay.

She had just poured herself an anxiety-reducing glass of wine when the doorbell went.

Evie stood outside, her arm round Jasmin, who was looking

surprisingly cheerful for someone who had spent the afternoon in a stuffy office with a Home Office inspector.

'We got it!' Evie announced joyfully. 'Permission to stay in the UK. Woop woop! The stamp on her passport will follow!' She proceeded to dance round the kitchen in a passable imitation of the can-can.

'Jasmin, that's fantastic news!' cried Gina. 'This calls for fizz!'

She searched in the fridge for the bottle of top-notch Cava she'd been keeping for an appropriate occasion. Champagne was beyond her everyday budget and, in Gina's view, Cava was far more delicious than its more popular sister, Prosecco.

'Unless you'd like a soft drink?' she asked, remembering Jasmin's background.

Jasmin laughed. 'No thanks. Do as the natives do, my grandmother told me.' They clinked glasses.

'To Jasmin's victory over red tape and prejudice!' Evie raised her glass.

'And to your wonderful skill in persuading them!' seconded Jasmin. 'Every time the man suggested a problem, Eve already had the answer! I don't think he'd come across anyone like her before. She was wonderful! I can't thank her enough.'

Gina smiled at the fate of some junior official finding himself face to face with the ball of energy that was her best friend.

'It was interesting to practise such different law,' Evie admitted. 'Though I'm not sure I'd want to do it full-time. Now, make sure you keep this somewhere very safe.'

Jasmin stopped dancing and grasped the passport she was holding out, then suddenly her face crumpled.

'What's the matter?' Evie asked. 'Are you feeling all right?'

'It was getting my passport back – it reminded me. You

know that nice Mr Napier is trying to help the workers at Mad Mike's to get their permissions to stay. The trouble is, Mr Marshall took their passports and claims he can't find them and, without passports, Daniel says there's nothing he can do. The night I went to ask for my passport, Mr Marshall put his hands on me . . .' She closed her eyes, looking as if the memory made her physically ill. 'He was laughing and saying he kept the passports in a place where no one would think of looking. I think he had been drinking, because he kept mumbling about smuggling being an honourable profession.'

'Not much strikes me as honourable about that man,' said Gina.

'No, but he kept going on about being a gentleman. It was really weird.'

'My dear girl,' Evie put an arm round her protectively. 'For the moment, with the atmosphere so flammable, I wouldn't go round telling anyone about this.'

'But what about their passports?' Jasmin's fists balled subconsciously. 'They are powerless without them!'

Gina and Ruthie weren't the only people who'd given in to the lure of the sunshine on a weekday when they would usually be working.

Stuart Nixon was walking down one of the more colourful streets in Brighton with his daughters Jessica and Maddy on a rare day off. They had already been passed by a juggler, a punk couple with pink Mohicans who looked as if they had walked straight out of the Seventies, a mime artist in whiteface dressed as Marcel Marceau, and a giggling bunch of nouveau flower children. 'I love this place!' Stuart announced. 'It's like walking back into my misspent youth.'

'I can't imagine you misbehaving!' teased Jessica.

'That's exactly my problem,' he replied. 'Actually, I was quite a looker. You won't believe it, but I was called Sexy Stu. They said I looked like John Travolta in *Saturday Night Fever!*'

His daughters both fell about laughing, provoking Stuart to take immediate action. Before they could stop him, he transformed himself into the white-suited star and discoed down the street so convincingly that the juggler, mime artist and Mohicans all started to laugh and spontaneously clap his performance.

'Dad,' Maddy appeared from behind a corporation flower bed. 'I didn't know you could disco!'

'You aren't the only ones who've been young, you know,' he laughed as the small crowd started to disperse. 'I haven't always been the pillar of Southdown's business community you see before you!'

'Wow, Dad!' endorsed Jessica. 'No wonder people remember you. Hot on the dancefloor, or what?'

'It was only school disco stuff,' he sighed, shepherding them towards the shelter of a nearby brasserie. 'And it was a long time ago. Let's have some lunch. I need a little sit-down.'

'Your fans'll be disappointed,' Jess pointed to the two old ladies on a bench who were still clapping.

'When you've got it, you've got it, Dad!' said Maddy, taking his arm.

'Let's have some wine,' announced Stuart as they sat down. 'And a big glass of water after that!'

They were enthusiastically attacking their main courses when Stuart took a large sip of his wine and enquired, in a deliberately casual tone, how they would feel if he spent some of his week in Croydon? 'There's an estate agency opening specializing in commercial property and I've been asked if I'd like to join. So I thought I'd run it by you.'

'But why the hell would you want to go to Croydon?' asked Maddy, wrinkling her nose. 'It's nothing but office blocks and shopping malls. Its chief recommendation is that it's quite near Central London. Most people view it as being sent to Siberia!'

'Hang on,' Jessica intervened with the terrifying perceptiveness one's children occasionally possess. 'This is about *her*, isn't it? She's the type who won't leave London, so little lapdog here is going to follow her at a safe distance!'

'I thought I was John Travolta,' protested Stuart, laughter in his voice.

'She won't appreciate it, Dad,' Jessica continued relentlessly. 'It reminds me of that awful bit in *Far from the Madding Crowd* when dull but faithful Gabriel Oak announces to beautiful Bathsheba: "At home by the fire, whenever I look up, there you will be. And whenever you look up, there will I be." That man's practically a stalker!'

'That's supposed to be one of the most romantic scenes in English Literature!' protested Maddy. 'He really loved her. When I fall in love, I'd want the man to be just like that.'

'The difference between my daughters in a nutshell!' Stuart commented affectionately. 'One wants independence at all costs. The other likes the idea of having a man to protect her. What's a mere male to do?'

'Not move to Croydon!' Jessica dipped down and kissed him on the top of his bald head. 'Anyway I'm right,' she insisted. 'Your Eve's like Bathsheba, always wanting to be smarter than the men. And they're both quite selfish. I can't see her changing any time soon.'

'Bathsheba did,' insisted Maddy, in a rare challenge to her feisty sister.

'Eve won't,' stated Jessica. 'I've seen the type before.'

And as the crème brûlée with passion fruit coulis arrived, Stuart was able to reassure himself that the best course was probably to steer somewhere between the opposing opinions of his two beloved daughters.

Sixteen

Once she was home, her London life swallowed Evie up like a hungry giant spying a tasty morsel. She knew that if she were to count the number of emails and messages that waited for her attention, she might be tempted to leap aboard the next train back to Southdown.

Divorce was always in demand, and it was no surprise to Evie that the vast majority of her clients were women. And she happened to believe passionately in getting the best deal for them. She smiled at the memory of Stuart saying he did the same when it came to the family home being sold. He was right: divorce was easier, though obviously just as painful, for the rich, but if the only asset you possessed was the family home, the equation was much more difficult.

She glanced out of her window at the peaceful gardens outside their office, such a contrast to the super-charged atmosphere inside. At least, given the private nature of their work, they had their own space and hadn't – like so many offices – gone over to open-plan and the nightmare of hot-desking. Evie could shut her door and say what she wanted without being overheard. Two pigeons were perched on her windowsill. The male was cooing loudly, ruffling up his neck and spreading out his tail before attempting to jump on the disinterested female.

'I know your game, mate,' commented Evie as her assistant announced the new client who had come to unfold the agonizing story of how she had ended up in a divorce lawyer's office.

The supreme irony was that though each client thought their story belonged absolutely and uniquely to them, Evie could practically recite it to them before they even opened their mouths.

Such was the predictable nature of human behaviour.

And though she might seem impenetrably efficient, Evie cared deeply about her clients and would listen sympathetically to their story, then fight for them with every legal instrument she could lay her hands on.

As her assistant knocked on the door and began to usher in a distressed-looking woman, for almost the first time she could recall, Evie had to will herself to devote her entire attention to her client.

Gina woke up from her dream and found she was sweating profusely. Someone had been banging on the front door and she'd known it was Mark and that she shouldn't let him in, and yet despite everything in her deep subconscious, she'd run downstairs and there he was on the doorstep telling her it was all a terrible mistake.

She sat up, furious with herself. Had she learned nothing? She snapped on the radio to find Glen Campbell singing 'Wichita Lineman', one of the most haunting songs ever written, about hearing his beloved's voice singing in the wires, and how he would want her for all time.

If the radio hadn't been wired in she would have thrown it against the wall. And then she began to laugh. OK, there were times when life seemed to conspire against you, but look at the sun shining in the sky, and here she was starting a new life at her age. 'Gina Greenhills,' she decided to make up her own mantra, 'you are not a perfect and unique soul, you're quite imperfect, but then so are most people. You're doing your bloody best in a horrible situation, and for that you deserve to feel pretty bloody proud. And you've got a lot to do today, so be grateful for that, for in the end we aren't saved by yoga, or even mindfulness, but by stuff we have to get up and do. So get up and do it!'

Tomorrow she was due to present her valuation to the family. It struck her that it might be helpful to get some insurance quotes as well. If they were high, Maudie might decide to use that as her excuse for blithely going on with life as she always had done. It struck her that it might be as well to arm Maudie with a rough valuation for the manor itself, and that Stuart Nixon would be the perfect person to provide it. Acting on the impulse, she made an appointment with his office to drop in later and talk to him.

Most of the morning was taken up with talking to specialist insurance brokers who had experience in dealing with historic buildings like the twelfth-century manor house.

By the time she'd done that she felt she deserved a break and decided to walk into town. After her hard work it was a shock to remember that in high summer Southdown was a holiday resort full of families vying for space on the crowded beach and old ladies in hats sitting in the bus shelters across the road, nursing cups of tea and gossiping. It might not have the sophistication of St Tropez or Marbella, but it certainly had its unique cocktail of sunshine (mostly), friendly chatter, the scent of hot dogs, takeaway pints in plastic glasses and overweight men with their tops off.

Gina was smiling at how lucky she was as she passed Giovanni's Italian restaurant and glimpsed Daniel Napier, wearing a suit instead of his usual denim, in the window table with Rebecca Boyd. They were deep in discussion with a laptop open in front of them. The sudden fear that they might be looking at houses to buy together flashed into her mind. How could she convince Daniel that he was the one she was really interested in?

She was so preoccupied with the idea that she stepped into the road without looking and a delivery scooter with an L-plate swerved so abruptly to avoid her that both of them ended up falling. The next thing she knew, Daniel was standing over her, his face clouded with concern, while the young driver, who had picked himself up, vociferously complained that it wasn't his fault and that the pizzas he was delivering were all ruined. Daniel quickly handed the youth some cash and he drove happily off while Gina got to her feet with Daniel's help.

'Are you all right?' he asked anxiously.

'Yes, I'm fine.' Gina brushed the dirt off her dress. 'The only thing that's injured is my pride. It was entirely my fault.'

'I know,' he grinned. 'I saw the whole thing.'

'I was preoccupied about something.' She smiled up at him, hoping that mind-reading was one of his numerous skills.

'Are you sure you're OK? I could run you down to A&E.'

Gina was on the point of saying, no, she was absolutely fine, when it struck her that it could be the perfect opportunity to explain about Mark. 'I think I'm OK, but I suppose it might be wise to check for concussion. I did rather whack my head on the pavement.' Gina crossed her fingers as she offered this outrageous lie.

'Here, sit on this wall,' he instructed her gently. 'I'll only be a moment.'

She pretended not to watch as he went back to the restaurant to pacify the furious-looking Rebecca, who was clearly uttering the words 'Silly woman'.

'You and Rebecca looked very busy,' she commented as they set off in his car, dreading any answer that included the words house-hunting.

'It sounds ridiculous, but it's the launch of the car wash,' he shrugged, looking faintly embarrassed. 'We've got a lot of small investors and I wanted to find a way of thanking them and making them feel involved. I did think of giving them all a free car wash, but Rebecca insists that because we've had council backing as well, we need to make a big show of thanking the bigwigs and the Harpers hotshots. So we're hiring a marquee and throwing a party in the car park.'

Gina could just hear Rebecca's voice selling him all this and wanted to grab that scooter and run her over.

'Thanks for paying that young man. How much was it?' She reached for her bag.

'Really, don't worry. I was just so relieved you were all right.'

'And the boy? Was he OK too?'

'Yes. I think he was nervous the police might get involved, so he was only too happy to scoot off.'

They were nearing the hospital, which meant it was now or never to explain about Mark.

'Daniel, the other day, when you came round—' she began.

'With the embarrassing doughnuts,' Daniel cut in with a shy smile that took her right back to their dancing school days and made her want to grab the wheel and kiss him on the spot.

Instead of which they were interrupted by the mee-maw of an emergency ambulance and Daniel had to pull rapidly out of its path. 'I think I'd better drop you here,' he apologized. 'There are never any free spaces in the hospital car park. Text and let me know what they say, won't you?' He leaned across and opened the door for her.

Reluctantly Gina climbed out. She waved as he edged his way round the ambulance and drove away, leaving her in a ridiculous quandary. Should she sit on a bench somewhere until it was time for her meeting with Stuart Nixon or actually go into the hospital?

Gina Greenhills, she told herself, *you do get yourself into some stupid situations*. Instead of wallowing in self-analysis, she played one of the silly games she'd devised to make herself feel better: *If this were a movie, what would Sigourney Weaver do?*

Lie.

She waited until the ambulance had delivered its patient, then followed the crew into reception and sat on a plastic chair while she rang for a cab to take her home.

As soon as she got there, she made a reviving coffee and rang Stuart.

'I'm so sorry to miss our appointment. I had a bit of a contretemps with a delivery scooter.'

'Oh my God, are you all right?'

'Fine, thank you. He was going very slowly. More of a shock. I'd requested a meeting so I could ask a favour . . . This may sound a bit off-the-wall, but I'm due to present the Great Valuation of Maudie's antiques to the family tomorrow and I thought it would make sense to have an estimate of what Rookery Manor itself might be worth. That way, I can give them an idea of the whole package. Obviously, I'm only talking ballpark . . .'

'Can you give me a little while and I'll see if I can find anything remotely similar? It's not exactly your four-bed executive home!'

Absolutely,' Gina replied gratefully. 'I'm here all day.'

She could hear a hesitation on the line and guessed he wanted to ask about Evie.

Deciding to give him at least a titbit, she went on: 'By the way, here's something to impress your daughter: Evie's managed to get Jasmin her official permission to stay!'

'That's fantastic news!'

'Isn't it just! After hearing the awful situation Jasmin was in, she read up on how immigration works and managed to secure a meeting for Jasmin with a Home Office inspector at their HQ in Croydon. It's a real coup – she said it was as rare as hen's teeth to pull off something like that, these things usually take months—'

'Funnily enough I bumped into her in Croydon when she was trying to set it up.'

'What on earth were you doing in Croydon?'

'It's a long story.' She could tell he was reluctant to reveal more.

'Why don't you congratulate her yourself? I'm sure she'd appreciate it, especially if you bumped into her when she was trying to set it all up. Look, Stuart . . . I probably shouldn't say this, but Evie really likes you!'

'Does she?' replied Stuart, sounding as if he'd just been awarded the golden apple. 'You mean it's worth my while hanging in there?'

'Yes, definitely,' Gina confided. Evie would kill her if she knew, but Stuart was exactly the kind of man for her.

'Thank you! And I'll get back to you with this information as soon as I can. Bye.'

Gina went up to her new bedroom and surveyed her wardrobe. Sadly she had no suitable garment to transform her into a super-confident antiques expert tomorrow. And anyway, judging from *Antiques Road Trip*, most people in this world of strange alchemy where things seemed to be worth either a fortune or much less than you thought for no apparent reason, people looked a bit of a mess.

She selected a simple shift dress in a shade somewhere between peach and terracotta, plus some beige slingbacks which went with everything. She then rooted through her jewellery case for a dramatic necklace that looked faintly as if it might have come from Tutankhamen's tomb.

The really important thing, of course, was not how she looked but what she said. It was, she realized, one of the hardest presentations she would ever have to make, fraught with conflicting loyalties on all sides. After telling her how grateful she was, both for the work Gina had put in on the valuation and for cheering Maudie up so much, Lucy had said she would invite the whole family to attend – even Susan, the meek sister who preferred to hide away in the Lake District. Maudie, she remembered, had already invited Rosa and Awful Ambrose.

Gina had almost finished planning her speech when Stuart rang.

'I've looked at a number houses of a similar type. Rookery Manor's proximity to the sea gives it a definite advantage and the fact that Southdown is two hours from town rather than Cornwall's five. Much depends, of course, on the buyer. If you managed to hook a hedge fund manager or someone with big City bonuses, I would say maybe £2 million. If it's a local buyer, that'll certainly fall to £1.5 million. I hope that's helpful.'

'Fantastic,' Gina replied gratefully. 'Since it's purely as a favour, I'll have to buy you a drink to thank you.'

'You've thanked me already,' replied Stuart, and she could imagine the smile on his face as he explained why: 'You told me Eve likes me!'

Now all he had to do was persuade Evie to tell him herself.

Seventeen

Gina surveyed herself in the mirror of the downstairs cloak-room at the manor and took a deep breath. She wasn't going on stage at the National Theatre, for God's sake, simply presenting some figures to a nice old lady, her equally nice niece, their mousy sister, a Syrian girl who had lost everything and an unpleasant couple who no one seemed to like much anyway, oh, and no doubt Mrs B, the housekeeper, who would certainly find a way of listening in.

By the time she arrived, holding her notes, they were all gathered in the drawing room, and to her amusement she saw they had dressed for the occasion too. The scene struck her as pure Poirot and she almost got the giggles, but finally managed to arrange her features into a pleasant, if slightly formal, smile.

'Hello, everyone,' she began, taking in that Maudie was sitting in her favourite chair, a high-backed one in red velvet with arms – one of a set of eight that had turned out to be worth much more than Gina had initially supposed. 'I'd like to begin with why I'm here in the first place. I was first invited by Lucy,' she paused and smiled in Lucy's direction, 'since she was aware of the great value of some of the items in the house and felt that it would benefit the family to get a rough estimate of the whole. As it happened, the invitation came at an opportune time for me. As you probably know I have for many years run a valuation company with my husband. We parted company and I took the opportunity to come here.

'I had not previously known Maudie,' Gina continued, 'but she gave me the warmest of welcomes, insisting that I treat my stay less as an exercise in valuation than as an English holiday!' There was general laughter at this, except from Rosa and Ambrose, who looked about as amused as the stone heads carved on the pillars in the driveway.

'You'll be relieved to know I only took her partly at her word, and managed to combine the work with enjoying one of the most beautiful landscapes in the world which also, of course, happened to be the place where I grew up and where I have come back to live. But I was unprepared for Maudie's unique personality, which combines warmth with extraordinary knowledge. She has the eye of a true collector who buys some things simply because she likes them, irrespective of their financial worth' – she indicated the eccentric mix that crowded every shelf and tabletop in the room – 'along with those she recognizes to be of great value. I think we should celebrate that.'

Lucy, smiling proudly at her great-aunt, led the clapping, which startled Maudie so much she had to wipe a tear from her eye.

Out of the corner of her eye, Gina noticed Ambrose exchange a withering look with his wife.

'So,' she resumed, 'on to the antiques. I'd like to go through some of the most valuable items before I offer my view of the whole, and where better to start than with your ancestress Lady Elizabeth Tyler . . .' She pointed to the portrait above the fireplace of a rather plain, unsmiling lady in a blue silk dress and matching lace cap staring down at them with a disapproving eye.

'I hope you're not going to say there's a family likeness,' chipped in Maudie.

'Despite her looks,' Gina continued, 'she was a well-known benefactress who helped local orphans.'

Gina saw Maudie's quick glance at Jasmin. 'I'm glad to hear that,' she announced firmly.

'More to the point. It's unsigned, but your family have always believed it's by Gainsborough and the experts I've consulted back that up. It's in the brushwork, apparently. Gainsborough was a master of light feathery strokes that led to great naturalness. You can also show its provenance. A similar portrait, also unsigned, has been sold by Bonham's for £31,000.'

'Goodbye Great-Great-Great Granny,' murmured Ambrose, but for some reason no one laughed at his joke.

'Although you love most of your collection, Maudie,' Gina continued, 'there was one piece of furniture you said you particularly disliked!' She indicated a small carved cabinet designed to be kept on a table, made of intricately carved rosewood. 'I believe it was brought back from India by another Tyler in the seventeenth century.'

'It has twenty-one drawers in it!' protested Maudie apologetically. 'I kept on having to go through half of them to find anything!'

'Maybe you're just supposed to admire it, Maudie,' teased Lucy.

'But it's hideous!'

'Not everyone thinks so,' smiled Gina. 'A cabinet almost its twin sold at auction in Devon for £35,000!'

'Bloody hell,' murmured Lucy.

Rosa, Gina noted, had got out a notebook and was starting to not very discreetly keep a tally.

'Now, if I could ask you all to get up for a moment, we'll go to the old hall.' They tended to forget that Rookery Manor was so ancient it had a large hall, rarely used now, which would once have been the centre of the house, where guests were greeted and dined, and where the servants and animals would have slept when the family had gone to bed. It was now occupied by an enormous table made of wood hewn from Elizabethan sailing ships.

'I always thought that table was worth a lot,' confided Rosa smugly.

'Actually, it's not the table,' Gina pointed out. 'It's the carpet.'

'The carpet!' Rosa shrieked. 'People come in here all the time with muddy boots!'

'That's because it's a home, Rosa dear,' Maudie pointed out, trying to repress a twinkle.

They all stared at their feet.

'It's a very old Feraghan Mahal from West Iran,' Gina continued calmly. 'It's huge, and the colour is good.'

'But carpets like this go for nothing,' protested Ambrose. 'You'd need a bloody palace!'

'Times have changed,' replied Gina. 'It isn't just the local dealers plus a few old ladies and the odd gambler hoping to make a few quid who go to auctions these days. Even small auctions are international now, via phone and internet, so the market for things has broadened dramatically.'

'You should watch *Flog It*, Ambrose,' advised Lucy with a wink.

'And how much did one of these go for?' Ambrose sneered. 'Twenty grand?'

'Good guess,' Gina replied sweetly. '£23,400!'

'Oh my God,' Rosa almost fainted. 'Get off it, everyone. I'll tell Mrs B to clean it up at once!'

'I'd ask the experts first,' advised Maudie gaily. 'Mrs B might be tempted to spray it with Vanish and ruin it.'

A choking sound from the anteroom next door confirmed that the enthusiastic housekeeper must have been eavesdropping on their conversation.

'I must say, Gina,' Lucy congratulated, 'you've been doing a very thorough job. I hadn't realized this would be quite such a long and fascinating session. I need to call my husband, so why don't I ask Mrs B to make coffee? She's so helpful, I'm sure she wouldn't mind.' Lucy knew perfectly well that the housekeeper would be listening in. 'Perhaps someone could go to the kitchen and ask her?'

The sound of scuttling from next door confirmed that Mrs B had indeed overheard and was on her way back to the kitchen now.

They all followed Lucy, with Rosa hopping like a demented hare to protect the newly valuable carpet.

On the way back to the drawing room Gina slipped into the cloakroom again. It had gone OK so far. Her plan was to stun them all so much with the value of the manor's antiques that they forgot to ask about the missing objects. She smiled at herself in the mirror. *It's all about building up the drama. Your heroine Sigourney could tell you a thing or two about that!*

'Gina dear,' Maudie greeted her when she rejoined them, 'I'm on the edge of my seat. I can't wait for what's coming next!'

They finished their coffee, plus some stale gingernuts that

Mrs B had produced, and followed Gina to the small sitting room, which in a grander era and been called the library.

In a huge glass case Maudie kept a lot of her small finds from antique markets and the occasional online bid.

'Surely there's nothing valuable in there!' Rosa protested. 'That's what Maudie calls her gewgaw case; nothing but trinkets and baubles.'

'There's one thing that's a bit more than a trinket,' Gina announced calmly. 'I don't think we should pick it up, but I've brought a torch so you can take a closer look. It's that blue octagonal tile in the middle.'

'What's so special about that?' Ambrose enquired scathingly. 'What use is one tile anyway?'

'It's very special indeed!' Maudie spoke with such suppressed passion all eyes switched to her. 'It came from an architectural dig.'

'But surely that's illegal?' demanded Ambrose gleefully.

'I was given it,' Maudie replied, her gaze slipping away into the past. For a second she seemed to lose all sense of time and place, and a small smile lit up her features, making her look almost like a young girl.

'It was him, wasn't it?' whispered Gina. 'The man in Damascus?'

'Yes,' replied Maudie simply.

'What on earth's she burbling on about?' whispered Rosa loudly. 'I told you she was losing it. She shouldn't be living here on her own.'

'I'm not on my own, Rosa,' replied Maudie with so much dignity that Rosa looked embarrassed. 'I have Jasmin.'

'And Mr and Mrs B,' added Jasmin, with a smile at the coffee-pot-wielding housekeeper.

Maudie briefly touched her hand, appreciating her sensitivity, a quality notably missing in her great-niece and awful husband.

'It's probably late thirteenth or early fourteenth century,' continued Gina. 'A very similar one came up last year. The auction house's estimate was £7,000,' she continued.

'£7,000!' Ambrose huffed. 'For tat like that? These antique people live in a mad world!'

'So Gina,' Lucy asked appreciatively, beginning to guess her clever technique, 'You say that was the estimate. How much did it actually fetch?'

'£123,500,' replied Gina calmly. 'To a bidder in Oman.'

'I need to sit down,' Rosa shook her head. 'I might just go into the other room for a moment.'

'Before you do,' smiled Gina, 'take a look at the picture on the far wall.'

'The Laura Knight?' asked Lucy. 'I love that painting. I wouldn't mind having that one day if no one else wants it.' Immediately realizing how this must sound, she turned to her great-aunt. 'Maudie, how horrible of me! Please forgive me.'

'Of course you can have it,' Maudie assured her. 'It deserves to go to someone who loves it.'

'Hang on,' Ambrose intervened, 'wait till we hear what it's worth.'

'It's an oil painting of Sennen Cove in Cornwall,' Gina explained. 'Laura Knight is better known for painting figures, so this is unusual. One very much like it was sold last year at Markham's.'

'Go on,' Ambrose almost drooled.

'Half a million pounds.' Gina tried not to smile at the expression on his face.

'Oh my God,' even mousy Susan gasped at that.

Maeve Haran

'I can't take all this in,' spluttered Ambrose. 'I think I'll go next door and sit with my wife for a moment.'

Gina could picture them both in the other room, frantically adding up the tally in Rosa's notebook.

'And now for my favourite,' Gina smiled round at the remaining group, aware that the tension was rising and grateful for Rosa and Ambrose's absence.

'My dear,' breathed Maudie, 'the great Sarah Bernhardt couldn't enthral me more. Whatever is it?'

Gina went back to Maudie's gewgaw cabinet. 'It's this.' She took out a delicate headband painted with leaves and pansies with large purple stones adorning it.

'Isn't it pretty?' Maudie said tenderly. 'I think I was imagining myself when I was young, being a bit of wood sprite! People always told me I was like a nymph: pretty and hard to pin down.'

The room went quiet as they all imagined her as she must have been, elusive and beautiful as a butterfly.

'We always forget,' Lucy murmured discreetly to Gina, 'old age is us, only a bit older!'

'I picked it up in the antiques market in Brighton. Don't tell me it's valuable!'

'It's only a hunch, and you'd need an expert to look at it, but I think it's by Rene Lalique!'

'But I thought he only did glass,' protested Lucy. 'I'm actually rather a fan of Flog It, and they have glass by him coming up now and then.'

'Before he started making glass he was famous for his Art Nouveau jewellery,' Gina replied.

'And how much would this be?'

'There was an auction in Paris recently and something similar fetched €160,000.'

'I don't need to sit down,' Maudie announced. 'I need a drink!'

'Altogether it must come to about three quarters of a million quid!' Lucy blurted. 'I think I'll join you!'

They trooped out to the kitchen where, by some extraordinary coincidence, or possibly because she had slipped back to listen, Mrs B was already opening a bottle of chilled Sauvignon.

'Haven't we got any champagne?' enquired Maudie.

'Not chilled I'm afraid, madam,' replied Mrs B grandly.

'This'll do nicely,' insisted Lucy. 'The sight of white wine with frosting all over the glass is one of my small pleasures in life!'

'I do love you, Lucy dear,' said Maudie. 'And the Laura Knight is yours – whatever Rosa's husband may think.'

'Do I hear my name being used in vain?' Ambrose appeared in the kitchen behind them. 'What's going on here?'

'We're celebrating our riches,' announced Maudie, sipping her wine contentedly.

'Estimated riches,' he corrected. 'It isn't worth anything until you sell it.'

'Thank you, Ambrose.' Maudie pointedly didn't offer him a glass. Nothing daunted, he walked up to the kitchen table and helped himself. 'You do realize the total comes to—'

'Three quarters of a million quid!' chorused Maudie, Lucy, Gina and Jasmin spontaneously.

'And how much is it insured for?' demanded Rosa, who had materialized behind her husband.

'Precisely nothing,' announced Maudie. 'And that's the way it's going to stay until we decide to sell my treasures, thus alerting the world and potential burglars to their value.'

The rumpus that ensued was exactly what Gina had hoped for. Arguments and accusations flew round the room like fireworks on Bonfire Night.

And as she'd hoped, in the ensuing clamour, no one remembered to ask Gina what had happened to the missing objects.

'Oh my God!' Ruthie leaned so far over her cappuccino in Costa the next morning that she ended up with chocolate froth on her capacious chest. 'So no one even *asked* about the missing stuff?'

Gina shook her head and giggled. 'Not a sausage! It was money that did it. They were so staggered at the size of the valuation, not to mention Maudie's blank refusal to insure any of it, that a good old family war broke out. You should have heard them. The fall of the Roman Empire had nothing on them. It's sad, though, in a way. Rookery Manor's such a special place and it'll be heartbreaking if it really does go to Rosa and Awful Ambrose. Can you imagine how gruesome they'll be when they're lord and lady of the manor?'

The thought was so appalling they both stared at their coffees in silence.

'Have you heard the latest on Daniel Napier?'

'No, what is the latest on Daniel Napier?'

'Gossip is they're hiring a marquee to fill half the car park. This launch is going to be massive.'

'I wish he wouldn't,' Gina insisted, her brow puckering anxiously.

'Why ever not? Well, apart from the fact it gives Rebecca Boyd the chance to go "Look what I've got!" about Daniel.'

'Because of Mike Marshall. He's not stable and it's one thing to open a rival car wash, but publicly rubbing the man's face in it by throwing a huge party is asking for trouble. It'd be much better to open without any fanfare at all. Especially seeing as it's an ethical car wash.'

262

'Not with that Rebecca on the scene. You can bet your last bitcoin she's behind the scale of the thing.'

Ruthie had to dash off, leaving Gina to pay the bill. She stayed at the table for a moment and looked at her phone.

A photograph of Mark appeared on the screen along with an invitation from iPhone to watch their last trip to Madrid. Cursing her phone, yet unable to resist, she watched the compilation set to music of them both together at the Prado, taking in Flamenco at the Café Ziryab, laughing as they got drenched at Cybele's fountain and eating tapas by the port. And after she'd watched it she took a deep breath and deleted every photograph of him she had on her phone, except those of him with the girls. To delete those would be unfair to them. Then she sent the girls a message: *Missing you both. Southdown lovely. Come and visit soon.*

Maudie had just had her hair done and was definitely looking her best. The girl had said her hair was the most beautiful of all her clients', still shining and soft and not at all thin like some older peoples'. Maudie wasn't so sure about that but forgave her because the result was so stunning. Even though she wasn't going anywhere, she put on her most stylish black frock, the one that so complimented the bright whiteness of her immaculate French pleat.

So when she bumped into Rosa and Ambrose, who had once again let themselves into the house unannounced, she was at her most *grande dame*.

'What are you two doing here?' she greeted them unceremoniously.

'There was something we forgot to ask you yesterday.' Even Ambrose looked slightly sheepish at their uninvited appearance.

'What? I was hoping for a morning's peace and quiet after

having the lot of you here yesterday. If you've come to pester me about insurance, you can go home right now.'

'No, no,' Rosa soothed, in a tone that made Maudie think of a weasel if it could speak in a human voice. 'Of course that's up to you.'

Since Maudie had heard Rosa assert only yesterday that she had lost her marbles, she treated this new acceptance with a large pinch of salt.

'Spit it out then,' Maudie folded her arms across her chest in a martial manner.

'We want to know what has happened to the missing objects.'

Maudie's narrow chest swelled and her eyes sparkled with anger. 'Since it has nothing whatever to do with you, I think perhaps it's time you left before you say anything more you might regret.'

'But Maudie . . .' protested Ambrose.

'Go!'

They swept out of the room in what Maudie decided was a pathetic attempt at dignity. She moved across and placed herself in the cover of the magnificent brocade curtains to watch them depart.

Except that they didn't. Five minutes passed, then ten. She assumed they'd gone to pump Mrs B for information and stormed regally off to confront them.

Just in time she realized they weren't in the kitchen but examining the objects that Gina had earmarked as the most valuable. To her horror, Rosa was holding the thirteenth-century tile given to Maudie by Fahad.

'Pity if I dropped it,' she joked to her husband.

'Rosa,' he replied as if he were addressing an out-of-line subordinate, 'that isn't even funny. Put it back.'

'Certainly,' she snapped. 'It's hideous anyway. I wouldn't even give it house room. That's quite nice though' – she indicated the Laura Knight oil of a Cornish landscape – 'reminds me of that one my friend Sue did of Fowey.'

'Except this one's worth half a million and Sue's was a painting by numbers.'

'It wasn't,' protested Rosa haughtily, 'she went to art class at the tech.'

'I'd sell it all,' Ambrose shrugged, running a hand along the £35,000 cabinet. 'And the house must be worth a million at least. We could go and live in the South of France.'

'With all those expats! What about my book group! We're reading James Joyce's *Ulysses*!' protested Rosa.

Standing behind the door, Maudie repressed a snort. If the rest of Rosa's book group were self-righteous pseudo-intellectuals like her, she doubted they'd recognize James Joyce if he hit them with a bit of bladderwrack!

'You could start your own club,' suggested Ambrose in a tone of the serpent tempting Eve. 'Meet on a sunny terrace under the vines.'

'With a glass of Provencal rosé!' Rosa sighed.

Suddenly the most wonderful inspiration came to Maudie, breathtaking in its outrageousness, and yet with a satisfying logic of its own.

For a moment she was back in Damascus with the only man she'd ever loved.

But to be fair on her family, she had to be sure.

She turned round and slipped back upstairs, where she made a call to Gina.

'Gina, dear, I wanted to thank you for your masterly performance yesterday. It was quite brilliant.'

'We got away with it, didn't we, Maudie? About the Chagall and stuff.'

'Unfortunately, no. Rosa and Ambrose have been back this morning asking questions.'

'I'm so sorry, Maudie, I hope it wasn't awful.'

An impish smile lit up Maudie's still-pretty features. 'I rather enjoyed it actually. I told them to get lost. But look, Gina dear, could you do me a favour? Your friend Eve, could you ask her down? There's something I want to ask her to do. It would be a professional assignment, obviously.'

'Of course I will, Maudie.' She could tell from the slight shake in Maudie's voice that this was something exceptionally important to her. 'I'll ask her at once.'

'Thank you, dear. I know I've told you many times, but I'm so very glad you agreed to come to the manor.'

'And I'm just grateful you asked me,' said Gina truthfully. There was no doubt in her mind that Lucy's invitation to come down to Southdown had changed her life for the better.

'Eve, can I have a word?'

This was the question Evie dreaded most from the firm's senior partner, since it usually meant she was going to be offered a particularly sensitive case that would involve the kind of diplomacy she most hated.

'Actually, I'm rather busy at the moment,' she lied. 'Something time sensitive,' she added, trying to look harassed and intense at the same time.

'I see,' the partner replied frostily. 'Well, perhaps you could spare me five minutes of your valuable time when you find yourself a little freer.' His entire bearing conveyed the message that if she wanted to be really valued by her employers she was going about it the wrong way. He stalked back past the expensive wood panelling over the luxurious thick pile carpet and shut his door firmly. It wasn't quite a slam but it wasn't far from it.

The thing was, while it was supposedly every lawyer's dream to rise to the top of their firm, Evie had always resisted it. A lone wolf, she found she couldn't stick the office politics, the kowtowing and back-stabbing the process involved. Today, however, the senior partner's attitude had been frostier than usual. She didn't quite know what this meant for her future, but it probably meant something.

So she was in an unusually reflective mood when Gina's call came through asking her to visit Southdown and see Maudie. It could mean more immigration advice, of course, but she suspected it was something more and was intrigued. There was a mystery here, and Evie loved mysteries. When she wasn't working, she loved to bury herself in one of the whodunnits that packed her bookcases.

Fortunately it was Friday so the senior partner would soon be catching his early train back to his rectory in the Home Counties, where all his neighbours reaped the rewards of similar success stories to his own.

She put in a call on Maudie's landline and was answered by Mrs B.

'Oh goody,' enthused the housekeeper. 'Mrs Tyler will be so delighted to hear from you. She keeps asking if you've been in touch. Shall I take the phone to her? It's one of those modern jobbies you can carry about,' she added proudly, as if this innovation were cutting-edge technology.

'Eve dear,' Maudie grabbed the phone, as excited as a child at Christmas. 'I can't tell you how pleased I am you called. Now I want to make it clear this is a proper commission which I insist on paying for.' She paused as if to build up her courage. 'I want you to try and find Jasmin's mother's birth certificate. I know it won't be easy as she was adopted when she was a baby. I expect Gina has already told you that I had a baby I had to give away in Damascus. I think Jasmin may be my granddaughter.'

Evie weighed this bombshell against the senior partner's request and had absolutely no problem deciding which to go for. There was no guarantee she would find the missing document, or that Jasmin would indeed turn out to be Maudie's grandchild. But as she had told Maudie long ago, much of her job was already about finding things out that people – usually errant husbands – wanted to keep hidden.

And she was bloody good at it.

'The answer's yes,' Evie replied instantly. 'I'm owed a lot of time off and the firm always says it believes in sabbaticals, though no one's ever dared take one. I'll be the trailblazer. Give me a little time to think about what I need to know and I'll come to the manor.'

'Eve, my dear, 'Maudie almost gulped, 'I can't thank you enough.'

'Then don't. I'll be in touch soon, but let's keep this as discreet as possible. You, me, Jasmin and Gina. No one else should know at this stage.'

'I quite understand. Goodbye, dear.'

As she put away her phone, Evie realized she hadn't felt as excited as this since she was a young lawyer starting out in her career.

She only hoped for everyone's sake it was going to work out the way Maudie wanted.

Eighteen

'Absolutely brilliant,' Rebecca Boyd's narrow chest swelled visibly, 'we've got the mayor! He's agreed to declare the car wash open. That's a big deal, Daniel.'

'Except that I've already asked Maudie Tyler.'

'That batty old lady!' replied Rebecca scornfully. 'Give her some soft soap about business etiquette meaning you have to have the mayor instead.'

'I think you'll find Maudie Tyler is quite well-versed in business etiquette,' Daniel replied drily. 'Her husband taught me a lot when I was starting out.'

They were in the Portakabin at the far end of the car park which had previously been a rubbish tip until Harpers had allowed them to make it the nerve centre for the car wash with a dedicated area added on for the workers to take their breaks. To the delight of the staff, there was even a shiny new shower and WC.

She gave him one of her dazzling smiles. 'I'm sure you'll find a way. What on earth are you watching?' She indicated the video on Daniel's laptop.

'I'm learning the Ten Car Wash Commandments from Ronny, car wash king of Florida!'

'Isn't it a bit late for that? Given that we're about to open?'

'It turns out Ronnie's quite instructive,' Daniel laughed. 'And reassuringly we've done most of what he suggests.'

'You can't be paying attention to some YouTube video!' she announced derisively.

'Ronny didn't get where he is today without knowing everything about car washes,' replied Daniel with a grin. 'Did you know that free vacuums can boost your business by 5 per cent?'

'I'm sure that's very useful,' she tutted impatiently.

'It's all about the customer experience, Rebecca,' corrected Daniel. 'It even shows you where to site the vacuum machines so that the rest of the car wash flows properly.'

'Can I remind you of something? This isn't Florida, it's Southdown!'

'You know, Rebecca . . .' He wondered for a moment if anyone had ever called her Becky. Looking at that fearsomely determined face, he doubted it. 'You shouldn't take everything so seriously. Have a laugh occasionally!'

Rebecca's eyebrows rose almost into her well-organized hairline. 'I often laugh when things are funny.'

The memory of Gina's infectious laughter filled his head as he recalled her expression when she realized she had sugar all over her chin and he'd brushed it off. With almost brutal firmness he banished the thought from his mind. What was the point of thinking about her when she had a husband who was clearly still around?

Rebecca might not have Gina's appealing softness but she was at least unattached. Though how she had taken over quite so much of organizing the car wash launch, or made it into such an embarrassingly big event, he wasn't at all sure.

* * *

Evie was weighing up whether to opt for the independence of booking a room for herself at the Jolly Sailor versus asking another favour from Gina. In the end she decided that, since it was Gina who'd got her into this, she wouldn't mind putting her up again. Gina, of course, might wonder why Evie was involving herself in the concerns of Southdown people again, and that was a question Evie wasn't too sure of herself, except that she liked Maudie and wanted to help her. But, as Gina would be the first to point out, Evie didn't usually rearrange her life unless there was a large fee involved, and in this case she hadn't even thought about money, just trying to make an old lady happy, which was by no means a certain outcome.

But at least she could give it a try.

Gina, of course, was delighted. 'That's terrific – when are you coming?'

'Would tomorrow be too soon?' Evie replied. 'The senior partner keeps cutting me in the corridors, it'll be nice to get away from the chill.'

'But why is he doing that?'

'Oh, I turned down a big case he wanted me to do.'

'So that you could come down here and help Maudie?' asked Gina.

'I'm interested in her story and thought maybe my particular skills could help her.'

'Right.' Gina didn't mention it, but she wondered if the feisty Jessica had really got to her or if there were other things in Southdown that were drawing her friend back. She did hope so. Naturally, she kept these speculations to herself. 'I'm going to an auction in Bewick in the morning but I could pick you up from the station there at lunchtime. It's on the Southdown line.'

'That would be perfect. And then I'd better pop up to the manor, if that's all right with you. There are a few facts I

271

need to get straight with Maudie before I start. Oh, and Gina, don't worry about Mark. I'll still be keeping a close eye on that as well.'

'Thanks, Evie. I was wondering,' replied Gina, grateful she didn't have to worry that Evie's mind would be on matters far removed from her friend's divorce.

As Evie stretched out in the first-class carriage on the train the next day she sipped an early lunchtime gin and tonic and stared out of the window trying to pin down the emotion she was feeling, and to her utter astonishment, realized it was excitement.

The truth was she had prided herself on not being like other women: needing a husband and family to validate her. She could validate herself, thank you. She'd believed it gave her a kind of strength, an immunity to the worries she saw befalling others – Gina with a husband who'd cared more about gambling and then left her for another woman, or Ruthie with children who still depended on her in their thirties, with grandchildren climbing out of the woodwork.

But now, she wasn't sure. Suddenly she wanted to test herself, to take risks that were not just professional. Was it meeting Stuart again after all these years? But Stuart, like Gina, wasn't a free agent. His daughters were part of his life, and Jessica at least had made it pretty clear what she thought of Evie. Besides, she was a city girl; London was her beating heart. Wasn't it?

She looked out of the window at the blazing blue sky and imagined the busy beach at Southdown, families lying out rugs and umbrellas, blowing up pink flamingo floats and pestering their parents for ice creams, and found she was smiling.

By the afternoon she was sitting with Maudie on her sunny terrace, surrounded by nodding hollyhocks, pink rambling roses, Canterbury bells and the occasional blue delphinium.

'Are you admiring nature's paintbox?' Maudie enquired. 'It's perfect, isn't it?'

'I suspect you had a hand in it as well as nature,' said Evie.

'Only using nature's tools. Now, what would you like to know? And first, may I just say how much I appreciate what you have done for Jasmin already, and now for me as well.'

'I'm enjoying it. Perhaps you could tell me the story. You'll feel more relaxed if you try and imagine you were telling it to a friend not a lawyer. That's what I tell my clients.'

Jasmin arrived with a pot of the rose-scented tea. 'Do you need me at all?' she asked shyly.

'I would love a chat later,' Evie replied with a smile. 'But I think it's better I talk to both of you individually, if that's all right?'

'Of course. I'm here whenever you need me. Oh, and Maudie, great news! We've got our first booking!'

Jasmin skipped away, looking delighted.

'She's certainly happy here,' commented Evie.

'Eve,' Maudie's gnarled fingers clutched hers tightly. 'She's the delight of my life. I feel like childless Anne in the Bible when she's told she's going to have a baby!'

Maudie sipped the rose tea and closed her eyes. When she spoke again it was in a voice that seemed younger and full of passion. 'That was the scent that was all around us when it happened. Damascus roses. I didn't mean it to happen, Eve, even though I loved him to distraction! I knew it was wrong. I had a perfectly kind husband, but he was much older than me and he was always so busy. Gerald even welcomed me seeing so many things with Fahad. I think in some roundabout way it made him feel less guilty that we hadn't been able to have children. I didn't know where the problem lay, with my husband or me, but he wasn't the kind of man you could ask about things like that.'

She turned so that she was in profile and stared into the beauty of the downs beyond. 'We had been to visit an architectural site, a tomb, not grand like Tutankhamun's, but exciting. He had got special permission for us to be there and we were alone. You were never alone out there; servants everywhere, my husband's assistants, drivers. It was another world. But there we were. Completely alone. And somehow, though we were surrounded by rock, there was this scent of roses. And this feeling, the most powerful I've ever felt, of being out of time, when the past and the present all seemed to fuse into that one moment, and suddenly it seemed not just right but inevitable and somehow God-given. Not the God of Sunday service, but some other mysterious force. And it happened.'

She turned her face back to face Evie full-on. 'Do I sound like a madwoman, my dear?'

Evie smiled ruefully. 'Who knows? They say love is a kind of madness. What happened next?'

'I found I was pregnant. I couldn't believe it at first. There was no one I could tell, certainly not Gerald. I'm not a small woman, fortunately. Stately is the word people used for me and thank goodness for it. I'm tall and large boned. I started putting my hair up like this and people looked at that instead of my body. I began to wear flowing clothes and they thought I was just another crazy Englishwoman trying to look like Lady Hester Stanhope, that explorer they called the Queen of the Desert!'

'What about your husband?'

Maudie shrugged expressively. 'He was one of those men who don't notice the things in front of him as long as the water's hot and the meals are on time. To be frank he cared more about geopolitics than his own home. But I couldn't tell him the truth. He would have been shocked beyond measure. So I sort of pretended to myself it wasn't happening.'

'But people must have noticed? Your servants? Your friends?'

'I played the eccentric card, cutting myself off, reading a lot. I told them I was writing a novel.' She laughed bitterly. 'I could have too. A forbidden love story. It'd probably be a film by now. The outside world was too worried about war and politics. So was my husband. Things were always shaky politically, and no one was interested in an eccentric Englishwoman.'

'But how did you actually have the baby?' asked Evie, fascinated. 'Your servants would have guessed. Servants always know everything.'

Saba was my close servant and she stuck by me. The others all came from her family and they kept quiet. Maybe it was kindness, maybe they hoped for a bribe. I think they liked our household and didn't want to see it broken up. A midwife appeared – another of their relations. My husband was away, thank God. There were whispers, of course, but he wasn't the type to notice gossip. So I gave my baby away and life went on.' The catch in her voice told Evie everything she wasn't saying about the grief she'd buried.

'Maudie, I'm sorry.'

'Thank you. But don't be. I began to rebuild my life. I was developing a genuine interest in archaeology, but then it started to get dangerous and we came home. The timing for me personally was perfect, but I still weep for the country and its people.'

'Maudie,' Evie's voice became serious. 'Even if you gave the baby away, there must have been a birth certificate. Did you go to the High Commission and register the birth?'

'Yes,' Maudie replied in a whisper of a voice. 'I did.'

'And who did you put for the father?'

'Unknown. Of course they raised an eyebrow, but there was so much going on outside that was important they didn't pursue it further.'

'And the actual date? And the name of the father? I will need these to proceed.'

As if she couldn't bear to speak the name out loud, Maudie wrote it down on a piece of paper, together with the date, and handed it to Evie.

'Thanks, Maudie. That's definitely something to start with. I'll get on to it at once.'

As she set off back to Southdown in a taxi, it struck Evie that of course there wasn't a British High Commission in Damascus any longer. No wonder Maudie had found information hard to track down. Evie smiled. She'd had far tougher challenges than this. To find out what happened to Maudie's baby next would be difficult but not, she hoped, impossible.

'Come for an evening swim – it'll do you good!' Gina suggested.

Evie had been solidly pursuing leads all yesterday, Gina noted, and it had obviously been proving very frustrating. 'It's too late to work anyway, and far too beautiful!'

Reluctantly Evie agreed, still harbouring doubts about braving the cool waters of the English Channel.

'Look,' Gina tempted, 'you can sit on the beach under a big towel if you don't like it, but at least give it a try!' She handed Evie an enormous blue bath sheet.

'OK. I've probably done enough for today.'

'You're not going to have to go out there, are you?' Gina asked nervously.

'It wouldn't be any help. I've got a contact in Beirut who's much more suitable for asking delicate questions than I am. Times have changed so much. They'd only see me as colonialist interloper.'

'I'll go and get my swimming things,' said Gina. 'Parking should be easy at this time of day.'

But Gina was wrong about this. The extreme beauty of the day and the feeling that summer would soon be over had gone to Southdowners' heads and the beach was as crowded at seven in the evening as it had been at three.

'Ooh,' laughed Gina, 'we're turning into the Germans! Have you noticed on holiday how they stay out from dawn till sundown to get that must-have all-over tan.'

'And quite often take all their clothes off,' teased Evie. 'Feel like a skinny dip?'

'No way!' Gina replied, horrified. 'In the hidden river, fine, but I don't want to frighten the children! Let's sit and take in the scenery for a moment.'

So they placed themselves side by side on the towel and looked around them. It was a picture of quite extraordinary beauty. The light was changing into dusk with a pearly glow on the water that made it seem entirely magical. The line of the setting sun across the water sparkled like glitter sprinkled on a home-made Christmas card.

'People tell me it's shoals of whitebait that cause the sparkle,' commented Gina. 'But I prefer to believe it's nature's paintbox, as Maudie puts it.'

A lone paddleboarder crossed in front of the setting sun and was frozen momentarily in pink luminescence. Evie quickly captured it on her camera.

She showed the picture to Gina. 'What a stunning image,' Gina said admiringly. 'You could win a contest with that!'

By now the paddleboarder had landed on the beach and was walking towards them. Evie would have known her anywhere. It was Stuart's spiky daughter, Jessica.

'Boarding alone, tonight?' asked Evie conversationally.

'So it would seem,' replied Jessica tersely.

'Is that safe?' Gina asked, realizing too late the criticism implied in the question.

'Yes, for an experienced boarder who knows what they're doing. I wouldn't recommend it for your friend.' The hostility was more than apparent in her tone.

'Her friend wouldn't be so foolhardy,' Evie shrugged, refusing to take the bait. 'I'm off for a swim. Gina, why don't you come in a minute.'

They both watched Evie walk across the beach and slip into the sea.

'What's she doing back here?' Jessica enquired rudely. 'It isn't even the weekend.'

'Perhaps it's because she's turning down cases and risking her career to help an old lady find out something important.'

'Very kind of her,' replied Jessica sarcastically. 'Then she goes back and screws the rich for the rest of the week.'

'As a matter of fact she's already taken time off work to learn enough immigration law to help Jasmin get permission to stay here, thank you very much. And for no fee whatsoever.'

'Right.' Jessica looked slightly abashed. 'Sorry. That's good of her.'

'She says she enjoyed it.'

'Is that why she's back?' The tinge of suspicion had returned.

'I imagine partly it is, but I really can't speak on her behalf. Why don't you ask her yourself?'

There was a slight smile on Jessica's face. 'I wouldn't dare, to be honest.'

'You've got Evie wrong, you know,' replied Gina. 'She can be incredible fun, as well as kind and generous beyond belief.'

'I'll take your word for it,' said Jessica. She started to walk away along the shingle just as Evie emerged from the waves and shook her hair like a large and aristocratic dog.

'What was all that about?' she enquired. 'Let me guess, you told her about plucky, generous Eve getting Jasmin leave to stay, didn't you?'

'I'm proud of you!' Gina defended herself.

'I know. But I can handle self-righteous millennials perfectly well myself!'

Evie spent the next day following up suggestions that might lead to more information in her search for the birth certificate, but all of them had turned out to be dead ends. Uncharacteristically, by the end of the day she was not only exhausted but beginning to doubt her own capacities.

From outside her window came the alluring scent of a barbecue, with an appropriately Levantine combination of hot coals, lamb and rosemary.

'Ruthie's coming to supper,' Gina reminded her. 'You've been working so hard! Come and have a glass of refreshing rosé.'

'You don't know how tempting that sounds!'

'Is it hard going?'

'An understatement! I only hope my contact in Beirut is doing better than I am.'

Gina wondered for a moment who would be paying the 'contact' and knew at once it would be Evie herself. For an instant she felt really annoyed with Jessica for being so rude.

Then she remembered how long the two girls had had their father to themselves; clearly they saw Evie as a threat.

The funny thing was, as Evie's friend, she knew what a great addition she would be to their family: generous, supportive and, Gina suspected, eager to encourage their relationship with their father rather than sabotage it. But it was an argument Gina didn't know how to make and she realized everyone involved would kill her if she tried. She also knew how easy it was for chances like this to disappear into thin air. This should be the best opportunity, here, now, for Evie to get together with Stuart while she was staying in Southdown, but Gina couldn't for the life of her think how to make it happen.

Ruthie had no such scruples.

After helping herself to an enormous rosé, she instantly turned to their friend. 'So, Evie, have you seen anything of Sexy Stu since you've been here?'

'I've been too busy for social arrangements,' Evie replied crisply and deftly changed the subject to ask Ruthie what she'd been up to lately.

'Sorry, was I being tactless as usual?' enquired Ruthie. 'Robin says the only reason I have a mouth is to put my foot in it. Nuff said.'

'We did bump into Jessica on the beach,' Gina couldn't resist adding.

'Those girls!' snapped Ruthie. 'They're that protective, you'd think *they* were married to him! On the other hand, here's a question: is Stuart such a nice, kind man because of having those daughters, or are the daughters the way they are because of having such a nice kind man as a father?'

'That's too deep for me,' Evie grinned. 'Gina, that lamb smells delicious.'

'Jasmin showed me how to do it. It's not gas or firelighters but a proper charcoal grill like you get in restaurants. How do you like your lamb, girls?'

'Practically baa-ing for me, please,' requested Ruthie.

Gina tried not to giggle. 'Veggie correctness hasn't arrived in Southdown yet,' she explained to Evie.

'So I see. Pink for me, please,' said Evie, 'and don't say "like your men", please, Ruthie.'

'Why would I?' protested Ruthie, looking bewildered. 'It isn't even funny.'

'So,' Ruthie asked as they sat down to eat at the white garden table. 'Have you received your invite to the big launch yet?'

'What big launch is this?' enquired Evie. 'This lamb's as good as it smells, by the way.'

'Thanks,' replied Gina, her lips twitching with suppressed laughter. 'I think Ruthie's referring to the opening of our new car wash. It seems to be Southdown's major event.'

'Oh for God's sake!' Evie shook her head and wondered how she could even faintly consider moving here.

'Come on now, Evie,' chided Gina. 'It is a big deal. Daniel says a lot of small investors have put money in it because they feel guilty about using your average hand car wash. I think it's a brilliant idea of Daniel's, and I will certainly be getting my car cleaned there.'

'Let's hope it's not going to be ice-cream wars all over again,' replied Evie. 'It got really nasty in Glasgow between rival ice-cream sellers. Mind you, that was about drugs and stolen goods. I can't see that happening in sleepy Southdown.'

'I saw the film,' Ruthie nodded sagely. 'It had that Clare Grogan in – you know, the one who bounces around singing "Happy Birthday"!'

Ruthie sprang up to give an instant demonstration.

'Thank God we're not in public.' Evie shook her head, but a moment later they were all dancing round the terrace singing "Happy Birthday" loud enough to frighten the birds.

When they sat down again, Ruthie returned to the subject of Southdown's big event: 'Honestly, it's going to be a big do. I'm taking Gina shopping so she won't turn up in another of her bin liners.'

'It's a pity I'm not around more to keep an eye on you two,' commented Evie.

'Well,' Ruthie replied blandly, 'you could easily put that right, couldn't she, Gina.'

Evie ignored the Ruthie-sized hint. 'I wonder if they're inviting the delightful Mr Marshall?'

'Not if they've got any sense,' Gina replied. 'Personally I think all this razzamatazz about the opening is understandable but a big mistake.'

'It's that bossy Rebecca who's behind it,' announced Ruthie, her mouth full of lamb.

'There is that,' conceded Gina. 'But I'm serious, Ruthie. He's not the kind of man who's going to take it well. To Mike Marshall it'll be a red rag to a bull.'

'I'm afraid you're right, but let's not spend our evening thinking about him,' said Evie. 'Now where's that bottle of rosé got to?'

Nineteen

'For God's sake, Rebecca, please don't tell me you've invited Mike Marshall to the launch?' Daniel enquired tersely.

'Certainly I have,' Rebecca shrugged her bony shoulders. 'He can make some nasty comment about idiots opening businesses they know nothing about to the local paper and he'll feel much better about the whole thing.'

'And what if the investors who've put their hard-earned money into Desperate Dan's read that and get scared?'

'It's a risk we have to take. This way we're more in control of the story.'

'I hope you're right.'

'I shouldn't worry,' she put an arm round his neck and tried to kiss him. 'I'm nearly always right.'

To her annoyance, Daniel turned his head away. Maybe she'd gone too far this time and should have consulted him first. But that wasn't the way she intended to lead her life once she'd persuaded him to get married, so why start now?

'He probably hasn't got a tux anyway, so he'll just say he's otherwise engaged.'

'That's the other thing. Making the whole thing black tie. It's ridiculously pretentious.'

'No it isn't. It's supposed to be ironic. Witty. A car wash launch with a dress code like Glyndebourne. It's funny.'

After all the times Daniel had wished Rebecca would display a sense of humour, now that it had finally emerged it only served to underline how very different it was from his own.

Worse than different. Ill-advised and provocative. He was genuinely tempted to end the relationship right away, but that would be unfair given all the work she had put into the launch. He resolved to wait till the launch was over and make up his mind then.

'Right,' Ruthie announced to Gina in the tone her family had come to recognize as non-negotiable, 'we're going shopping. No more hiding your figure in an upmarket bin bag. I've seen the perfect dress for you.'

'Ruthie . . .' Gina attempted to protest, 'I really don't have a lot of spare cash for splurging on clothes at the moment.'

'Then it's just as well your dream dress is in the window of that new Oxfam boutique. It's in the posh end of town next to the expensive clothes shops. You spend money and do good at the same time. I don't think you can argue with that.'

Gina followed Ruthie, smiling ruefully. You had to admit, Ruthie thought of everything.

The shop itself was stylishly arranged so that it didn't have the air of a charity outlet. It was colour-coordinated so that each section of the store offered different shades of one colour so that the overall effect was of a rather enticing rainbow. The window itself had concentrated on shades of red from scarlet to plum and, bang in the middle, on a display model, was a sculpted dress with scrolled-down shoulders in red satin. It was certainly eye-catching. 'There you go,' insisted Ruthie. 'Absolutely bloody perfect.'

'Ruthie,' protested Gina, 'this is ridiculous. That dress is so not my style.'

'Isn't that the point?'

'Well, it's *your* point.'

'Try it on. If you hate it, we'll look for another baggy outrage so you can blend in with the marquee and not be noticed.'

She pulled back the thin curtain that passed as a changing room door and shoved Gina and the dress in. 'You have to promise to come out and show me before you put your clothes back on and run out of the shop. Agreed?'

'Agreed,' conceded Gina.

She took off her top and trousers and reached for the dress, avoiding looking at her semi-naked body in the mirror in case she got a nasty shock. To her surprise, the dress was made by a well-known designer who must have been going through their tarty phase. It even had a silky feel-good lining so that it slipped down over her body like water rippling over stones.

An arm suddenly snaked round the curtain holding a pair of beige slingbacks with three-inch heels which just happened to be exactly the right size because Ruthie had brought them along with her.

'Ready yet?'

'As ready as I'll ever be,' replied Gina, deciding not to take a peek till she was outside the cubicle.

Trying not to feel foolish, she swept aside the curtain and stepped out.

'Wow, you look amazing!' Ruthie insisted in such a loud voice that all the other shoppers turned to look too. 'She does, doesn't she?' Ruthie appealed to her impromptu audience.

'She does indeed,' congratulated a lady of much their own vintage.

'Not bad,' conceded a young woman who was probably the granddaughter.

'We'll take it,' Ruthie announced. 'My gift. No arguing or I'll be mortally offended and not speak to you for a month.'

'Promise?' Gina teased. She had to admit the dress had an impact. It suited her shiny dark hair, and the slope of the shoulders somehow echoed her slanting cheekbones, commonly acknowledged as her best feature. 'All right,' she conceded, 'it doesn't look anything like me, but it does look good.'

'Go on, give us a twirl!'

Feeling hideously embarrassed, Gina did as she was told and found everyone in the shop had started clapping. Gina took a bow and joined in the happy laughter.

She only hoped it would have a similar effect on Daniel Napier.

Evie sat in Gina's sunny kitchen and tried to ignore the glorious weather outside and concentrate on her laptop. The wonder of modern technology was that she could continue to keep an eye on her usual work while at the same time doing her best to access any information that would help trace Jasmin's background. She had questioned the girl gently to discover if she knew anything useful, but it was obvious that Jasmin had been told very little about herself and had no suspicion that the grandmother she loved might have adopted her mother as a baby. How much adopted children should be told was a hot potato in every culture and these events would have happened well over fifty years ago when times and moral attitudes were very different.

Evie sighed and checked to see that no more messages from her contact in Beirut had come through. Nothing yet but Evie refused to be discouraged. If they drew a blank in the end they'd just have to accept it. But Evie had recognized Maudie as a kindred spirit – as daring and determined as she was herself – and it would mean a great deal to her to be able to make the old lady happy.

In her quiet way, Maudie was the backbone of her family and loved by more people than she probably suspected.

Evie turned her back on the blazing sunshine and with dogged determination made herself go back to her laptop. At almost six o'clock she was rewarded by a brief message from her contact. It wasn't much, but it was the first bit of encouraging news she'd had, and that was enough for Evie. She decided it was time to find a glass of wine and watch the evening sun lighting up the glorious landscape from Gina's terrace.

'Maudie, those guests I told you about have confirmed their booking!' Jasmin told her excitedly. 'It's a Mr and Mrs Williams. Where do you think we should put them?'

'Oh, I think the four-poster room on the top floor, don't you? The one that Gina stayed in? It has the best views from the back of the house and it's a little bit separate, which will be nice for them and us.'

'I'll make up the bed then,' Jasmin volunteered. 'I promised Mrs B the work wasn't going to fall on her, and I'd like to be useful! I've been feeling guilty living in your beautiful house and not doing anything to help.'

Maudie took her hand. 'Jasmin dear, you have brought sunlight into my declining years! Besides, having guests was your idea, and if it works out, it really might mean I can stay here and not have to move into a flat like Rosa keeps telling me! I've lived here for fifty years and every inch is familiar and beloved.'

They stood for a moment taking in the sights and smells of

Rookery Manor, which meant so much to Maudie. The bright sunlight caught the dust particles in the air and made them shine like microscopic jewels against the warmth of the wood panelling and the bright colours of the Persian rugs scattered over the floor. The air was fragrant with furniture polish mingling with the scent of roses in the large arrangement on the drawing room table and the lavender from the path outside. It was a house that felt loved and lived-in.

Jasmin went off to look for sheets and pillowcases, plus the bucket of cleaning products Mrs B kept in the pantry, and tried not to think of the homes belonging to her family she had left behind her.

'She's a hard worker, that girl,' Mrs B commented to her husband.

'And the old lady's a different person now the lass is here,' agreed the taciturn Mr B, looking out of the kitchen window. 'Aye aye, here come the busybodies!' he added.

A moment later the kitchen door opened and Rosa and Ambrose marched in.

Rosa was waving a copy of the local tourist bulletin. 'Mrs B, do you know anything about this?'

She showed Mrs B the pull-out with an advert circled in pink Dayglo pen: *Come and experience life in a medieval manor for the price of a Premier Inn.*

'Good morning, Mrs Winstanley. Oh yes,' laughed Mrs B, 'Mrs Tyler was very pleased about thinking that up. Fair chortled away to herself she did, didn't she, Mr B?'

Mr B nodded his bobble hat up and down.

'Yes, but surely it's unfair on you?' Rosa suggested sweetly. 'The extra work, I mean? You have enough to do already.'

'The girl's doing it,' Mr B informed her with relish. 'She's upstairs making the bed for the first guests now. She's doing the cooking, n'all. Says her grandmother taught her how to cook English-like.'

'I think we need to have a word with Maudie,' snapped Ambrose. 'Do you know where she is?'

'Deadheading roses, I shouldn't wonder,' replied Mrs B. 'She doesn't think Mr B does it proper, being a man and all.'

Rosa exchanged a look with her husband at Maudie's batty logic.

'They've changed their tune,' murmured Mr B when they'd gone. 'Pretending to give a tinker's cuss about us! Usually they're spouting off about you and me being an idle pair what could be replaced by a con-cee-erge.'

'Jealous, as usual, I shouldn't wonder. That Mrs Winstanley would be jealous of a fly if it landed on Mrs Tyler.'

'Would you want to stay on if they get the house?' Mr B asked.

'I'd be packed before they read the will!'

'And I'd be joining you,' he endorsed with a wink.

'That's a relief, you silly old sod. Now, where are those onions you promised? Jasmin's going to show me her roast chicken and she wants one to shove up its bum.'

'Funny ideas, some people,' marvelled Mr B, shaking his head.

'Nonsense, my old auntie from Hebden Bridge used to do it, with sage n'all.'

'Oh well,' shrugged Mr B, 'that's Yorkshire. What do you expect?'

Meanwhile, Rosa had tracked down Maudie and was outlining all the possible perils and pitfalls of entertaining paying guests.

As soon as they'd gone, Maudie went to look for Jasmin. She had just finished spring-cleaning the room so that the wooden floor glowed and all the surfaces in the en suite bath-room sparkled and shone in the early evening sunlight. Fresh towels were laid on the bed and she had placed a wrapped chocolate on top of the pillow. There was even a tray with a teapot, kettle and cups and saucers, together with a selection of teabags and a milk jug ready to be filled with fresh milk.

'I know how you English like your tea in bed!' laughed Jasmin.

'My goodness, you've been busy!' said Maudie.

'I like to do a job properly,' the girl replied modestly.

'How about another evening swim? I'll phone Gina now and see if she can come and get you, and try and wrest Eve away from the laptop for a while!'

Jasmin's young face turned serious. 'You are all so kind to me! The way you have accepted me in your life.'

Maudie opened her arms and folded the girl into her Youth Dewed embrace.

Gina was only too delighted to agree, and fifteen minutes later she scooped up Jasmin and bundled a reluctant Evie into the car.

'But I haven't brought my swimming things,' protested Evie.

Gina pointed to a bulging Waitrose bag on the back seat. 'I raided your room. I hope you don't mind?'

'I've hardly got any secrets from you after all these years,' replied Evie. 'I keep reading articles about wild swimming and didn't think I was going to be indulging in any, and look at me now!'

'I'm not sure swimming in the sea at Southdown counts as wild swimming! But our secret river swim,' she grinned over her shoulder at Evie, who had settled down next to her swim-ming things, 'that would definitely count!'

They were driving through the town when Jasmin turned anxiously to Gina. 'Could we stop for a moment? That girl at the bus stop. She was a friend of mine at the car wash. She looks so upset. Could I just talk to her?'

'Of course,' Gina pulled the car in.

'I won't be long,' promised Jasmin, and dashed across the road to the girl, who was leaning miserably against a bus shelter.

Five minutes later they hugged each other and Jasmin came back, almost in tears herself.

'Poor girl,' she explained. 'Mr Marshall won't let them have their passports – he claims he can't find them! And I've been so lucky that you helped me, Eve.' She hesitated a moment. 'I know you don't want me to talk about it, but I wish I understood what he meant when he said he'd put the passports somewhere only smugglers knew about, where no one would find them.'

Gina felt a sudden frisson of fear remembering the time she and Ruthie had bumped into him at the famous smugglers' caves. She'd wondered at the time what the hell he was doing there. Could he have been hiding passports?

But why hide them in a tourist attraction when he could so much more easily lock them away? On the other hand, someone with his warped sense of humour would probably think it hilarious for a modern-day people trafficker to conceal things in a place where historic smugglers were celebrated, knowing that tourists passed through every day without suspecting.

'I wonder . . .' she began, then stopped.

'What?' persisted Jasmin, eager for anything that might help her friend.

'Ridiculous really, but Ruthie and I bumped into him when we were looking round Southdown's smugglers' caves and I wondered if he could have put them there.'

'Come on,' Evie could see how scared Jasmin was and

deliberately changed the subject. 'Let's get down to the beach! We could all do with a swim to clear our heads!'

Ten minutes later they were lying on their backs in the deliciously deep, clear water trying to think of nothing but how beautiful it was and how lucky they were to have the sea on their doorstep. But for once it didn't work. Gina kept seeing that face looming out of the darkness and leering at Ruthie and her; as hard as she tried, there was no way she could forget about it.

Since it would be impossible to put off the mayor now that Rebecca had invited him, Daniel decided to go and explain everything to Maudie in person.

It was a beautiful evening for heading out of town and into the downs. The fields were the colour of a lion's mane, waving in the breeze, the corn not yet harvested against a ridiculously blue sky. He wondered how many people had returned to Rookery Manor down this narrow lane over the centuries, from marriages and funerals to baptisms and battles. It was unique in the area for its rich history. He hoped it would go on in the future, creating more stories, and not end up becoming either a boarding school or a country hotel run by strangers with no appreciation for its history.

'Daniel Napier!' Maudie greeted him with an impish smile. 'Have you come to invite me out? I could be ready in five minutes!'

Daniel laughed, knowing perfectly well when he was being teased. Maudie had had a soft spot for him ever since he'd first come to the manor to visit her late husband. Even in those days, Daniel could remember thinking what an odd couple they were, her husband so dry and businesslike; Maudie so full of life and laughter.

'Come on, I'm not serious. Let's have a drink on the terrace.' She rang a bell and Mrs B appeared. 'What would you like? I know – how about a Buck's Fizz made with blood oranges? I read about it in my magazine. Apparently, it's all the rage in London cocktail bars.'

'Absolutely,' Daniel smiled. 'I'd hate to be out of fashion.'

'Nonsense!' Maudie roared with laughter. 'I bet you don't give a toss about fashion!'

Daniel pretended to look injured. 'I hope you don't deduce this from my appearance? I put my best suit on to visit the lady of the manor!'

'Daniel, I'm flattered. I bet you don't know the other thing that's in fashion?'

Daniel shook his head, waiting to be enlightened.

'Espresso martinis! Isn't that funny! I had one with my toast and marmalade yesterday. It certainly beats Nescafé!'

'Maudie . . .' laughed Daniel, greatly enjoying himself, 'I know it's an espresso, but I don't think you're supposed to have it for breakfast!'

Their drinks arrived and Maudie held hers up so that the setting sun caught the red of the blood orange and lit it up like a jewel. 'Cheers! And to what do I owe the honour of your visit, Daniel?'

'I came to apologize about a misunderstanding. A while ago I asked you to come and open the car wash, but it seems the mayor has been invited too.'

'It *seems*?' Maudie asked, raising an eyebrow. Ruthie had quietly filled her in with stories of ruthless Rebecca and how she was A Bad Thing.

'Yes. The opening is being mostly organized by Rebecca Boyd. I'm sure you know her?'

'That bossy woman who runs the lettings agency? She looks

like the type who'd invite the mayor. And was it her idea to dress everyone up in monkey suits?'

'She thinks it's witty,' apologized Daniel.

'Ludicrous, more like. And inappropriate,' Maudie expostulated. 'It is the opening of a car wash, after all, even if it is a rather unique one.'

'I'm with you, as it happens,' agreed Daniel.

Maudie grinned. 'Remember this, Daniel. If you don't agree now, you certainly won't agree later. And believe me, I know.'

'You're reading far too much into this, Maudie. Rebecca and I aren't contemplating anything long term.'

'That's what men always think. Women usually have other plans. Be careful, Daniel. You're a very special person and I'd hate to see you make a stupid mistake.'

Before Daniel had time to reply, a car drove up and parked in the front drive. Jasmin and Gina got out and waved.

'Come and join us for a drink on the terrace,' insisted Maudie.

Gina, conscious of having both wet hair and streaky mascara, hesitated, but Maudie had spotted an opportunity and certainly wasn't going to let it go.

'Gina, dear,' she enquired smilingly as they both sat down. 'Rebecca Boyd – wasn't she the woman who wouldn't help you when you were trying to track down Daniel from your dancing school days?'

Gina flushed slightly but couldn't repress a grin when she realized what Maudie was up to. 'She was probably trying to protect her client's privacy.'

'Or make sure she spiked the competition,' Maudie announced gaily. 'I can't stand possessive women. I was telling Daniel he really ought to watch out. Gina, what do you think?'

Gina avoided looking at Daniel. 'I can't win here, because I hate women bitching about other women, but Rebecca was spectacularly unhelpful. It almost seemed that she didn't want me to find her client.'

'Of course she didn't,' pronounced Maudie. 'You're far too attractive to have as competition, even if you don't see it yourself. Isn't she, Daniel?'

Daniel laughed. 'I'm delighted to know about all these ladies you believe are fighting over me. But if I have to give the golden apple to anyone, Maudie, it has to be to you.'

'That's very pretty, Daniel, and I quite forgive you about not wanting me to open the car wash. I'm sure Ms Boyd knows best.'

As Daniel drove home he wondered what Maudie was up to, and if she knew that Gina's husband was still on the scene.

Twenty

_____

On the day of the car wash opening, Maudie was dressed and ready by teatime.

'I don't have many social occasions in my life these days,' she announced with an impish smile, 'so I like to make the most of them when I do! And it may only be the opening of a car wash, but everyone who's anyone in Southdown will be there!'

She was certainly making the most of this occasion. She had chosen the smartest of her black dresses and not only had her hair done specially but had topped it with a tiny pillbox hat adorned by a single ostrich feather. The effect was theatrical in the extreme, but no one was going to spoil it by pointing out that she looked as if she had wandered off the set of *My Fair Lady* or that people probably didn't wear hats to car wash openings.

Jasmin, by contrast, was wearing a demure dress in grey with a white collar. A choice that seemed designed to make her blend into the background rather than draw the eye.

Gina arrived in a taxi to fetch them at 6 p.m.

'Gina, darling, you look fabulous!' Maudie stood back to

admire the red dress. 'It's so different to your usual style, but I like it. It reveals a whole new side to your personality!'

'The cheap hooker side?' laughed Gina. 'Blame Ruthie! She made me buy it. And I have to say I've been losing my nerve ever since I put it on.'

'Well, don't. You look terrific in it!' Maudie insisted.

'And given the situation, it couldn't be more appropriate!' seconded Evie, who had appeared from the library, still in her workaday jeans since she wasn't going with them.

'What on earth do you mean?' Gina asked. 'Given that I'm going to the opening of an ethical car wash in a dress from Oxfam?'

'I came to bring you the news that your decree nisi has just come through and pretty soon you're going to be a free woman!'

'Oh my God, Evie,' Gina replied, stunned. She'd longed for this moment so much and now it was here she felt sad as well as elated. She hoped her daughters wouldn't be too hurt, though they kept assuring her that half their friends' parents were divorced already.

Evie was watching her, surprised at her muted reaction. But then, Gina reminded herself, Evie had never been married.

'You are happy, aren't you?' Evie finally enquired. 'I mean, this is what you wanted?'

'Of course, I'm very happy,' Gina threw herself into her friend's arms. 'And thank you so much for everything you've done!'

'Congratulations, Georgina!' seconded Maudie. 'This calls for champagne. Mrs B! Mrs B! Bring some champagne and four glasses. Mrs Greenhills is celebrating her divorce!'

'Funny old world,' Mrs B confided to her taciturn husband of fifty years as she took the bottle out of the fridge. 'In our day it was getting married we celebrated!'

Mr B smiled. 'Well, it's good there's progress in some things!'

'You watch yourself, Bill Browning!' was Mrs B's lively riposte.

They toasted Gina's approaching freedom in Maudie's favourite vintage champagne glasses. 'To Ms Georgina Greenhills,' Maudie announced, careful to stress the 'Ms' this time. 'May your next choice be a wiser one!'

'Who says there's going to be a next choice?' Gina protested, laughing.

'In that dress? You'll be fighting them off!' insisted Maudie.

'So who's going to tell Daniel about the decree nisi?' Evie whispered to Maudie as she helped her on with her coat.

'I think I might find a way,' replied Maudie with a wink. 'It'd be worth it just to annoy that Boyd woman. Now, I think we'd better get going.'

The far end of the enormous car park had been closed off for the event and as they arrived they had to admit Rebecca had done a good job. Giant posters of iconic American cars, from Chevrolets to Mustangs, hung from the fences, and the guests were being welcomed with car-related music, from the Beatles' 'Drive My Car' to Tracy Chapman's 'Fast Car', cleverly culminating in the bouncy blues of 'Car Wash' by Rose Royce. At the supermarket end drinks and nibbles were served under a large blue canopy as the photographer from the *Southdown Gazette* clicked happily away. Later the mayoral limo would be the first car to go through the new facility and he would cut a ribbon to declare it open.

The mayor had already arrived in black tie, rendered even fancier by his mayoral chain. The guests ranged, Gina noted, from relaxed bigwigs from Harpers who were used to formal occasions to the rather gauche stiffness of council members who didn't approve of all this nonsense of having to hire evening dress and tackle a dickie bow. The small investors were mainly of a type. The ladies in their flowery dresses, holding hands with husbands in baggy chinos and faded linen shirts with socks and sandals despite the dress code. They could easily have been waiting in the queue for the Chelsea Flower Show or a National Trust property. The occasional brave individual stood out in a splash of pink hair or leopard skin.

Rebecca certainly looked eye-catching in a slinky black dress with a fishtail train which, to Gina's delight, people kept treading on.

But to her eyes the best dressed was Daniel himself.

'Look, Maudie,' she breathed, her gaze fixing on his luxuriant dark hair and laughing eyes, 'he's wearing a velvet jacket just like the one he wore to dancing school!'

'Is that so?' said Maudie, wondering when she could break the news to him about Gina's divorce. 'He's definitely the most attractive man here!'

'Hello, ladies,' Daniel greeted them, 'if you don't mind the rather archaic expression, but it somehow suits all this ridiculous get-up. Welcome to our rather embarrassing charade. Get yourselves a drink and remember, underneath all this nonsense, it is for a good cause!'

'One question, Daniel,' Gina asked softly.

'If it's PR-related,' he smiled back, 'you'd better ask Rebecca, otherwise fire away.'

'It's about your jacket,' she felt almost embarrassed asking. 'Is it the one you used to wear to dancing school?'

'I'm afraid the moths got that,' replied Daniel. 'This was the nearest I could find. I'm stunned you can remember.'

Unconsciously she put out a hand and stroked it.

'By the way,' he said softly, his eyes on hers, 'that's quite a dress.'

'Ruthie made me buy it. She said I mustn't wear one of my usual bin bags.'

'Ruthie was right.'

Across the crowd Rebecca's hawklike gaze landed on Gina and Daniel, and in seconds she was there beside them, holding her phone.

'Great dress, Gina,' she purred. 'It almost looks expensive.'

Gina regarded her suspiciously, wondering what was coming next.

'Seeing as it came from the Oxfam shop.' Smirking with delight at the opportunity to embarrass her rival, she held up her phone to show Daniel a photo of the shop window with the dress displayed.

'But that's fantastic!' he congratulated, sounding even more impressed. 'We should have made everyone do that. It's so fitting to launch an ethical business wearing charity shop clothes, so two good causes get to benefit. How clever of you, Gina.'

'Very clever,' Rebecca endorsed hollowly.

'Where did you get your dress, Rebecca?' replied Gina, keeping her voice carefully neutral. 'It must have cost a bomb.'

At this, Rebecca suddenly remembered she needed to check the mike for the speeches.

On her third glass of supermarket rosé, supplied by Harpers, Maudie spotted an opportunity and dived in.

'Daniel! I think this a wonderful idea. Many congratulations. By the way, we ought to congratulate Gina too. She got her decree nisi today!'

Daniel stared at Gina, almost speechless with surprise. 'I didn't know you were still getting divorced!'

Gina pulled in her tummy and discreetly pushed out her breasts to make sure the red dress displayed her curves to their best advantage. She was about to reply when the conversation was dramatically interrupted.

'Evening, Daniel, Ms Greenhills,' Mike Marshall looked as if he had chosen his dress suit two sizes too small to emphasize the bulging muscles of his torso and upper arms. 'So, when are you going to show us how this sham of a car wash works?'

Something about the blatant superiority of his tone triggered alarm bells in Gina.

'Any minute now, Mr Marshall. And thanks for coming. There is plenty of room in Southdown for both of us, after all.'

'Except that you are deliberately humiliating me with all this shit about being ethical, trying to imply that I am not.'

Daniel looked him in the eye. 'Well, are you? I've heard otherwise.'

'Then maybe you shouldn't listen to rumours,' he replied nastily. 'For the sake of your new venture.'

'Come on, time for the speeches,' Rebecca interrupted, grabbing Daniel by the arm.

'Good luck, Mr Napier,' said Mike, with the same smug superiority. He then marched off towards his car and drove away with Gina watching him thoughtfully.

The mayor's speech was brief and funny, and Daniel then invited him to come and press the button to start their first-ever car wash.

'I'm glad cars aren't usually as big as yours,' joked the new manager, indicating the mayoral limo, and the four cloth-wielding young men and women on the team laughed dutifully as the mayor pushed the button.

Instead of the sound of water flowing for the first cleaning stage, there was complete silence, followed by throat clearing and the occasional muffled laugh. The photographer from the local paper couldn't believe his luck.

'What's the problem?' Daniel asked the new manager, but he was looking as baffled as anyone else. In the front row Gina felt a tug on her red dress. It was Jasmin, beckoning her to follow.

'It's the pressure washer,' she stated in a low voice. 'It happened once at Mike's and I watched him put it right.'

'Let's go then.' Gina led Jasmin as unobtrusively as possible through the crowd to the cabin that served as the nerve centre of the car wash.

'I can do it, but I need a wrench,' whispered Jasmin, pulling on the lever as hard as she could.

'Right, I've got one in my car,' replied Gina.

She discarded the red heels and ran barefoot through the car park, trying to stay as unobtrusive as possible, which was quite difficult in a clinging red sheath dress. Thank God her car wasn't far away and the wrench exactly where it should be. She dashed back and handed it to Jasmin, who took hold of the large metal nut on the end of pressure washer unit. Gina grabbed the wrench at the same time and they both pulled with all their strength. From up by the canopy they heard a sudden shout of triumph mingled with relief, like a goal in the final minute of a football match. The car wash had started operating.

Daniel appeared at the door of the cabin, surprised to find them in there. 'Thank God it's going. Did you find a fault in the unit?'

'It was Jasmin,' admitted Gina. 'She'd seen Mike mend theirs in the past.'

'You were the one who had the wrench,' Jasmin insisted on sharing the glory. 'We couldn't have done it without that!'

'Which reminds me,' laughed Gina. 'Where are my shoes? Not that I can put them on. My feet are filthy from running around in the car park!'

'I'll wash them for you once this lot have gone,' offered Daniel, indicating the guests who had started to drift home, 'with the pressure washer,' he added with a grin. 'Thanks for saving the day. Can you imagine how embarrassing it would have been if our new ethical car wash wouldn't function on its first outing!'

'We're grateful to be of service, aren't we, Jasmin?'

Jasmin smiled and nodded.

'I'm assuming it was deliberate?' asked Daniel.

'What do you think?'

'I think Mike Marshall is currently laughing all the way home.'

'He won't be when he hears we fixed it!' Gina grinned.

'Can you keep my name out of it?' pleaded Jasmin, suddenly terrified.

'Of course. He can blame me.'

And he certainly found out the next morning when the *Southdown Gazette* landed on his mat with the headline LOCAL HERO OPENS ETHICAL CAR WASH blazed across its front page.

'It's not over yet, Mr Ethical Napier,' he muttered savagely, 'as you'll be finding out.'

'So how did the red dress go down?' Ruthie had appeared at the manor not long after breakfast, brandishing the local paper. 'Not that I need to ask. A whole page of photos, and for some reason you appear in three of them!'

Gina snatched the paper, half excited, half appalled.

There she was, listening to an extremely dull councillor

pontificating on the subject of whether they should bring back free deck chairs to the seafront as they'd had when Gina was growing up. Then Gina trying to look engrossed while the mayor's wife indiscreetly sounded off on her pet topic of the hideous new incinerator the council had installed which everyone local hated. Finally, there was Gina smiling straight at the camera and raising her glass in a toast.

'Look closely at the background. There's someone who can't take his eyes off you!' Ruthie pointed out.

Evie grabbed the paper from her. 'She's right. Look at Daniel, toasting you back! I bet the vamp in black will have something to say about that!'

Gina giggled. 'They should have photographed me ten minutes later, running across the car park in bare feet!'

'My God, Gina, what happened?' demanded Ruthie.

'Mike Marshall tried to sabotage the whole thing and wonderful Jasmin knew how to put it right, but she needed the wrench from my car to do it.'

'There's no mention of any of that in the paper,' puzzled Ruthie.

'That's because we managed to get away with it. Think how awful it would have been if it hadn't worked!'

'Sounds like you need a pat on the back, so it's a good thing I've booked Luca's at eight!'

'What are we celebrating?' asked Gina.

'Your decree nisi, of course! Divorce parties are all the thing now. They're all over Instagram.' She turned to Evie. 'Have you told Sexy Stuart you're in town?'

Evie shrugged. 'It's not worth it. Those daughters of his can't stand me and they're a huge part of his life. I'm not going to create a situation where he has to choose. I've seen enough wicked stepmothers in my work, thank you, and I'm not prepared to be one of them, so let's forget it. He's bald as a coot anyway,' she added unconvincingly.

'As a matter of fact,' corrected Ruthie, 'coots aren't bald. Besides, Stuart's eyes make up for it. He's got the sparkliest eyes in Southdown, haven't you noticed?'

Gina collapsed in giggles.

'You should start a dating agency and call it Looking on the Bright Side,' Evie replied.

'Can I help it if I'm a cock-eyed optimist?' enquired Ruthie, pretending to look injured.

'Dinner at Luca's is a very nice idea,' Evie conceded. 'Gina, are you going to wear The Dress again?' Evie asked.

'Yes, Gina. I really think you should!' endorsed Ruthie.

'People will have seen it so often after all the pictures in the paper they'll start asking for its autograph!' Gina replied. 'I'll see you later, girls. I've got to go and ring my own daughters and tell them the news. What time did you say at the restaurant?'

'Aperol spritzes at eight.'

'Great. We'll get a cab,' announced Gina. 'I know what's it's like when you're on the Aperol!'

She waved goodbye and got into her car, thinking during the drive back through the peaceful countryside of what she was going to say to Sadie and Lisa.

As it turned out, they already knew. Mark had called Sadie when Lisa happened to be there and told them the news. They seemed to be taking it remarkably calmly, though Lisa's voice broke a little when she asked her mother how she was.

'I'm fine, thank you,' replied Gina, trying to keep her voice steady. 'Sad that it should have come to this, but feeling relieved as well.'

'That's just how we feel,' agreed Sadie. 'You're not too old to start again, Mum,' she added.

'Thank you, darling,' she smiled, thinking of Daniel and whether he'd ever escape the bony clutches of Rebecca Boyd.

Luca's was a lovely old-fashioned Italian restaurant on the seafront, where they still thought the height of sophistication was pink tablecloths with candles stuck in chianti bottles wrapped in straw. The walls were lined with paintings of the Ponte Vecchio and the Piazza San Marco, and there was traditional Italian music playing, which, if you closed your eyes, made you feel you could actually be in some small mountain village in Italy.

For some reason the place always made Gina think of the scene in *Lady and the Tramp* where the two dogs start eating the same piece of spaghetti and end up kissing. Charm was something that didn't come with Michelin stars, and Luca's was overflowing with the stuff.

Ruthie had pushed the boat out fashion-wise and was wearing a linen shift in a yellow so bright it made you want to reach for your sunglasses. Gina had given in to Ruthie's entreaties and wore the now famous red dress. Even Evie, usually the most understated of dressers, had surrendered to the prevailing mood and worn blue palazzo pants with a colourful top.

By eight o'clock the place was packed with early diners and families who'd come straight from the beach, loaded with buckets and spades and airbeds, knowing that Luca, being Italian, loved families and would put up with a bit of sand on the floor. The adults were glowing with sun cream, some of them a telltale red from overdoing it, the children universally tanned like little biscuits, all of them bubbling over with holiday happiness.

'So, *belle signore*,' the owner Luca finally fought his way over to them, 'what are we having tonight? My special is *vitello*, veal, but we only use happy calves, and what is he going to do, the boy cow who is no good for milk except to make a lovely dish for the *signorine*?'

'That logic is definitely Mediterranean,' murmured Evie as soon as Luca was out of earshot, seating some other customers while they pondered the menu.

'Poor little calves,' Gina couldn't help commenting. 'I hope they were happy.'

Ruthie opted for her beloved calamari, followed by spaghetti carbonara, improbably with *zucchini fritti* on the side; while Gina chose *fegato Veneziana*.

'You know that's actually calves' liver, don't you?' announced Evie as she settled uncompromisingly on the veal special. 'I don't eat much meat these days,' she offered as her defence. 'I'm practically pescatarian.'

'I thought that was a star sign,' teased Ruthie. 'So, how's your search for Jasmin's mother going?'

'Very slowly. I've been on the point of giving up at least twice, which isn't like me. But my contact has had a bit of a breakthrough, so I'll stick with it for the moment.'

'Aren't your bosses going bananas?' enquired Ruthie.

'Quite probably, but I don't care as much as I thought I would,' Evie replied.

'Ah ha,' pointed out Gina. 'It's the celebrated Southdown syndrome you warned me about. Sun, Sea and – what's the other one? – definitely not Sex in my case . . .'

'Sleep?' suggested Ruthie, and they all fell about laughing.

'Hang on,' Gina recovered first. 'Isn't that Stuart Nixon and the Difficult Daughter over there?'

'Ruthie,' Evie asked sternly. 'Did you by any chance tell Stuart we were coming here tonight?'

'Me?' replied Ruthie, all innocence.

'Yes, you,' persisted Evie.

'I might have. I did bump into him in the second-hand bookshop, and we had a lovely long chat about Ian Rankin. We both like a good crime novel.'

'You'll be the victim of a crime if you're not careful,' threatened Evie. 'Quite possibly strangulation with spaghetti carbonara!'

'Perhaps I'd better change my order,' replied Ruthie, mock-penitent.

'Oh God, he's getting up!' blurted Evie, holding on to the arms of her chair. Neither of them had heard a tone of panic from their cool and competent friend before. 'Don't look, either of you!'

However, it wasn't Stuart who approached them but Jessica. 'Hello all, you look like you're having fun.'

'We are,' replied Ruthie gaily.

'Actually,' she continued, not looking nearly as sure of her ground as usual. 'It was Eve I wanted to speak to, or rather apologize to. Look, I realize I've been rude and hostile, and it really isn't on. I hope you'll accept my apology and that we can start again.' She gave a smile that made her look more like a guilty child than an assertive twenty-nine-year-old. 'Jessica Nixon. Nice to meet you.' She held out her hand as if this really were their first meeting.

Evie smiled back. 'Eve Beeston. Good to meet you too.'

On the other side of the room Stuart raised his glass in silent toast.

Evie felt a leap of optimism. Was she going to let herself believe in this as a real possibility after all these years had passed?

Twenty-One

'Maudie, the guests are here!' Jasmin shouted excitedly up the stairs. They had driven a long way and had asked if they could arrive early and drop off their things.

Mr B, once he'd realized that Jasmin really was shouldering the burden of work rather than him or his wife, had decided to throw his enthusiasm behind the venture. As Mrs B had pointed out, the old lady was more likely to stay here if she could earn a bit for the upkeep – which included their wages – and stop those nasty Winstanleys from getting her to move into town and hand the place over to them.

He opened the passenger side of their car and greeted the arrivals with an old-fashioned bow designed to make them overlook his overalls and bobble hat and imagine they were arriving at the Ritz. 'Welcome to Rookery Manor. The Honourable Mrs Tyler will be down in a moment to greet you.'

'Thanks,' replied Mr Williams, looking somewhat overwhelmed. 'Where do we park the car?'

'Round by the stables. But if you'd like to get out your bags, I could do it for you.'

By the time Jasmin peeped out of the drawing-room window she saw a small man watching Mr B driving off in his very expensive car with a look of extreme trepidation as his equally small wife stood staring up at the manor.

Moments later Maudie appeared, wearing one of her most dramatic dresses and holding her hand out to them as if she were royalty. 'Welcome, dear guests! Breakfast is laid out for you in the small saloon. We didn't know what you'd want so we've provided everything from bacon and egg to muesli and porridge!'

'Oh,' Mrs Williams shot a look at her husband. 'That's so kind of you, but we don't eat breakfast. We thought we were only dropping off our things.'

'But why don't you eat breakfast?' Maudie enquired curiously.

'We believe it's better for the system. It keeps down your blood sugar and blood pressure,' explained Mrs Williams apologetically.

'How absolutely fascinating!' Maudie replied, as if Mrs Williams had revealed the secret of life. 'Jasmin, could you show these lovely people their room?' She turned to Mr Williams. 'I realize you may be wanting to dash off, but if not I'd be delighted to give you a tour of the house. It's steeped in history, you know.'

The couple followed Jasmin, smiling all the way to their room.

When Jasmin returned, Maudie swept her into her arms. 'Dearest girl, this is going to be such fun! I'd forgotten how much I enjoy being a hostess. And I've already learned something new. I think I might stop having breakfast!'

'Here, Bill, you'd better eat up this bacon and eggs,' Mrs B instructed her husband after Jasmin had cleared it away. 'It's a crime if it goes to waste. Never heard such nonsense in my life. Not eating breakfast because it's good for you! My nan always said it was the most important meal of the day!'

'Did you hear Mrs Tyler saying she might try doing it herself?' replied her husband. 'She's going to love this palaver, ain't she?'

'Heh heh,' sniggered Mrs B. 'It's going to get right up that Rosa's stuck-up nose!'

When Evie arrived to work in the small room she'd been allocated in the manor, the Williams' had departed on their trip and she found an important message waiting for her from her contact in Beirut.

She was reading it when Maudie knocked on the door. 'Sorry to disturb you, dear, but I've been thinking and this morning it sort of came to a head.'

'What's that, Maudie?'

'It's about Jasmin. I've decided to call off the search for her birth certificate. The thing is, I couldn't love her any more even if she were my granddaughter.' Evie could see for herself how Maudie glowed at the mere mention of the girl. 'She's brought light into my life, you see. I hadn't realized how lonely I was until Jasmin came along and cheered me up, and this idea of having guests – it's just perfect! And it's wonderful that they're actually paying. To me it'll be like the old days, when this house was full of people and laughter. I hope I haven't put you to all this trouble for nothing, I feel very guilty that you've sacrificed your success to come down here.'

'I haven't,' Evie insisted. 'Like you I've found something out, something I've fought hard against admitting. Call it age, losing my edge, or finally seeing the light, but I'm not really interested in going back to my old life. When I return to London, I'm going to make some big changes.' She led Maudie to a chair and sat down next to her. 'But I have news that is far more important than my cliched admissions. You're right to call off the search – because we don't need to look any more.'

She reached for Maudie's hand with its gnarled blue veins that revealed her true age in a way her appearance did not. 'Jasmin *is* your granddaughter. My contact has tracked down the all-important adoption certificate. The baby you gave away was renamed Nadia. And Nadia is Jasmin's mother.'

Evie felt a shudder run through Maudie and held on to her tightly.

'My daughter,' she repeated. 'My daughter Nadia.' And then as if reality finally struck. 'Is my daughter Nadia still alive?'

'I'm afraid not.' Evie bowed her head. 'She died of cholera at forty-five.'

'Oh, my poor Nadia. If I hadn't given her away . . .' she began, then made herself stop. 'Is there any other family?'

'It seems not,' Evie replied gently. 'Her adopted father – the professor she mentioned – died during the war. That's why the grandmother brought her up from when she was about ten, because her mother was dead too.'

Maudie stared into the distance as if she were transporting herself through time and space. 'My granddaughter,' she repeated softly and began to cry. 'I suppose I'd better decide the best time to tell everyone. Will you be able to get a copy of her new birth certificate, do you think?'

'It's here now on my laptop,' Eve replied gently. 'My contact sent a scan to me. Would you like me to print it out?'

'Yes,' Maudie nodded, still looking as if she were in a dream. 'Then it'll seem more real.'

Evie walked across the room to the printer and pressed the button. She handed the printout to Maudie.

Maudie stared at the birth certificate and started to smile. 'She really is my granddaughter. How utterly wonderful!'

Turning to back to Evie, she grasped her hand, the tears spilling over down her cheeks. 'My dear girl, I can't thank you enough. I knew if anyone could do it, you could. You're so clever and determined. I suppose the next thing for me to do is tell the family.'

Evie suppressed a smile, imagining how popular the revelation would be with some of Maudie's family members.

'And now I have to go back to London.' She tapped her laptop tellingly. 'Communication from the senior partner,' she winked.

'But you will come back!' Evie begged. 'You're one of us now.'

'It's very tempting. I've been far happier here than I expected. Who knows?'

Maudie watched Evie get her things together and wondered if Gina would be able to persuade her to stay. She suspected the one person who could change her mind hadn't yet asked her.

What was the matter with men these days?

The next thing she had to do was invite the family to come round, and she would break the news to them.

'Are you really going back to London tomorrow?' Gina asked Evie. 'I'm going to miss you so much!'

They were sitting in Gina's garden, enjoying the last of the setting sun and sharing a bottle of chilled rosé.

'I have to if I want to keep my job,' Evie replied. 'And though I admit Southdown's been a revelation, I'm not quite ready to chuck it all in and take the plunge like you did.'

'I had the temptation of this house, remember? And a very generous legal adviser who told me to go for it.'

'And you don't have any regrets?' enquired Evie.

'None!' insisted Gina. 'I love the lifestyle here and I can still run the business – and go swimming in the sea at the same time.'

'I envy you that. I've decided to make some changes and cut back on my workload.'

'Good for you!' Evie's reduced workload, mused Gina, would still be three times other people's.

Evie lay back admiring Gina's bronzed skin and compared it enviously with her own much paler look. That was another thing she'd like to change. Should she share the news about Jasmin with her friend, she wondered, but decided it would be fairer to let Maudie break the news herself.

'Where shall we go for dinner for your last night?' Gina broke into her thoughts.

'I liked that pub on the seafront.'

'The Langdon Arms? Let's go there then. Ruthie's hoping to drop in later.'

'Great. I have to do a bit of packing first.'

'I'll book for 8 p.m. then.'

Evie went up to the room she was staying in to sort out her things. She'd only been here for ten days but it had begun to feel like home again and leaving would be quite a wrench. She tried to remind herself of all the things she loved about London: its sophistication, the galleries, restaurants and wine bars, her job. It struck her that what she didn't have was friends. With such a busy working life she'd never felt she needed them. Now, having spent so much time with Gina and Ruthie, she realized how much she'd miss them.

Then there was Stuart.

She wasn't going to let herself think about Stuart and his sparkly eyes. If he'd wanted to get closer to her, he could have, but he hadn't even tried.

The Langdon Arms was buzzing with Friday-night drinkers, spilling out so that they filled not only the terrace in front of the pub but right out across the pavement into the road. The stalwarts at the bar stood with their pints listening to the happy shouts of the teenagers riding the rollercoaster on the promenade or watching the bright lights of the giant wheel and the pier beyond. There was a heady holiday feeling everywhere.

'How can you leave all this?' Gina asked, gesturing round her.

'With difficulty – and believe me, I never thought I'd say that!'

'You could still change your mind,' tempted Gina.

'No reason to. I'm a Londoner at heart.'

'So, what are you having?'

'Since it's my last night I'm going to push the boat out and have scampi and chips!'

'Ooh, and you such a sophisticate. Oh well, you'll be back to your sea bass and kale soon enough.'

'To the joys of London Town!' Evie raised her glass just as she caught sight of Stuart laughing with his two daughters across the crowded bar and felt a jolt of disappointment.

Jessica, noting a subtle change in her father, followed his glance. The reason was patently obvious. Eve and Gina were at a table on the other side of the pub.

'You should say hello,' she said firmly. 'I think they're about to go into the restaurant. Now's your chance.' And she gave him a very unsubtle shove.

'Stuart!' Gina greeted him, sensing slight embarrassment on his part. 'We're having a farewell dinner for Evie. She's going back to London tomorrow. Why don't you join us? I'm sure they'd be happy to add another place.'

He glanced at Evie and for the briefest of moments their eyes locked, then he gestured back towards his daughters.

'I'm out with Jessica and Maddy, I'm afraid.'

Don't ask them too, Evie willed her friend, but fortunately Gina had more sense than to force the situation.

'I hope you'll be back again soon?' enquired Stuart.

Why did he always keep a distance and never ask her out? Evie wanted to scream.

'I'm not sure about that,' she replied, looking him straight in the eye. 'I suspect Real Life beckons and I'm usually pretty busy.'

He seemed on the verge of saying something, then changed his mind. 'Well, goodbye then and good luck.'

Across the room Jessica watched him anxiously.

When he rejoined them, she put her arm round him. 'I've ordered you another drink. You're going to need it when you hear what I've got to say. Look, Dad, I was completely wrong about Eve. She's one of the good ones and you'd be mad to let her go.'

Stuart's sparkly eyes fixed on her affectionately. 'I'm glad you've changed your mind, and that you're big enough to do admit it, but Eve is a city girl through and through. You said moving to Croydon would be like being sent to Siberia, but so would Southdown to someone like her.'

'Dad!' Jessica replied passionately. 'People have relationships across continents! You're talking about sixty miles!'

'I'm sorry to let you down, but I'm not the type for a relationship with someone who loves the city and finds my hometown the acme of provincial. I've thought about it, Jessica, and the truth is, I'm too old!'

Jessica shrugged. 'Only you know what you really want, but I'm surprised at you, Dad. It's not like you to be a coward!'

* * *

'So what's this summons from Maudie all about?' Rosa asked her younger sister in her usual pugnacious tone.

Lucy was lying on her enormous white sofa with her equally enormous white husky, which she treasured for its bright blue eyes that exactly matched her cushions. She also loved his gentle nature. She'd called him Saff, short for Sapphire, only less pretentious, she hoped, and they were both indulging their guilty pleasure of watching *Poirot* on TV. Lucy loved the programme but was beginning to get fed up with the fact it was sponsored by mobility aids and thinking she might have to change her allegiance to something younger.

'I'm sorry, Rosa, but I don't follow your drift,' Lucy replied irritably. Rosa was the sort of person who never watched television at all, not even when everyone else was watching. 'What's what all about?'

'This summons from Maudie,' repeated Rosa. 'Haven't you looked at your phone lately? She wants us all to go to the manor tomorrow afternoon.'

Lucy glanced at the TV where Poirot was about to gather all the suspects in the library as he always did.

'Perhaps she's going to tell us she's changing her will or something.'

'But she hasn't told us what's in it at the moment!' objected Rosa.

'Well maybe she's going to tell us then.'

'It's highly inconvenient anyway,' moaned Rosa. 'I have a committee meeting I'll have to miss. And Ambrose is going to have to come back from London early for it.'

'I expect we could survive without you,' Lucy replied naughtily, knowing there was no way on earth that the pair would miss it.

'It's so high-handed,' Rosa went on. 'As if she were royalty or something.'

'Well, clearly it's something important to her,' sighed Lucy. 'Now, if that was all . . .'

'She could have had a diagnosis,' Rosa volunteered.

Observing the way Rosa had cheered up at the prospect, Lucy remarked drily, 'I wouldn't get your hopes up. If you ask me, Maudie's indestructible!'

'No need to sound so superior!' flashed back Rosa. 'Just because you married the richest man in Southdown!'

'Try not to be so embittered, Rosa. We all know you and Ambrose want the manor.'

'Only because we care about it! Family means a lot to us. And Rookery Manor's a very special place.'

'Indeed. Then I'll see you tomorrow at this family meeting. In the meantime, I have urgent business I must attend to, so bye for now,' she insisted, practically pushing her sister out of the penthouse.

Rosa imagined her rushing off to a hairdresser appointment or session at the beauty parlour, while the truth was Lucy wanted Poirot to tell her whodunnit before she had to take the dog for a walk and sort out supper.

Gina had just waved Evie off the next morning and was trying not to think how much duller life would be without her, when her phone rang. It was Becky, the helpful young Waddington's intern she'd spoken to about the missing Chagall.

The thought of that awful Gavin Miers putting his hand on her knee flashed into her mind and she felt angry all over again. Why did he think she was fair game just because she'd split from her husband?

'That Chagall you were asking about, Ms Greenhills,' said Becky. 'It seems we did sell it after all. I'm sorry I wasn't aware of that when you rang, but Mr Miers was in charge of the transaction. I only came across the paperwork yesterday, and when I asked him about it, he said it was none of my business, that I was only an intern.'

Gina could hear the righteous indignation of the young in the girl's tone. It reminded her of her daughter Sadie.

'Do you happen to know who the seller was?' Gina asked, keeping her voice neutral.

'That was the other odd thing. Mr Miers said it was being sold anonymously. And yet somebody definitely brought it in,' replied the girl.

Gina's throat tightened in sudden tension. 'Do you happen to know who?

'No, except that my friend Suze – she's another intern – heard Mr Miers call him Ambrose. Is that any help to you?'

Gina gulped back her astonishment and made herself sound normal. 'Very helpful indeed, thanks.'

'Great. By the way . . .' Gina could hear nervousness creep into the girl's previously confident tone. 'Could you not mention how you found out?'

'Absolutely. And thanks again.'

As she put her phone back in her pocket, Gina wondered why the girl had taken the risk of calling. Maybe she simply suspected something dodgy was happening and couldn't do anything about it herself. Or perhaps Gavin Miers had tried it on with her too.

If so, he'd obviously picked the wrong person.

Had it not been for Becky's call, Gina would have gone on assuming that Maudie was the one who had sold the lithograph in order to provide for Jasmine. Rather than upset Maudie by questioning her about the theft, she had let it go, telling herself Maudie was entitled to trade in her treasures for much-needed cash if she chose to do so. The more she thought about it, the more incensed she was that the money the Chagall sold for had been pocketed by the Winstanleys.

Still, there was a certain satisfaction in discovering that the seller was Awful Ambrose, especially after the way he and Rosa had accused her of the theft, telling Maudie that she'd had it authenticated beforehand solely to increase its sale value. From the start, they'd seemed consumed with jealousy and resentment at the way Maudie had taken to her, but she'd never have imagined they would stoop so low. Then again, obsession made people act in strange ways.

But what to do with this information? For the moment, Gina resolved to keep the knowledge to herself until she decided how best to use it.

Twenty-Two

Next morning, as she drove towards the manor for the meeting, Gina noticed that the queue for Desperate Dan's was so long that it snaked right round the car park and into the main road.

She'd decided to give it a try since, as usual, she had left far too much time for the journey and besides, she'd love to see how it was doing.

Brilliantly, it seemed. More than that, the atmosphere here was completely different to its rival. Instead of haunted, anxious faces, the workers here were smiling and exchanging jokes with each other. Someone had given them the uniform of polo shirts in an optimistic yellow which suited the mood of the place. The other thing she noticed was how smoothly the process seemed to work and how clean the premises were. OK, they were new, but it also reflected good management and a sense of pride. Mike Marshall must be fuming.

As she queued for the free vacuum she decided to top up her tyres – always a nightmare process in Gina's eyes. The display showing how full your tyres were baffled her, as did knowing whether any air was actually getting through to them.

Inevitably she'd end up looking so hopeless that some bossy bloke would step in to offer patronizing assistance.

'Can I be of any help?' enquired a voice behind her as she struggled to find the cap on the passenger-side tyre which she'd just dropped. Who made these things so damn tiny anyway?

To her annoyance, it was Daniel Napier. Now she was going to seem like a complete idiot instead of the strong modern woman she aspired to be.

'Everyone finds these machines tricky,' he shrugged, 'except the occasional irritating know-all.'

He crouched down, elegantly managing to avoid soiling his pale chinos, and expertly filled each tyre in turn.

'You seem to be going gangbusters here,' commented Gina.

'Yes, we're very pleased.' Weakly, she found herself wondering if the 'we' meant him and Rebecca Boyd and whether, now that the place was launched, she would back off. Probably too much to hope.

'And how are you enjoying your house?' asked Daniel.

'Love it. Mainly because it's so different from when my parents lived there!' She was on the brink of adding, 'Why don't you come and have a look?' when they were interrupted by someone Gina recognized. It was the young woman who'd been crying at the bus stop. The one Jasmin had stopped to talk to, who was desperate to find her confiscated passport.

'Could you give this to Jasmin?' She handed Gina a grubby note with Jasmin's name on the front. 'Soon, please,' she added with an air of quiet desperation.

'Of course. I'll give it to her today.'

'I wonder what that's all about,' said Daniel when she'd gone.

'I don't know,' replied Gina, conscious he shared her anxiety, 'but I'd better keep an eye on Jasmin.'

'Be careful,' he reached out a hand and touched hers, and Gina, who was trying so hard to be independent and self-sufficient, felt herself melt disgracefully at the thought of someone who would look out for her.

'I will. I've got to go up the manor. Maudie's called a family meeting and I'm included. I suspect it's to tell them her new idea for making the manor pay for itself.'

'And what's that?'

'Filling the place with paying guests so Maudie can pretend it's the kind of grand house party she's always longed for.'

'And how will the family feel about that?'

'I'll report back as soon as I know.'

'Do that. And Gina . . .' he hesitated for a fraction of a second.

'Yes?'

'Take care of yourself.'

Gina smiled, wondering how they could get beyond this chilly politeness.

It wouldn't be long before she got an answer. But not in the way she was expecting.

The meeting had been set up in the dining room, which was so large and grand they rarely used it. Today six coffee cups were set out on the long table, next to a huge rose bowl filled with blooms from the garden, whose scent pervaded the whole room. But the dominating presence was undoubtedly a vast portrait of Maudie in a dramatic black ball gown, painted in the manner of John Singer Sargent.

Maudie glanced round at her audience: Lucy smiled back, fascinated to hear what her great-aunt had to say; Gina sat towards one end trying to keep a low profile at such an intimate family occasion; Rosa already looked aggressive even though she had no idea what was to come; Ambrose managed in some accomplished manner to look both bored and resentful at the same time; Jasmin simply looked down, modest and self-effacing, and Mrs B took an unnecessarily long time to serve the coffees in the hope of catching the drift of what seemed a momentous occasion.

'Thank you for coming. I'm sure you're all wondering what this is about.' Maudie straightened her back and raised her head, as if to give herself confidence. 'I'm going to tell you a story,' she began. 'As we're in what dear Jasmin calls a fairy-tale manor, I'll tell it to you in the form of a fairy tale.' Rosa darted a look of obvious dislike at Jasmin, who was still looking modestly at the table. 'And like all good fairy tales it has a happy ending.'

'Actually, they don't,' pointed out Ambrose fussily. 'A lot of fairy tales end with people being eaten by wolves or turned into toads.'

'I fear that's too much to hope in this case,' Maudie replied, looking straight at him. 'May I go on?'

Ambrose sat down ungraciously.

'A long time ago a young girl married an older man whom she admired very much. In the habit of the times, she didn't know him very well, but she did choose him herself. Her parents were concerned because he was nearer their age, but she was a headstrong girl and she got her way. He joined the British Cultural Commission, and they were posted to exciting places: Cyprus, Morocco and then to Damascus.'

'Where Jasmin comes from,' noted Ambrose, raising an eyebrow.

'Exactly,' smiled Maudie, pausing a moment.

'Don't keep us on tenterhooks,' Rosa chipped in cynically. 'We're all gripped. Tell us more about our heroine.'

'She was young with a thirst for adventure. Her husband was too busy to join in, but he was happy that she should be shown around by a younger colleague who would take her to all the wonderful historical places and bring them to life for her.'

'Possibly rather rash of him,' observed Ambrose.

Lucy stared at him, beginning to guess what was coming next.

Maudie ignored him.

'The young wife became very close to the colleague. He was all the things her husband was not: attentive, tender, full of life and learning. She fell in love with him and became pregnant.'

'But didn't anyone notice?' asked Lucy.

'She wore the eccentric clothes favoured by famous lady explorers of the era. Her faithful servant helped her and told her she must hide from public view and give the baby away as soon as it was born.'

'Why is she telling us all this?' Rosa stage-whispered to Lucy.

'Wait and see,' replied Lucy. 'I expect you'll find out in a minute.' She glanced at Jasmin, whose face had taken on a stony quality, though whether it was from disapproval of such a colonial tale or attentiveness, Lucy couldn't tell.

'You were always slow, Rosa,' needled Ambrose.

'Those were very different times,' continued Maudie, aware of the intensity of their attention, 'and the young wife felt she had no choice. So the baby was adopted and not long afterwards they were posted back to England. Our heroine was very, very sad. Her husband had a portrait commissioned to try and cheer her up.' She glanced at the vast picture on the wall above them with dislike.

'Oh my God,' blurted Rosa. 'She's talking about herself!'

Looking on, Gina tried not to smile at the outrage in Rosa's tone.

'The couple moved from London to Southdown,' continued Maudie. 'They bought a fairy-tale manor house. And then, many years later, something wonderful happened!'

'She gets pregnant again?' suggested Ambrose rudely.

'Shut up, Ambrose,' Lucy hissed. 'Everyone else is interested.'

'The husband died but the widow lived on to a great age. One day she sees a girl working in a car wash who looks totally out of place. She strongly reminds her of someone.'

'The younger colleague,' suggested Ambrose smugly.

'Oh my God, you don't mean . . .' The colour drained from Rosa's face.

'Yes, Rosa, full marks,' said Ambrose, shaking his head. 'I'm assuming you think the baby you gave away was Jasmin's mother?'

'But that would mean . . .'

Rosa's face in that moment reminded Gina of a landed fish gasping for breath.

'Exactly so,' endorsed Ambrose, smiling unpleasantly. 'If the baby Maudie gave away was Jasmin's mother, which I suspect is the drift of the story, then Jasmin would be Maudie's granddaughter.'

They all stared at the girl, who looked for a moment like a cornered animal.

'But how can you be sure?' demanded Rosa, beginning to see the implications of Maudie's revelation.

'With great difficulty. Because of the tragic situation in her country, records are hard to find, but then the wonderful Eve arrived and she managed to track down the adoption and birth certificates.'

Maudie's gaze switched to Jasmin, an expression almost of

pleading in her eyes. 'My dearest girl, believe me, I could not be happier!'

Jasmin's response was to rise slowly from the table. 'If you will all excuse me, I would like a little time to think about this.' And she ran from the room.

Gina rose at the same time.

'Give her a few minutes,' counselled Lucy gently. 'Just to take in the shock. Have you any more surprises for us, Maudie?' she enquired.

Maudie smiled at her gratefully. 'As a matter of fact, I do.' She stood up so that, in a dramatic evocation of the passing years, the Maudie of today was silhouetted against the youthful version in the black dress. 'I have made a decision,' she announced firmly. 'I know I am growing older, but I wanted you all to know that I will not be moving from here.' She avoided Rosa's eyes as she added: 'Especially not to a sensible flat on the seafront with a concierge.'

Rosa shot a look at her husband, who stared stonily ahead. 'For the moment, Rookery Manor is going to become a B and B to cover the costs of its upkeep. I have always loved being a hostess and Jasmin is happy to do the organizing and even help make beds. My granddaughter and I are going to do it together.'

Gina could hear the pride ringing in her voice.

'It'll be a huge amount of work,' protested Rosa.

'Jasmin is happy to do the work,' repeated Maudie. 'Her aunt ran a guesthouse and she helped with everything. We have a couple staying here already. They seem to like it.'

As if in endorsement of this, Mrs B put her head round the door. 'Sorry to interrupt, but the guests were asking for Jasmin.'

'I'll go and find her,' Maudie announced, getting to her feet. 'I will be back shortly.'

'My God,' Rosa shook her head as Maudie departed. 'Do you believe this crazy claim?'

Lucy smiled. 'A birth certificate is pretty good evidence to support the claim, I'd have thought.'

Upstairs, Maudie and Jasmin sent their paying guests on their way with detailed guidance on how to find the Fishermen's Museum in the centre of town.

'Let's sit down here for a moment,' Maudie indicated a sofa with a very deep back and rope ties where they would be almost invisible.

'You really are my grandmother?' Jasmin asked as they sat down, her dark eyes fixed on Maudie's fading blue ones.

'I really am.' She folded Jasmin into her soft embrace. 'I'll show you the certificate later.'

Jasmin closed her eyes and breathed in Maudie's perfume. 'My grandmother Teta also wore perfume,' she whispered, and began to cry, overcome with conflicting emotions of hope about a new life and loyalty to the woman who had brought her up.

'Your grandmother Teta sounds a wonderful woman.' Maudie gently stroked the girl's dark hair. 'You are lucky, Jasmin. You have two grandmothers. Teta, whose memory you honour, and the undeserving Maudie.'

'You are very deserving,' Jasmin replied, raising a tentative hand to Maudie's face. 'I think Teta would have been glad for me.'

'Then I hope I will live up to Teta's expectations,' replied Maudie, with a watery smile. 'Now, I think we should go back to your new family. Before they kill each other!'

'All families kill each other,' laughed Jasmin as she helped Maudie up from the depths of the sofa.

'Right. Into battle!'

Mrs B had had the good sense to provide more coffee in their absence. Maudie made a mental note to thank her later.

'Hello, everyone,' she apologized. 'Sorry about the interruption. We have sent our guests happily off to the Fishermen's Museum.'

'Would you like some coffee, Maudie?' asked Jasmin and went off to fetch her a fresh cup.

'Perhaps it is better I make my announcement with my granddaughter out of the room,' Maudie said. 'I wanted to let you know that I am putting the ownership of Rookery Manor and its contents into a trust. The trust will be in favour of my granddaughter, on the condition she makes sufficient profit to keep the place on its feet.'

'This is ludicrous! You know nothing about the girl!' accused Ambrose.

'I know enough. And I believe I know something about character.' Maudie announced, looking beadily at Rosa.

'But what about the rest of us?' demanded Rosa. 'Is everything going to the girl you've only just met?'

'To my granddaughter,' Maudie reminded her. 'There will be other legacies in my will, of course,' she reassured.

'Maudie,' Ambrose adopted another tack. 'Is this wise? We have heard from Gina how much your possessions are worth. You surely will not be handing those to Jasmin as well? I mean, what about the things that have been disappearing? Can you be sure there is no connection to Jasmin's arrival at the manor?'

Even Rosa looked appalled at this suggestion.

Gina fixed Ambrose with a penetrating stare. 'I would be careful about making random accusations of theft, if I were you, Ambrose,' she announced pleasantly. 'I have received some very interesting information about the individual who sold the missing Chagall through Waddingon's.'

'Have you indeed . . .' stumbled Ambrose, suddenly fixing all his attention on the piece of paper in front of him.

'But, Maudie,' persisted Rosa, ignoring the treacherous undercurrents, 'Jasmin is a lovely girl, and no doubt very efficient, but she has none of the deep affection for the manor that Ambrose and I do.'

Maudie turned towards the pair with the sweetest of smiles on her face. 'But Rosa, dear, correct me if I'm wrong, but didn't I overhear the two of you arriving at the decision that, despite your deep affection for the manor, you intended to sell it and move to the South of France?'

For the first time anyone could remember, Rosa Winstanley was entirely lost for words.

By the time Jasmin reappeared with Maudie's coffee, almost everyone had disappeared.

'Round one to you, Maudie,' grinned Lucy as she kissed her great-aunt goodbye.

'Game, set and match, I hope,' replied Maudie, beginning to look exhausted after such an emotional encounter. 'You don't mind about the manor, do you, Lucy love? You're the only one of my other relations I'd want to leave it to. Would you have wanted to live here?'

'Not unless you gave me carte blanche to demolish it and build a Le Corbuisier concrete nightmare?' laughed her great-niece.

'I don't think the planners would let you,' replied Maudie. 'Though you never know nowadays. Jasmin dear, I'm going to take this coffee upstairs and have a nap.'

'I'll come with you,' offered Lucy. 'And carry that cup for you.' She removed the cup from Maudie's shaking hand. 'It's been quite a morning for you.'

'Have they all gone?' whispered Jasmin to Gina, looking nearly as worn out as Maudie.

'Not sure,' replied Gina. 'Don't worry about them though. Lucy's nice and I'm pretty sure Rosa and Awful Ambrose will keep their distance now. How are you? Has this all been a difficult shock?'

'Maudie was so kind,' replied Jasmin, close to tears. 'She told me she is not replacing my grandmother but wants only to share the honour with her.'

'Maudie has been so happy since she saw you in the car wash that day.'

'It was a lucky day for me.'

'And for Maudie.' They held each other for a brief moment before Gina remembered her mission.

'Jasmin, I saw a friend of yours – I recognized her from the time she was crying at the bus stop – she handed me this and asked me to give it to you. She said it was important.'

Jasmin read the letter and stood stock-still, as if she'd been turned to stone by a bad witch from Maudie's fairy tale. At last she managed to speak. 'My friend's been told she can get help. But she has to have her passport. The one Mike Marshall hid from her.'

'And you think you know where he put it?' asked Gina.

Jasmin nodded. 'I'm going to have to try and get it for her.'

Involuntarily Gina's hand went out to her. Daniel had been right to worry. 'If you do go, I'm coming with you.'

Twenty-Three

Evie sat on her usual bench in Embankment Gardens and looked around her. It was her favourite time of day, when the dusk was painting everything with its pearly light and most people had gone home. Most of her fellow lawyers seeking peace would go to the Temple Gardens or Lincoln's Inn Fields, but she preferred the flower-filled expanse of this place.

Cleopatra's Needle and the river were just across the road. On her way she'd walked past the last watergate in London where Tudor boats would have moored in the fifteenth century. Then there was dear old Robert Burns. The words of perhaps his most famous poem had leapt into her head: 'My love is like a red, red rose'. They left her unmoved. Maybe that was her trouble.

She thought of the huge pile of work that had waited for her on her return. She didn't grudge it. Jessica might imply that it wasn't important, but everyone suffered hurt during divorce, and if she could help she still wanted to as much as ever.

The thought of Jessica brought Southdown to mind. Would Gina be going for an evening swim in the glassy water with its path of shining light?

Really, what *was* the matter with her today? She'd sat on this bench countless times before, but tonight for the first time she noticed it bore a memorial inscribed on a small brass plate: *In Memory of Mary W. Bates, forever missed by her husband, children and grandchildren.* She noted with a shock that Mary had been the age that she was now.

She wasn't usually given to mawkish sentimentality, but she couldn't help wondering what would be put on her bench. But then, she wouldn't have husband, children or grandchildren to put it there in the first place.

Enough of this, she told herself, you need a drink. She gathered her things and walked towards her favourite wine bar, Casks, only five minutes away, where she dropped in for a drink most evenings on her way home.

As she turned into Villiers Street she noticed some idiot in a white suit and sunglasses was causing a disturbance at the far end. Really, what kind of fool went around dressed like that?

To her horror she realized he was walking towards her. Worse: *dancing* towards her. People were stopping to stand and stare. As he got closer, she realized he had some kind of speaker in his pocket which was blaring out a Bee Gees song. He was really near now. Was he some kind of busker or performance artist? She recognized the song as 'More Than a Woman'.

Just as she was about to say something rude about not accosting women in the street, he whipped off his sunglasses.

Oh my God, it was Stuart Nixon!

And he was holding a hand out to her just like Travolta in the dance contest in *Saturday Night Fever*! Worse, everyone was clapping and shouting, and she would look a complete idiot if she refused.

'For pity's sake, Stuart,' she hissed, trying to remain her usual cool and composed self. 'What the fuck are you doing?'

'Asking you to dance,' he grinned. 'Blame Jessica. This is her idea – and think how foolish I'll look if you turn me down.'

'Go on, lady,' shouted the flower vendor outside the tube station. 'Give the lad a chance!'

'But I don't know the moves,' she pleaded.

'Just follow what I do.'

She put down her laptop bag, assuming she'd never see it again, and took his hand.

To her surprise, her body seemed to take over from her mind and she began to feel like the heroine of one of her favourite romcoms; Julia Roberts perhaps, or Meg Ryan.

By the time they got to the final chord she was laughing with pure pleasure.

And then, to the delight of the crowd, he was kissing her.

For a moment she forgot that she was in her work clothes, standing in the middle of a crowd in Villiers Street, and kissed him back.

'I hoped I'd find you here,' he grinned when they finally drew apart. 'I'd hate to waste a good suit.'

'John Travolta wasn't bald,' Evie pointed out, pulling his head towards her and dropping a kiss on the top of his head.

'He probably is now,' replied Stuart with a grin. 'Time for some champagne, I think.'

She'd been so carried away she'd forgotten all about the laptop containing her entire working life. Now she looked around for it anxiously.

'I believe you might need this,' said a disturbingly familiar voice.

She jerked round to find the senior partner holding out her laptop bag, his face as stony as Cleopatra's Needle.

'Perhaps I'm to congratulate you?' he enquired, bracket-faced.

'I was coming to that bit,' said Stuart, turning her round to face him. 'I don't mind if I have to live in London, but I can't give up the only chance of happiness I've had in years. Besides,' he added, 'my daughters would never forgive me if I let you go. Will you marry me?'

Evie hesitated for a second, struggling with all that she knew about marriage and its high failure rate.

'Come on, Eve,' encouraged the senior partner, 'I can't stand here all day holding your laptop.'

She looked up at Stuart's sparkly eyes and remembered the kindness he'd showed to so many people, and knew she could do with some of that.

'Yes,' she replied. 'I will.'

Everyone around them began to clap again, but even louder this time.

'Congratulations,' the senior partner commented to Stuart as the clapping began to subside, 'on winning a wonderful woman.' His face softened and Evie expected some sentimental recollection of his own engagement. Instead, a mischievous expression Evie had never seen before spread across his features. 'I used to fancy myself as a bit of a Travolta back in the day.'

Evie reached out and took her laptop, trying not to picture the senior partner in a white suit with his chest hair showing.

'Good luck to you both.' He walked off, smiling, no doubt imagining himself in his heyday breaking out the moves to 'Stayin' Alive'.

'Well, you never know about people, do you?' marvelled Evie.

'That's the joy of them,' agreed her betrothed, leading her towards the nearby wine bar. 'Our celebration awaits.'

She pointed to his pocket, from which the Bee Gees were still loudly emanating. 'And maybe now you could turn off the music?'

Twenty-Four

Going back to the caves to look for the hidden passports was a frightening prospect, but it would be safer if they went together. Her conscience wouldn't let Jasmin go alone, and having two of them would mean that one could at least look out for any potential danger. And after all, she reminded herself, this was Southdown on a Tuesday in summer. What could really happen?

'The best time to go would be right before closing,' Gina stated, trying to sound more confident than she felt. 'I'm no expert but I did visit them with my friend, and have a rough idea of the layout, which I suspect is more than you?'

'I hate caves,' apologized Jasmin. 'I used to hide when my father tried to take me.'

'Has Maudie got a proper torch? It would be much more use than phones.'

'I'll ask Mrs B,' suggested Jasmin. 'She knows everything.' She went off in search of the housekeeper, who turned out to be in the farthest corner of the manor looking for something in the loft.

'Now what would you be wanting with a torch?' enquired Mrs B.

Jasmin sensed it would be best to say as little as possible to the gossipy and overprotective housekeeper. 'I have lost the catch on a necklace,' she bluffed, hoping her honest nature didn't shine through. 'It would be easier to find with proper light.'

'I'll see if I can find it. Mr B's probably nicked it for his shed.'

'I wonder, what are those two up to?' she enquired of her husband, not expecting an answer. He never knew what was going on and was even less interested. There had been something shifty in Jasmin's manner that Mrs B's ever-vigilant radar had picked up despite all attempts to put her off the scent. 'I think I'd better keep an eye out.' She picked up the powerful torch and took it back to the house to find Jasmin.

'I've looked up the opening times of the caves and they close at five, so I suggest we get there for four thirty when it's less busy,' suggested Gina in a low voice.

She saw the terrified look on Jasmin's face. 'What if we were trapped there for the night?'

That was certainly a frightening thought and, as usual with anything scary, Gina decided the best course was to ignore it. 'Providing the passports are where we think he put them we should be able to get in and out again in ten minutes. There's a funicular lift up the cliffside which will make it even quicker.'

'The torch you asked for, Jasmin dear,' Mrs B had materialized as silently as the ghost of any unfortunate hanged for smuggling.

'I won't ask what you're up to, but it's clearly an adventure,' offered Mrs B, taking in the fear that seemed to be rooting Jasmin to the spot. The girl was practically shaking!

As neither of them responded to this sally she turned away, her mind whirring with the information she'd gleaned. What caves did they mean? If they were going to use the funicular it meant either a clifftop walk, the dismal cafe that overlooked the town, or – yes, of course that was why they'd need a torch – the smugglers' caves! But what on earth were they planning to do in the caves at closing time? And what was all that about passports? For the hundredth time she wished her husband had been of a more enquiring nature so they could try and solve this mystery together.

There was something going on here, Mrs B decided. This was no ordinary outing, or why would the normally sensible Gina look so rattled? And Jasmin so outright scared? Someone ought to be keeping an eye on those two. But who? Mr B would be no bloody good.

And then she thought of someone who might help.

Parking was always tricky in the height of summer, so Jasmin and Gina got the bus down to the old town and walked through the crowded back streets towards the funicular. This was the sophisticated end of the town made up of second-hand book-shops, antiques markets and vintage clothes emporia. They walked past a half-timbered inn with laughing sunburnt drinkers spilling out onto the pavement, making the most of their last days of holiday. The other end of town was more raucous. Tattooed overweight men with their tops off – not a good look, Gina decided – amassed pints of beer on every available surface from windowsills, pavements and the dividing walls between the pub and the seafront. Here families wandered up and down, clutching children's hands, Dayglo airbeds and massive ice-cream cones topped with chocolate or chopped caramel. It was all so reassuringly normal.

Beyond the old town were rows and rows of tall, narrow fishermen's huts fashioned from black planks, as high as bell-towers, where – in the days when Southdown boasted a large fishing fleet – nets would be hung to dry from the highest rafters. Now they looked almost like characters in an action-adventure film who might uproot and form an army to fight against an evil monster. If the monster turned out to be Mike Marshall, she hoped they'd be on their side.

Gina tried to take in some of the holiday mood which surrounded them but her concern for Jasmin, who was looking pale and nervous, and her own mounting fears meant that she was almost grateful when they reached the funicular and left it all behind.

Back at Rookery Manor, Mrs B was standing by the house phone, which, ever since its installation, had been sited in a highly inconvenient spot under the main staircase. Maudie had always held that this was a very good thing since it discouraged guests from making lengthy phone calls at her expense. Despite much advice to get rid of it now that the smartphone had arrived, Maudie insisted it was useful for finding her mobile, and worth keeping just for that.

'I know I'm right,' Mrs B announced to no one in particular. 'I'm going to phone that nice Mr Napier.' Like Gina's own friends, Mrs B had been taking a lively interest in the budding romance, and greatly approved of it. 'He'll know what to do, I'm sure.'

Daniel was halfway through showing a grandee from the town hall, who had realized the PR value of having helped fund this venture, round the car wash when his phone buzzed in his pocket. He realized a call from the manor was sufficiently unusual that he'd better take it.

'Hello, Mrs Browning,' he asked when Mrs B excitedly identified herself. 'What can I do for you?'

'It's Jasmin and Gina, Mr Napier. They've gone to the smugglers' caves!'

Daniel was not immediately able to see why a visit to Southdown's premier tourist attraction might be a problem, but Mrs B soon filled him in on what she'd overheard, plus a few lurid speculations of her own.

'The thing is, Mr Napier, they're deliberately going at closing time and they've taken a torch! I didn't mean to overhear,' she added, flustered. 'I was handing over the torch – Mr B had it in his shed. I'm concerned they've got themselves into some kind of trouble. You should have seen Jasmin. She was white as a Greek yogurt!'

'Thank you for letting me know. You did the right thing,' reassured Daniel, who was beginning to piece together a dangerously worrying scenario as he spoke. 'I'll go down there myself and see what's going on.'

'Will you, Mr Napier? That's such a relief. I'll say goodbye then. Oh and, er, don't worry about returning the torch.'

Daniel would have laughed out loud if he didn't have to shuffle off the grandee he was showing round and get down to the caves in record time.

'Yes, Mr Wentworth,' he reassured the astonished official as he ushered him out, hating himself for sounding so pompous, 'I do think we can all be proud of at least trying to do something to help in this time of such great turmoil in the world.'

'That's a good quote,' replied the man, 'mind if I write it down?'

The funicular should have been fun. In a few minutes you were transported from the crowded and noisy streets of Southdown to the glorious beauty of a clifftop view. On a clear day locals said you could see France. But neither Gina nor Jasmin were in the mood to appreciate peace or beauty today.

Jasmin was looking so pale and shaky that Gina put her arm round the girl. 'Are you really sure you want to go ahead with this?' she asked gently. 'I'm sure she would understand if you said it wasn't possible.'

'No she wouldn't!' Jasmin flashed back passionately. 'I have been given a chance and I must do what I can to help her. Without her passport she is trapped.'

'Yes,' Gina replied humbly. 'I can see that. Let's go then. I'll lead the way and you must stay close.'

As Gina had hoped, it was so near closing time that no more visitors were expected and the entrance was unmanned. She helped Gina over the turnstile and followed immediately behind.

Ahead was a long, narrow passageway hewn from the rock with niches all the way down where electric candles burned. She remembered that it seemed more like the entrance to a monastery than underground caves and possessed an aura of almost religious peace. She sensed the girl in front relax a little.

At the end of the passage, they found themselves in the wide cave where a large figure with a brutal, unnerving face was carved into the rock wall. Gina recalled that it was supposed to be a pre-Christian figure and that pagan religious rites were carried out here, so she hurried Jasmin on into the next cavern.

This one was full of tableaux of smuggling scenes and definitely more Yo Ho Ho in its atmosphere. It was interesting how much smuggling seemed to have been tolerated historically. The famous Kipling rhyme came into her mind again: 'Brandy for the Parson, Baccy for the Clerk, Watch the wall, my darling, While the Gentlemen go by.'

Why, she wondered, should smugglers be called Gentlemen? Surely a lot of them were vicious thugs?

A jolly-looking smuggler with rosy cheeks and a barrel on his shoulder stared out at them, so lifelike they had to stop and stare.

And then, with all the drama of a stage show, the lights went out and they were engulfed in darkness. Jasmin let out a piercing shriek before Gina put a hand over her mouth to stop her. 'Don't worry, we've got a torch, remember!'

She riffled through her shoulder bag until she found it buried underneath her wallet and a Sainsbury's Bag for Life. Only she could go on a dangerous rescue mission with a Sainsbury's bag!

Gina willed herself to be calm when she recognized where they were. 'I think it's through there. I remember that crazy-looking man.' She pointed to a figure with mad, staring eyes illuminated in the powerful beam of the torch. He was staring down at something and wielding a truncheon. 'There should be a wooden box near here.'

Gina shone the torch at the cavern floor. Just below the figure was a small platform. On it a kind of pirate chest with iron handles was displayed with the top thrown open. Gina bent down to examine it. There were bottles of brandy and rum, some lengths of silk and a packet of loose tea. She lifted the silk and just as her hand searched for anything that felt like a passport, a voice rang out through the dark behind them insisting, 'I didn't do it!' in tones of utter desperation. Gina gasped and sprang back as the lights suddenly came up.

The voice had come from the figure of the young man Gina remembered, who rattled the bars piteously. In the next tableau about three feet along, the same desperate young man dangled from a gibbet, stone dead.

'You're feeling sorry for him, aren't you?' someone snarled from out of the darkness.

They both whipped round to find Mike Marshall staring at them. 'We used to be called Gentlemen once upon a time, given the proper respect. Are these what you're looking for?' He held out the passports.

Jasmin jumped forward to try and grab them and found herself being grabbed instead, powerful arms trapping her in a mock-embrace.

Gina glanced around, desperate to find something that could be used in self-defence. Trying to look cowed and terrified, she pretended to turn away and put her hands over her face, at the same making a grab for the truncheon held by the effigy and praying it wasn't stuck down. To her relief it came away smoothly, and she stuffed it into her jacket.

'So,' Mike continued, his voice thick with a horrible kind of pleasure. 'Two pretty ladies, at my mercy. What am I going to do with you both?'

'Maybe smugglers were called Gentlemen,' intervened a voice Gina instantly recognized, 'because they stuck to brandy and rum.'

Mike attempted to whip round just as the barrel belonging to the rosy-cheeked figure they'd passed earlier rolled at speed along the cave floor and knocked his feet from under him. The impact made him release his hold on Jasmin, who darted like a terrified gazelle across the cavern to where Daniel Napier had emerged from the shadows, dropping the passports at the same time.

'You self-satisfied shit,' hissed Marshall. 'It was fine here till you showed up with your fucking liberal superiority.' The muscles in his arms bulged from under his T-shirt in fury. 'Do you think I'm finished with you?'

'That's enough, Mr Marshall. It'd be better for you if kept

your counsel.' A uniformed police officer stepped forward into the light.

Before Marshall had time to review his options, Gina heard the click of handcuffs and felt her whole body shudder with relief.

'Our victim support officer will look after the young woman,' said the policeman, indicating Jasmin, who was standing with closed eyes leaning on Daniel's shoulder.

'Don't worry, it'll be all right,' Gina reassured her.

Jasmin nodded, looking exhausted, as a young female officer – who, Gina noted with relief, was about Jasmin's own age – led her off.

Five minutes later Gina and Daniel stood alone in the cavern, accompanied by effigies of smugglers of one sort or another.

'My God, I was glad when I heard your voice,' Gina admitted, struggling against collapsing. 'How on earth did you get the police to come with you?'

Daniel's reply was to pull her into his arms. 'Are you sure you're all right?' he asked, looking down at her.

'I am now,' she replied, nestling gratefully into his shoulder.

'You weren't in any real danger, but I can see it must have felt as if you were.'

'Too bloody right,' she replied indignantly. 'The man's a maniac. And he certainly doesn't like you.'

'Satisfying, isn't it?' he grinned. 'The police have been interested in Mr Marshall's activities for some time. All they needed was some evidence, which you have thoughtfully provided.'

'Hang on . . .' it had felt so natural for Daniel to appear when he was needed that she realized she had no idea how he'd known they were there. 'How the hell did you know we'd gone to the caves?'

'Mrs Browning from the manor phoned me.'

'Of course she did. We borrowed a torch from her. Amen to having a housekeeper who's such a busybody. You really are a bit of a local hero, aren't you, Mr Napier?'

'I don't know,' he replied, holding her even more firmly. 'Me with the barrel, you with that truncheon you hid down your jumper. I thought we made a pretty good team.'

He leaned down and touched her face with infinite tenderness. 'You look shattered. I think I should take you home.'

Gina had absolutely no argument with Daniel taking her anywhere.

'And administer a large G&T as soon as possible.'

'Sounds heavenly,' she agreed, trying to pretend to be a rational human being.

Fifteen minutes later she had opened her front door and let him lead her to straight to her sunny terrace, where she almost collapsed into the arms of a cushioned garden chair. She closed her eyes and made herself breathe deeply. It was all OK. Especially the bit where Daniel had kissed her.

He had only no sooner poured them two large G&Ts than the doorbell rang.

'I'll go,' he announced, suppressing his obvious irritation at the interruption, to find Maudie, her whole face puckered with anxiety, standing on the doorstep. 'Where is Jasmin?' she blurted before any form of greeting.

'A nice young policewoman is looking after her,' Gina replied, jumping up from her garden chair. 'Jasmin knew where Mike Marshall had hidden some of his workers' passports in the smugglers' caves. Some joke of his that smugglers should be seen as gentlemen like the old-time smugglers in the eighteenth century they celebrate there. Anyway, he was hiding in a cave and jumped out on us, but Daniel here burst in with the police and they arrested him.'

'Good Lord! Is Jasmin at the police station? She'll be terrified! You know how scared she is of officialdom, because where she comes from you can't trust anyone. I must go and find her!'

'Do you want me to come with you?' offered Gina, trying to hide her reluctance.

Maudie took one swift glance at their brimming drinks, and the expression on Daniel's face, and refused point-blank. 'I'm the Honourable Maud Tyler, remember. I can lay it on with a trowel when I need to. I don't think the local constabulary has encountered anything like me.'

'I wish them luck,' grinned Daniel.

'They'll need it,' confirmed Maudie with a very unladylike expression on her aristocratic features.

When she arrived at Southdown's police station with its reassuring blend of Dickens and *Dixon of Dock Green*, still boasting the old-fashioned blue lantern outside, she found the place was already in an uproar because a Ms Rebecca Boyd was looking for the missing Daniel Napier.

'I know he went to the caves because he told the workers at the car wash that was where he was going. So, where the fuck is he?' demanded Rebecca.

'I imagine he's gone home,' suggested the police officer who had arrested Mike Marshall. 'It's too late to go back to work, even to a car wash.'

Maudie pondered the situation for all of five seconds. She had never liked the pushy Rebecca Boyd, and she knew perfectly well she had designs on Daniel and had done her best to make sure he didn't take an interest in Gina.

'He's gone home with Gina,' Maudie announced gleefully. 'She was the heroine of the day, protecting Jasmin from that lowlife Mike Marshall. Anyone with half a brain can see that the reason Daniel dashed to the caves was because Gina was in danger. I'm sure he cared about Jasmin too, but it was Gina he was really concerned about!'

'What arrant nonsense,' Rebecca insisted. 'He went to make sure Mike Marshall was apprehended, that's all.'

'Believe what you like, dear,' replied Maudie at her most *grande dame*. 'But I'll tell you another thing: Gina looked ten times better than you the other night, even if her dress did come from a charity shop.' A door opened at the end of the room and Jasmin appeared with a young police officer.

'Jasmin!' Maudie shrieked. 'My darling girl, are you all right?'

'Yes, thanks to you, Maudie, and thanks to Daniel—'

'—and Gina!' interposed Maudie with a saintly expression.

'My friend has her passport back and that evil man's been arrested!'

'I'll take you home now, dear girl,' Maudie enfolded Jasmin in her arms. 'You're safe!'

'Safe,' repeated Jasmin, as if the word were a precious jewel she was holding in her hand. 'Yes. I am safe.'

'If I were you, dear,' Maudie counselled Rebecca, 'I'd go home and settle down with a ready meal and some nice reassuring television.'

'When I need your advice, I'll ask for it,' snapped Rebecca and marched out of the police station.

After all the hard work she'd put in with Daniel Napier, Rebecca Boyd wasn't about to give up without a fight. Gina lived in Downview Crescent, she knew, though she had no idea what number. When she arrived, she was relieved to find there were only six houses. But which one was Gina's?

She parked round the corner, out of view, and spotted an old lady with long-handled secateurs who was giving her perfectly trimmed hedge an unnecessary going over. She looked just the type who would know all the gossip.

'Excuse me,' Rebecca enquired. 'Can you tell me which house Georgina Greenhills lives in?'

The neighbour gave her a speculative look. 'That'd be number nine,' she announced. 'Only I wouldn't disturb her, if I were you. She's got her new beau with her and they looked pretty loved-up, as my granddaughter would say.'

Rebecca's eyes narrowed in anger. 'I only asked where she lived, not some kind of *Love Island* speculation about sex!'

The neighbour watched her march angrily towards number nine, then called out, 'Your generation didn't invent sex, you know. People have been doing it for generations!'

Rebecca knocked furiously on the door of 9 Downview Crescent.

After almost five minutes a slightly dishevelled Daniel Napier answered it.

'You're only going to regret this!' Rebecca insisted before he could get a word out. 'Remember what I said. Sex with an ex is always a mistake.'

'And do you remember what I replied? That Gina and I were only fifteen. All we attempted was ballroom dancing.'

'I hope you're not going to be disappointed when you do!' Rebecca threw back her head and stuck out her chest in an attempt to look alluring. 'Goodbye, Daniel.'

'Goodbye, Rebecca.'

No sooner had the door closed than Gina's mobile began to ring. In case it might be Sadie or Lisa, Gina went to look for it. Inevitably it was down the back of the sofa. It wasn't either of her daughters but Evie.

'Gina, I never thought I'd say this,' breathed Evie, sounding more excited than Gina had ever heard her before. 'I'm only bloody engaged!'

'Oh, Evie, I can't tell you how delighted I am.'

'And we want you to be a bridesmaid!'

'I suppose there's a first time for everything,' replied Gina. 'Of course, I'd be delighted.' She exchanged a loving smile with Daniel, who was sitting next to her on the sofa, laughing. 'And I'll put some fizz in the fridge so we can celebrate properly as soon as you can get here.'

She said her goodbyes and Daniel took the phone from her and put it down the back of the sofa again.

'Talking of first times for everything,' he held out a hand to her. 'Shall we go upstairs?'

'That's the most unromantic offer of sex I've ever had!' replied Gina teasingly.

'How about this then?'

Daniel swept her into his arms and carried her up the stairs.

'Now, Ms Greenhills,' he murmured lovingly into her ear. 'I hope I'm not going to be disappointed!'

'Do you know, Mr Napier,' she reached up to undo the buttons on his shirt, 'I have the strongest feeling you won't be.'

After that, for some reason, neither of them felt like talking.

With Thanks

———

To all the friends I had fun with as a teenager growing up in Worthing; for Jo Cruddas who not only helped me move house but gave me useful ideas for the book as well as invaluable insights into antiques valuation; to Fiona Shackleton for her wisdom and kindness; to Deborah Taylor for her extremely useful advice on the complex rules of immigration; and to everyone at my local car wash whose happy attitude partly inspired this story.

**If you enjoyed *In the Summertime*, then you'll
love these other titles by Maeve Haran . . .**

The Greek Holiday

**There's nothing like friendship and
sunshine to get you through . . .**

Penny, Dora, Nell and Moira had always meant to keep in touch,
but life got in the way.

So when Penny gets an unexpected legacy, she decides not to tell
her overbearing husband but to spend it instead on a reunion
on the sun-drenched Greek island they visited at eighteen. But
many years later, what was a tiny village full of donkeys and
cafes is now a major tourist attraction. And the friends have to
face the fact that their own personal difficulties can't always
be cured by a holiday in the sun.

On the way back to Athens, they stop at a tiny island, not yet on
the tourist map. In Kyri, they find an opportunity to contribute
to a community needing their help and, at the same time,
to recapture lost romance and have some healing fun.

But will they relearn the most valuable lesson of all:
the true importance of their friendship?

More laughter and love in . . .

In a Country Garden

Are your best friends the last people you should end up living with?

Lifelong friends Claudia, Ella, Laura and Sal celebrated sixty as the new forty, determined not to let age change things. But now they are looking at the future and wondering how to make growing old more fun.

Why not live together – helping and supporting each other when any of them need it – and still keep enjoying life? Joined by Claudia's reluctant husband, Sal's energetic new fiancé, and the intriguing Mrs Lal, they ignore the protests of their children and pool their resources into a manor house in the country. Only Laura holds out, determined she still has some living to do, especially now she has met the dashing Gavin through an online dating app.

Life and love certainly haven't finished with them in what the locals dub a new-age old-age commune. But are your best friends the last people you should end up living with?

Find more sunshine and friendship in . . .

An Italian Holiday

Sometimes you have to go through
the clouds to find the sun

Springtime in glorious Southern Italy can go to your head.
Especially if you're escaping not just miserable weather but
an overbearing husband, the embarrassingly public loss
of your company, an interfering mother who still tries to run
your life or the pain of a husband's affair with a girl young
enough to be his daughter.

As the sun ripens the lemons in the groves that tumble down
the hillsides and the Mediterranean dazzles beneath them,
bossy Angela, extrovert Sylvie, unconfident Claire and
mousy Monica leave their trapped lives behind, and begin
to blossom in quite unexpected ways.

Packed with memorable characters, *An Italian Holiday*
is a witty and entertaining reminder of why going a little mad
in the sunshine can sometimes be exactly what you need.

Escape to the château in . . .

A Very French Wedding

Even dreams can have their complications . . .

Steph, Jo and Meredith have been friends since school. Their
lives have all taken very different paths across the years, but
when Meredith buys a romantic château in an idyllic village
in the Dordogne she finds she can't do it alone – so who
better to enlist for help than her two old friends? Together
they hope to bring the château back to life and create the
most romantic wedding venue in France.

And it seems that the nearby village of Bratenac has much
more to offer than sun, wine and delicious French food when
a handsome chef and his equally charming son, a *vigneron*
from New Zealand, not to mention the local ladies' luncheon
club and a British bulldog named Nelly, all join the party.